THE
❌ SILVER SWORD ❌

David Zindell

TOR
fantasy

A TOM DOHERTY ASSOCIATES BOOK
NEW YORK

THE SILVER SWORD

Copyright © 2001, 2007 by David Zindell

The Silver Sword was originally published in 2001, in substantially different form, by Voyager, an imprint of HarperCollins UK, as the second half of *The Lightstone*. The Tor edition has been specially revised by the author.

Edited by Claire Eddy

Map by Richard Geiger

A Tor Book
Published by Tom Doherty Associates, LLC
175 Fifth Avenue
New York, NY 10010

www.tor.com

Tor® is a registered trademark of Tom Doherty Associates, LLC.

ISBN-13: 978-0-7653-5592-8
ISBN-10: 0-7653-5592-2

First Tor Edition: May 2007
First Tor Mass Market Edition: April 2008

Printed in the United States of America

0 9 8 7 6 5 4 3 2 1

TO MY DAUGHTERS, JUSTINE AND JILLIAN,
*who journeyed with me on many long and magical walks
through Ea and helped generate this story with their pointed
questions, blazing enthusiasm, dreams, and delight*

ACKNOWLEDGMENT

I would like to thank my editor, Claire Eddy, for her many insights and suggestions that made this a better book in many, many ways.

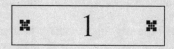

1

THE ANGELS, IT is written, at the beginning of time sang into creation the stars. With the aid of the Lightstone, their golden voices brought forth out of the black void Solaru, Aras, Varshara, and a million other bright bursts of fire. I have heard the stars sing back. All men and women can apprehend the heavens' music as well as the angels, but who can hold inside such blazing, infinite songs? Only one, I believe, who finds the golden Cup of Heaven in which to contain their light, in whatever place on earth this greatest of all gelstei has been lost.

At the western edge of the world, the stars shine the same as those of the Morning Mountains of my home. Having called my six companions and me across the length of Ea on a great quest, these bright points of light put a song in each of our hearts and led us back east. Bright hopes we held, and bright gelstei, too: a ruby firestone, a bit of black jade, a scryer's clear sphere that gave visions of the future. Other ancient crystals we had gained on our long journey; into my hands had come the legendary silver sword, Alkaladur. Must I, I wondered, use this Sword of Fate to fight the Red Dragon named Morjin as we had for so many months and miles—perhaps even to the death? Or would my blade's shining silustria point the way toward the Lightstone as told in the ancient songs?

In the warmest days of Marud in the year 2812, as we sailed across the Dragon Channel from the Island of the Swans to Surrapam on a stout bilander called the *Snowy Owl*, these questions burned through my mind. Through my blood still burned the kirax that one of Morjin's assassins had struck into me with a poisoned arrow. The pain of this foul substance would always torment me, even as in some mysterious way it connected me to the foulness of Morjin's mind and heart. Miraculously, though, whenever I gripped my newly acquired sword and pointed it toward the stars, the fire of the kirax seemed to go away.

"So, that sword seems almost to have been made for you." Kane, the fiercest of my friends, spoke these words to me on the last night of our voyage. We stood on the deck of the *Snowy Owl,* looking for warships on the glistening black waters to the east. "And even as it now belongs to you, you belong to it."

It was a strange thing for him to say, but then Kane was a strange man. He was tall, like the Valari people from which I came, and he had the same bright, black eyes as did my brothers and my father, King Shavashar Elahad. But his hair had turned white, and he wore it cropped short instead of long and black and tied with brightly colored battle ribbons. And where the bold faces of my people most often recalled those of hawks or eagles, Kane's grim visage brought to mind the wildness and fury of a tiger. He moved, too, with all the power of such a beast. At times, though, as when we stood together looking up at the stars, he came alive with a terrible beauty, and then he seemed the most graceful and glorious of men.

"Well, I am a Valari warrior, aren't I?" I told him. "And isn't it said that a warrior's sword is his soul?"

I looked down the length of Alkaladur's blade, double-edged and sharp enough to cut steel. Its silustria, hardest of all substances except the gold gelstei of the Lightstone, caught the starlight and cast it back with a silvery sheen. The sword's maker had set seven diamonds into its black jade hilt, carved with swans like unto those of my family's emblem. A great round diamond formed the sword's pommel stone. When I pointed the sword to the east, the silustria filled with a bright white radiance as it flared in resonance with the lost Lightstone.

"It is said," Kane told me, "that this sword has many powers, and you have called upon one of them. But *you* have many powers, too, eh? Soon enough, I think, this sword will call upon all that dwells most deeply within you, Valashu Elahad."

I thought about this as I listened to the ship's timbers creaking and the wind whipping at the sails. I looked out across the deck. There, near the bow, stretched out beneath their traveling cloaks, lay four of our other friends: Master Juwain of the Great White Brotherhood; the minstrel Alphanderry; Lady Liljana Ashvaran of Tria; and Atara Ars Narmada, daughter of Ea's greatest king, warrior of the Manslayer Society—and the woman I loved. Already, it seemed, whenever Alkaladur's deepest light pierced my heart, I felt myself opening to passions almost too beautiful to bear.

"What are you looking at, my friend?" a low, rumbling voice called out to me.

Just then, Prince Maram Marshayk, the seventh member of our company, came staggering out of the darkness with a bottle of brandy clenched in his huge hand. A great, dense beard bloomed from his heavy face; he stood nearly as tall as Kane, and was even thicker in his body and limbs, though less from hard sinew than jiggling fat. He wore a stained cloak over his rather ostentatious scarlet woolens, while on each of his fingers he sported a jeweled ring. Of all my friends, he had suffered the worst from the rigors of our quest—or, at least, had complained the most about them.

"Why aren't you sleeping, Maram?" I asked in a low voice.

"Ah, why must you answer a question with a question?" He belched loudly as he looked through the darkness at me—and my sword. "I am not sleeping because one of Captain Kharald's fine sailors offered to share this fine brandy with me. And because it's too lovely of a night to sleep. *And*, most of all, because whenever I close my eyes, I can still smell the perfume of Lalaiu's hair upon my face, and that keeps me awake."

He spoke of the Maiian woman that he had left behind on the Island of the Swans. Listening to the wistfulness that came into his heavy voice, I could almost believe that he loved her.

"The question," he said to me, glancing at Atara, "is why *you* aren't making the most of this splendid night and taking a few moments of joy with *your* beloved while you still can?"

I felt my cheeks burning with the heat of my blood. I looked at Atara, whose beautiful blue eyes had finally closed in sleep. Her long blond hair half-covered the most beautiful face I had ever seen. At that moment, I thought, she looked much more like a gentle maiden than a skilled warrior who had vowed to slay a hundred of her enemies before marrying. And I remembered well enough my promise to her father, King Kiritan of Alonia: that before taking her hand in mine, I would find the Lightstone and bring it into the City of Light. This, surely, was not vainglory on my part (or not just), but only good sense. With all of Ea about to go up in flames, who would want to marry anyone and bring children into the world—unless the Lightstone *was* found and war ended forever?

"You know why," I said quietly to Maram.

As Maram's brown eyes softened with his regard for me, I thought that he *did* know the real reason that I could not take Atara to me, the deepest and most painful reason that I tried to keep a secret, even from myself. And I loved him for that.

"Someday," he promised me, "I'll stand with you in Tria when you wed Atara. *If* we make it across this water without the damn Hesperuk warships attacking us. And across Surrapam without running into the damn Hesperuk army. And then through the mountains without . . ."

For a while, as we stood with the salty sea wind blowing at our faces, Maram recited a litany of all the dangers he supposed might lie ahead of us. Then his attention fell upon my sword, and he said, "There might have been much blood upon this blade, once, but surely the ages have washed it clean. I have to tell you that I'm not ready to see you bloody it again."

"Nor am I," I told him. "It might be that we can reach our journey's end in peace."

"It *might* be," Maram sighed out. "But already, Morjin has sent an assassin to murder you. And a great bear he made into a ghul. And the damn Grays with their stone eyes that nearly sucked out our souls. And in Tria, more assassins, with that damn Kallimun priest, and of course that monster Meliadus in the Vardaloon—not to mention whole plagues of mosquitoes, leeches, and ticks. Ah, am I forgetting anything?"

If he *had* forgotten any of Morjin's assaults, I would not remind him, for he needed no extra fuel to stoke the fires of his vivid imagination.

"And what if Morjin finds you with his damn illusions again?"

"Then I will fight them off, as I have before," I reassured him.

"We can only hope so," he said with a belch of brandy. "But now we propose to cross Surrapam in secret—what if someone gives us away? What if Morjin somehow *sees* you carrying that bright sword of yours? Even with twenty Alkaladurs, you couldn't fight off the whole damn Hesperuk army!"

His words seemed to hang in the air as the ship pitched and rolled beneath us and sent up a salty spray. Then Captain Kharald, pacing the deck midships, walked over to us. His heavy boots thumped across worn wood. He was a heavyset man dressed in a thick wool shirt, pantaloons, and a black belt from which hung a spyglass and a cutlass. The dark of full night bled away the colors of his bright red hair and his green eyes, but I could easily make out the careworn lines of his blunt face. As captain of a ship running the Dragon Channel with a hold full of grain for his starving people, he had many cares and concerns.

"That is a great sword you gained on the island," he said to me. "I've never seen its like."

I stood pointing Alkaladur down toward the deck of the ship. It wouldn't do for Captain Kharald—or anyone—to see it light up like a star.

"A great sword indeed," he went on, stroking his beard. "And it's said that you Valari are the greatest warriors in the world."

His rough, wrinkled face, in the light of the waning moon, tightened with calculation. But he said no more to me that night. He bade Kane, Maram, and me to lie back down with our friends to take some rest. Then he walked over to the *Snowy Owl*'s mainmast to check on the lookout in the crow's nest high above us.

As we rejoined our other friends and tried to sleep, I had to fight back a gnawing sickness in my belly. I felt too poignantly Captain Kharald's dread of the Hesperuks who had invaded Surrapam. What would it be like, I wondered, to see my land ravaged by one of Morjin's murderous and crucifying armies?

With a strong wind blowing at our backs, we fairly flew across the glittering waters of the Dragon Channel. It took us only a day and night, altogether, of fast sailing to complete our passage. Fortune favored us, for the lookout gave no cry of alarm as to Hesperuk warships, but only called out near dawn that he had sighted Surrapam. There, in the morning, at Artram, the last of Surrapam's free ports and therefore crowded with ships coming and going through its bustling harbor, we made landfall. Immediately we set to work bringing our horses up from below deck and down the gangplank onto the dock.

I led forth, keeping a firm hold on the reins of Altaru, my fierce black stallion, so that he wouldn't rear up and strike out at any of Captain Kharald's crew with his great hooves. Atara, walking beside her roan mare, Fire, came next. She had a gift for gentling horses—perhaps inherited from her grandfather's people. Like most of the fierce Sarni who roam the grasslands of the Wendrush, she stood tall and straight, with a great strength that seemed to well up from her lithely muscled body. The Surrapamers crowding the dock stared at her in wonder. Although Atara had the same blond hair and brilliant blue eyes as the many Thalunes common in Surrapam, she carried herself with a barbaric grace. She certainly had the look of a barbarian, with her black leather armor studded with steel and the leather trousers beneath her traveling cloak. Her bare, brown arms showed circlets of gold, and a torque of lapis and gold shone from her neck. And no Thalune woman would wear a sword at her side or bear a bow and arrows as if ready to put a shaft through any man who insulted her.

It did not take long for the rest of our companions—Kane, Maram, Master Juwain, Liljana, and Alphanderry—to join us on the dock. As we stood checking our horses' loads, Captain Kharald came down the gangplank to speak with us.

"I have just had news," he told us, standing in close. "All the countryside north of the Maron River is lost. King Kaiman has rallied our army and is making a stand near Azam only forty miles from here. It seems our wheat is needed very badly."

I watched the lean, hungry-looking Surrapam dockmen who had already gone to work unloading the bags of wheat from the *Snowy Owl*'s holds. From nearby smithies down Artram's busy streets came the sounds of hammered steel and the clamor of preparations for war.

Captain Kharald looked from Atara to Maram, and then at Kane and me. And he said, "Your swords are needed badly, too. Would you be willing to raise them against the enemy that you say you oppose?"

I remembered Thaman, his countryman, who had requested help from the Valari in Duke Rezu's castle; in the months since then, I thought, it had gone very badly for his people.

"We do indeed oppose him," Liljana said in her calm, controlled voice. "But there are other ways of fighting the Red Dragon than with *this*."

She set her hand on the hilt of the cutlass that she had reluctantly strapped to her side in Tria, upon her vow to make the quest. Despite this weapon, few would mistake her for a warrior. She was middling old, with iron-gray hair bound tight and coiled like a matron's and a rather stout body that seemed all softness and curves. Her round, almost jolly face readily broke into warm smiles. With her wide hips and great breasts, one could easily imagine her as a mother of many children—and a grandmother of many more. It always surprised people, I thought, to discover that beneath her comely exterior, she possessed a will of steel.

"I think," Captain Kharald said to her, nodding toward her sword, "that you might do very well fighting the Red Dragon with *that*. But you still might help. Cooking for our soldiers. Or caring for the wounded."

Liljana remained quiet while she studied Captain Kharald with her wise hazel eyes. I sensed that she did want to tend to Surrapam's wounded warriors and make them well—as she did almost everyone in the world.

"And you, Master Juwain," Captain Kharald said, turning slightly, "are a healer, are you not?"

Master Juwain, short and compact and tough as old tree roots, slowly nodded his bald head. His rather ugly face shone with the keenest of intelligence as he considered Captain Kharald's words. I saw torment working at his luminous gray eyes. I noticed him pressing his hand against the pocket of his woolens where he kept his varistei: the green healing crystal that he had been given far away in a magical wood.

"I am a master healer," he said to Captain Kharald without pride. "But even such as I can do little when the dogs of war are loosed upon the world."

"What little you can do would be greatly appreciated. Even one life saved is one more soldier who might recover to fight the Dragon. And one less grieving mother."

At this, Master Juwain bowed his head in thought, and stared down at the ground.

"And you, minstrel," Captain Kharald said, looking at Alphanderry, "such a voice you have! Such a gift with music! You could sing to the soldiers before battle and put the fire of the angels into their hearts."

Alphanderry's soft, sad eyes brightened at this. He was a slender man, handsome of face and form, and at once lively and dreamy in his manner. His black, curly hair seemed to catch the sun's rays in a crown of light. Upon his back he bore a six-stringed mandolet, from which he could summon the most beautiful of melodies. Everything about him—his fine, tapering fingers, his sensual lips, the poise of his head, his innate curiosity and imagination—bespoke his deep love for beauty.

"I would gladly play for the soldiers," Alphanderry told Captain Kharald. "But then it seems that I must gladly die, for the Hesperuks will surely prevail."

He spoke these words simply and almost happily, as if fate was only fate and should be celebrated as with everything in life—and later sung about with passion and reverence.

But his carefree way seemed only to irritate Maram, who huffed out, "Well, *I* am not so ready to die, gladly or otherwise. And I don't think you are either."

At this, Alphanderry just shrugged his shoulders as he smiled at Maram.

"Val," Maram said to me, "would you talk some sense into our foolish friend?"

In answer, I could only let my hand rest upon Alkaladur's hilt as I looked from Alphanderry and then at Captain Kharald.

"Val," Maram said again, this time in alarm, "please don't tell me that you're thinking of offering King Kaiman your sword!"

Now all the rest of my friends looked at me, too. I thought it strange that although I was the youngest of our company, at only a score of years, it had fallen upon me to be their leader.

"Captain Kharald and his people," I said to Maram, "have given us their aid."

"For which we paid them good gold!"

I considered this as I turned toward Atara. And she told me, "Whatever we do, Surrapam will fall."

I wondered what visions she might have seen in her scryer's crystal, and I asked her, "Have you *seen* this, then?"

Her bright blue eyes fixed on mine. "Any soldier in King Kaiman's army could see that. A child could, Val."

A clacking sound on the wharf drew my attention. There, two boys in front of a sailmaker's shop played with wooden swords. And I said to Atara, "Yes, the *children*."

Atara looked at them, too, and said with some certainty: "If we stay, we *will* die. Surely, though, knowing this cannot be the basis for determining the rightness or wrongness of such a course."

"It can for *me*!" Maram said.

At that moment, a whirl of little crimson and silver lights broke out of the still air above us. Flick, the strange being that had attached himself to us in the Lokilani's wood, spun about like a constellation of stars. He remained invisible to Captain Kharald and others who had not partaken of the wood's magic. But to me, he seemed to speak in bright bursts of radiance that I could almost understand.

Then Kane caught my attention, and shot me a look that struck deep into my soul. I could almost feel his heart surging savagely in time with my own. His purpose dwelled with *my* purpose, and that was both a bright and a terrible thing. I recalled that my father, in the course of his kingship, had from evil necessity had to make many hard decisions.

Finally I turned to Captain Kharald and said, "It is one thing to risk one's life in a noble cause, and another to throw it away. Even a hundred regiments arrayed against the Red Dragon wouldn't be enough to bring him down. But the finding of the Lightstone might be."

Captain Kharald's face reddened with anger and disappointment. "Then you intend to continue your quest?"

"Yes, we must. It is our calling."

Captain Kharald drew in a long breath and held it before letting it out slowly in a deep sigh. "Well, go in the One's light then. Perhaps you'll find your Cup of Heaven before Morjin does—and before he slaughters us all. I wish you well, Valashu Elahad."

I wished him well, too, and so did the others. And then, after clasping his rough hand, we mounted our horses and rode north through Artram's narrow streets.

The choice of this direction was Kane's. Ever alert for enemies and Kallimun spies, he spared no effort in trying to throw potential pursuers off our scent. Artram was a rather small city of stout wooden houses and the inevitable shops of sailmakers, ropemakers, and sawyers working up great spars to be used in fitting out the many ships docked in her port. There were many salteries, too, preserving the cargoes of cod and char that the fishing boats brought in from the sea. Most of these shops, however, were now empty, their stores having been requisitioned by King Kaiman's quartermasters. In truth, there seemed little food left in the city, and little hope for defeating Hesperu's ravaging armies, either.

Everywhere we went, we saw marks of woe upon the Surrapamers' gaunt faces. It pained me to see the children eyeing our well-fed horses and full saddlebags. Like Thaman and Captain Kharald, they were mostly red of hair, fair of skin, and thick of body—or would have been in better times. Though nearly beaten, they carried themselves bravely and well. Were we, I wondered, truly doing the right thing by deserting them?

I resolved that if I ever returned to Mesh, I would speak out strongly for helping them, if only by taking the field against the Red Dragon.

Maram surprised us all by stopping to pull off his rings one by one and giving them to various beggars who crossed our path. After slipping his third ring into the hand of a one-legged old warrior, Kane chided him for such conspicuous largesse. And Maram chided *him*, saying, "I can always get more rings, but he'll never get another leg. I regret only that I have only ten fingers, with ten rings to give."

And then Liljana pointed out that Maram might very well want to reserve his rings to trade for food, as we had completely run out of coins, silver or gold. Maram fell silent for a few moments as he considered this. Then once again, he found the best of himself, tapping the gold medallion that King Kiritan had given those vowing to make the quest. And he said, "Atara is the finest shot I ever saw, and we can always hunt for food. And as it once was, we shall have to hope that people will honor our quest and provide us hospitality."

The afternoon found us a few miles outside of the city, in a region of rich black earth and once-prosperous farms. But the King's quartermasters had come here, too. Smokehouses that should have been stuffed with hanging hams were empty; barns that should have been full of dried barley and corn held only straw. Most of the grown men having been called to war, or already laid low by it, the fields of wheat were tended by women, children, and old men.

When we were sure that no one had followed us out of Artram, we turned east toward the mountains. Although the great Crescent Mountains were said to be very tall, we could not see even the tallest of their peaks, even though they lay only sixty miles away. For Surrapam was a land of clouds and mists and a sempiternal coolness clinging like moistened silk to its lush fields. That day, a thin drizzle sifted slowly down through the air. Although it was full summer, and the height of Marud at that, its chill made me draw my cloak tightly around me.

And yet, despite the gloom, it was a rich, beautiful land of evergreen forests and emerald fields glowing softly beneath the sky's gentle light. I could see why the Hesperuks might wish to conquer it. The farther we rode across its verdant folds, the more it seemed that we were journeying in the wrong direction. But three times that day I drew Alkaladur, and each time its faint radiance pointed us east. And east we must continue, I thought, even though great battles and the call to arms lay behind us.

We camped that night in a stand of spruce trees beside a swift stream. Its waters were clear and sweet, and full of trout, nine of which Alphanderry and Kane caught for our dinner. Maram summoned forth a fire from some moist sticks, while Liljana set to with her pots and pans. It was the first time she had cooked a full meal for us since before Varkall.

We ate our fried fish in the silence of those soft woods. For dessert, we had blackberries, for these shiny little fruits grew abundantly in thickets along the roads we had ridden. Then I sat by the fire with my new sword unsheathed, and we were ready to discuss the journey that still lay before us.

"I'm afraid that the Lightstone must still dwell to the east of us," Master Juwain said. "And I think it's more than a coincidence that Khaisham lies directly along the line which Val's sword has shown."

It was not the first time he had said this. Ever since the Island of the Swans, when it became clear that our journey might take us as far as Khaisham and the great library there, he had gazed off in its direction with a new excitement in his calm gray eyes.

"I still don't see how the Lightstone could be there," Maram said. "The Library has been searched a hundred times, hasn't it?"

"Yes," Master Juwain said. "But it's too vast ever to be searched fully. The number of books it holds is said to be thousands and thousands."

Kane smiled at this and said, "I've been to the Library once, many years ago. The number of its books is thousands *of* thousands. Many of them have never even been read."

A new idea had suddenly come to Master Juwain, who sat

rubbing his hands together as if in anticipation of a feast. "Then perhaps one of them holds the Lightstone."

"You mean, holds knowledge about it, don't you, sir?" Maram asked.

"No, I mean the Cup of Heaven itself. Perhaps one of the books has had its pages hollowed out to fit a small golden cup. And so escaped being discovered in any search."

"Now *there's* a thought," Maram said.

"It's as I've always told you: When you open a book, you never know what you'll find there."

We talked for quite a while about the Library and the great treasures it guarded: not just the books, of course, but the paintings, sculptures, jewelry, and collections of unknown gelstei, many of which dated from the Age of Law—and whose purpose neither the Librarians nor anyone else had been able to fathom. For Master Juwain, a journey to the Library was an opportunity of a lifetime. And the rest of us were eager to view this wonder, too. Even Atara, who had little patience for books, seemed excited at the prospect of beholding so many of them.

"I think there's no other choice then," she said. "We should go to this library, and see what we see."

And so, despite Maram's objections that Khaisham lay five hundred miles away across unknown lands, we decided to journey there unless my sword pointed us elsewhere or we found the Lightstone first.

To firm up our resolve, we broke out the brandy and sat sipping it by the fire. This distillation of grapes, ripened in the sun far away, warmed us deep inside. Alphanderry began playing his mandolet, and much to everyone's surprise, Kane joined him in song. His singing voice, which I had never heard, was much like the brandy itself: rich, dark, fiery, and aged to a bittersweet perfection—and quite beautiful in its own way. He sang to the stars far above us, which we could not see; he sang to the earth that gave us form and life and would someday take it away. When he had finished, I sat staring at my sword as if I might find my reflection there.

"What do you see, Val?" Master Juwain asked.

"That's hard to say," I told him. "It's all so strange. Here we are drinking this good brandy—and it's as if the vintner who made it left the taste of his soul in it. In the air, there's the sound of battle, even though it's quiet tonight. And the earth upon which we sit: can you feel her heart beating up through the ground? And not just *her* heart, but everyone's and everything's: the nightingale's and the wood vole's, and even that of the Lord Librarian in Khaisham half a world away. It beats and beats, and there's a song there—the same strange song that the stars sing. And truly, it's a cloudy night, but the stars are always there, in their spirals and sprays of light, like sea foam, like diamonds, like dreams in the mind of a child. And they never cease forming up and delighting: it's like Flick whirling in the Lokilani's wood. And it's all part of one pattern. And we could see the whole of it from any part if only we opened our eyes, if only we knew *how* to look. Strange, strange."

Maram staggered over to me, and touched my head to see if I had a fever. He had never heard me speak like this before; neither had I.

"My friend, you're drunk," he said, looking down at Alkaladur. "Drunk on brandy or drunk on the fire of this sword—it's all the same."

Master Juwain looked back and forth between the sword and me. "No, I don't think he's quite drunk yet. I think he's just beginning to see."

He went on to tell us that everyone had three eyes: the eye of the senses; the eye of reason; and the eye of the soul. This third eye did not develop so easily as the others. Meditation helped open it, and so did the attunement of certain gelstei. "All the greater gelstei quicken the other sight," he said, "but the silver is especially the stone of the soul."

The silustria, he said, had its most obvious effects on that part of the soul we called the mind. Like a highly polished lens, the silver crystal could reflect and magnify its powers: logic, deduction, calculation, awareness, insight, and ordinary memory. In its reflective qualities, the silver gelstei might also be used as a shield against energies: vital, physical, and particularly mental. A sword made of silustria, he thought, could cut through all things material as the mind cuts through ignorance and darkness, for it was far harder than diamond. In fact, in its fundamental composition the silver was very much like the gold gelstei, and was one of the two noble stones.

"But its most sublime power is said to be this seeing of the soul that Val has told of. The way that all things are interconnected."

"So," Kane said, looking at me. "Just so."

Alphanderry, who seemed to have a song ready for any occasion, sang an old one about the making of the heavens and earth. Its words, written down by some ancient minstrel long ago, told of how all of creation was woven of a single tapestry of superluminal jewels, the light of each jewel reflected in that of every other. Although only the One could ever perceive each of the tapestry's shimmering emeralds, sapphires, and diamonds, a man, through the power of the silver gelstei, might apprehend its unfolding pattern in all its unimaginable magnificence.

" 'For we are the eyes through which the One beholds itself and knows itself divine,' " Alphanderry quoted. Then he said, "What wonders would we behold if only we had the eyes to see them?"

"Divine, you say?" Maram muttered. "The One might be, but I certainly am not. I think the mountains soon enough will freeze this poor, poor mortal flesh of mine."

Alphanderry smiled at this as if Maram had challenged him to a game. Then he offered us another song, also old and beautiful, and also about creation. It told of the breath of the One. When the One inhaled, all things drew in and progressed toward the center of creation: the Ardun, men and women of the earth, advanced in their powers of body, mind, and soul to be called Star People, while these beings eventually found exaltation as the immortal Elijin. And those of this first order of angels, after ages, became the great Galadin who could not be harmed in any way or die. Except that they *could* die, after ages of ages, in a fiery burst into light, when they found greater life as the blessed leldra in union with the One. And then the One breathed out, in light and music, and the leldra sang into creation a new universe. Stars and comets they made, bright moons and suns and the many earths from which men and women would someday take their being—and find within themselves the ageless longing to be more. And so the One breathed in and out, on and on forever, and all the universes of the angels and men were without end.

As Alphanderry sang on and on through the night, his beautiful voice filled with his own longing that he might someday recapture the very words and music of the angels. We all listened to him, and none so intently as Maram.

"Ah, well," Maram said after Alphanderry had finally finished. He yawned and drank the last of his brandy. "I'm off to bed, and I can only hope my *snoring,* in and out, doesn't disturb you too badly. I must tell you that, despite your fine company, I miss Lalaiu. So I'm off to behold her in my dreams."

He stood up, yawned again, rubbed his eyes and then patted Alphanderry's head. "And *that,* my friend, is the only part of this wonderful tapestry of yours I care to see tonight."

Alphanderry's song left me wide awake and fairly trembling with a vast excitement as I tried to perceive the jeweled tapestry into which my life was woven—and strove even harder to see with the eye of my soul. For a long while I stayed awake listening to Maram snoring, and to Atara's softer breathing, out and in. How was it possible, I wondered, that even in sleep I could feel her love for me? I took out my sword, and pointed its bright blade toward the eastern horizon. How was it possible, I wanted to ask the Galadin who dwelled in the stars, that I could feel the Lightstone calling me toward my fate?

The next morning, after a breakfast of porridge and blackberries fortified with some walnuts that Liljana had held in reserve, we set out in good spirits. We rode across fallow fields and little dirt roads, neither seeking out the occasional farmhouses we came across nor trying to avoid them. This part of Surrapam, it seemed, was not the most populated. Broad swaths of forest separated the much narrower strips of cultivated land and settlements from each other. Although the roads through the giant, moss-hung trees were good enough, if a little damp, I wondered what it would be like when we reached the mountains, where we might find no roads at all.

Maram, too, brooded about this. As we paused to make a midmorning meal out of the clumps of blackberries growing along the roadside, he pointed ahead of us and said, "How are we to take the horses across the mountains if there are no roads for them? The *Crescent* Mountains, Val?"

"Don't worry," I told him, "we'll find a way."

When Kane pointed out that we could always skirt around the great mountain chain by journeying north, Maram groaned, "But that would add another three hundred miles to our journey! Let's at least try crossing the mountains first."

At this, Atara laughed and said, "Your laziness is giving you courage."

"It would give me more if you could *see* a road through the mountains. Can you?"

But in answer, Atara popped a blackberry into her mouth and slowly shook her head.

As we set out again, I wondered at the capriciousness of each of our gifts and the various gelstei that quickened them. Among us, we now had six; only Alphanderry lacked a stone, and so great were our hopes after my gaining Alkaladur that we were sure he would find a purple gelstei somewhere between Surrapam and Khaisham. Although Master Juwain brought forth his green varistei with greater and greater frequency, he admitted that drawing upon its deepest healing properties might be the work of a lifetime. Kane, of course, kept his dark stone mostly hidden and his doubts about using it secret as well. Could the black gelstei, I wondered, possibly steal away some of Morjin's evil power even as it damped the fires of the red gelstei? No one seemed to know. Liljana's blue figurine might indeed aid her in mindspeaking, but there were no dolphins or whales to be found in Ea's interior, and none among us with her talent. As she had promised to look away from the running streams of our thoughts unless invited to dip into them, she had little opportunity to gain mastery of her stone. And mastery she would need, I thought, if ever she turned her mind toward Morjin. As for Atara, she gazed into her scryer's sphere as often as I searched the sky for the sun. What she saw there, however, remained a mystery. I gathered that her visions were as uncertain as blizzards in spring, and blew through her with sometimes blinding fury.

Maram's talent proved to be the most fickle of any of ours—and the most neglected. Where he should have been growing more adept in using his firestone, he seemed almost to have forgotten that he possessed it. As he had said, his dreams were now of Lalaiu; at any one time, I thought, he was able to pour his passions into one vessel only. At the end of the day, after we had covered a good twenty-five miles through a deepening drizzle, he tried to make a fire for us with his gelstei. But the long red crystal brightened not even a little and remained dead in his hands.

"The wood is too wet," he said as he knelt over a pile of it that he had made. "There's too little light coming through these damn clouds."

"Hmmph, you've gotten a fire out of your crystal before with as little light," Atara chided him. "I should think the test of it is at times such as these rather than in waiting for perfect conditions."

"I didn't know I was being tested," Maram fired back.

"Our whole journey is a test for all of us. And all our lives might someday depend on your firestone."

Her words cut deep into me and remained in my mind as I stayed awake meditating. For I had a sword that I must learn to wield—and not by crossing blades with Kane every night during our fencing practice. Although Alkaladur might indeed be hard enough to slice through the hardest steel, it had more vital powers that I was only beginning to sense. It would take all my will, I thought, all my awareness to find myself in the silvery substance of the sword and it in me.

Later, toward midnight, Atara admitted that she couldn't sleep either. She came over to sit with me by the fire, and she said, "*Everything* might someday depend on your sword. And your gift."

She reached out with her long finger to trace the zags of the lightning-bolt scar cut into my forehead. I could feel the pulses of her life—and much else—passing from her flesh into mine. Kane called my ability to experience other's passions and pains as my own the *valarda*, and said that many of the Star People and all of the angels possessed this grace. For most of my life, it had seemed more of a curse. Too often, as when Atara looked at me with her own fiery passion pouring out of her, I felt myself utterly burning away as by the blaze of the sun.

"But what does the *valarda* have to do with my sword?" I asked her.

"I can't quite see that yet," she said, peering at Alkaludur's shining blade. "But it seems that in opening your heart to others, you also open yourself to your fate."

"My fate," I murmured, turning west to stare through the misty dark. "Are we *truly* doing the right thing? To run away from Morjin's armies?"

"We are running away from nothing, Val. *Everything* lies ahead of us."

She pressed her hand into mine, and looked at me. And I said, "Perhaps it does. But I will never avoid battle with Morjin's creatures again."

I felt a cold, sick fear shoot through her veins as she told me, "You needn't seek them out. Battles we'll fight, whatever we do."

"Do you mean, fight battles with *this*?" I asked, lifting my sword a little higher. "Battles against Morjin?"

In answer, she only smiled at me and gazed at me with her beautiful eyes.

"Morjin," I murmured again, staring at the fire's red flames.

She squeezed my hand as she said, "But you must not hate him, don't you see? It is as Kane said: the *valarda* joins you to Morjin, and is your greatest vulnerability. But your greatest strength, too."

I shook my head at this, and said, "How can I not hate a man who has subjugated half of the world's kingdoms and claims dominion over all Ea? A man who has gained immortality through his evil sorcery and aspires to be an Elijin? The Lord of Lies he is, the Lord of Illusions—the Great Beast."

"He *is* the Lord of Illusions," she said to me, "and if you would fight them off, you must open yourself to everything that is within your sword."

I smiled at this as I gripped Alkaladur's black jade hilt. "Is that a piece of friendly advice or a prophecy?"

Her full lips tightened in anger a moment before she said, "*This* is a prophecy that you would do well to remember: 'The seven brothers and sisters of the earth with the seven stones will set forth into the darkness. The Lightstone will be found, the Maitreya will come forth, and a new age will begin. A seventh son with the mark of Valoreth will slay the dragon. The old world will be destroyed and a new world created.' "

As she finished reciting Ayondela Kirriland's famous prophecy that had set knights across Ea vowing to make the quest, she again touched the scar marking my forehead. And she told me, "Without the brightness of your sword, Val, we will never find our way through the dark—or through Morjin's illusions. And without the brightness of your *heart*, we will never create anything new in this world, you and I."

She kissed my lips then, and stood up to go off to bed. I couldn't quite tell if she slept very much after that, but I did not. For hours, as Kane prowled the perimeter of our encampment looking for enemies, I sat by the fire gazing at my mysterious and beautiful sword.

Morning brought with it only a little sun, which lasted scarcely long enough for us to saddle the horses and break camp. It began to rain again, but much of its sting was taken away by the needles of the towering trees above us. Here were hemlocks and spruce two hundred feet high, and great king firs perhaps even higher. They formed a vast shield of green protecting against wind and water, and sheltering the many squirrels, foxes, and birds that lived here. Despite the pull of my sword, which I drew out often, I might have been content to ride through this lovely forest another month, for its smells of mosses and wildflowers pleased me greatly. Soon, however, the trees gave way to more farmland, cut with numerous streams running down from the mountains. In this more open country the rain found us easy targets, and pelted us with icy drops that streaked down through the sky like silver arrows. It soaked our garments, making a misery of what should have been an easy ride. And then late in the afternoon, we had a stroke of luck. When we knocked at the door to one of the farmhouses, we found a poor widow whose freckle-faced son, Jaetan, agreed to point out a path that might lead over the mountains.

That night Kane gave the widow a young buck that he had hunted for supper; she shared with us a few eggs and a little stale bread. Our beds we had to make in her barn, but at least it was dry enough. We set out the next morning just after first light with Jaetan leading the way on a bony-looking old nag that was too big for him. As Jaetan admitted, he was only thirteen—too young to ride off with his older brother to war. And yet, I thought, I had gone to war at that age. It gladdened my heart, even as I filled with not a little pride, that even in the hour of their greatest need, the Surrapamers were not so war-loving as we Valari.

After a couple of hours of riding up a gradually ascending dirt road, we came to a notch between two hills where the road seemed to disappear into a great, green wall of vegetation. Jaetan pointed into it and told us, "This is the old East Road. It's said to lead into Eanna. But no one really knows because no one goes that way anymore."

"Except us," Maram muttered nervously.

Jaetan looked at him and told him, "The road is good enough, I think. But it's said that there are still many bears in the mountains, Master Maram."

"Oh, excellent," Maram said, staring into the woods. "Bears, is it now?"

We thanked Jaetan for his hospitality, and then Jaetan rode back toward his mother's house and warmth of the hearth that awaited him.

"Well," Maram said, "if the old maps are right, we've sixty miles of mountains to cross before we reach Eanna. I suppose we'd better start out before the bears catch our scent."

But we saw no sign of bears all that day, nor the next nor even the one following that. The woods about us, though, were thick enough to have hidden a hundred of them. As the hills to either side of us rose and swelled into mountains, the giant trees of western Surrapam gave way to many more silver firs and nobles. These graceful evergreens, while not so tall as their lowland cousins, grew more densely. If not for the road, we would have been hard-pressed to fight our way through them. This narrow muddy track had been cut along a snake-like course. And it turned like a snake, now curving south, now north, but always making its way roughly east as it gradually gained elevation. And with every thousand feet higher upon the green, humped earth that we stood, it seemed that the rain poured down harder.

Making camp in these misty mountains was very much a misery. The needles of the conifers, the bushes, the mosses and ferns about our soaked sleeping furs—everything the eye and hand fell upon was dripping wet. That Maram failed yet again with his fire dispirited us even more. When the day's first light fought its way through the almost solid grayness lying over the drenched earth each morning, we were glad to get moving again, if only because our exertions warmed our stiff bodies.

Three times the road failed us, vanishing into a mass of vegetation that seemed to swallow it completely. And three times Maram complained that we were lost and would never see the sun again, let alone Khaisham. But each time, with an unerring sense, Atara struck off into the forest, leading us through the trees for half a mile or more until we found the road again. It was as if she could see much of the path that lay before us. It made me wonder if her powers of scrying were much greater than she let on.

On the fourth day of our mountain crossing, fortune turned our way. The rain stopped, the sky cleared, and the sun shined down upon us and warmed the world. The needles of the trees and the bushes' leaves, still wet with rain, shimmered as if covered with millions of melting diamonds. For the first time, we had a good view of the great peaks around us. Snow and ice covered these spurs of rock, which pushed up into the sky to the north and south of us. Our little road led between them; the ground that we still had to cross was not really a gap in the mountains, but only a stretch where they rose less high. Although we had covered a good thirty miles, as the raven flies, we still had heights to climb and as many more miles before us.

We broke then for our midday meal in a sparkling glade by a little lake. Maram, who still had his talent with flint and steel, struck up a fire, which Liljana used to roast a rock goat that Atara had managed to shoot. After some days of cold cheese and battle biscuits, we were all looking forward to this feast. While the meat was cooking, Maram discovered a downed tree trunk, hollowed and swarming with bees.

"Mmm, honeycomb," he said to me as he pointed at it and licked his lips.

I watched from a safe distance as he built up another fire from wet twigs to smoke the bees out of their home. It took quite some time, and many blows of the axe, but he finally pulled out a huge, sticky mass of waxen comb dripping with golden honey. That he suffered only a dozen stings from his robbery amazed me.

"You're brave enough when you want to be," I said to him as he handed me a piece of comb.

"I'd take a thousand stings for honey," he said, licking the golden, glistening comb. "In all the world, there's nothing sweeter except a woman."

He rubbed some honey over the stings along his hands and face, and then we returned to the others to share this treasure.

We all gorged on the succulent goat meat and honey, Maram most of all. After he had finished stuffing his belly, he fell asleep on top of the dewed bracken near some bushes that Kane called pink spira. The rays of sun playing over his honey-smeared face showed a happy man.

We let him finish his nap while we broke our makeshift camp. After our water bags had all been filled and the horses packed, we made ready to mount them and ride back to the road. And then, just as Liljana pointed out that it wouldn't do to leave Maram sleeping, we heard him murmuring behind us as if dreaming: "Ah, Lalaiu, so soft, so sweet."

I turned to go fetch him, but stopped dead in my tracks. For what my eyes beheld then, my mind wouldn't quite believe: There, across the glade, in a break in the bushes above Maram and bending over him, crouched a large, black she-bear. Her shiny snout pressed down into Maram's face as she licked his lips and beard with her long, pink tongue. She seemed content lapping up the smears of honey that the careless Maram had left clinging there. And all the while, Maram murmured in his half-sleep, "Lalaiu, ah, Lalaiu."

I might have fallen down laughing at my friend's very mistaken bliss. But bears, after all, were bears. As it was midsummer, I feared that she had young cubs nearby.

Slowly and quietly, I reached out to tap on the elbow of Kane, who had his back to the bear as he tightened the cinch of his horse. When he turned to see what I was looking at, his face lit up with many emotions at once: concern, hilarity, contempt, outrage, and bloodlust. Quick as a wink, he drew forth his bow, strung it, and fit an arrow to its string. This movement alerted the others as to Maram's peril—and the horses, too. Altaru, facing the wind, finally turned to see the bear; he suddenly reared up as he let loose a tremendous whinny. Then the other horses added their voices to the great chorus of challenge and panic splitting the air. We had all we could do to keep hold of their reins and prevent them from running off. With Kane's bay stamping about and threatening to split his skull with a flying hoof, he couldn't get off a shot. And it was good that he didn't. For just as Maram finally awakened and looked up with wide eyes into the hairy face of his new lover, the bear started at the sudden noise and peered across the glade as if seeing us for the first time. She seemed more astonished than we were. It took her only a moment to gather her legs beneath her and bound off into the bushes.

"Oh, my Lord!" Maram called out upon realizing what had happened. He sprang up and raced to the lake's edge, where he knelt to wash his face. Then he said, "Oh, my—I was nearly eaten!"

Atara, keeping an eye out for the bear's return, walked up to him and poked a finger into his big belly. "Hmmph, you're half a bear yourself. I've never seen anyone eat honey the way that you do. But the next time, perhaps you should be more careful how you eat it."

That day we climbed to the greatest heights of our mountain crossing. This was a broad saddle between two great peaks, where lush meadows alternated with spirelike conifers. Thousands of wildflowers in colors from blazing pink to indigo brightened the sides of the road. Marmots and pikas grazed there, and looked at us as if they had never seen our kind before. But as they fed upon the seeds they found among the flowers, they kept a close watch for the eagles who hunted them. We watched for them, too. Maram wondered if the Great Beast could seize the souls of these circling birds and turn them into ghuls as he had the bear at the beginning of our journey.

"Do you think he's watching us, Val? Do you think he can see us?"

I stopped to draw my sword and watch it glow along the line to the east. Its fire was of a faint white. In the journey from Swan Island, I had noticed that other things beside the Lightstone caused it to shine. In the glint of the stars, its radiance was more silver, while the stillness of my soul seemed to produce a clearer and brighter light.

"It's strange," I said, "but ever since Lady Nimaiu gave me this blade, the Lord of Lies seems to have a harder time finding me, even in my dreams."

I looked up at a great, golden eagle gliding along the mountain wind, and I said, "There is no evil in these creatures, Maram. If they're watching, it's only because *they're* afraid of us."

My words seemed to reassure him, and we began our descent through the eastern half of the Crescent range with good courage. For another three days, beneath the strong mountain sun, we rode on without incident. And then, on the first day of Soal, with most of the great Crescent range at our backs, we came out of a cleft in the foothills to see a vast plain opening to the east. It was like a sea of grass, yellow-green, and colored with deeper green lines where trees grew along the winding watercourses. Another hour's journey would take us down into it.

"Eanna," Kane said, pointing down into this lovely land. "At least, this was once part of the ancient kingdom. But we're far from Imatru, and I doubt if King Hanniban holds any sway here."

We left the road only a couple of miles from the mountains. It turned south, whether toward some lost city in this pretty country or toward nowhere, none of us could say. The Red Desert, Kane told us, lay not so very far in that direction, and its drifting vermilion sands and dunes had swallowed up more than one city over the millennia.

Even hundreds of miles north of the heart of it, we felt a whiff of its heat. But after the freezing rains of the mountains, we welcomed this warming of the air, for it was dry like the breath of the stars and clean, and did not smother us. That night, beneath the constellations that hung in the heavens like a blazing tapestry, it felt quite cool—not so much that it chilled our bones, but rather that bracing crispness that sharpens all the senses and invites the marvel of the infinite.

The moon rose over the world like a gleaming half-shield; beneath it, from far out across the luminous earth, wolves howled and lions roared. I dreamed of these animals, and of a great silver swan that flew so high it caught the fire of the stars. When I awoke in the morning to a sky so blue that it seemed to go on forever, I felt this fire in me, warming my heart and calling me to journey forth toward the completion of our quest.

We rode steadily all that day and the next, and the two following that. It was hard for me, used to the more circumscribed horizons of mountainous or wooded country, to see just how far we traveled each day. But Atara had a better eye for distances here. She put the tally at a good fifty miles. So it was that we crossed almost the whole length of southern Eanna in very little time. And in all that wide land, dotted with cottonwood trees with their shimmering silver-green leaves, we saw no people.

"I should think *someone* would live here," Liljana said on the fifth morning of our journey across the steppe. "This is a fair land indeed."

Later that day, however, we came across some nomads who solved the mystery of Eanna's emptiness for us. The head of the thirty members of this band, who lived in tents woven from the hair of the shaggy cattle they tended, presented himself as Jacarun the Elder. He was a whitebeard whose bushy brows overhung his suspicious old eyes. But when he saw that we meant no harm and wanted only to cross his country, he was free with the milk and cheeses that his people got from their cattle—and with advice as well.

"We are the Telamun," he explained to us as we broke from our journey to take a meal with his family. "And once our tribe was great."

He told us that generations of war had reduced the Telamun to little more than a few dozen families; he lamented that their days as a free people were almost over, for others were now eyeing his family's ancient lands.

"King Hanniban has been having trouble with his barons, it's said, so hasn't yet been able to muster the few companies that it would take to conquer us," he told us. "But some of the Ravirii have come up from the Red Desert—they butchered a family not fifty miles from here. And the Yarkonans, well, in the long run, they're the real threat, of course. Count Ulanu of Aigul—they call him Ulanu the Handsome—has it in mind to conquer all of Yarkona in the Red Dragon's name and set himself up as king. If he ever does, he'll turn his gaze west and send his crucifiers here."

He called for one of his daughters to bring us some roasted beef. And then, after fixing his weary old eyes on Kane and my other friends, he looked at me and asked, "And where are you bound, Sar Valashu?"

"To Yarkona," I said.

"Aha, I thought so! To the Library at Khaisham, yes?"

"How did you know?"

"Well, you're not the first pilgrims to cross our lands on way to the Library, though you may be the last." He sighed as he lifted his staff toward the sky. "You see, no one goes to Yarkona anymore—it's an accursed land."

He advised us that, if we insisted on completing our journey, we should avoid Aigul and Count Ulanu's demesne at all costs.

We ate our roasted beef then, and washed it down with some fermented milk that Jacarun called *laas*. After visiting with his family and admiring the fatness of their cattle—and restraining Maram from doing likewise with their women—we thanked Jacarun for his hospitality and set out again.

Soon the steppe, which had gradually been drying out as we drew further away from the Crescent Mountains, grew quite sere. The greens of its grasses gave way to yellow and umber and more somber tones. New shrubs found root here in the rockier soil: mostly bitterbroom and yusage, as Kane named these tough-looking plants. They gave shelter to lizards, thrashers, rock sparrows, and other animals that I had never seen before. We put quite a few miles behind us, though not so many as on the four preceding days. The horses, perhaps sensing that they would find less water and food to the east, began moving more slowly as if to conserve their strength. And as we approached the land that Jacarun had warned us against, we turned our gazes inward to look for strength of our own.

And then, at the height of the afternoon's blaze, something in the wavering distances caught my attention. The horizon seemed to melt into the earth and sky like a ripple of quicksilver. My whole being tingled with a dreadful anticipation. On our ride down from the mountains, Master Juwain had tried to explicate the mirages of the hotter lands we had entered. The fire of the sun, he told us, heated up the air closest to the roiling ground, and like a lens the air bent light and cast it into our eyes in ways that dazzled and fooled us. And now, as I feared that Morjin had found us again with one of his illusions, I felt a sickness build inside me as with the charge in the air before a lightning stroke. It was as if the fire of his foul breath could bend and twist something inside a man and make him see things that did not exist.

Atara, looking at me from the top of her horse, seemed to sense what was happening. And she cried out to me, "Val— your sword!"

As Kane, Master Juwain, and my other friends turned toward me, I drew Alkaladur from its sheath. I pointed it east, straight into the heart of the illusion forming up and falling down upon me—and toward the distant Lightstone. My sword flared a brilliant white then. And the secret sword that I carried inside myself seemed to blaze with a clear and numinous radiance. All at once, I felt the air clear, and something inside me, too. A fresh wind seemed to blow across the world and through my soul.

"It is gone!" I called out to Atara, and the others. "In truth, the illusion never took hold!"

I tried to explain what I thought had happened, and Master Juwain listened attentively. He said to me, "It is the power of the silver gelstei. And *your* power, too. You are growing stronger, Valashu Elahad. And wiser."

"Ha—he's as strong as the silustria itself!" Kane called out. "Or could be, someday."

As Maram turned to marvel at my sword and beam his great faith in me, Kane cut him off with a savage look. And he growled out, to both Maram and me: "Don't be too pleased with yourselves just yet. Every strength, as with life and death, is paired with its opposite. Don't think that Morjin can't feel how you warded off his damn illusion. And so will want to wreak his revenge on you all the more."

Kane, I thought, detested self-congratulation and complacency. For him, even a great victory was only a step toward the next battle. And I wondered yet again on what anvil his soul had been forged.

After that we rode on toward the east. I kept a firm grip on my sword. I could not feel even the slightest haze of illusion working at me; it seemed almost that I had finally become invisible to Morjin.

Just before dusk, with the sun casting its longest rays over a glowing, reddened land, we came to a little trickle of water that Kane called the Parth. From its sandy banks, we looked out on the distant rocky outcroppings of Yarkona. There, I prayed, we would at last find the end of our journey and our hearts' deepest desire.

2

THE MOON THAT night was just past full and tinged a glowing red. It hung low in conjunction with a blazing twist of stars that some called the Snake constellation and others the Dragon.

"Blood Moon in the Dragon," Master Juwain said. He sat sipping his tea and looking up at the sky. "I haven't seen such-like in many years."

He brought out his book then, and sat reading quietly by the firelight, perhaps looking for some passage that would turn his attentions away from the stars. And then Liljana, who had gone off to wash the dishes in a small stream that led back to the Parth, returned holding some stones in her hand. They were black and shiny like Kane's gelstei but had more the look of melted glass. Liljana called them angels' tears; she said that wherever they were found, the earth would weep with the sorrow of the heavens. Atara gazed too long at these three, droplike stones. I felt a great heaviness descend upon her heart like a storm cloud, but she sat quietly sipping her tea and saying nothing.

We slept uneasily that night, and Kane didn't sleep at all. He stood for hours keeping watch, looking for lions in the shadows of the moon-reddened rocks or enemies approaching across the darkling plain. Alphanderry, who couldn't sleep either, brought out his mandolet and sang to keep him company.

And so the hours of night passed, and the heavens turned slowly about the rutilant earth. When morning came, we had a better look at this harsher country into which we had ventured. Yarkona, Master Juwain said, meant the "Green Land," but there was little of this hue about it. It was neither true steppe nor quite desert; the sparse grass here was burnt brown by a much hotter sun. The yusage had been joined by its even tougher cousins: ursage and spiny sage, whose spiked leaves discouraged the brush voles and deer from browsing upon them. We saw a few of these cautious animals in the early light, framed by some blackish cliffs to the east. These sharp prominences had a charred look about them, as if the sun had set fire to the very stone.

Kane told us we had made camp in Sagaram, a domain that some local lord had carved out of this once-great realm a century before. We looked to him for knowledge that might help us cross it. But as he admitted, he had come this way many years ago, in more peaceful times. Since then, he said, the boundaries of Yarkona's little baronies had no doubt shifted like a desert's sands, perhaps some of them having been blown away by war altogether.

"Aigul lies some sixty miles to the north and east," he told us. "Unless it has grown since then, and its counts have annexed lands to the south."

These lands we set out to cross on that dry, windy morning. Sagaram proved to be little more than a thin strip of shrubs and sere grasses running seventy miles or so along the Parth. By early afternoon, we had made our way clear into the next domain, although no river or stone marked the border, and we didn't realize it at the time. It took some more miles of plodding across the hot, rising plain before we found anyone who could give us directions. This was a goatherd named Jartak who lived in a little stone house by a well in sight of a striking rock formation to the east of us.

"You've come to Karkut," he told us as he shared a little cheese and bread with us. He was a short man, neither young nor old, with a great flowing tunic pulled over his spare frame and tied at the waist with a bit of dirty rope. "To the north of us lie Hansh and Aigul; to the south is the Nashthalan. That's mostly desert now, and you'll want to stay well to the north of it if you're to come to Khaisham safely."

While his two young sons watered our horses, we poured some of our brandy into his cup and asked him if he could tell more about his land.

"My business is herding goats, so what do I know?" he muttered. "But it's common knowledge that Count Ulanu wishes to conquer the whole of Yarkona in the bloody Red Dragon's name. Everyone looks to the Librarians of Khaisham to oppose him, for Khaisham remains strong."

"But what of your domain?" I asked him.

"What of it?" he said, shaking his head. "You ask painful questions. Well, I can tell you that Duke Rasham is a good enough man, but it's said that some of his lords have gone over to the Kallimun."

"But has your duke never sought help from Khaisham in holding his realm together?"

"Of course he has," he told me. "But there have been murders of those who speak for joining arms with Khaisham. You should be careful in Karkut, I'm sorry to say, Sar Valashu. These are evil times."

"It would seem that we must take care wherever we go in Yarkona."

"That is true," he said. "But there are some domains you must avoid at all costs."

We waited for him to say more, and Maram finally called out, "Which ones, then?"

Jartak looked to his right and then to his left as if he worried that someone might be listening to our conversation. I felt his fear like a snake working at his insides. But then he told us, "Stay clear of Aigul, of course. And to the west of those crucifiers, Brahamdur, whose baron and lords are practically Count Ulanu's slaves. And Sagaram—you were lucky to cross it unmolested, for they've been forced into an alliance with Aigul."

"All right, all right," Maram said with both irritation and disquiet, "then we'll set our course south of those domains."

"But you can't," Jartak told him.

"Why not, damn it?"

"Because to the north of us, between here and Aigul, Hansh has nearly lost its freedom as well. It's said that soon Count Ulanu will press Hansh levies into his army."

Maram, of course, didn't like the news he was hearing. He looked at Jartak and half-shouted, "But how are we to reach Khaisham, then?"

"The route through Madhvam would be the safest," Jartak said, naming the domain just east of us. "They have only swords and spears for Count Ulanu, though I haven't heard that they have any quarrel with pilgrims."

But Madhvam, as Maram learned, adjoined Aigul to its north, and that was too close for him. "What if this Ulanu the Handsome attacks Madhvam while we're crossing it?"

"That's unlikely," Jartak said. "A knight stopping at my well only two days ago told that Count Ulanu has just marched against Sikar. The fortifications of that city are the strongest in all Yarkona."

Maram took a gulp of his brandy and said, "Ah, I should think that the Librarians' opposition of Count Ulanu—and Sikar's—would lead all the free domains to join against him."

"Well, I should think that, too, but what do I know?" Jartak said. "I'm afraid many lords think otherwise. They say that if Count Ulanu's conquest is inevitable, they should join with him rather than wind up nailed to crosses."

"Nothing's inevitable," Kane snarled, "except such cowardly talk."

Now Maram poured himself another cup of brandy and sat staring at the dark liquid. Then he said, "If the Red Dragon desires the conquest of Yarkona so badly, I don't see why he doesn't just send an army to reduce it. Sakai isn't so far from here, is it? What could stop him?"

At this, Jartak began laughing and said, "Send an army through the White Mountains? That is the land of the Ymanir."

He went on to say that the Ymanir were also called the Frost Giants; they were savage men nearly eight feet tall and covered with white fur, who were known to kill all who entered their country and eat them.

And with that image planted in our minds, we finished our little meal and thanked Jartak for his hospitality. All that hot afternoon we rode along the route that he had advised. We found the Nashbrum, a smallish river that ran down from the mountains and seemed to narrow and lose substance to the burning earth as it flowed toward the Nashthalan. We paralleled it almost all the way to Madhvam, and then spent the next day passing through that sere land. We encountered no one who possessed the will to try to stop us. Toward mid-afternoon, some big clouds formed up and let loose a quick burst of thunder and rain. It lasted only long enough to wet the sharp rocks that tore at our horses' hooves. It was a measure of our desire to reach Khaisham that we still made a good distance that day. By the time the sun had left its fierceness behind it in the waves of heat radiating off the glowing land, we found ourselves in the domain of Virad. To the north of us, and to the east, too, the knifelike peaks of the White Mountains caught the red fire of the setting sun.

"Well, that was a day," Maram said. He wiped the sweat from his dripping brown curls and dismounted. "I'm hot, I'm thirsty, I'm tired. And what's worse," he said, pressing his nose to his armpit, "I stink. This heat is much worse than the rain in the Crescent Mountains."

"Hmmph," Atara said to him, "it's only worse because you're suffering from it now. Just wait until our return."

"If we *do* return," he muttered. He scratched at some beads of sweat in his thick beard as he looked about. "Val, are you sure this is Virad?"

I pointed along the river where it abruptly turned north across the rocky ground about five miles ahead of us. "Jartak told us to look for that turning. There, we're to set our course to the southeast and so come to the pass of the Kul Joram after another forty miles."

According to Jartak, a spur running down from the White Mountains separated Virad from Khaisham, and the pass was the only way to cross it.

"Well, then, we must have ridden clear across Madhvam today."

"Too far," Kane said, coming over to us and studying the terrain around us. "We pressed the horses too hard. Tomorrow we'll have to satisfy ourselves with half that distance."

That night we fortified our camp with some of the logs and branches we found down by the river. The moon, when it rose over the black hills, was waning though still nearly full. It set the wolves farther out on the plain to howling: a high-pitched, plaintive sound that had always unnerved Maram—and Liljana and Master Juwain, as well. To soothe them, Alphanderry plucked the strings of his mandolet and sang of ages past and brighter times to come when the Galadin and Elijin would walk the earth again. His clear voice rang out across the river, echoing from the ominous-looking rocks. It brought cheer to us all; but it also touched Kane with a deep dread I felt pulling at his insides like the teeth of something much worse than wolves.

"Too loud," Kane muttered at Alphanderry. "This isn't Alonia, eh? Nor even Surrapam."

After that Alphanderry sang more quietly, and the golden tones pouring from his throat seemed to harmonize with the wolves' howls, softening them and rendering them less haunting. But then, above his beautiful voice and those of the wolves, from the north of us where the river turned into some low hills, came a distant keening sound that was terrible to hear.

"Shhh," Maram said, tapping Alphanderry's knee, "what was that?"

Alphanderry put down his mandolet and listened with the rest of us. Again came the far-off keening, and then an answering sound, much closer, from the hills to the east. It was like the shrieking of a cat and the scream of a wounded horse and the cries of the damned all bound up into a single, piercing howl.

"That's no wolf!" Maram called out. "What is it?"

Again came the howl, closer and fiercer: OWRRRUULLL!

Kane jumped to his feet and drew his sword. It seemed to point of its own toward the terrible sound.

"Do you know what that is?" Maram asked him, also drawing his sword.

Now all of us, except Master Juwain, took up weapons and stood staring at the moonlit rocks across the river.

"Ah, for the love of woman, Kane, please tell us if you know what we're facing!"

But Kane remained silent, staring off into the dark. The cry came again, but it seemed to be moving away from us. After a while, it faded and then vanished into the night.

Maram turned toward Kane as if it was he who had called forth the hideous voices and said, "Wolves don't howl like that."

"No," Kane muttered, "but the Blues do."

"The Blues! Who or what are the Blues?"

It was Master Juwain who answered Maram. He knelt by the fire, reading from his book as he quoted from the Visions: " 'Then came the blue men, the half-dead whose cries will wake the dead. They are the heralds of the Red Dragon, and the ghosts of battle follow them to war.' "

He closed his book and said, "I've often wondered what those lines meant."

"They mean this," Kane said. "None of us will sleep tonight."

He told us then what he knew of the Blues. He said that they were a short, immensely squat and powerful people, a race of warriors bred by Morjin during the Age of Swords. It was their gift—or curse—to have few nerves in their bodies and so to feel little pain. This gift was deepened by their eating the berries of the kirque plant, which enabled them to march into battle in a frenzy of unfeeling wrath toward their foes. The berries also stained their skin a pale shade of blue; most of their men accentuated this color by rubbing berry juice across their skin so that the whole of their bodies were blemished a deep blue the color of a bruise. Most of them, as well, displayed many scabs, open cuts, and running sores across their arms and legs, for in their nearly nerveless immunity to pain, they were wont to wound themselves and take no notice of the injury. But others couldn't help noticing them: they went into battle naked wielding huge steel axes. They howled like maddened wolves. They killed without pity or feeling as if their souls had died. Because of this, they were called the Soulless Ones or the Half-Dead.

"It was said that the Blues had all perished two ages ago," Kane told us. "But I've long heard it rumored that there was some terror hidden in the White Mountains—other than the Frost Giants, of course."

We all looked at the great, snowcapped peaks glistening in

the moonlight. And then Maram said, "But we're still a good forty miles from the mountains. What would the Blues be doing in the hills of Yarkona?"

"That is what I would like to know," Kane told him. Then he clapped him on the arm and smiled his savage smile. "But not too badly. And not tonight. Now why don't we try to sleep? Alphanderry and I will take the first watch. If the Blues come back to sing for us, we'll be sure to wake you."

But the Half-Dead, if such they really were, did not return that night. Even so, none of us got much sleep. By the time morning came, we were all red-eyed and crabby, almost too tired to pull ourselves onto our footsore horses. We prayed for a few clouds to soften the sun. Each hour, however, it waxed hotter and hotter so that it threatened to set all the sky on fire.

We rode through a land devoid of people. After we turned southeast at the bend in the river, we sought out the few scattered huts along the rocky plain to gather knowledge of the country through which we passed. But the huts were all empty, deserted it seemed in great haste. Perhaps, I thought, the cries of the Soulless Ones had driven their owners away.

Late that morning, we saw some vultures circling in the sky ahead of us. As we rode closer, the air thickened with a terrible smell. Maram wanted to turn aside from whatever lay in that direction, but Kane was eager as always to see what must be seen. And so we pressed on until we crested a low rise. And there before us, growing out of the sage and grass like trees, were three wooden crosses from which hung the blackened bodies of three naked men. Vultures, perched on the arms of the crosses, bent their beaks downward, working at them. When Kane saw these death birds, his face darkened and his heart filled with wrath. He charged forward, waving his sword and growling like a wolf to drive the vultures away.

"How I hate these damn birds!" he raged. "They make a mockery of the One's noblest creation."

We rode up to him, holding our cloaks over our noses against the awful stench. I forced myself to look up at these husks of once-proud men, which iron nails and the iron-hard beaks of the vultures had reduced so pitifully. To Kane, I said, "You didn't tell us that the Blues learned the defilements of the Crucifier."

"I never heard that they did," he said, looking at the crosses. "This may be the work of some lord who has gone over to the Kallimun."

"What lord?" Liljana asked, nudging her horse closer to Kane. "Jartak said that the lords of Virad looked to Khaisham for leadership."

"So, it seems that some of them may look to Aigul."

I dismounted Altaru and walked over to the center cross. I reached out and touched the foot of the man who had been nailed to it. His flesh was soft, swollen, and hot—as hot as the burning air itself.

"We should bury these men," I said.

Kane thrust his sword toward the rock-hard earth. "We *should* bury them, Val. But it would take us a day of digging, eh? And whoever put them here may come back and find us."

And so, after a saying a prayer for the three men who had ended their lives in this desolate place, we mounted our horses and resumed our journey. But as we rode over the hot, tormented earth, Alphanderry wet his throat with a little blood from his cracked lips and gave us a song to hearten us. He made a hauntingly beautiful music in remembrance of the dead men, singing their souls up to the stars behind the sky. Despite the terrible thing we had just seen, his words were in praise of life:

> Sing ye songs of glory,
> Sing ye songs of glory,
> That the light of the One
> Will shine upon the world.

"Too loud," Kane muttered as he scanned the low hills about us.

But Alphanderry, perhaps concentrating on an image of the Lightstone that lay somewhere before us, raised up his voice even louder. He sang strongly and bravely, with a reckless abandon, and his voice filled the countryside. Even the grasses,

I thought, sere and stunted here, would want to weep at the sound of it.

"Too damn loud, I say!" Kane barked out, flashing an angry look at Alphanderry. "Do you want to announce us to the whole world?"

Alphanderry, however, seemed drunk on the beauty of his own singing. He ignored Kane. After a while, strange and wonderful words began pouring from his lips in a torrent that seemed impossible to stop.

"Damn you, Alphanderry, come to your senses, will you?"

As Kane glowered at Alphanderry, he finally fell quiet. The look on his face was that of a scolded puppy. To Kane, he said, "I'm sorry, but I was so close. So very close to finding the words of the angels."

"If the crucifiers come upon us here," Kane said, "not even the angels will be able to help us."

Even as he said this, Atara pointed at a far-off hill. I looked there and thought I saw a hazy figure vanish behind it.

"What is it?" Kane asked, squinting.

Atara, who had the best eyes of any of us, said, "It was a man—he seemed dressed in blue."

At this news, Maram sat swallowing against the fear in his throat as if he could so easily make it go away.

"I'm sorry," Alphanderry said again. "But maybe the blue man didn't see us."

"Foolish minstrel," Kane said softly. "Let's ride now, and hope he didn't."

And so we set out again, riding as swiftly as we dared. And with each mile we covered, the air grew hotter so that it fairly roiled with the stench of death. We entered a country of rolling swells of earth like the waves of the sea; some were a hundred feet high and broken with rocky outcroppings. We kept a reasonably straight course, winding our way down their troughs. After a while, I felt a sick sensation along the back of my neck as if the vultures were watching me. I stopped and turned toward the left; I looked toward the top of a rise even as Atara did, too.

"What is it?" Maram said, reining up behind us. "What do you see?"

We had been told to avoid Aigul, and so we had. But Aigul han't avoided us. Just as Maram swallowed another mouthful of air and belched in disquiet, a company of cavalry broke over the rise and thundered down the slope straight toward us. There were twenty-three of them, as I saw at a glance. Their mail and helms gleamed in the sun. And holstered and up-raised from a horse near their leader was a long pole from which streamed their standard: a bright white banner showing the coils and fiery tongue of a great red dragon.

"Oh, my Lord!" Maram cried out. "Oh, my Lord!"

Liljana, who had drawn her sword, looked about with her calm, penetrating eyes and said to me, "Do we flee or fight, Val?"

"Perhaps neither," I said, trying to keep my voice calm. I turned, pointing toward the right, where a hummock stood like a grass-covered castle. "Up there—we'll face them up there."

It took us only a few moments to gain what little protection the hummock's height provided us. Its top was nearly flat, per-haps fifty yards across; we sat on our horses there as we watched the men approach. I didn't remark what we could now see quite plainly: that next to this great lord, who bore upon his white surcoat another red dragon, rode three naked men whose bodies seemed painted blue. Their mountain ponies carried them up our hummock with greater agility than did the war-horses of their heavily armored companions. Each of the three men was short and immensely muscled, and each brandished in his knotted fist an immense steel axe.

"I'm sorry," Alphanderry said to Kane, who had his sword drawn as his black eyes stared down at the approaching com-pany.

"It's not your sorrow that we need now, my young friend," Kane said with a grim smile, "but your strength. And your courage."

The company drew up in a crescent on the slope below us. And then their leader, along with the standard-bearer and one of the blue men, rode forward a few paces. He was a quick-eyed man with a vulpine look to his hard face, which seemed all angles and planes, like pieces of chipped flint. Many would have called him handsome, a grace that he seemed to relish as he sat up straight on his horse in all his vanity and pride. His eyes were almost as dark as his well-trimmed beard; they fixed upon me like poisoned lances that pierced my heart.

"Who are you?" he called out to me in a raspy voice. "Come down and identify yourselves!"

"Who are you," I said to him, "who rides upon us like robbers?"

"Robbers, is it? Be careful how you speak to the lord of this domain!"

I traded a quick look with Kane and then Atara, who held her strung bow down against her saddle. Jartak had told us that Virad's lord was Duke Vikram, an old man with scars along his white-bearded face. To this much younger man below us, I said, "We had heard that the lord of this domain is Duke Vikram. You do not fit his description."

The man exulted. "Duke Vikram is dead. I'm the lord of Virad now. And of Sikar and Aigul. You may address me as Count Ulanu."

It came to me, all in a moment, what the terrible stench in the air must be: the taint of many corpses rotting in the sun. Somewhere near here, I knew, a battle had recently been fought. And Count Ulanu claimed the lordship of Virad by right of conquest.

"You have my name, now give me yours," the count said to me.

"We're pilgrims," I told him, "only pilgrims bound for Khaisham."

"Pilgrims with swords," he said, looking at Kane, Maram, and Liljana. Then he turned his gaze on me and studied my face for a long time. "It's said that the Valari look like you."

I slipped my hand beneath my cloak as I rested it on the hilt of my sword. I noticed Maram gripping his red crystal in his free hand even as Liljana held her blue stone to her head.

"What's that you've got in your hand?" Count Ulanu barked at her.

But Liljana didn't answer him; she just sat staring at him as if her eyes could drink up all the challenge in his and still hold more.

Count Ulanu bent his head to whisper something to one of the Blues, whose large, round head was shaved and stained darkly with the juice of the kirque berries, even as Kane had said. One of his ears was missing, and the skin about the hole was all scabbed over. Along his side, he showed an open wound, probably from a sword cut; in the dark red suck of it squirmed many white maggots eating away the decaying flesh there.

"You picked an evil time for your pilgrimage," the count said, looking up at us. His voice had now softened as if he were trying to lure a reluctant serving girl into his chambers. "There has been unrest in Sikar and in Virad. Both Duke Amadam and Duke Vikram were forced to ask our help in putting down rebellions. This we did. We've recently fought a battle not far from here, at Tarmanam. Victory was ours, but sadly, Duke Vikram was killed. A few of the rebellious lords and their knights escaped us. They'll likely turn to outlawry now and fall upon pilgrims such as you. That is why we must ask you to lay down your arms and come with us for your own protection."

I sat on top of Altaru, sweating in the burning sun as I listened to him. I smelled the acridness of his sweat and that of the knights about him. I knew that he was lying, even if I couldn't quite tell what the truth really was. I noticed Liljana suddenly close her eyes; it was strange how she seemed to be staring straight at him even so.

"You might ask us to lay down our arms," Kane told him, with surprising politeness, "but we must respectfully decline your request."

"I'm afraid we must to do more than ask," Count Ulanu said, his voice rising with anger. "Please lay them down now and come with us."

"No, we can't do that."

"When peace has been restored, we'll provide you an escort to Khaisham so that you may complete your pilgrimage."

"No, thank you," Kane said icily.

"You have my word that you'll be treated honorably and well," Count Ulanu said, smiling sincerely. "There's a tower for guests at Duke Vikram's castle—it overlooks the Ashbrum River. We'll be happy to set you up there."

Now Liljana's nose pointed straight toward him as if she were sniffing out poison in a cup. She opened her eyes to stare at him. "He speaks the truth: there are many towers of wood now at the duke's castle. He intends to set us on these crosses with the duke's knights and his family above the river."

The sudden rage that empurpled Count Ulanu's face just then was terrible to behold. He whipped out his saber and pointed it at Liljana as he shouted, "Damn you, witch! Give me what's in your hand before I cut it off and take it from you!"

Liljana opened her hand to show him her blue gelstei. Then she smiled defiantly as she closed her hand about the stone and stuck her fist out toward him.

"Damn witch," the count muttered.

"There was a battle at Tarmanam," she said to all who could hear. "But there were no rebellious lords—only those faithful to Duke Vikram, who has been cruelly tortured to death."

In her frightfully calm and measured way, she went on to tell us something of what she had seen in the count's mind. She said that he and his army had marched into Sikar even as Jartak had told us. But there had been no siege of the mighty fortifications there. As soon as the count's engineers had set up their catapults and battering rams, his army had been joined by a host of Blues. And then Kallimun priests within the city had assassinated the Duke of Sikar and his family; they had thrown open the city gates. Hostages had been taken and threatened with crucifixion. The Sikar army had then gone over to the count, taking oaths of loyalty to him and his distant master. Thus Sikar had fallen in scarcely a day.

Count Ulanu had then gathered up both armies—and the companies of Blues. In a lightning strike, he had swept south, into Virad. Duke Vikram and his lords had had no time to watch events unfold in Sikar and to sue for peace on favorable terms; their only choice was to surrender unconditionally or to ride out to battle. With the Khaisham Librarians still preparing to send a force to Sikar, much too late, Duke Vikram chose to fight alone. But his forces had been slaughtered and many of the survivors crucified. And now his captured family awaited the same fate, imprisoned in his own castle.

"It was treachery that took Sikar," Liljana said to us. "And now this lying count promises us more treachery with every breath."

Two of the count's knights, clad in mail and armed with wicked-looking, curved swords, nudged their horses closer to their master. Then the count told Liljana: "You know many things but not the one that really matters."

"And what is that, dear Count?"

"In the end, you'll beg to be allowed to bow before me and kiss my feet. How long has it been, old witch, since you've kissed a man?"

In answer, Liljana again held out her fist to him, this time with her middle finger extended.

The count's face filled with hate, but he had the force of will to channel it into his words: "Why don't you try looking into my mind now?"

Then he, this priest of the Kallimun, turned upon her a gaze so venomous and full of malice that she gave a cry of pain.

"What a gracious lord you are!" she said. She continued to stare at him despite her obvious anguish. "I should imagine that all Yarkona has remarked on your exemplary manners."

I knew what she intended, and I approved her strategy: she was trying to use her blue gelstei and all the sharpness of her tongue to provoke the count into an action against us. For surely there must be a battle between us; it would be best if we forced the count and his men to fight it, here, upon this high ground, charging up this hill. This was our fate, perhaps written in the moon and stars, and I could see it approaching as clearly as could Atara. And yet it was also my fate that I must first speak for peace.

"Count Ulanu," I said, "you are now lord of Sikar and Virad by conquest. But surely the lords of Khaisham are preparing to take them back. Why don't you withdraw your men so that we may continue our journey? When we reach Khaisham, we'll speak to the Librarians concerning these matters. Perhaps a way can be found to restore peace to Yarkona without more war."

It was a poor speech, I thought, and Count Ulanu had as much regard for it as I.

"Pilgrims, are you?" he muttered. "Seven of you, what's to be done with seven damn pilgrims?"

As the hot wind rippled the grasses about the hill, the Blue warrior with the shaved head impatiently turned to speak to the count. His words came out in a series of guttural sounds like the grunts of a bear. From his neck dangled a clear stone, which gleamed in the fierce rays of the sun. It was a large, square-cut diamond like those that are affixed to leather breast-pieces to make up the famed Valari battle armor. The other Blues sported identical gems. I saw in a flash how these Blues had acquired such stones: they had been ripped free from the armor of the crucified Valari after the Battle of Tarshid an entire age ago. For three thousand years, Morjin had hoarded them against the day they might be needed. As now they were. For clearly he had bought the service of the Blues' axes with these stolen diamonds.

"Urturuk here," the count said, nodding at the scabrous Blue, "suggests that we do send you on to Khaisham. Or at least your heads."

Like a perfect jewel forming up in my mind, I suddenly saw what Morjin's spending of this long-hoarded treasure portended: that he had finally committed to the open conquest of not only Yarkona but all of Ea.

"The Librarians," the count said, "must be sent some sign that they've forfeited the right to receive more pilgrims."

While the horses, ours and theirs, nickered nervously and pawed the earth, Count Ulanu stared up the grassy hill at us, deciding what to do.

And then Liljana smiled at him and said, "But haven't you already made your request to the Librarians?"

Again, the rage returned to Count Ulanu's face as he gazed

at Liljana with all his hate. And she stared right back at him, taking perhaps too much delight in her power to provoke him. Then she told us of the hidden thing that she had so painfully wrested from the count's mind.

"After Tarmanam," she called to him so that all his men could hear, "didn't you send a rider to Khaisham demanding a tribute of gold? And didn't the Librarians send you a book illumined with gilt letters? A book of manners?"

Her revelation of the Librarians' rebuke and the count's secret shame proved too much for him. The count's hand tightened on his horse's reins, pulling back its head until it screamed in pain. And then the count himself suddenly pointed his sword at us and screamed to his men, "Damned witch! Take her! Take them all! And be sure you take the Valari alive!"

This command pleased the three Blues who clanked their great axes together and, in harmony with the ringing steel, let loose a long and savage howl.

Then twenty knights kicked their spurs against their screaming horses' flanks, and the battle was joined.

THE COUNT HIMSELF led the charge up the hill. He was daring enough to show brave, but cunning enough to know that his knights wouldn't let him ride right onto our swords unprotected and alone. As their horses wheezed and sweated and pounded up the steep slope, two of his knights spurred their mounts slightly ahead of him to act as living shields. And it was well for him that they did. For just then, behind me, a bowstring twanged and an arrow buried itself in the lead knight's chest. I heard Atara call out, "Twenty-three!" A few moments later, another arrow sizzled through the roiling air, only to glance off the count's shield. And then he and his men were upon us.

The first knight to crest the hill—a big, burly man with fear-maddened eyes—drove his horse straight toward me. But owing to his uphill charge, he had little momentum and less balance in his saddle; with Altaru's hooves planted squarely in the earth, the point of my lance took him in the throat and drove clean through him. The force of his fall ripped the lance from my grasp. A wheeze of bloody breath escaped from his ruined throat and filled me like a scream. It built louder and louder until it seemed that the earth itself was shrieking in agony as it split asunder beneath me.

"Val!" Kane called out from somewhere nearby. "Draw your sword!"

I heard his sword slice the air and cleave through the gorget surrounding a knight's neck. I was vaguely aware of Maram fumbling with his red crystal and trying to catch a few rays of sun with which to burn the advancing knights. Master Juwáin, to my astonishment, scooped up the shield of the man I had unhorsed; he held it, protecting Liljana from another knight's sword as she tried to urge her horse toward Count Ulanu. Behind me, to the right and left, Atara and Alphanderry worked furiously with their swords to beat back the attack of yet more knights who were trying to flank us along the rear of the hill and take us from behind.

"Val!"

With a trembling hand, I drew forth Alkaladur. The long blade gleamed in the light of the sun. The sight of the silver gelstei shining so brilliantly dismayed Count Ulanu and his men, even as it drove back the darkness engulfing me. My mind suddenly cleared. A fierce strength flowed up my hand into my arm, a strength that felt as bottomless as the sea. It was as if I were drawing Altaru's surging blood into me, and more, the very fires of the earth itself.

The Bright Sword flared white then, so brilliant and dazzling that the nearest knights cried out and threw their arms over their eyes. But other knights and the three Blues pressed toward me. Kane was near me, too, cutting and killing and cursing. Horses collided with each other, snorted and screamed. Altaru turned his wrath on any who tried to harm me. An un-horsed knight tried to hammer my back with his mace; Altaru kicked out, catching him in the chest and knocking him over. And then, even as Urturuk, the Blue with the missing ear, came for me with his huge axe, Altaru backed up to trample the fallen knight with his sharp hooves. He struck down with tremendous force, again and again until the knight's head was little more than white bones and broken brains beneath his crumpled helm.

"Val—on your right!"

I narrowly pulled back from Urturuk's ferocious axe blow, which would have chopped through Altaru's neck. Altaru furi-ously bit out at Urturuk, taking a good chunk of flesh from his shoulder. Urturuk seemed not to notice this ugly wound. He drove straight toward Altaru again, his mouth fairly frothing with wrath, this time trying to split open his skull—or mine.

At last I swung Alkaladur. It arced downward in a silvery flash, cutting through the axe's haft and into Urturuk's bare chest, cleaving him nearly in two. The spray of blood from his opened chest nearly blinded me. I almost didn't see one of the count's knights coming at me from the other side. But a sudden whinny and tensing of Altaru's body told me of his attack. I whirled about, swinging Alkaladur again. Its terri-ble, star-tempered edge cut through both shield and the mailed forearm behind it, and then bit into the steel rings covering the knight's belly. He cried out to see his arm fall away like a pruned tree limb, and plunged to the ground screaming out his death agony.

"Take him!" Count Ulanu screamed to his knights scarcely a dozen yards from me. "Can't you take one damned Valari!"

With knights now pressing us on all sides, I urged Altaru to-ward Count Ulanu. But Liljana, with Master Juwain still hold-ing out the shield to protect her right side while Kane bulled his way forward on her left, had already reached him. She struck her sword straight out toward his sneering face. The point of it managed to slice off the tip of his nose even as one of his knight's horses knocked into hers. Blood streamed from this rather minor gash. But it was enough to unnerve Count Ulanu—and his men.

"The count is wounded!" one of his captains shouted. "Fall back!"

Although it hadn't been Count Ulanu who ordered this ignoble retreat, he made no move to gainsay his knight's command. He himself led the flight back down the hill. Two of his knights guarded his back as he turned his horse—and paid with their lives. Kane's sword took one of them clean through the forehead while I pushed the point of mine through the other's armor into his heart. And suddenly the battle was over.

"Do we pursue?" Maram called out, reining in his horse. He was either battle-drunk, I thought, or mad. "I'll give them a taste of fire, I will!"

So saying, he drew out his gelstei and tried to loose a bolt of flame upon Count Ulanu and his retreating knights. But although the crystal warmed to a bright scarlet, it never came fully alive.

"Hold!" I called out. "Hold now!"

Atara, who had her bow raised, fired off an arrow, which split the mail of one of the retreating knights. He galloped away from us with a feathered shaft sticking out of his shoulder.

"Hold, please!"

With the three men I had killed lying rent and bleeding on the grass, I could barely keep from falling, too. Kane had dispatched two knights and the other two Blues. Atara had added two more men to her tally, while Maram, Alphanderry, Liljana, and Master Juwain had done extraordinarily well in beating off the assault of armored knights without taking any wounds themselves. But now the agony of the slain took hold of my heart. A doorway showing only blackness opened to my left. The nothingness there beckoned me deeper toward death than I had ever been. To keep from being pulled inside, I held on to Alkaladur as tightly as I could. Its numinous fire opened another door through which streamed the light of the sun and stars. It warmed my icy limbs and brought me back to life.

"Val, are you wounded?" Master Juwain asked as he came up to me. Then he turned to take stock of the corpse-strewn hummock and called out to the rest of our company, "Is anyone wounded?"

None of us were. I sat on top of the trembling Altaru, gaining strength each moment as I watched the last of Count Ulanu's men disappear over the same ridge from which they had come.

"What now, Val?" Liljana said to me as she wiped the count's blood from the tip of her sword. "Do we pursue?"

"No, we've had enough of battle for one day. And we don't know how close the rest of the count's army is." I looked up at the blazing sun and then out across Yarkona's rocky hills, calculating time and distances. To Liljana, to my other battle-sickened friends, I said, "Now we flee."

They needed no further encouragement to put this hill of carnage behind us. We eased the horses down its grassy slopes. And then we urged them to fast canter toward the east. The pass into Khaisham called the Kul Joram, I guessed, lay a good twenty-five or thirty miles ahead of us. And beyond that, we would still need to ride another twenty miles to reach the Librarians' city.

We kept up a good pace for most of five miles, but then one of the packhorses threw a shoe, and we had to go more slowly as the sun-scorched turf gave way to ground planted with many more rocks. It was dry and hot, and the glazy blue sky held not the faintest breath of wind. The horses sweated even more profusely than did we. They kept driving onward through the murderous heat, snorting at the dust, making choking sounds in their throats and gasping until their nostrils and lips were white with froth. When we came across a little stream running down from the mountains, we had to stop to water them lest our dash across the burning plain kill them.

Alphanderry, gazing back in the direction from which we had come, spoke to all of us, saying, "I'm sorry, but this is all my fault. If I hadn't opened my mouth to sing, we'd never have been discovered."

I walked up to him and laid my hand on the damp, dark

curls of his head. I told him, "They might have found us in any case. And without your songs, we'd never have had the courage to come this far."

"How far *have* we come?" Master Juwain said, looking eastward. "How far to this Kul Joram?"

Liljana brushed back the hair sticking to her face as she caught my eye. "There's something I must tell you, something else I saw in the count's filthy mind. After Tarmanam, he sent a force to the Kul Joram to hold it for his army's advance into Khaisham."

Maram, bending low by the stream to examine the hooves of his tiring sorrel, straightened up and said, "But this is terrible news! How are we to cross into Khaisham, then?"

"Don't you give up hope so easily. There is another pass."

"The Kul Moroth," Kane spat out as he gazed into the wavering distances. "It lies twenty miles north of the Kul Joram. It is an evil place, and much narrower, but it will have to do."

Maram pulled at his beard as he fixed Liljana with a suspicious look. "I thought you promised that you'd never look into another's mind without his permission? This was a sacred principle, you said."

"Do you think I'd have let that treacherous count nail you to a cross because of a principle?" Liljana said. "Besides, I promised you, not him."

Master Juwain came up to examine me and said, "It seems that you're growing ever more able to put up shields against others' agonies."

"No, it's just the opposite," I said, thinking of the three men I had slain. "Each time a man goes over now, it carries me deeper into the death realm. But the *valarda,* even as it opens me to this void, also opens me to the world. To all its pain, yes, but to its life as well. The sword that Lady Nimaiu gave me only aids in this opening. When I wield it truly, it's as if the soul of the world pours into me."

So saying, I drew Alkaladur and held it gleaming faintly toward the east.

"Then the sword lends you a certain protection against the vulnerabilities of your gift."

"No, it is not so, sir. Someday when I kill, the death realm will grab hold of me so tightly that I'll never return."

Because there was nothing for him to say to this, he stood looking at me quietly even as the others fell silent, too.

Then Atara, scanning the horizon behind us, drew in a quick breath as she pointed toward the west. "They're coming. Don't you see?"

At first none of us did. But as we stared at the far-off hills until our eyes burned, we finally saw a plume of dust rising into the sky.

"How many are there?" Maram asked Atara.

"That's hard to say," she told him.

But even as we stood there beneath the quick beatings of our hearts, the dust plume grew bigger.

"Too many, I think," Kane said. "Let's ride now. We'll have to leave the packhorses behind. They're practically lame and slowing us down."

We made a quick redistribution of those vital stores that the packhorses carried, filling our mounts' saddlebags as full as we dared. Then we said good-bye to these faithful beasts that had carried our belongings so far. I prayed that they would wander over Yarkona's mounded plains until some kind farmer found them and put them to work.

With pursuit now certain, we set out for the Kul Moroth. We rode hard, pressing the horses to a full gallop until it became clear that they couldn't hold such a pace. Altaru and Iolo were strong enough, and Fire, too, but Kane's big bay and Liljana's gelding had little wind left for such heroics. Master Juwain's sorrel seemed to have aged greatly since setting out from Mesh, while Maram's poor horse was in the worst shape of any of our mounts. His sore hoof, now bruised by hot stones, was getting worse with every furlong we covered.

"Perhaps you should just leave me behind," Maram gasped as he urged his limping sorrel to keep up with us. "I'll ride off in a different direction. Perhaps the count's men will follow me, instead of you."

It was a courageous offer, if a little insincere. I thought that he might hope that our pursuers would follow us instead of him.

"On the Wendrush," Atara said from on top of Fire, "that is how it must be. Where speed is life, a war party is only as fast as its slowest horse."

Her words greatly alarmed Maram, who had no real intention of simply riding away from us. She saw his disquiet and said, "But this is not the Wendrush and we are no war party."

"Just so," I said. "Our company will reach Khaisham together or not at all. We have a lead; now let's keep it."

But this proved impossible to do. As the ground grew even drier and rougher, Maram's sorrel slowed his pace even more. And the plume of dust behind us grew closer and thickened into a cloud.

"What are we to do?" Maram muttered. "What are we to do?"

And Kane, bringing up the rear, answered him with one word, "Ride."

And ride we did. The rhythm of our horses' hooves beat against the ground like the pounding of a drum. It grew very hot. I squinted against the sun pouring down upon the rocks to the east of us. Its rays, I thought, were like fiery nails fixing us to the earth. Dust stung my eyes and found its way into my mouth. Here the soil tasted of salt and men's tears, if not those of the angels. Here, in this burning waste, it would be easy for horse and man to perish, sweated dry of all their water.

After some miles, all my thoughts turned toward visions of water. I remembered the deep blue stillness of Lake Waskaw and the rivers of Mesh; I thought of the soft white clouds over Mount Vayu and its glittering snowfields melting into rills and brooks. I began to pray for rain.

But the sky remained clear, a hot and hellish blue-white that glared like fired iron. And the cloud of dust following us grew ever nearer.

"The Count," Kane observed bitterly, looking back, "can afford to leave his laggards behind."

As the hours passed, we entered terrain in which a series of low ridges ran from north to south like dull knife blades pushing up the earth. They paralleled the mountain spur still ahead of us where, if Kane's memory proved true, we would find the Kul Moroth. In most places, we had no choice but to ride up and over these sunbaked folds. This hot, heaving work tortured the horses. From the top of one of them, where we paused to rest our faithful and sweating friends, we had a better view of the men pursuing us.

"Oh, Lord!" Maram groaned. "There are so many!"

For now, beneath the roiling column of dust drawing closer to the west, we saw perhaps five hundred men on horses following the dragon standard. I thought I caught a glimpse of another red dragon set against a white surcoat: surely that of Count Ulanu leading the pursuit. There were many knights behind him, both heavy cavalry and light, and even a few horse archers accoutered much as Atara. A whole company of Blues on their swift, nimble ponies galloped after us as well. It seemed that Count Ulanu had summoned the entire vanguard of his army to help him wreak his vengeance upon us.

During the next hour of our flight, clouds began moving in from the north and darkening the sky. They built to great heights with amazing quickness. Their black, billowing shapes blocked out much of the sun. It grew much cooler, a gift from the heavens for which we were all grateful.

Count Ulanu's men, though, drew as much relief from the approaching storm as did we. He sent some of his horse archers galloping forward in a wild dash finally to close with us. They fired off a few rounds of arrows, which fell to earth out of range.

"Hmmph, archers shouldn't waste arrows so," Atara said. "If they come any closer, I'll spare them a few of mine."

They did come closer. As we ascended yet another ridge, a feathered shaft struck the earth only a dozen yards behind Kane's heaving bay. Atara's great recurved bow was strung and ready; I thought that she would wait until gaining the crest of the ridge before turning to shoot back at them.

The rapidly cooling air about us seemed charged with anticipation and death. The sky rumbled with great rolling waves of thunder. I felt an itch at the back of my neck as if something were pulling at my hair. And then a bolt of lightning flashed down from the clouds and burned the air. It struck the ridge above us, and sent a blue fire running along the rocks. Balls of hail fell, too, pelting us and pinging off my helmet. Master Juwain and the others made a sort of canopy of their cloaks, holding them up to protect their heads. And still the lightning streaked down and set the very earth to humming.

It seemed folly to climb toward the ridgeline where the lightning was the fiercest. But behind us rode six archers firing off death from their bows. These steel-tipped bolts struck even closer than did the lightning. One of them glanced off my helmet like a piece of hail—only with much greater force. The sound of it dinging against the steel caused Atara to turn in her saddle and finally fire off a shot of her own. The arrow sank into the belly of the lead archer, who fell off his horse onto the hail-shrouded earth. But the others only charged after us with renewed determination.

I was the first to the ridge, followed in quick succession by Alphanderry, Liljana, Master Juwain, Maram, and Kane. Atara rode more slowly, the better to make her shots and fight her arrow duel. Another two found their marks, and she called out, "Twenty-eight!" Just as she reached the ridgetop, however, with the sky's bright fire sizzling the very rocks, the hail began to fall much harder. It streaked down from the sky at a slant like millions of silver bolts. Her arrows crashed into these hurtling balls of ice with sharp clacking sounds, sometimes shattering them into a spray of frozen chips and snow. The hail deflected the advancing archers' arrows, too. They fired off many rounds to no effect. But one of their arrows ripped through Atara's billowing cloak just before two more of hers raised her count to thirty. Then the remaining archer, sighting his last arrow with great care, fired off a desperate shot. Lightning flashed and thunder rent the sky, and somewhere beneath these terrifying events came the even more terrible twang of his bowstring. And then I gasped to see a couple feet of wood and feathers sticking out of Atara's chest.

"Ride!" she choked out as she kicked her horse forward. "Keep riding!"

It wasn't fear that drove her on through the pain of such a grievous wound nor even will but regard for us and what must happen if her strength failed. I felt this in the way that she waved on Master Juwain every time he turned his worried gaze toward her; it was obvious in her brave smiles toward Kane and especially in the bittersweet protectiveness that lit up her face whenever she looked at me. Of all the courageous acts I had witnessed on fields of battle, I thought that her jolting ride across the final miles of Virad was the most valorous.

Liljana, galloping by her side, suggested that we must stop to offer her a little water. But Atara waved her on, too, gasping out, "Ride, ride now—they're too close." There was blood on her lips as she said this.

Soon the thunder and rain stopped, and the dark clouds boiled above us as if threatening to break apart. The mountainous spur marking Khaisham's border came into view. It was a barren escarpment of reddish rock perhaps a thousand feet high. It stood like a wall before us. Along its length, it was cut with fissures starkly defining great rock forms that looked like pyramids and towers. From the miles of plain that still lay between us and it, it was hard to make out much detail. But I prayed that one of these dark openings into the upfolded earth would prove to be the pass named the Kul Moroth.

So began our wild dash toward whatever safety the domain of Khaisham might afford us. Count Ulanu and his men were thundering closer with each passing minute. We rode as fast as we could considering the lameness of Maram's horse and Atara's injury. I felt the jolts of pain that shot through her body with every strike of her horse's hooves; I felt her quickly weakening in her grip upon the reins as her vitality drained out of her. She was coughing up blood, I saw, not much but enough.

Kane pointed out a rent in the rocks ahead of us a little larger than the others. We rode straight toward it over the stony ground. Now, from behind us along the wind, came the high-pitched howling of the Blues; it chilled us more cruelly than had any rain or hail. It seemed to promise us a death beneath steel-bladed axes of enemies mad for revenge.

Death was everywhere about us. We felt it immediately as we found the opening to the Kul Moroth. As Kane had warned us, it seemed an evil place. Others, I knew, had died here in desperate battles before us. I could almost hear their cries of anguish echoing off the walls of rock rising up on either side of us. The pass was dark in its depths, and the sunlight had to fight its way down to its hard, scarred floor. And it was narrow indeed; ten horses would have had trouble riding through it side by side. The ground was uneven and strewn with many rocks and boulders. Other boulders, and even greater sandstone pinnacles, seemed perched precariously along the pass's walls and top as if ready to roll down upon us at the slightest jolt.

We drove the horses forward as quickly as we dared. And then, just as we made a turning through this dark corridor and caught a glimpse of Khaisham's rough terrain a half-mile ahead of us, Atara let loose a gasp of pain and slumped forward, throwing her arms around Fire's neck. She could go no farther. My first thought was that we would have to lash her to her horse if we were to ride the rest of the distance to the Librarians' city.

But this was not to be. I dismounted quickly, and Master Juwain and Liljana did, too. We reached Atara's side just as she slipped off her saddle and fell into our arms. We found a place where the fallen boulders provided some slight protection against Count Ulanu's advancing army, and there we laid her down, against the cold stone.

"There's no time for this!" Kane growled out as he gazed back through the pass. "No time, I say!"

"Oh, Lord!" Maram said, coming down from his horse and looking at Atara. "The poor lamb!"

Now Alphanderry dismounted, too, and so did Kane. His dark eyes flashed toward Atara as he said, "We've got to put her back on her horse."

Master Juwain, after examining Atara, looked up at Kane and said, "I'm afraid the arrow pierced her lights. We can't just lash her to her horse."

"So, what can we do?"

"I've got to draw the arrow and stanch the bleeding somehow. If I don't, she'll die."

"So, if you do she'll die anyway, I think."

There was no time to argue. Atara was coughing up more blood now, and her face was very pale. Liljana used a clean white cloth to wipe the bright scarlet from her mouth.

"Val," she whispered to me as the slightness of her breath moved over her blue lips. "Leave me here and save yourself."

"No," I told her.

"Leave me—it's the Sarni way."

"It is not my way," I told her. "It is not the way of the Valari."

From the opening of the pass came the sound of iron-shod hooves striking stone and a terrible howling growing louder with each passing moment.

"Go now, damn you!"

"No, I won't leave you."

I drew Alkaladur, then. The sight of its shimmering length cut straight through to my heart. I would kill a hundred of Count Ulanu's men, I vowed, before I let anyone come close to her. I knew I could.

Just then a fierce howling split the air.

"They come!" Maram said, taking out his red crystal.

As Master Juwain brought forth his wooden chest and searched through its clacking steel instruments, Alphanderry laid his hand upon Atara's head. He told her, "I'm sorry, but this my fault. My singing—"

"Your singing is all I wish to hear now," Atara said, forcing a smile. "Sing for me, now, will you? Please?"

Master Juwain found the two instruments that he was looking for: a razor-sharp knife and a long, spoonlike curve of steel with a little hole in the bowl near its end. Just then Alphanderry sang out:

> *Be ye songs of glory,*
> *Be ye songs of glory,*
> *That the light of the One*
> *Will shine upon the world.*

Maram, with tears in his eyes, stood above Atara as he tried to position his gelstei so that it caught what little light filtered down to the floor of the pass. He called out, "I'll burn them if they come close! My Lord, I will!"

The wild look in his eyes alarmed Kane. He drew out his black gelstei and stood looking between it and Maram's stone.

"Hold her!" Master Juwain said to me as he looked down at Atara.

I put aside my sword, sat and pulled Atara onto my lap. My hands found their way between her arms and sides as I hung on to her tightly.

Master Juwain cut open her leather armor and the softer shirt beneath. He grasped the arrow and tugged on it, gently. Atara gasped in agony, but the arrow didn't move. Then Master Juwain nodded at me as if admonishing me not to let go of her. Sighing sadly, he used the knife to probe the opening that the arrow had made between her ribs and enlarge it, slightly. Now it took both Liljana and me to hold Atara still. Her body writhed with what little strength she had left. And still Master Juwain wasn't done tormenting her. He took out his spoon and fit its tip to the red hole in Atara's creamy white skin. Then he pushed his elongated spoon down along the arrow, slowly, feeling his way, deep into her. He twirled it about, and from deep in her throat came a succession of strangled cries. At last Master Juwain smiled with relief. I understood that the hole at the spoon's tip had snagged the tip of the arrow point; its curved flanges would now be wrapped around the point's barbs, thus shielding Atara's flesh from them so that they wouldn't catch as Master Juwain drew the arrow. This he now did. It came out with surprising smoothness and ease.

And so did much blood. In truth, it ran out of her like a bright red stream, flowing across her chest and wetting my hands with its warmth.

And all the while, Alphanderry knelt by her and sang:

> *Be ye songs of glory,*
> *Be ye songs of glory,*

That the light of the One
Will shine upon the world.

"Maram!" I heard Kane call out behind me. "Watch what you're doing with that crystal!"

The quick clopping of many horses' hooves against stone came closer, as did the hideous howling, which filled the pass with an almost deafening sound that pounded at our hearts.

Kane glanced down at Atara, who was fighting to breathe, much air now wheezing out of her chest along with a frothy red spray.

"So," he said. "So."

Master Juwain touched her chest just above the place where the archer's arrow had ripped open her lungs. Everyone knew that such sucking wounds were mortal.

"She's bleeding to death!" I cried out. "We have to stanch it!"

Master Juwain stared at her, almost frozen in his thoughts. "The wound is too grievous, too deep. I'm sorry, but I'm afraid there is no way."

"Yes, there is," I said. I reached my bloody hand into his pocket where he kept his green crystal. I took it out and gave it to him. "Use this, please."

"I'm afraid I don't know how."

"Please, sir. Use the gelstei."

He sighed as he gripped his healing stone. He held it above Atara's wound. He closed his eyes as if looking inside himself for the spark with which to ignite it. "I'm afraid there's nothing," he said.

Maram, breaking off his fumblings with his crystal, said, "Ah, perhaps you should read from your book. Or perhaps meditation would—"

"There is no time," Master Juwain said with uncharacteristic vehemence. "Never enough time."

The horrible howling drew suddenly closer, almost as if it came from inside my own chest.

"Atara," I whispered. Through my hand, I felt her pulse

weakening. I felt her life ready to blow out like a candle flame in an ice-cold wind.

"Please, sir," I said to Master Juwain, "keep trying."

Again, Master Juwain closed his eyes even as his hand closed tightly around the gelstei. But soon he opened them and shook his head.

"One more time. Please."

"But there is no rhyme or reason to using this stone!" he said bitterly.

"No reason of the mind," I said to him.

Atara began moving her lips as if she wanted to tell me something. But no words came out of them, only the faintest of whispers. The touch of her breath against my ear was so cold it burned like fire.

"What is it, Atara?" In her eyes was a look of faraway places and last things. I pressed my lips to her ear and whispered, "What do you see?"

And she told me, "I see you, Val, everywhere."

In her clear blue eyes staring up at me, I saw my grandfather's eyes and the dying face of my mother's grandmother. I saw our children, Atara's and mine, who were worse than dead because we had never breathed our life into them.

A door to a deep, dark dungeon opened beneath Atara then. I was not the only one to look upon it. Atara, who could always see so much, and sometimes everything, turned and whispered, "Alphanderry."

Alphanderry stood up and smoothed his tunic, stained with sweat, rain, and blood. He smiled as Atara said, "Alphanderry, sing, it's time."

Just as Count Ulanu and the knights of his hard-riding guard showed themselves down the pass's dark turnings, Alphanderry began walking toward them. I didn't know what he was doing.

"Oh, my Lord!" Maram said above me. "Here they are!"

The Blues riding behind Count Ulanu began singing with a fearful glee as they clanked their axes together.

And Alphanderry, with a much different voice, sang out, *"La valaha eshama halla, lais arda alhalla. . . ."*

His music had a new quality to it, both sadder and sweeter than anything I had ever heard before. I knew that he was close to finding the words that he had so long sought and opening the heavens with their sound.

"Valashu Elahad!" Count Ulanu called out as he rode with his captains and crucifiers inexorably toward us. "Lay down your weapons and you will be spared!"

And then, as the count reined in his horse and stopped dead in his tracks, Alphanderry began singing more strongly. The count looked at him as if he were mad. So did his captains and the knights and Blues behind him. But then Alphanderry's song built ever larger and deeper, and began soaring outward like a flock of swans beating their wings up toward the sky. So wondrous was the music that poured out of him that it seemed the count and his men couldn't move.

Something in it touched Master Juwain, too, as I could tell from the faraway look that haunted his eyes. He was staring into the past, I thought, and looking for an answer to Atara's approaching death in the fleeting images of memory or in the verses of the *Saganom Elu*. But he would never find it there.

"Look at her," I said to Master Juwain. I took his free hand and brought it over Atara's and mine so that it covered both of them. "Please look, sir."

There was nothing more I could say to him, no more urgings or pleadings. I no longer felt resentment that he had failed to heal Atara, only an overwhelming gratitude that he had tried. And for Atara, I felt everything there was to feel. Her weakening pulse beneath my fingers touched mine with a deeper beating, vaster and infinitely finer. The sweet hurt of it reminded me how great and good it was to be alive. There seemed no end to it; it swelled my heart like the sun, breaking me open. And as I looked at Master Juwain eye-to-eye and heart-to-heart, he found himself in this luminous thing.

"I never knew, Val," he whispered. "Yes, I see, I see."

And then Master Juwain, who turned back to Atara, did look and seemed suddenly to see her. He found the reason of his heart as his eyes grew moist with tears. He found his greatness, too. Then he smiled as if finally understanding something. He touched the wound in her chest. Then he held the varistei over it, the long axis of the stone exactly perpendicular to the opening that the arrow had made. He took a deep breath and then let it out to the sound of Atara's own anguished gasp.

I was waiting to see the gelstei glow with its soft, healing light. Even Kane, despite his despair, was looking at the stone as if hoping it would begin shining like a magical emerald. What happened next amazed us all. A rare fire suddenly leaped in Master Juwain's eyes. And then viridian flames almost too bright to behold shot from both ends of the gelstei; they circled to meet each other beneath it before shooting like a stream of fire straight into Atara's wound. She cried out as if struck again with a burning arrow. But the green fire kept filling up the hole in her chest, and soon her eyes warmed with the intense life of it. A few moments later, the last of the fire swirled about the opening of the wound as if stitching it shut with its numinous light. As it crackled and then faded along her pale skin, we blinked our eyes, not daring to believe what we saw. For Atara was now breathing easily, and her flesh had been made whole.

It seemed that neither Count Ulanu nor his men witnessed this miracle, for Liljana's and Master Juwain's backs blocked their view of it. And before them unfolded a miracle of another sort. As Alphanderry stood in all his glory facing down the vanguard of an entire army, his tongue found the turnings of the language that he had sought all his life. Its sounds flowed out of him like golden drops of light. And words and music became as one, for now Alphanderry was singing the Song of the One. In its eternal harmonies and pure tones, it was impossible to lie, impossible to see the world other than as it was because every word was a thought's or a thing's true name.

Nothing like this song had been heard on Ea since the Star People first came to earth ages ago. Its terrible beauty was almost impossible to bear. With every passing moment, Alphanderry's words became clearer, sweeter, brighter. They dissolved time as the sea does salt—and hatred, pride, and bitterness. They called us to remember all that we had lost and might yet be regained; they reminded us who we really were. Tears filled my eyes, and I looked up astonished to see Kane weeping, too. The stony Blues had belted their axes for a moment so that they might cover their faces. Even Count Ulanu had fallen away from his disdain. His misting eyes gave sign that he was recalling his own original grace. It seemed that he might have a change of heart and renounce the Kallimun and Morjin, then and there with all the world witnessing his remaking.

In the magic of that moment in the Kul Moroth, all things seemed possible. Flick, near Alphanderry, was spinning wildly, beautifully, exultantly. The walls of stone around us echoed Alphanderry's words and seemed to sing them themselves. High above the world, the clouds parted and a shaft of light drove down though the pass to touch Alphanderry's head. I thought I saw a golden bowl floating above him and pouring out its radiance over him as from an infinite source.

And so Alphanderry sang with the angels. But he was, after all, only a man. One single line of the Galadin's song was all that he could call forth in its true form. After a while, his voice began to falter and fail him. He nearly wept at losing the ancient, heavenly connection. And then the spell was broken.

Count Ulanu, still sitting on his war horse in his battle armor, shook his head as if he couldn't quite believe what he had heard. It infuriated him to see what a dreadful sculpture he had made of himself from the sacred clay with which the One had provided him. His wrath now fell upon Alphanderry for showing him this. And for standing between him and the rest of us. A snarl of outrage returned to his face; he drew his sword as his knights pointed their lances at Alphanderry. The Blues, with unfeeling fingers, gripped their axes and readied themselves to advance upon him.

And again they roared out their fierce war cry! OWRRUL-LLLL!

At last, with the howls of the Blues drowning out the final echoes of Alphanderry's music, I grabbed up my sword and leaped to my feet. Kane gripped his gelstei as his wild black eyes fell upon Maram's red crystal.

"I'll burn them!" Maram called out. "I will, I will!"

The clouds above the pass broke apart even more, and rays of light streamed down and touched Maram's firestone. It began glowing bright crimson.

Alphanderry, who had marched many yards down the pass away from us, turned and looked up toward his right. Something seemed to catch his eye. For a moment, he recaptured his joy and something of the Star People's lost language as he cried out: "Ahura Alarama!"

"What?" I shouted, gathering my strength to run to his side.

"I see him!"

"See who?"

"The one you call Flick." He smiled like a child. "Oh, Val . . . the colors!"

Just then, even as Count Ulanu spurred his horse forward, Maram's gelstei flared and burned his hands. He screamed, jerking the blazing crystal upward. A great stream of fire poured out of it and blasted the boulders along the pass's walls. Kane was now working urgently with his black crystal to damp the fury of the firestone. But it drew its power from the very sun and fed the fires of the earth. The ground around us began shaking violently; I went down to one knee to keep from falling altogether. Stones rained down like hail, and one of them pinged off my helmet. Then came a deafening roar of great boulders bounding down the pass's walls. In only a few moments, the rockslide filled the defile to a height of twenty feet. A great mound stood between Alphanderry and the rest of the company, cutting off his escape. And keeping us from coming to his aid. We couldn't even see him.

But we could still hear him. As the dust choked us and settled slowly down, from beyond the heaped-up rubble I heard him singing what I knew would be his death song. For I knew that Count Ulanu, who spared no mercy for himself, would find none for him.

My hand gripped the hilt of my sword so fiercely that my fingers hurt; my arm hurt even as I felt Count Ulanu's arm pull back and his sword thrust downward. Alphanderry's terrible cry easily pierced the rocks between us. It pierced the whole world; it pierced my heart. My sword fell from my hand, even as I clasped my chest and fell myself. A door opened before me, and I followed Alphanderry through it.

I walked with him through the dark, vacant spaces up toward the stars.

■   4   ■

THE CITY OF KHAISHAM was built on a strong site where the plains of Yarkona come up against the White Mountains. Directly to its east was Mount Redruth, an upfolding of great blocks of red sandstone that looked like pieces of a rusted iron breastplate. Mount Salmas, to the east and north, was more gentle in its rise toward the sky and slightly higher, too. Its peak pushed its way above treeline like a bald, rounded pate. Out from the gorge between these two mountains rushed a river: the Tearam. Its swift flow was diverted into little channels along either side of it in order to water the fields to the north and west of the city. The city itself was built to the south of the river. A wall following its curves formed the city's northern defenses. It rose up just above the Tearam's banks and ran east into the notch between the mountains. There it turned south along the slopes of Mount Redruth for a mile before turning yet again west through some excellent pasture. The wall's final turning took it back north toward the river. This stretch of mortared stone was the wall's longest and its most vulnerable—and therefore the most heavily defended. Great round towers rose up along its length at five-hundred-foot intervals. The south wall was likewise protected.

The men and women of Khaisham had good reason to feel safe in their little stone houses behind this wall, for it had never been breached or their city taken. The lords of Khaisham, though, desired even more protection for the great Library and the treasures it held. And so long ago they had built a second, inner wall around the Library itself.

This striking edifice occupied the heights at the Khaisham's northeast corner, almost in the mouth of the gorge, and thus further protected by the Tearam and Mount Redruth. Unlike Khaisham's other buildings, which had been raised up out of the sandstone common in the mountains to the east, the Library had been constructed of white marble. No one remembered whence this fine stone had come. It lent the Library much of its grandeur. Its gleaming faces, which caught and reflected the harsh Yarkonan sun, showed themselves to pilgrims even far out on the pasturage to the west of the city. The centermost section of the Library was a great, white cube; four others, forming its various wings, adjoined it to the west, south, east, and north so that its shape was that of a cross. Smaller cubes erupted out of each of these four, making for wings to the wings. The overall effect was that of a great crystal, like a snowflake, with points radiating at perfect angles from a common center. Above its great main doorway, burnt into the marble there in block letters, were these words: PRESERVE ART ABOVE ARTIFACT, WISDOM ABOVE KNOWLEDGE. PRESERVE MEMORY ABOVE ALL.

We came to Khaisham from the Kul Moroth almost directly to the west. I was never to remember very much of this twenty-mile journey, for I was conscious during only parts of it. It was I, not Atara, whom my companions had to lash to a horse. At times, when my eyes opened slightly, I was aware of the rocky green pastures through which we rode and the shepherds tending their flocks there. More than once, I listened as Kane seemed to sigh out the name Alphanderry with his every breath. I watched as his eyes misted like mirrors and he clamped shut his jaws so tightly that I feared his teeth would break and the splinters drive into his gums. At other times, however, the darkness closed in upon me, and I saw nothing. Nothing of this world, that is. For the bright constellations I had longed to apprehend since my childhood were now all too near. I could see how their swirling patterns found their

likeness in those of the mountains far below them—and in
Flick's fiery form, and in a man's dreams, indeed, in all
things. In truth, from the moment of Alphanderry's death, I
was like a man walking between two worlds and with my feet
firmly planted in neither.

It was just as well, perhaps, that I couldn't touch upon my
companions' grief. Can a cup hold an entire ocean? With the
passing of Alphanderry from this world, it seemed that the
spirit of the quest had left our company. It was as if a great
blow had driven from each of us his very breath. I was dimly
aware of Maram riding along on Alphanderry's horse and
muttering that instead of burning the Kul Moroth's rocks, he
should have directed his fire at Count Ulanu and his army. He
voiced his doubt that we would ever leave Khaisham now. The
others were quieter though perhaps more disconsolate. Liljana
seemed to have aged ten years in a moment, and her face was
deeply creased with lines that all pointed toward death. Master Juwain was clearly appalled to have saved Atara only to
lose Alphanderry so unexpectedly a few minutes later. He
rode with his head bowed, not even caring to open his book
and read a requiem or prayer. Atara, healed of her mortal
wound, looked out upon the landscape of a terrible sadness it
seemed that only she could see. And Kane, more than once,
when he thought no one was listening, murmured to himself,
"He's gone—my little friend is gone."

As for me, the sheer evil of Morjin and all his works chilled
my soul. It pervaded the world's waters and the air, even the
rocks beneath the horses' hooves; it seemed as awesome as a
mountain and unstoppable, like an avalanche, like the fall of
night. For the first time, I realized just how slim our chances
of finding the Lightstone really were. If Alphanderry, so
bright and pure of heart, could be slain by one of Morjin's
men, any of us could. And if we could, we surely would, for
Morjin was spending all his wealth and bending all his will toward defeating all who opposed him. Just who were we to
succeed when so many had failed?

By the time we found our way past Khaisham's gates and
into the Library, my desolation had only deepened as a cold

worse than winter took hold of me and would not let go. For four days I lay as one dead in the Library's infirmary, lost in dark caverns that had no end.

My friends nearly despaired of me. Atara sat by my side day and night and would not let go my hand. Maram, sitting by my other side, wept even more than she did, while Kane stood like a statue keeping a vigil over me. Liljana made me hot soups which she somehow managed to make me swallow. As for Master Juwain, after he had failed to revive me with his teas or the magic of his green crystal, he called for many books to be brought to our room. It was his faith that one of them might tell of the Lightstone, which alone had the power to revive me now.

It was the Lightstone, I believe, no less the love of my friends, that brought me back to the world. Like a faint, golden glimmer, my hope of finding it never completely died. Even as Liljana's soups strengthened my body, this hope flared brighter within my soul. It filled me with a fire that gradually drove away the cold and awakened me. And so on the thirteenth day of Soal, and the one hundred and fifteenth of our quest, I opened my eyes to see the sunlight streaming through the room's south-facing windows.

"Val, you've come back!" Atara said. She bent to kiss my hand and then she pressed her lips to mine. "I never thought . . ."

"I never thought I'd see you again either," I told her.

Above me, Flick turned about slowly as if welcoming me back.

We spoke of Alphanderry for a long while. I needed to be sure that my memory of what happened in the Kul Moroth was real and true, and not just a bad dream. After Atara and my other friends attested to hearing Alphanderry's screams, I said, "It's cruel that the most beloved of us should be the first to die."

Maram, sitting to my left, grasped my hand and squeezed it almost hard enough to break my bones. Then he said, "Ah, my friend, I must tell you something. Alphanderry, while dearer to all of us than I could ever say, was not the most beloved. You are. Because you're the most able to love."

Because I didn't want him to see the ocean of anguish flowing within me just then, I pressed my hand against my face for a few moments. When I looked out at the room again, everything was a blur.

Master Juwain was there at the foot of my bed, reading a passage from the Songs of the *Saganom Elu:* " 'After the darkest night, the brightest morning. After the gray of winter, the green of spring.' "

Then he read a requiem from the Book of Ages, and we prayed for Alphanderry's spirit; I wept as I silently prayed for my own.

Food was then brought to us, and we made a feast in honor of Alphanderry's music which had sustained us in our darkest hours, in the pathless tangle of the Vardaloon and in the starkness of the Kul Moroth. I had no appetite for meat and bread, but I forced myself to eat these viands even so. I felt the strength of it in my belly even as the wonder of Alphanderry's last song would always fill my heart.

After breakfast, Kane brought me my sword. I drew forth Alkaladur and let its silver fire run down its length into my arm. Now that I was able to sit up and even stand, weakly, I held the blade pointing toward the Library's eastern wing. The silustria that formed its perfect symmetry seemed to gleam with a new brightness.

"It's here," I said to my companions. "The Lightstone must be here."

"If it is," Kane informed me gravely, "we'd better go look for it as soon as you're able to walk. Much has happened these last few days while you've slept with the dead."

So saying, he sent for the Lord Librarian that we might hold council and discuss Khaisham's peril—and our own.

While we waited in that sunny room, with its flowering plants along the windows and its rows of white-blanketed beds, Kane reassured me that the horses were well tended and that Altaru had taken no wound or injury in our flight across Khaisham from the pass. Maram admitted to having to leave his lame sorrel behind. If he took any joy from inheriting and riding Alphanderry's magnificent Iolo, he gave no sign.

Soon the door to the infirmary opened, and in walked a tall man wearing a suit of much-scarred mail over the limbs of his long body. His green surcoat showed an open book, all golden and touched with the sun's seven rays. His face showed worry, intelligence, command, and pride. He had a large, jutting nose scarred across the middle and a long, serious face with a scar running down from his eye into his well-trimmed gray beard. His hands—long and large and well formed—were stained with ink. His name was Vishalar Grayam, the Lord Librarian, and like his kindred, he was both a scholar and a warrior.

After we had been presented to each other, he shook my hand, testing me and looking at me for a long time. And then he said, "It is good that you've come back to us, Sar Valashu. You've awakened none too soon."

He went on to tell me what had happened since our passage of the Kul Moroth. Count Ulanu, he said, raging at the mysterious rockslide, had sent many of his men scrambling over it. They had all perished on Kane's and Maram's swords. Kane had then led the retreat from the pass, and Count Ulanu hadn't been able to pursue us. By the time he had raced his men south to the Kul Joram, our company had nearly reached Khaisham's gates.

Count Ulanu had then sent for his army, still encamped near Tarmanam in Virad. It had taken his men four days to march across eastern Yarkona, pass through the Kul Joram, and encamp outside of Khaisham. Now the forces of Aigul and Sikar, and the Blues, were preparing to besiege the city's walls.

"And if that isn't bad enough," the Lord Librarian told us, "we've just had grievous news. After Sikar's fall, Inyam and Madhvam made a separate peace with Aigul. And so we can't expect any help from that direction."

And worse yet, he told us, Brahamdur, Sagaram, and Hansh had agreed to send contingents to aid Count Ulanu.

"Then it seems all of Yarkona has fallen," Maram said gloomily.

"Not yet," Lord Grayam told him. "We still stand. So does Sarad."

"But will Sarad come to your aid?" I asked him.

"No, I doubt if they will. I expect that they, too, in the end, will do homage to Count Ulanu."

"Then you stand alone," Maram said, looking toward the window like a trapped beast.

"Alone, yes, perhaps," the Lord Librarian said. He looked from Kane to Atara and then me. Lastly, he fixed Maram with a long, penetrating gaze.

"Then will you make peace with the count yourselves?" Maram asked.

"We would if we could," the Lord Librarian said. "But I'm afraid that while it takes two to make peace, it only takes one to make war."

"But if you were to surrender and kneel to—"

"If we surrendered to Count Ulanu," the Lord Librarian spat out, "he would enslave those he didn't crucify. And as for our kneeling to him, we Librarians kneel to the Lord of Light and no one else."

He went on to tell us that the Librarians of Khaisham were devoted to preserving the ancient wisdom, which had its ultimate source in the light of the One. Theirs was the task of transcribing old, crumbling volumes collected from around the world and illuminating new manuscripts. Perhaps their noblest effort was the compilation of a great encyclopedia indexing all books and all knowledge—which was still unfinished, as Lord Grayam sadly admitted. But their foremost duty was to protect the Library's treasures, even unto their deaths. Toward this end, they made vows and trained with swords almost as diligently as with their pens.

"You've taken vows of your own," he said, nodding toward my medallion. "We are fortunate to be joined by a company of such talents. I would hope that someday you might tell of what happened in the Kul Moroth. How strange that the ground should shake just as you passed through it! And that rocks should have blocked Count Ulanu's pursuit. And such rocks! The knights I sent there tell me that many of them were blackened as if by lightning."

Maram turned to look at me then. But neither of us—or our other companions—wished to speak of our gelstei.

"Well, then," Lord Grayam said, "you're good at keeping your own counsel, and I approve of that. But I must ask your trust in three things in order that you might have mine. First: If you find here anything of note or worth, you will bring it to me. Second: You will take great care not to harm any of the books, many of which are ancient and all too easy to harm. Third: You will remove nothing from the Library without my permission."

I touched my medallion and told him, "When a knight takes refuge in a lord's castle, he doesn't dispute his rules. But you must know that we've come to claim the Lightstone and take it away to other lands."

The Lord Librarian bristled at this as his hand found the hilt of his sword. "Does a knight in your land then enter his lord's castle to claim for his own his lord's most precious possession?"

"The Lightstone," I told him, remembering my vows, "is no one's possession. And we seek it not for ourselves but for all Ea."

"A noble quest," he sighed, relaxing his hand from his sword. "But if you found the Cup of Heaven here, don't you think it should remain here where it can best be guarded?"

I managed to climb out of bed and walk over to the window. There, below me, I could see the many houses of Khaisham, with their square stone chimneys and brightly painted shutters. Beyond the city streets was Khaisham's outer wall, and beyond it, spread out over the green pastures to the south of the city, the thousands of tents of Count Ulanu's army.

"Forgive me, Lord Librarian," I said, "but you might find it difficult guarding even your own people's lives now."

Lord Grayam's face fell sad and grave, and lines of worry furrowed his brow as he looked out the window with me.

"What you say is true," he admitted. "But it is also true that you won't find the Lightstone here. The Library has been searched through every nook and cranny for it for most of three thousand years. And so here we stand, arguing over nothing at a time when there is much else to do."

"If we're arguing over nothing," I said, "then surely you won't mind if we begin our search?"

"So long as you abide by my rules."

If we abided by his rules, as I pointed out to him, we would have to bring the Lightstone to him should we be so fortunate as to find it.

"That is true," he said.

"Then it would seem that we're at an impasse." I looked at Master Juwain and asked, "Who has the wisdom to see our way through it?"

Master Juwain stepped forward, gripping his book, which Lord Grayam eyed admiringly. Master Juwain said, "It may be that if we gain the Lightstone, we'll also gain the wisdom to know what should be done with it."

"Very well then, let that be the way of it," Lord Grayam said. "I won't say yea or nay to your taking it from here until I've held it in my hands and you in yours. Do we understand each other?"

"Yes," I said, speaking for the others, "we do."

"Excellent. Then I wish you well. Now please forgive me while I excuse myself. I've the city's defenses to look to."

So saying, the Lord Librarian bowed to us and strode from the room.

I counted exactly three beats of my heart before Maram opened his mouth and said, "Well, what are we waiting for?"

I drew my sword and watched the light play along its gleaming contours.

"You must follow where your sword leads you," Master Juwain told me, clapping me on the shoulder. Then he picked up a large book bound in red leather. "But I'm afraid I must follow where this leads me."

He told us that he was off to the Library's stacks to look for a book by a Master Malachi.

"But, sir," Maram said to him, "if we find the Lightstone—"

"Then I shall be very happy," Master Juwain told him. "Now why don't we meet by the statue of King Eluli in the great hall at midday? This place is vast, and it wouldn't do to lose each other in it."

Liljana, too, admitted that she wished to make her own researches among the Library's millions of books. And so she followed Master Juwain out the door, leaving Maram, Kane, Atara, and me behind.

The infirmary, as I soon found, was a rather little room off a side wing connected by a large hall to an off-wing leading to the Library's immense south wing. Upon making passage into this cavernous space, I realized that it would be easy to become lost in the Library, not because there was anything mazelike about it, but simply because it was huge. In truth, the whole of this building had been laid out according to the four points of the world with a precise and sacred geometry. Everything about its construction, from the distances between the pillars holding up the roof to the great marble walls, seemed to be that of cubes and squares. And of a special kind of rectangle, which, if the square part of it was removed, the remaining smaller rectangle retained the exact proportions of its parent. What these measures had to do with books puzzled me. Kane believed that the golden rectangle, as he called it, symbolized man himself: no matter what parts were taken away, a sacred spark in the image of the whole being always remained. And as with man, even more so with books. As any of the Librarians would attest, every part of a book, from its ridged spine to the last letter upon the last page, was sacred.

There were certainly many books. The south wing was divided into many sections, each filled with long islands of stacks of books reaching up nearly three hundred feet high toward the stone ceiling with its great skylights. Each island was like a mighty tower of stone and wood, leather and paper; stairs at either end of an island led to the walkways circling them at their different levels. Thirty levels I counted to each island; it would take a long time, I thought, to climb to the top of one should a desired volume be shelved there. Passing from the heights of one island to another would have taken even longer but for the graceful stone bridges connecting them at various levels. The bridges, along with the islands stacked with their books, formed an immense and intricate latticework that seemed to interconnect the recordings of all possible knowledge.

As I walked with my friends down the long and seemingly endless aisles, I breathed in the scents of mildew and dust and old secrets. Many of the books, I saw, had been written in Ardik or ancient Ardik; quite a few told their tales in languages now long dead. By chance, it seemed, we passed by shelves of many large volumes of genealogies. Half a hundred of these were given over to the lineages of the Valari. I couldn't help opening an old book that traced the ancestry of Telemesh back son to father, generation to generation, to the great Aramesh. This gave evidence to the claim that the Meshian line of kings might truly extend back all the way to Elahad himself. My discovery filled me with pride. It renewed my determination to find the golden cup that the greatest of all my ancestors had brought to earth so long ago.

Alkaladur's faintly gleaming blade seemed to point us into an adjoining hall that was almost large enough to hold King Kiritan's entire palace. Here were collected all the Library's books pertaining to the Lightstone. There must have been a million of them. It seemed impossible that each of them had been searched for any mention of where Sartan Odinan might have hidden the golden cup after he had liberated it from the dungeons of Argattha. But a passing Librarian, hastily buckling on his sword as he hurried through the stacks to Lord Grayam's summons, assured us that they had. There were many Librarians, he told us, and there had been many generations of them since the Lightstone had become lost at the beginning of the Age of the Dragon. That his generation might be the last of these devout scholar-warriors seemed not to enter his mind. And so he excused himself and marched off toward his duty atop the city's walls.

We walked slowly through this vast hall, with its even vaster silences and echoes of memory, into an eastern offwing. And then into a side wing, and still my sword seemed to point us east. After some time, we came to an alcove off a small room lined with painted shields and various artifacts.

We determined that we had reached this wing's easternmost extension. We could go no farther in this direction.

"We must try another wing," Kane said to me. "If your sword still shows true, then let's find our way to the east wing."

Our search thus far had taken up the whole morning and part of the afternoon. Now we spent another hour crossing the Library's centermost section, also called the great hall. It dwarfed even the south wing, and was filled with so many towering islands of books and soaring bridges that I grew dizzy looking up at them. I was grateful when we passed into the east wing and through one of its off-wings to find a side wing where the Librarians had put together an impressive collection of lesser gelstei. These were presented in locked cabinets of teak and glass. Atara gasped like a little girl to see so many glowstones, wish stones, angel eyes, warders, love stones, and dragon bones gathered into one place. We might have lingered there if Alkaladur hadn't pointed us down a long corridor leading to another side wing. The moment that we stepped into this chamber, with its many books of ancient poetry, my sword's blade warmed noticeably. And when we crossed into an adjoining room filled with vases, chalices, jewel-encrusted plates, and the like, the silustria flared so that even Atara and Maram noticed its brightness.

"It's here! It must be here!" Maram called out. And then a moment later, he gave a great shout and said, "I see it!"

Like a maddened bull, he pushed past me and blundered his way into the room straight toward a stand holding up a golden chalice. But in his great urgency, he knocked against another stand where sat a little bowl that seemed to have been carved out of a single, immense pearl. The bowl crashed against the floor, sending up nacreous splinters. Maram paid this sacrilege no attention. He grasped the chalice in both hands and held it above his head as he cried out, "The Lightstone! The Lightstone!"

Kane now strode across the room to get a better look at the chalice. Then he snapped at Maram, "You fat fool! If that's the true gold, then a coin can outshine the sun."

So saying, he reached out and wrenched the chalice from Maram's grasp. He opened his mouth to reveal his long, white teeth. And then he bit down hard on the rim of the chalice. He showed Maram, and all of us, the marks his teeth had made in the soft gold.

"But I was certain the Lightstone was here!" Maram said. "Val, your sword . . ."

His voice died as he noticed that my sword was still flaring. I swept it about the room. As it aligned with the chipped bowl on the floor, it flared even more brightly. I stared at the bowl, and saw what my friends saw, too: that the missing chip of pearl had revealed a gleam of gold.

Quick as a cat, Kane scooped up the bowl and set it back on its stand. Then he said to me, "We must break it open. Strike it with your sword, Val. Strike, I say."

And so I did. Without waiting for doubt to freeze my limbs, I swung Alkaladur in a flashing arc toward the bowl. Kane had taught me to wield my sword with an almost perfect precision; I aimed it so that its edge would cut the pearl to a depth of a tenth of an inch, but no more. The impossibly sharp silustria sliced right into the soft pearl. This thin veneer split away more easily than the shell of a boiled egg. Pieces of pearl fell with a tinkle onto the stand. And there upon it stood revealed a plain, golden bowl.

"Oh, my Lord! Oh, my Lord!"

Kane, ignoring the stricken look on Maram's face, picked it up. It took him only a moment to peel away the pieces of pearl that still clung to the inside of the bowl. Its gleaming golden surface was as perfect and unmarked as the silustria of my sword.

"It is the Lightstone!" Maram cried out.

A strangeness fell over Kane then. His face burned with wonder, doubt, joy, bitterness and awe. After a very long time, he handed the bowl to me. And the moment that my hands closed around it, I felt something like a sweet, liquid gold pouring into my soul.

"I wish Alphanderry was here to see this," I said as I passed the bowl to Maram.

We held council and decided that we must find Liljana and Master Juwain. But it was they who found us. A few moments later, Liljana stepped into the room, followed by Master Juwain. Immediately, Maram showed them the bowl and told them, "I've found the Lightstone! Look! Look! Behold and rejoice!"

As Master Juwain's large gray eyes grew even larger, I gazed at this golden bowl. It was one of the happiest moments of my life.

"So this is what you've been shouting about," Master Juwain said, examining the bowl. "We've been looking all over for you—did you know it's past midday?"

In this windowless room, time seemed lost in the hollows of the bowl that Maram held up triumphantly. In defense at missing our rendezvous by King Eluli's statue, he said again, "I've found the Gelstei!"

"What do you mean, you found it?" Atara asked him.

"Well, I mean, ah, if I hadn't knocked the bowl over . . ."

"I'm afraid you haven't found the Lightstone," Master Juwain said.

Maram looked at him in such disbelief that he nearly dropped the bowl. I wondered if Master Juwain had ruined his sight in reading his books all day. And Kane just stared at the bowl, his black eyes full of mystery and doubt.

Master Juwain took the bowl from Maram as Liljana stepped closer. He looked at us and said, "Have you put it to the test?"

"It is the Gelstei, sir," I said. "What else could it be?"

"If it's the true gold," he told me, "nothing could harm it in any way. Nothing could scratch it—not even the silustria of your sword."

"But Val has already struck his sword against it!" Maram said. "And see, there is no mark!"

In truth, though, Alkaladur's edge had never quite touched the bowl. Because I had to know if it really was the Lightstone, I brought out my sword again. As Master Juwain held the bowl firmly, I drew my sword across it. And there, cut into the gold, was the faintest of scratches.

"I don't understand!" I said. There was a sudden emptiness in my belly.

"I'm afraid you've found one of the False Gelstei," he told me. "Once upon a time, more than one such were made."

He went on to say that in the Age of Law, the ancients had applied all their art toward fabricating the gold gelstei. After many attempts, the great alchemist Ninlil Gurmani had succeeded in making a silver gelstei with a golden sheen to it. Although it had none of the properties of the true gold, it was thought that the Lightstone might take its power from its shape rather than its substance alone. And so this gold-seeming silustria was cast into the form of bowls and cups, in the likeness of the Cup of Heaven itself. But to no avail.

"I'm afraid there is only one Lightstone," Master Juwain told me.

"So," Kane said, glowering at the little bowl that he held. "So."

"But look!" I said, pointing my sword at the bowl. "Look how it brightens!"

The silver of my sword was indeed glowing strongly. But Master Juwain looked at it and slowly shook his head. And then he asked me, "Don't you remember Alphanderry's poem?

> *The silver sword, from starlight formed,*
> *Sought that which formed the stellar light,*
> *And in its presence flared and warmed*
> *Until it blazed a brilliant white.*

"It flares," he said, "but there is no blazing brilliance, is there?"

In looking at my sword's silvery sheen, I had to admit there was not.

"This bowl is of silustria," Master Juwain said. "And so your sword finds a powerful resonance with it. It is what pointed you toward this room, away from where the Light-stone really lies."

The hollowness inside me grew as large as a cave, and I felt sick to my soul. And then the meaning of Master Juwain's words and the gleam in his eyes struck home.

"What are you saying, sir?"

"I'm saying that I know where Sartan Odinan hid the Light-stone." He set the bowl back on its stand and smiled at Liljana. "We do."

I finally noticed Liljana holding a cracked, leather-bound book in her hands. She gave it to him and said, "It seems that Master Juwain is even more of a scholar than I had thought."

Beaming at her compliment, Master Juwain proceeded to tell us about his researches in the Library that day—and during the days that I had lain unconscious in the infirmary.

"I began by trying to read everything the Librarians had collected about Sartan Odinan," he said. "While I was waiting for Val to return to us, I must have read thirty books."

A chance remark in one of them, he told us, led him to think that Sartan might have had Brotherhood training before he had fallen into evil and joined the Kallimun priesthood. This training, Master Juwain believed, had gone very deep. And so he wondered if Sartan, in a time of great need, seeking to hide the Lightstone, might have sought refuge among those who had taught him as a child. It was an extraordinary intuition which was to prove true.

Master Juwain's next step was to look in the Great Index for references to Sartan in any writings by any Brother. One of these was an account of a Master Todor, who had lived during the darkest period of the Age of the Dragon when the Sarni had once again broken the Long Wall and threatened Tria. The reference indicated that Master Todor had collected stories of all things that had to do with the Lightstone, particularly myths as to its fate.

It had taken Master Juwain half a day to locate Master Todor's great work in the Library's stacks. In it he found mention of a Master Malachi, whose superiors had disciplined him for taking an unseemly interest in Sartan. Master Juwain, searching in an off-wing of the north wing, had found a few of Master Malachi's books, the titles of which had been in-dexed, if not their contents. In *The Golden Renegade,* Master Juwain found a passage telling of a Master Aluino, who was said to have seen Sartan before Sartan died.

"And there I was afraid that this particular branch of my search had broken," Master Juwain told us as he glanced at the False Gelstei. "You see, I couldn't find any reference to Master Aluino in the Great Index. That is not surprising. There must be a million books that the Librarians have never gotten to—with more collected every year."

"So what did you do?" Maram asked him.

"What did I do? Think, Brother Maram. Sartan escaped Argattha with the Lightstone in the year 82 of this age—so the histories tell. And so I knew the approximate years of Master Aluino's life. Do you see?"

"Ah, no, I'm sorry, I don't."

"Well," Master Juwain said, "it occurred to me that Master Aluino must have kept a journal, as we Brothers are still encouraged to do."

Here Maram looked down at the floor in embarrassment. It was clear that he had always found other ways to keep himself engaged during his free hours at night.

"And so," Master Juwain continued, "it also occurred to me that if Master Aluino had kept a journal, there was a chance that it might have found its way into the Library."

"Aha," Maram said, looking up and nodding his head.

"There is a hall off the west wing where old journals are stored and sorted by century," Master Juwain said. "I've spent most of the day looking for one by Master Aluino. Looking and reading."

And with that, he proudly held up the fusty journal and opened it to a page that he had marked. He took great care, for the journal's paper was brittle and ancient.

"You see," he said, "this is written in Old West Ardik. Master Aluino had his residence at the Brotherhood's sanctuary of Navuu, in Surrapam. He was the Master Healer there."

No, no, I thought, it can't be. Navuu lay five hundred miles from Khaisham, across the Red Desert in lands now held by the Hesperuks' marauding armies.

"Well," Atara asked, "what does the journal say?"

Master Juwain cleared his throat and said, "This entry is from the fifteenth of Valte, in the year 82 of the Age of the

Dragon." Then he began reading to us, translating as he went:

Today a man seeking sanctuary was brought to me. A tall man with a filthy beard, dressed in rags. His feet were torn and bleeding. And his eyes: they were sad, desperate, wild. The eyes of a madman. His body had been badly burned from the sun, especially about the face and arms. But his hands were the worst. He had strange burns on the palms and fingers that wouldn't heal. Such burns, I thought, would drive anyone mad.

All my healings failed him; even the varistei had no virtue here, for I soon learned that his burns were not of the body alone but the soul. It is strange, isn't it, that when the soul decides to die, the body can never hold on to it.

I believe that he had come to our sanctuary to die. He claimed to have been taught at one of the Brotherhood schools in Alonia as a child; he said many times that he was coming home. Babbled this, he did. There was much about his speech that was incoherent. And much that was coherent but not to be believed. For four days I listened to his rantings and fantasies, and pieced together a story which he wanted me to believe—and which I believe he believed.

He said his name was Sartan Odinan, the very same Kallimun priest who had burned Suma to the ground with a firestone during the Red Dragon's invasion of Alonia. Sartan the Renegade, who had repented of this terrible crime and betrayed his master. It was believed that Sartan killed himself in atonement, but this man told a different story as to his fate.

Here Master Juwain looked up from the journal and said, "Please remember, this was written shortly after Kalkamesh had befriended Sartan and they had entered Argattha to reclaim the Lightstone. That tale certainly wasn't widely known at the time. The Red Dragon had only just begun his torture of Kalkamesh."

A strange stillness inside Kane made me recall the Song of

Kalkamesh and Telemesh that Kane had asked the minstrel Yashku to recite in Duke Rezu's hall. I couldn't help thinking of the immortal Kalkamesh crucified to the rocky face of Skartaru, and his rescue by a young prince who would become one of Mesh's greatest kings.

"Let me resume this at the critical point," Master Juwain said, tapping his finger against the journal. "You already know how Kalkamesh and Sartan found the Lightstone locked in the dungeon cell and opened it."

And so he said that just as he and this mythical Kalkamesh opened the dungeon doors, the Red Dragon's guards discovered them. While Kalkamesh turned to fight them, he said, he grabbed the Cup of Heaven and fled back through the Red Dragon's throne room whence they had come. For this man, who claimed to have once been a High Priest of the Kallimun, had again fallen and was now moved with a sudden lust to keep the Cup for himself.

And now he reached the most incredible part of his story. He claimed that upon touching the Cup of Heaven, it had flared a brilliant golden white and burned his hands. And that it had then turned invisible. He said that he had then set it down in the throne room, glad to be rid of it—this hellishly beautiful thing, as he called it. After that, he had fled Argattha, abandoning Kalkamesh to his fate. The story that he told me was that he made his way into the Red Desert and across the Crescent Mountains and so came here to our sanctuary.

It is difficult to believe his story, or almost any part of it. The myth of an immortal man named Kalkamesh is just that; only the Elijin and Galadin have attained to the deathlessness of the One. Also, it would be impossible for anyone to enter Argattha as he told, for it is guarded by dragons. And nowhere is it recorded that the Cup of Heaven has the power to turn invisible.

And yet there are those strange burns on his hands to account for. I believe this part of his story, if no other: that his lust for the Lightstone burned him, body and soul, and drove him mad. Perhaps he did somehow manage to cross the Red Desert. Perhaps he saw the image of the Lightstone in some blazing rock or heated iron and tried to hold on to it. If so, it has seared his soul far beyond my power to heal him.

I am old now, and my heart has grown weak; my varistei has no power to keep me from the journey that all must make—and that I will certainly make soon, perhaps next month, perhaps tomorrow, following my doomed patient toward the stars. But I before I go, I wish to record here a warning to myself, which this poor, wretched man has unknowingly brought me: the very great danger of coveting that which no man was meant to possess. Soon enough I'll return to the One, and there will be light far beyond that which is held by any cup or stone.

Master Juwain finished reading and closed his book. The silence in that room of ancient artifacts was nearly total. Flick spun about slowly near the False Gelstei, and it seemed the whole world was spinning, too. Atara stared at the wall as if its smooth marble was as invisible as Master Aluino's patient had claimed the Lightstone to be. Kane's very soul blazed with frustration and hate, and I couldn't bear to look at him. I turned to see Maram nervously pulling at his beard and Liljana smiling ironically as if to hide a great fear.

And then, as from far away, through that little room's smells of dust and defeat, came a faint braying of horns and booming of war drums. I felt my heart beating out the same dread rhythm, again and again.

Maram was the first to break the quiet. He pointed at the journal in Master Juwain's hands and said, "The story that madman told can't be true, can it?"

Yes, I thought, as I listened to my heart and the pulsing of the world, it is true.

"Ah, no, no," Maram muttered, "this is too, too bad, to think that the Lightstone was left in Argattha."

The drums boomed even louder and seemed to sound out promises of doom from inside all things.

I looked at the False Gelstei sitting on its stand. I gripped the hilt of my sword as Maram said, "Then the quest is over. There is no hope."

I looked from him to Master Juwain and Liljana, and then at Atara and Kane. No hope could I see on any of their faces; there was nothing in their hearts except the beat of despair.

We stood there for a long time, waiting for what we knew not. Atara seemed lost within some secret terror. Even Master Juwain's pride at his discovery had given way to the meaning of it and a deepening gloom.

And then footfalls sounded in the adjoining chamber. A few moments later, a young Librarian about twelve years old came into the room and said, "Sar Valashu, Lord Grayam bids you and your companions to take shelter in the keep. Or to join him on the walls, as is your wont."

Then he told us that the attack of Count Ulanu's armies had begun.

5

WE RETREATED THROUGH the Library's halls and chambers to the infirmary, where I retrieved my helmet and Atara her bow and arrows. There we said good-bye to Master Juwain and Liljana. Master Juwain would be helping the other healers who would tend the Librarians' inevitable battle wounds, and Liljana decided that she could best serve the city by assisting him. As healers set out saws, clamps, and other gleaming steel instruments, Master Juwain embraced us one by one, and said, "Please don't let me see that any of you have returned to this room until the battle is won."

The young page who had found us earlier escorted Kane, Maram, Atara, and me out of the Library and through the gates of the inner wall. He led the way through the narrow city streets, which were crowded with anxious people hurrying this way and that. Many were women clutching screaming babies, on their way to take refuge in the Library's keep or grounds behind its inner wall. But quite a few were Librarians dressed as Kane and I were in mail, and bearing maces, crossbows, and swords. Still more were Khaisham's smiths, carpenters, masons, and other tradesmen. They were only poorly accoutered and armed, some bearing nothing more in the way of weaponry than a spear or a heavy shovel. At need, they would take their places along the walls with the Librarians—and us. But they would also keep the fighting men supplied with food, water, arrows, and anything else necessary to withstanding a siege.

The flow of these hundreds of men, with their carts and braying donkeys, swept us down across the city to its west wall. This was Khaisham's longest and most vulnerable, and there atop a square mural tower near its center stood the Lord Librarian. He was resplendent in his polished mail and the green surcoat displaying the golden book over his heart. Other knights and archers were with him on the tower's ledge, behind the narrow stone merlons of the battlements that protected them from the enemy's missiles. We followed the page up a flight of steps until we stood at the top of the wall behind the slightly larger merlons there. And then we walked up another flight of steps, adjoining and turning around and up into the tower itself.

"I knew you would come," the Lord Librarian said to us as we crowded onto the tower's ledge.

"Yes, but will they stay?" a nearby knight with a long mustache asked.

He turned to look down and out across the pasture in front of the wall, and there was a sight that would have sent even brave men fleeing. Three hundred yards from us, across the bright green grass that would soon be stained red, Count Ulanu had his armies drawn up in a long line facing the wall. Their steel-jacketed shields, spears, and armor formed a wall of its own as thousands of his men stood shoulder-to-shoulder slowly advancing upon us. To our left, half a mile away where

Khaisham's walls turned back toward Mount Redruth, I saw yet more lines of men marching across the pasture to the south of the city. And to the right, in the fields across the Tearam, stood companies of Count Ulanu's cavalry and other warriors. These men, blocked by the river's rushing waters, would make no assault upon the walls, but they would wait with their lances and swords held ready should any of Khaisham's citizens try to flee across it.

"We're surrounded," Lord Grayam told us as he watched the count's army march toward us. "So many—I had never thought he'd be able to muster so many."

Out on the plain below us, I counted the standards of forty-four battalions. Ten bore the hawks and other insignia of Sikar and another five the black bears of Virad. There were masses of Blues, too, at least two thousand of them, huddled and naked and holding high their axes—and letting loose their bone-chilling howls.

"We should have sent aid to Sikar," Lord Grayam said. "And we might have if we'd had more time. Too late, always too late."

From out across the rolling pasture came the booming of the enemy's war drums. It set the very stones of the walls to vibrating their terrible sound.

"No, that wasn't it," Lord Grayam said to a knight nearby whom I took to be one of his captains. "I was too proud. I thought that we could stand alone. And now but for Sar Valashu and his companions, we do."

Maram looked down at the advancing armies and took a gulp of air as if it were a potion that might fortify him. He seemed to be having second thoughts about joining the city's defense. Then he belched and said, "Ah, Lord Grayam, I must tell you that I'm no warrior, only a poor Brother and—"

"Yes, Prince Maram?"

Maram noticed that all the men at the top of the tower were looking at him. So were those along the wall below.

"—and I really shouldn't remain here, if I would only get in your way. If I were to join the others in the keep, then—"

"You mean, the women and the children?" Lord Grayam asked.

"Ah, yes, the . . . noncombatants. If I were to join them, then . . ."

Maram's voice trailed off; he saw that Kane and I were staring at him, too.

Again he gulped air, belched and rolled his eyes toward the heavens as if asking why he was always having to do things that he didn't want to do. And then he continued, "What I mean is, ah, although I'm certainly no swordmaster, I do have some skill, and I believe my blade would be wasted if I had to wait out this battle in the keep—unless of course you, sir, deem my inexpertise to be dangerous to the coordination of your defenses and would—"

"Good!" Lord Grayam suddenly called out, wasting no more time. "I accept the service of your sword, at least for the duration of the siege."

Maram shut his mouth then, having woven a web of words in which he had caught himself. He seemed quite disgusted.

"All of you," Lord Grayam said, "Sar Valashu, Kane, Princess Atara—we're honored that you would fight with us, of your own choice."

In truth, I thought, listening to the booming of the drums, we had little choice. Our escape was cut off. And because the Librarians had succored us in a time of great need, it would be ignoble of us to forsake them. And perhaps most importantly, Alphanderry's cruel murder needed to be avenged.

Maram looked out one of the crenels of the battlements. He muttered, "At least there's a good wall between us and them."

But the wall, I thought, as I looked down at the Librarians lined up along it, might not provide as much safety as Maram hoped. It was neither very thick or high; the red sandstone its masons had built with was probably too soft to withstand very long a bombardment of good, granite boulders. The mural towers, being square instead of round, were also more vulnerable, and the wall had no machicolation: no projecting stone parapet at its top from which boiling oil or lime might be dropped down upon anyone assaulting it. Even now, in the last moments before the battle, the city's carpenters were hurriedly nailing into place hoardings over the lip of the wall to extend it outward toward the enemy. But these covered shelters were few and protected the walls only near the great towers at either side of the vulnerable gates. Since they were made of wood, fire arrows might ignite them. To forestall this calamity, the carpenters were also nailing wet hides over them.

"Sar Valashu," Lord Grayam said to me as he placed his arm around the Librarian next to him, "allow me to present my son, Captain Donalam."

Captain Donalam, a sturdy-looking man about Asaru's age, grasped my hand firmly and smiled as if to reassure me that Khaisham had never been conquered. Then he excused himself, and walked down the tower's stairs to the wall, where he would command the Librarians waiting for him there.

We, too, took our leave of the Lord Librarian. We walked down the stairs to the wall, and took our places behind the battlements. Maram bemoaned being that much closer to the enemy. And with every passing moment, as the drums beat out their relentless tattoo and the first arrows began hissing through the air, the enemy marched closer to us.

It was hard to look upon them as they drew in upon the city in their lines of flashing steel. I counted the standards of twenty-nine of Aigul's battalions. Among them fluttered the much larger standard of Count Ulanu's whole army: the white banner stained bloodred with its great, snarling dragon. Near it, on top of his big brown horse, was Count Ulanu himself.

"Damn him!" Kane snarled beside me. "Damn him to eternal hell!"

Everyone could see that we had hard work ahead of us. Four great siege towers, as high as the walls and with great iron hooks to latch on to them, were being rolled forward across the grass. The moment they came up against the walls, many men would mount the stairs inside them and come pouring over the top. Three battering rams rolled toward the west wall's gates, too. But the most fearsome of the enemy's weapons were the catapults that had begun heaving boulders at the city. One of these was a mangonel, which flung its missiles in a low arc against the wall itself. Even as I drew in a deep breath and grasped the hilt of my sword, a great boulder soared across the pasture and crashed into the wall a hundred yards to the south, shattering its battlements in a shower of stone.

Now it begins, I thought, with a terrible pulling inside me. Again and always, it begins.

As I did before any battle, I built up walls around me. These were as high as the stars and as hard as diamond; they were as thick as the mountains that keep peoples apart. My will was the stone that formed them, and my dread of what was to come was the mortar that cemented them in place. Only in this way could I bear the agonies of men hit by flying rocks or pierced with arrows and the screaming that filled the air.

"Ashtoreth!" Maram cried out, calling upon the greatest of the Galadin. He hunched behind the stone merlon next to me. "Valoreth!"

Now the archers along the walls, working with crossbows or longbows, firing from the arrow slits at the centers of the merlons, shot out great sheets of arrows at Count Ulanu's men. Warriors began falling, in their ones and tens, clutching their chests and bellies. And the enemy's archers returned our fire in great black clouds of whining bolts that arched high and fell almost straight down upon the walls in a clatter of steel points breaking upon stone and too often finding their marks in a throat or a hand or an eye.

There is no pain, I told myself. Now there is only killing and death.

We had skilled archers of our own, and none so fine as Atara. She stood beside me, firing off arrows at a rate that the nearby crossbowmen couldn't match. And few could match the range of her powerful, double-curved horn bow, and none her accuracy. Every one of her shots, almost, struck some man of Aigul or Virad or one of the naked Blues.

"Thirty-two!" I heard her call out just after her bowstring had twanged yet again. And then, a few minutes later, "Thirty-three!"

Kane, Maram, and I might have taken our chances in this missile duel, but there were too few bows to be spared and even fewer arrows. In any case, the battle would not be decided by archers. When I dared to look out from the crenel beside me, I saw the many men behind the enemy's front lines bearing long ladders. The count's armies, even as they battered the gates, would try to take the city by escalade. It was the most dangerous kind of assault.

I was certain that it was the count's rage to capture us that had led him to these tactics. I knew this, as I knew many things now since gaining my silver sword. And Kane seemed to know it, too. While Atara fired off her arrows and Maram cowered behind the battlements muttering prayers to the heavens, Kane looked at me and said, "There can be no surrender for us, do you understand?"

"Yes," I told him. And then, as a great rock crashed into the wall below us and set the stones to shaking, I said, "They're going to scale the walls."

"So, Count Ulanu has the men—if he has the will to waste them."

"He has the will," I said.

As his armies' lines drew closer, their drums boomed even louder.

Now a new terror fell upon us as the Aigul archers began shooting off flaming arrows, trying to set the hoardings above the gates, and the gates themselves, on fire. This tactic rankled Maram. He clearly regarded this fulminous substance as his prerogative. Astonishing both Kane and me, he suddenly stood straight up as he reached his hand into his pocket.

"Fire, is it?" he said, taking out his red crystal. "I'll give them fire!"

Kane moved as if to grab Maram's arm, then checked himself. He looked at me, and we both knew that if there was ever a time for using the red gelstei's flame against living flesh, this was it.

"Be careful!" Kane hissed at him. "Remember what happened in the Kul Moroth."

It was exactly this memory, I thought, which moved Maram

to expose himself in the crenel. He knew, as did everyone, what would happen if we did not make a good defense here. And he saw that he had the power to harm the enemy grievously.

"I'll be careful," Maram muttered, gripping his crystal. "Careful to aim this at Count Ulanu's ugly face."

As Maram positioned the crystal and the sun's rays fell upon it, a lancet of fire suddenly streaked out through the air. It fell upon one of Count Ulanu's knights and cut through the mail covering him. He fell screaming from his horse, trying to claw off the rings of molten steel burning into his chest.

"Ai, a firestone!" another knight called out fifty yards from the wall as he looked up at Maram. "They have a firestone!"

This cry, picked up by others along the enemy's lines, practically halted the whole army's advance. Count Ulanu's warriors tried to cover themselves with their shields; they crouched behind their mantelets, those little rolling walls of wood that gave good protection against arrows if not fire. More than a few of them tried to duck down behind those warriors in front of them.

"Ai, a firestone! A firestone!" came their terrified cries.

The Librarians along the wall seemed only slightly less frightened by what they beheld in Maram's hand. They stared at him in amazement. Then Lord Grayam called down from the tower above us: "It is a good thing you stood with us after all, Prince Maram. I wondered about the Kul Moroth. The angel fire you've been given to wield may yet win this battle!"

But I was not so sure of this. Firestones, as I had learned from my grandfather's stories, were notoriously difficult to wield in battle. And Maram's was an old stone with an uncertain hand upon it. It took a long time in drinking in the sun's rays before spitting them back out as fire. And despite Maram's boast, he had yet to learn to aim his crystal with anything like an archer's precision with bow and arrow. The next bolt of flame loosed from his stone shot out and burned through the grass dozens of yards from Count Ulanu or any of his men.

"Have pity on the poor moles!" Atara called to him, smiling as she reached for more arrows.

Count Ulanu, too, saw that the terror of Maram's crystal might be worse than its sear. With his captains, he rode along his lines, calling out encouragements and urging his men forward.

"To the walls!" his voice carried out over the corpse-strewn pasture. "Be quick now, and we'll take them this very day!"

Archers on top of the walls fired their arrows at the count; one of these whining shafts, shot by Atara, embedded itself in his shield. But Count Ulanu seemed undeterred by this hail of death. Along with the knights of his guard, he bravely charged forward into it. Then his warriors from Aigul followed him, and a whole host of the screaming Blues ran toward us, too. Their war cries seemed to tear straight into our bellies.

"Damn them!" Maram called out.

A tremendous blast from his firestone burned a swath through one of Aigul's advancing companies. Twenty men fell like charred scarecrows. The men around them screamed and halted. But when no further fire issued forth, their captains got them moving again. They sprinted with their ladders straight toward the wall.

The enemy had more ladders than we did men. The moment these long wooden constructions touched the wall, the Librarians tried to push them away with forked poles. Many were the attackers that fell off, crying out as they thudded to the ground and perhaps breaking an arm or a leg. But many more fought their way up to the crenels. Here they were met with spear or mace or sword. The thousands of fierce, individual battles up and down the walls would determine whether the city was taken in this first assault.

Kane, working furiously at the crenel next to mine, stabbed out his sword six times, and six of the enemy's warriors flew out into space with mortal wounds reddening their bodies. Atara, to my right, stood firing arrows straight into the faces of anyone who showed themselves at the top of their ladders. And Maram stood behind me, still trying to get a flame from his glowing crystal.

"Raahhh! Burners of men!" a voice howled out.

One of the Blues came bounding up the ladder below my

crenel with the dexterity of a great, squat ape. His face, stained a dark blue, showed no emotion other than a rage to rip and rend. Foam gathered about his mouth as he let loose a terrible cry. He ducked beneath the thrust of my sword and nearly caught me with his axe. But I backed away, and its steel edge scraped along the sandstone of the merlon, sending out sparks. My next thrust drove deep into his muscle-knotted arm. He took as little notice of this spurting wound as I might a mosquito bite. With a dreadful quickness, he grabbed his axe with his other hand and swung it at me, all in one motion. Its edge bit almost through the mail covering my shoulder, shocking me and bruising the flesh beneath down to the bone. His next blow might have taken off my head if I hadn't swung my sword first, taking off his. Unbelievably, he stood headless at the mouth of the crenel for at least three heartbeats before toppling back from the wall.

There is no pain, I told myself. I stood blinking away the Blue's blood from my eyes and gasping for air. There is no pain.

Only my grip on Alkaladur kept me from falling off the rampart behind the battlements to the street below. My sword's shimmering silustria drew strength from the earth and sky, and I drew strength from it. Now other Blues showed themselves in the crenel in which I stood; my silver sword cut their naked bodies as if through plums. Some of Count Ulanu's knights followed them up the ladder. I had only a little more difficulty in cutting through their mail and killing them one by one.

But many of the Librarians along the walls had less success than Kane and I. Many had fallen, hacked apart, bleeding and crying out their death agonies. Fifty yards down the wall to the left, a squadron of Blues had broken through their defenses. They were rampaging about the battlements, swinging their axes at anything that moved and howling hideously even as they themselves were hacked apart.

One of the Librarians near me cried, "How are we to kill them if they don't know when they are already killed?"

From the tower high above the battlements, Lord Grayam's

strong voice suddenly called down to us: "Atara! Atara Ars Narmada! Our archers are fallen! Come up here now!"

Atara wasted no time in hurrying up the tower stairs to his summons. From this vantage high above the walls, she could shoot her arrows down at the Blues who now held an entire section of the wall.

Now two of the great siege towers had nearly been brought up flush with the walls. And one of the battering rams already had. A hundred yards from us, Count Ulanu's warriors had positioned it in front of the centermost of the west wall's gates. It looked almost like a small chalet, with its steeply pointed triangular frame covered in a housing of wooden planks and wet hides. Inside it, hung on chains from the sturdy frame, was a great tree trunk whose head was black iron cast into the shape of a ram. The men inside the housing swung the log back and forth so that the ram's head struck the wooden gate, again and again, back and forth, threatening to shatter it into splinters.

DOOM! two, three, four, DOOM! two, three, four, DOOM! two, three . . .

"Oh, no!" Maram said beside me. "They're going to break us in!"

He positioned his red crystal beneath the rays of the waning sun, but nothing happened. "What's wrong with this stone!" he wailed out. And then, in a much softer voice, "What's wrong with me?"

And still the great ram beat against the gates, and the whole world seemed ready to break into pieces. From the left came the yowling of the Blues, and from the tower above, the twang of Atara's bowstring as she fired arrows over our heads into them.

There is no pain, I told myself, hacking apart a young knight who had won through to the battlements. There is only killing and death.

"I'm out!" I heard Atara call down to a man in the street below.

And then someone cried out, "More arrows! Send up more arrows!"

One of the city's tradesmen, climbing halfway up the wall's steps from the street below, heaved a sheaf of arrows up to me. I grabbed it by the binding cord, and ran up the tower steps to deliver them to Atara.

"Are you all right?" I said to her, looking her over for wounds.

"I'm fine, Val," she said. Then she looked at my blood-spattered surcoat and mail and asked, "Are you all right?"

"For now," I said, cutting the cord around the sheaf of arrows.

As she fit one to her bowstring, Lord Grayam came over to me holding a long bow. He asked, "Can you work one of these as you wield your sword?"

"No," I said, "but I can shoot."

"Good—then aim your arrows at those Blues on the wall!"

From the tower's vantage, Atara began shooting her arrows into the Blues with a deadly accuracy. I did, too. Where I had once pulled aside my bow to keep from wounding a deer, I now found myself firing feathered shafts into men's naked bellies and throats. Astonishingly, many of the Blues fought on even with half a dozen arrows sticking out of them.

A few moments later a great boulder, hurled by the mangonel, nearly found its mark. It crashed into the wall below us where it joined the tower, and broke a hole there. When the dust had settled and the tower stopped shaking, I looked down to see that the boulder had caved in part of it and destroyed the stone stairway leading from the tower down to the walls.

And still the battering ram worked against the city's gates. I heard Maram cursing from thirty feet below me. Then I watched as he leaned out of a vacant crenel near Kane and held his crystal pointed toward the ram. A red fire that quickly built into swirling crimson flames leapt out from it. The flames fell upon the ram's housing like the breath of a dragon. In only moments, the wet hides nailed to the ram's frame steamed and began burning away as the wood beneath ignited in a great torment of fire. Screams split the air as the men inside it began burning, too.

More than one of Count Ulanu's men, upon witnessing this horror, turned to flee from the wall. Then ten more broke, and twenty, and soon whole companies from Aigul and Inyam were turning and running. Count Ulanu and his captains rode upon them, striking them with the flats of their swords and trying to turn back the tide of this uncalled retreat. But when men lose the courage to fight, there is little their leaders can do to make them.

For the moment, the enemy's attack failed and the world seemed to stand still. All I could hear was the cries and pleading of the wounded, and the long, dark, terrible shrieking inside me. Then I took note of a tremendous clamor coming from the south of the city. A knight on top of a wounded horse came galloping through the streets from that direction. He stopped just beneath our tower and called up to Lord Grayam.

"My Lord!" he gasped. "The Sun gate is broken! Captain Nicolam is holding the entrance, but we are too few! He begs you to send more men!"

It took only a moment for Lord Grayam to call down to his son, Captain Donalam, to lead half a company of knights to this new crisis along the south wall. Kane, who had a sense for where the battle was to be the fiercest, looked up toward me and smiled savagely as he favored me with a quick nod of his head. Then he gripped his bloody sword and joined Captain Donalam's knights. They climbed down the wall to the street and began running behind the knight's horse. I would have gone with them, but the tower's steps were broken, and I had no good way down to them.

Out on the pasture before the west wall, the enemy's war drums were booming again. Count Ulanu rode among his badly mauled battalions, screaming out orders and trying to re-form his men.

"No, no," Maram called out below me, "I'll burn him with starfire—I will!"

Flushed with the hubris of his recent triumphs, he stood leaning out between two of the battlements' arrow-scarred merlons. He pointed his gelstei toward Count Ulanu five hundred yards from us out on the pasture below. The slanting rays of the sun touched the firestone. It began to glow again, hell-ishly hot, it seemed to me. Ten thousand enemy warriors waited to see if its fire would fall upon them. Then Maram let out a cry as the sear of his stone burned his hand. He wailed as his fingers opened against his will, and he let go of it. It fell straight down in front of the wall like a shooting star.

"No!" Maram cried. "Oh, what have I done!"

"The firestone!" someone shouted. "He's dropped the fire-stone!"

The bright crystal, now quickly cooling to a blood red, lay on the green grass of the pasture beneath the wall. A hundred of the Librarians had seen Maram drop it. And ten thousand of the enemy had.

"Maram Marshayk!" Lord Grayam called out next to me. He looked down from the tower at Maram almost alone be-neath us. "The gelstei! You must retrieve the gelstei!"

Maram peered over the crenel at the firestone where it lay among the bodies of fallen warriors thirty feet below him. He shook his head and muttered, "No, no—not I."

Far out on the pasture, Count Ulanu had called up his archers, who brought their bows to bear at our section of the wall.

"Maram!" I shouted, looking down at him. I examined the broken masonry of the tower's stairway to see if there was any way I could climb down to him. There wasn't. "Maram, you must not let them gain the firestone! Go now!"

"No!" Maram shouted back at me. "I can't!"

"You can! You must!"

"No, no," he said angrily. "How could you ask this of me?"

Behind Count Ulanu, ten of his knights gathered in their horses' reins and turned their shining helms toward us.

"Maram!"

"No! No!"

Several Librarians near Maram chose that moment to haul themselves up over the battlements and climb down the out-side of the wall on the ladders that Count Ulanu's men had left there. Arrows killed them. They fell down on top of the heaps of the dying and the dead.

"Maram!" I called out again.

"No, no! I won't go! Are you mad?"

He pulled back behind his merlon just as a rain of arrows clacked against the wall.

Atara, standing next to me on the tower's ledge, looked down at Maram and said, "He'll never do it."

"Yes," I said to her, "he will."

Lord Grayam tapped me on the shoulder and pointed across the pasture to where a company of cavalry had now gathered behind the archers to charge toward the wall. He started to call for five more of his Librarians, to Maram's left, to go down to the gelstei. But Atara stayed his command. With a strange light her eyes, she said, "No, it must be Maram, if it's anyone."

"Maram!" I called again. "The seven brothers and sisters of the earth with the seven—"

"Now we're only six and Alphanderry is dead! And I will be, too, if you ask me to go down there! How can you?"

How could I ask him this, I wondered? And then another thought, as clear and hard as a diamond: How could I not? I knew that the success of the quest depended on his regaining the firestone, as might the fate of Khaisham and much more. The whole world, I sensed, turned upon this moment.

"Maram!" I called out, but there was a silence below me.

It is a terrible thing to lead others in battle. Maram and my companions had elected me to lead us on our quest, and lead I must. But since there was no way I could go down to the firestone myself, I had to persuade him to do so. I wanted to give him all my courage then. But all I could do was to show him his own.

"Maram," I said, though I did not speak with breath and lips. I drew Alkaladur and held it shining in the sun. Strangely, although I had killed many men with it, its silver blade was unstained, for the silustria was so smooth and hard that blood would not cling to it. Maram couldn't help seeing himself in its mirrored brightness. I opened my heart to him then and touched him with the *valarda,* this gift of the angels. My sword cut deep into him. And there, inside his own heart, he found a sword shimmering as bright as any kalama, if not so keenly honed.

"Damn you!" Maram called out to me. But his eyes told me just the opposite. And then, in a softer voice, which I could barely hear, he muttered, "All right, all right, I'll go!"

He turned to look out at what he must do, the muscles along his great body tensing as he gathered in all his strength. For a moment, I thought he was ready to go up and over the wall. And then he quickly pulled himself back behind the safety of the merlon. And still the drums along the enemy's lines beat almost as loud as my heart.

"I can't do this," he said to himself. And then a moment later, "Oh yes, you can, my friend." Again he faced the open crenel, and again he pulled back as he cried out, "Am I mad?"

And still a third time he rushed to the crenel. He put his hands upon the chipped stone there, gathered in his breath, looked out . . . and heaved up his breakfast in a bitter spew. And then, to my pride and his own, he pulled himself up and turned facing the wall to let himself down the ladder there.

"Atara!" I cried, sheathing my sword and grabbing up my bow. "Shoot now! Shoot as you've never shot before!"

Maram was climbing down the ladder with amazing speed as Count Ulanu's knights thundered across the pasture straight toward him. Atara's bow sang out, and so did mine—and those of the Librarians along the wall. Five knights fell from their horses with arrows sticking out of them. But the enemy's archers were now firing off arrows of their own. One of these struck Maram in his rump; he cried out in anger but kept climbing down the ladder. Then he suddenly let go of it and jumped the final five feet to the ground. He scooped up his crystal and leaped back toward the ladder.

Atara's bowstring twanged again, and another knight fell. I killed one, too—as did the archers along the wall. Thus the company of knights charging Maram melted beneath this hot rain of arrows. Only one of them managed to close the last twenty yards, slowing his horse as he neared the wall.

"Maram!" I called down to him. "Behind you!"

Maram, about to be robbed of his treasure and perhaps his life, whipped out his sword even as he turned and ducked beneath the knight's lance. Then he lunged forward and stabbed his sword into the knight's thigh. In its quickness and ferocity, it was a move worthy of Kane.

Just then one of Atara's arrows burned down and took the knight through his throat. He clung desperately to his horse even as Maram turned to race back up the ladder.

"I'm saved!" he cried out. "I'm saved!"

But he had spoken too soon. At that moment, an arrow whined through air and buried itself in the other half of his fat rump. It seemed to push him even more quickly up the ladder. So it was, with feathered shafts sticking out of either of his hindquarters, he reached the top of the wall and heaved himself up over the crenel. Taking care to jump immediately behind one of the merlons, he held up the firestone triumphantly.

"Behold!" he said to me. "Behold and rejoice!"

Then he gazed lovingly at the crystal in his hand as he said, "Ah, my beauty—did you really think I'd let anyone else have you?"

From the top of the tower, Lord Grayam called down to him, "Thank you, Maram Marshayk!"

Other Librarians nearby by took up the cry: "Maram Marshayk! Maram Marshayk!" In a moment, their exultation spread up and down the wall so that knights and archers were now cheering out: "Ma-ram! Ma-ram! Ma-ram! . . ."

The sound of so many voices lifted up in praise carried out across the pasture to where Count Ulanu sat on his horse. Hundreds of his men lay slaughtered beneath the wall, and only a few moments before, a whole company of his finest cavalry had perished. One of his siege towers and battering rams were now nothing but charred beams. And still Maram had his firestone. So when the enemy's bugles sounded again and Count Ulanu began pulling back his lines to make camp for the night, no one was surprised.

"Ma-ram! Ma-ram! Ma-ram! . . ."

A rope ladder was called for and cast up to the Lord

Librarian—and to Atara and me. We climbed down it and embraced Maram, taking care with his wounds. The blood dripping down his legs caused him to turn and look back at the arrows embedded in him. And then he gasped in outrage and pain, "Oh, my Lord, I'll never sit down again!"

"It's all right," I said to him, "I'll carry you, if I must."

"Will you?"

I gripped his hand in mine with great joy as I watched him holding his red crystal in the other. I said, "Thank you, Maram."

In his soft brown eyes was a fire brighter than anything I had seen lighting up his gelstei. "Thank you, my friend," he told me.

Lord Grayam came forward and clasped his hand, too. "You would do well, Prince Maram, to repair to the infirmary—with the other warriors wounded here today."

Maram managed a painful but proud smile. "We won, Lord Grayam."

Lord Grayam stared down though the ruins of the wall at the bloody ground beneath us. He said, "Yes, we won the day."

But the Librarians, too, had lost many men. Tomorrow, I thought, would be another day of battle and even more terrible.

SOON AFTER THAT a messenger arrived to give Lord Grayam news that made his face blanch and set his hand to trembling: The enemy had been thrown back from the Sun Gate, but in its defense Captain Nicolam had been killed and Captain Donalam and several knights captured. The gate itself was ruined beyond repair; Kane and a hundred knights stood in a line behind it in case Count Ulanu should order a night assault of the city.

"They've taken my son," Lord Grayam said. In his quavering

voice, there was sadness, outrage and great fear. "And if we try to hold as we did today, tomorrow they'll take the city."

He issued orders then to abandon the outer wall—and with it, most of Khaisham. So many Librarians had fallen that day, he said, that there were just too few left to hold this extended perimeter. It was an agonizing decision to have to make, but a good one, or so I judged.

And so all the citizens of Khaisham not killed or captured by Count Ulanu's men retreated behind the city's inner wall, which surrounded the Library. Between its blocks of red sandstone and the houses of the city, an expanse of ground five hundred yards wide had been left barren of any buildings or structures. This provided a clear field of fire for Lord Grayam's archers, who quickly took up their stations behind the wall's battlements.

We took Maram to the infirmary to have the arrows drawn and his wounds dressed. After we said good-bye to Master Juwain and Liljana and left them to a sleepless night of tending the wounded, we walked back through the Library. Almost everyone in Khaisham not dead or stationed along the walls had crowded into it. It was a vast place indeed, but it had been built to house millions of books, not thousands of people. It pained me to see aisle upon aisle of old men, women, and children camped out there, trying to rest upon little straw mats that they had put down to cover the cold stone floor.

After that, we took our places behind the battlements of the west wall. There we found one of Lord Grayam's knights speaking in low tones to Kane. It was very dark there, the only illumination being the fire of the torches in the courtyard below and the far-off glimmer of the stars.

"So," Kane said, pointing out at the strip of dark, barren ground that separated the walls from the rest of the city. "They'll try to move their siege engines in as close as they can before morning."

I looked across the barren ground down toward the houses of the city. With no one left to light their hearths, they were strangely dark. Beyond them, in the thicker dark, farther to the west, I could just make out the lines of the outer wall.

While we had been in the infirmary, Count Ulanu's engineers had breached its gates. The sounds of him bringing up his army lent a chill to the air. There came a squeaking of the axles of many wagons, and iron-shod wheels rolling over the paving stones of the empty streets. Thousands of boots striking stone, jangling steel, whinnying horses, hateful shouts, and the incessant howling of the Blues—this was the cacophony we had to endure those long hours after dusk in place of the nightingale's song or other music.

After a while, Lord Grayam walked down the battlements toward us and approached Kane. He told him, "Thank you for your work at the gate. It's said that but for your sword, the enemy would have broken through."

"My sword, yes," Kane said, nodding his head. "And those of a hundred others, Captain Donalam's foremost among them."

In the dim torchlight, I thought I caught a gleam of water in Lord Grayam's eyes. "I've been told that my son was stunned by an axe blow and thus taken before he could regain his wits."

Kane, who didn't like to lie, lied to Lord Grayam now. I sensed a terrible sadness in him as his dark eyes filled with a rare compassion. "I'm sure he never regained his wits. I'm sure he sleeps with the dead."

"Let us hope so—there's little enough hope left for us now."

To cheer Lord Grayam, and myself, I finally told him of what we had found in the Library earlier that day. I brought forth the False Gelstei and pressed the little bowl into his hands. As the night deepened, Kane and Maram recounted the story of Master Juwain finding Master Aluino's journal. And then Atara, whose memory was like a glittering net that seemed to gather in all things, quoted from it almost word for word.

"Is it possible that Master Aluino told true?" Lord Grayam exclaimed. "That the Lightstone is still in Argattha?"

He turned the False Gelstei about in his hands as if it might provide an answer to his question. Then he said to us, "This is why we fight. Do you see what treasures we have here? How can we let them be lost?"

He thanked me for telling him of our find and delivering the cup to him, according to our promise. And then he told us, "You're truly noble, all of you. With such virtue on our side, we might yet win this battle."

Time is strange. That night near the ides of Soal, as measured by the sands of an hourglass, was rather short as summer nights are. But as measured by the sufferings of the soul, it seemed to drag on forever. Count Ulanu's men were determined that none of us should sleep. The half-moon rose to the Blues' relentless howls, which grew louder and more ferocious as the world turned past midnight. From the darkness beyond the wall came a clamor of axes being struck together and of swords banging against shields. Iron hammers beat against nails as terrible screams split the night.

When the morning finally broke free from the gray of twilight and the forms of the dark earth began to sharpen, a terrible sight greeted all who stood behind the battlements. For there, set into the ground along the barren strip in front of the walls, were twenty wooden crosses. The naked bodies of men and three women were nailed to them. The rising wind carried their moans and cries up to us.

Atara, pressing close to my side as she looked out the crenel before us, let loose a soft cry: "Oh, no—look, Val! It's Alphanderry!"

I stared along the line of her pointed finger, peering out into the dawn. My eyes were not as keen as hers; at first all I could make out was the torment of men writhing on their blood-stained wooden towers. And then as the light grew stronger, I saw that the middlemost of the crosses bore the body of our friend. Cords running across his brow bound his head to the cross so that we could get a good look at his face. His eyes were open and gazed out at the sky as if he were hoping to catch sight of the rising sun.

"Is he alive?" Maram asked me.

For a moment, I closed my eyes, remembering. Then I

looked at the remains of Alphanderry as I felt for the beating of his heart. "No, he is dead. And five days dead at that."

"Then why crucify him? He's beyond all pain now."

"He is, but we're not, eh?" Kane said, clenching his fists in fury. If his fingernails had been claws, they would have torn open his palms. "Count Ulanu desecrates the dead in order to kill the hope of the living."

It was why he had crucified the others, too. These, however, were all still alive and all too keenly aware of the agonies that they suffered. It took at least two days to die upon the cross and sometimes much longer.

"Look!" one of the Librarians said, pointing at the cross next to Alphanderry's. "It's Captain Donalam!"

Captain Donalam, hanging there helplessly, his anguished face caked with black blood, looked up toward the wall in silent supplication. I saw him meet eyes with his father. What passed between them was terrible to behold. I felt Lord Grayam's heart break open, and then there was nothing left inside him except defeat and a desire to die in his son's place.

"Look!" another Librarian said. "There's Josam Sharod!"

And so it went, the knights on the wall calling out the names of their companions and friends.

Then someone called out our names. We turned to see Liljana climbing the stairs to the wall, bearing a pot of soup that she had made us for breakfast. She set it down and joined us in looking out at the crosses.

"Alphanderry!" she cried out as if he were her own child. "Why did they do this to you?"

"So," Kane growled, "the Dragon's priests make every abomination, seek every opportunity to degrade the human spirit."

Just then, from the masses of the enemy's foot soldiers gathered behind the line of crosses, four of Count Ulanu's knights rode toward us bearing a white flag. They stopped their horses beneath the walls and their proud-faced leader called up to Lord Grayam, requesting a parlay: "Count Ulanu would speak with you as to making a peace."

"We spoke yesterday," Lord Grayam called down. "What has changed?"

In answer, the knight looked back at the crosses behind him and the city's broken outer wall.

Lord Grayam stared down at his helpless son, and he finally said, "All right then, we shall speak with your bloody count."

The knight signaled to his three companions; they turned to ride back through the crosses and return to their lines, which were drawn up across the barren ground with the city's houses just beyond them. After a few moments, Count Ulanu and five more knights rode back toward the wall, their dragon standard flapping in the early morning wind.

As soon as he had halted beneath the battlements, I felt his malice beating out at us like a war hammer. He reserved the greatest part of his hate for Liljana. He stared at her with a pitilessness that promised no quarter. And she stared right back at him, at the wound her sword had gouged in his face. What was left of his nose was a black, cauterized sore and looked as if the bitterest of acids had eaten it off.

"Hmmph," Atara said, glancing at Liljana, "I suppose he'll have to be called Ulanu the Not-So-Handsome now."

For a few moments, Liljana and Count Ulanu locked eyes and contended with each other mind-to-mind. But Liljana had grown ever stronger and more attuned to her blue gelstei. It seemed that Count Ulanu couldn't bear her gaze, for he suddenly broke off looking at her. Then he spurred his horse forward a few paces and called out his terms to Lord Grayam: "Surrender and your people will be spared. Give us Sar Valashu Elahad and his companions, and there will be no more crucifixions."

"Supposing we believed you," Lord Grayam said, "what would befall my people upon surrender?"

"Only that they should do homage to me and swear to obey the wishes of Lord Morjin."

"You'd make us slaves," Lord Grayam said.

Count Ulanu pointed at the crosses and said, "How many more of the children of your domain are you prepared to see mounted thusly?"

"We cannot surrender the books to you," Lord Grayam said. At this, many of the Librarians along the wall grimly nodded their heads.

"Books!" Count Ulanu spat out. Then he reached into the pocket of his cloak and pulled out a large book bound with leather as dark as the skin of a sunbaked corpse. He held it up and said, "This is the only book of any value. Either other books are in accord with what it tells, and so are superfluous, or else they mock its truth and so are abominations."

I knew of this single volume of lies that he showed us: it was the *Darakul Elu,* the Black Book, which had been written by Morjin. It told of his dreams of uniting the world under the Dragon banner; it told of a new order in which men must serve the priests of the Kallimun, as they served Morjin—and that all must serve his lord, Angra Mainyu. It was the only book I knew that the Librarians refused to allow through the doors of the Library.

"We cannot surrender the books," Lord Grayam said, looking at the count's book with loathing. "We've vowed to give our lives to protect them."

"Are books more precious to you than the lives of your people?"

Lord Grayam squared back his tired shoulders and spoke with all the dignity that he could command. It was then that I learned what hard men and women the Librarians truly were. His words stunned me and rang in my mind: "The lives of men come and go like leaves budding on a tree in the spring and torn off in the fall. But knowledge is eternal—as the tree is sacred. We shall never surrender."

"We shall see," Count Ulanu snarled.

Lord Grayam pointed at the crosses and said, "If you have any mercy, take these people down from there and bind their wounds."

"Mercy, is it?" Count Ulanu shouted. "If it's mercy you want, that you shall have. We'll leave their fate in your hands—or should I say, those of your archers?"

And with that, he smiled wickedly and turned his horse to gallop with his knights back toward his lines.

"Ah," Maram said to me, "I'm afraid to know what he meant by that."

But the implication of his words soon became terribly clear. The Librarians along the wall began to call out to Lord Grayam to mount a sally outside the walls to rescue those who had been crucified. Lord Grayam listened for a few moments and then raised his hand to stay their voices. He pointed down at the enemy's army, where companies of cavalry had assembled in the spaces behind the front ranks of foot soldiers. And then he said, "Count Ulanu would like us to do just as you suggest. So that he could slaughter our knights while we attempted to rescue those for whom there can be no rescue other than death."

"Then what are we to do?" a sad-faced knight named Jonatham asked. "Watch them bake before our eyes beneath the sun?"

"We know what we must do," Lord Grayam said. The bitterness in his voice hurt me worse than the poison that Morjin's man had put into my blood.

"No, no, please," I said. "Let's make a sally, while we can."

A hundred knights called out to ride their warhorses into the face of the enemy and free the crucified women and men. But again Lord Grayam held up his hand and said, "You might kill many of the enemy, but there would be no time to pull our people down from their crosses. In the end, all of you would be killed or captured yourselves."

The Librarians, steeped in the wisdom of the books they guarded, bowed before this logic.

"Archers!" Lord Grayam called out. "Take up your bows!"

I stood stunned in silence as I watched the archers along the walls fit arrows to their bowstrings and the crossbowmen set their bolts.

"Every abomination," Kane said. "Every degradation of the spirit."

Atara, alone of the archers there, refused to lift her bow. Her brilliant blue eyes filled with tears and partially blinded her to sight of what must be.

"Ulanu the Merciful," Liljana said bitterly. "Ulanu the Cruel."

"No, no," I whispered, "they mustn't do this!"

"No, Val, they must," Kane said. "What if it were your brothers crucified out there?"

Every perversion, I thought, listening to the moans of the dying. What could be more perverse than to twist a man's love for his son into the necessity of slaying him?

"Fire!"

And so it was done. The Khaisham archers fired their arrows into their countrymen and friends. Set upon their crosses only seventy yards from the walls, they were easy targets, as Count Ulanu had intended them to be.

Lord Grayam slumped against the battlements as if he had fired arrows into his own heart. I listened for the cries of his son and the other crucified Librarians, but now there was only the moaning of the wind.

Kane stood staring at Alphanderry's body, whose arms were opened wide as if to ask the mercy of the heavens. After a while, his fury poured into me, as did his dark thoughts.

"We should at least ride out and recover the body of our friend," I said. "He shouldn't be left hanging for the vultures."

"So," Kane said, his eyes blazing into mine. "So."

I walked up to Lord Grayam and drew his attention to the enemy's ranks, where the massed cavalry had turned about and was making its way rank by rank back toward the rear. Obviously, since Count Ulanu's trap had failed, he had ordered their withdrawal. And I said to Lord Grayam, "It was impossible to rescue your people, truly. But it may be that we could bring back our friend's body and a couple of the others for burial."

"No, Sar Valashu," Lord Grayam said, "I couldn't allow that."

"The enemy isn't expecting a sally now," I said. "We could ride like lightning and return before Count Ulanu could mount an attack."

The knight named Jonatham called out to ride with us, and so did a dozen others. And then a hundred more along the wall turned toward Lord Grayam with a fire in their hearts and steel in their voices that could not be gainsaid. And so Lord

Grayam, not wanting their spirits to be broken like his own, finally agreed to our wild plan.

"All right," he said to me. "You and Kane may go and take ten others but no more. Go quickly before the enemy begins the day's assault."

Already, Count Ulanu's war drums were booming out their terror as bugles blared out and their battalions made ready to assault the walls.

I pulled on my helmet, as did Kane his. Maram, due to his wounds, would not be going with us. But Atara grabbed up some more arrows for her quiver, and the long, lean Jonatham came over to us, and we had two of our ten. He and Lord Grayam helped me in choosing the other eight knights for our sortie.

We gathered with our horses behind the sally port set into the inner wall's main gate. Its iron-studded doors were thrown open, and we rode out, the twelve of us, across the rocky, barren ground. We galloped forward in a thunder of pounding hooves. It took only seconds to cover the ground between the wall and the line of crosses, but this was enough time for Count Ulanu's archers to begin firing at us and for him to order his cavalry back through his lines to meet our unexpected charge.

An arrow pinged off my helmet and another struck my mail over my shoulder but failed to penetrate its tough Godhran steel. But some of the knights behind me weren't so lucky. One of them, a powerful Librarian named Braham, cried out as a whining shaft suddenly transfixed his forearm. Even so, we reached the crosses in good order. We would have a few moments, but no more, before Count Ulanu's knights fell upon us.

I steadied Altaru beneath Alphanderry's cross. Even desecrated and left to hang uncovered in shame, he retained a beauty and nobility that defied death. Cords bound his arms to the beam while iron spikes, bent over against the palms like clamps, pierced either hand. Another spike had been driven through his feet. I drew my sword then and touched it to the cords binding his head and arms; they parted like strands of grass. Then I swung Alkaladur three times, against Alphanderry's ankles and wrists. His body fell down toward me; Kane, who had brought his horse up close against mine, helped me catch it. We draped him across Altaru's back just in front of me. His hands and feet we had to leave nailed to the cross.

Jonatham and Braham likewise managed to recover the body of Captain Donalam, even as a rain of arrows poured down upon us. And then the arrow storm suddenly ceased. For Count Ulanu's knights rode upon us then, and his archers did not wish to kill them in trying to annihilate us.

Although we were outnumbered seven to one, we had that which overcame mere numbers. Atara, her blond hair streaming back behind her in the wind, rode about wildly firing off death with every bend of her great bow. Jonatham charged the enemy knights once, twice, three times, and his lance became an instrument of vengeance, piercing throat or eye or heart with a lethal accuracy. Kane's sword flashed out with the fury of lightning and thunder, while I wielded the Bright Sword with all the terrible art he had taught me. I rode Altaru straight into the enemy knights where they gathered like a knot of shields and horses, and no matter the armor protecting them, their limbs and heads flew from their bodies like blood sausages encased in steel. The sun rising over Mount Redruth cast its rays upon Alkaladur, which blazed with a blinding light. The sight of it struck terror into even those knights who had yet to come near it. As if they were of one mind, like a flock of birds, they suddenly turned about toward their lines and put their horses to flight.

We managed to cut down five more Librarians before the arrow storm began again. Then we retreated back through the sally port, bearing the bodies of friends and companions across our horses. As cheers rang out from the hundreds of Librarians along the walls, Lord Grayam came down to meet us. He thanked Jonatham and Braham for rescuing his son's body; he knelt down and kissed his son upon the lips. Then he stood up and said, "There is little time for a proper burial, but it will be a while yet before the enemy begins their attack. Let's do for the slain what we can."

We all made a procession then, and we went down into the vast crypt beneath the Library. Master Juwain and the families of the dead joined us there. In that dim, musty space of many thick columns and arches holding up the floor of the Library above us, we laid the dead in their tombs and covered them with slabs of stone. We prayed for their souls and wept. It would have been fitting for us to give a favorite song into the silences of that cold, vast space, but this was not the Librarians' way. And so my companions and I sang our praises of Alphanderry inside our hearts.

A messenger came to tell Lord Grayam that the enemy was advancing and his presence was requested on the walls. Those of us who would fight with him there followed him to the battlements. Kane, Maram, Atara, and I said good-bye to Master Juwain and Liljana, who returned to the infirmary to prepare for the terrible day that awaited us all.

We gathered again on the western wall where Lord Grayam had his post. He climbed up to the tower guarding the wall's gate, and Atara joined him there. Kane and I stood with the grim-faced knights beneath them along the wall where the fighting would be the fiercest.

Maram, hesitating a moment before climbing the tower, too, held up his red gelstei and said, "It is difficult to use this in battle. Difficult to aim. And the more fire I bring forth from it, the longer it takes to gather in the sun's rays for the next burst."

"It is an old crystal," Kane muttered. "It has lost much of its power."

"I don't believe this will be enough to win the battle."

"No, perhaps not. But it's kept us from losing it so far."

"Do you think so?"

"I think that if any survive to sing of the deeds that were done here, the name of Maram Marshayk will be mentioned first."

Such praise, coming from Kane, surprised Maram and pleased him greatly. After a few moments of thought, however, he looked down at the lines of the enemy gathered at the edge of the barren ground, and he said, "I still hate to use this against men."

"Ha, men," Kane snarled out. "Do true men crucify other men? Use your damn stone, I say! Burn these beasts of the Beast straight to hell!"

He stood next to me with his sword held ready to drink the enemy's blood. He stared down at the empty cross where Count Ulanu had put Alphanderry. I saw him scowling at the hands and feet that remained nailed to it. A dark and terrible storm built inexorably inside him, awaiting only the advance of Count Ulanu and his men for its fury to be unleashed.

As on the preceding day, the enemy's drums pounded out their promise of death, and Count Ulanu's steel-clad battalions marched in their gleaming lines toward the walls. The siege towers and battering rams rolled forward; the catapults hurled great stones crashing against the walls and the smooth marble of the Library itself. Arrows fell like rain, and fire flashed forth as screams rang out and men began dying.

During the first assault, Count Ulanu sent his finest knights against our part of the wall. They were almost harder to beat back than were the Blues, for they fought with greater skill, and their armor gave good protection against arrow and sword—all swords except Kane's kalama and Alkaladur. Our bloody blades made a carnage of their steel-clad bodies. Even so, many of them hurled themselves bravely over the battlements. They came at us in twos and tens, and worked their way behind us. Twice I saved Kane from a mace crushing in his helm, and three times he saved me. Thus our flashing swords forged deep bonds of brotherhood between us. For a few golden moments we fought back-to-back as if we were one: a single, black-eyed Valari warrior with four arms and two swords guarding both front and back.

There came a moment during the fiercest part of the attack when a dozen of these knights of Aigul won a bridgehead on the wall. Kane and I found ourselves separated, with the knights between us. They killed two Librarians standing near me, and a few more fighting near Kane. They had beards as black as Count Ulanu's and looked enough like him to have been his cousins; I thought they were some of the same knights that had pursued us into the Kul Moroth.

They taunted Kane, telling him that soon they would capture him and have the pleasure of nailing him to a cross as they had Alphanderry.

It was the wrong thing to do. For Kane fell mad then. And so did I. Working along the wall toward the south, I wielded my sword with all the fury of the blazing Soal sun that poured down upon us. And Kane fought like a demon from hell, slashing and thrusting and rending his way north. Together, our flashing swords were like the teeth of a terrible beast closing upon our enemy. They died one by one, and then suddenly, the three knights still alive lost heart before our terrible onslaught. Two of them hurled themselves over the battlements, taking their chances with broken legs or backs in their plummet to the hard ground below. The remaining knight, seized with terror, threw down his sword. He knelt before Kane, placed his hands together over his chest and cried out, "Quarter! I beg quarter of you!"

Kane raised his sword high to finish this hated enemy knight.

"Mercy, please!" the knight begged.

"So, I'll give you the same mercy your count gave my friend!"

The madness suddenly left me. I called out, "Kane! A warrior's code!"

"Damn the code!" he thundered. "Damn him!"

"Kane!"

"Damn him, I say!"

Kane's sword lifted higher as the knight looked at me, his eyes pleading like a trapped fawn's.

I raised high my sword then so that its silustria caught the sun's rays and threw them back into Kane's face. For a moment he stood there dazzled by this golden light. His sword wavered. Then he looked at me, and I looked at him. There was a calling of our eyes, Valari eyes: black, brilliant, and bottomless as the stellar deeps. There the stars shined, and there, too, Alphanderry's last song reverberated and sailed out toward infinity. I heard the haunting sound of it inside me, and in that moment, so did Kane. And in the opening of his heart, he began to remember who he really was and who he was meant to be. This was a bright, blessed being, joyful and compassionate—not a murderer of terrified men who had thrown down their weapons and asked for mercy. But he feared this shining one more than any other enemy. It was upon me to remind him that he was great enough of heart and soul that he need fear nothing in this world—nor that which dwelled beyond it.

"So," he said, suddenly sheathing his sword as tears filled his eyes. He stepped past the kneeling knight and came up to me. He touched my sword, touched my hand, and then clamped his hand fiercely about my forearm. A bright, blazing thing, secret until now, passed between us. And he whispered, "So, Val—so."

He turned his back on the knight, not wanting to look at him. The Librarians came to take the knight away to that part of the Library where captives were being held. And all the while, Kane stared up at the sky as if looking for himself in the light that kept pouring from the bright morning sun.

Three more times that long day, Count Ulanu's armies made assaults upon the wall. And thrice we threw them back, each time with greater difficulty and desperation. Kane's newfound compassion did not keep him from fighting like an angel of death, nor did my own stay the terror of the sword Lady Nimaiu had given me. But all our efforts—and those of Maram, Atara, and the Librarians—were not enough to defeat the much greater forces flung against us. Near the end of the third assault, with most of Count Ulanu's army in retreat from the walls, we suffered our greatest loss thus far. For one of the Blues, who had fought his way up to a section of wall where Lord Grayam stood with his sword trying to meet a sudden crisis, felled Lord Grayam with a blow of his axe. He himself was slain a moment later, but the deed was done. The Librarians set Lord Grayam down behind the wall's battlements. There he called for me and the rest of our company to come to him. While a messenger ran to summon Master Juwain and Liljana, I knelt with Kane, Atara, and Maram by his side.

"I'm dying," he gasped as he leaned back against the battlements.

I tried not to look at the bloody opening that the Blue had chopped into his belly. I knew it was a wound that not even Master Juwain could heal.

Jonatham and Braham called for a litter to carry the Lord Librarian to the infirmary. But he shook his head violently, telling them, "There's no time! Never enough time! Now please leave me alone with Sar Valashu and his companions. I must speak with them before it is truly too late."

This command displeased both Jonatham and Braham. But they did as he had asked, walking off down the wall and leaving us with him.

"The next attack will be the last," he told us. "They'll wait until sunset so that Prince Maram can't use his firestone, and then . . . the end."

"No," I said, as the blood bubbled from his belly. "There is always hope."

"Brave Valari," he said, shaking his head.

In truth, unless a miracle befell us, the next assault would be the last. I looked out along the broken walls at the dullness of Librarians' eyes and the exhaustion with which they held their notched and bloodstained weapons. A knowledge comes to men in battle when the battle is nearly lost. And now the enemy began re-forming themselves in their battalions in front of the houses of the glowing city. The Librarians peered out at this gathering doom as courageously as they could: without much fear but also without hope.

And then, from the tower to our left, one of the Librarians there pointed toward the west and shouted down, "They're coming! I see the standards of Sarad! We're saved!"

It seemed that we had our miracle after all. I stood to look out the crenel, beyond Count Ulanu's armies and the houses of the city, beyond even the broken outer wall to the west. And there, perhaps a mile out on the pasture, cresting a hill and limned against the setting sun, was a great host of men marching toward Khaisham. The red sun glinted off their armor; their standards, in a direct line with this fiery orb, were hard to see. I told myself that I could make out the golden lions of Sarad against a flapping blue banner. But then one of the Librarians, from the tower to our right, peered through his looking glass and announced, "No, the standards are black! And it is the golden dragons of Brahamdur!"

He then swept his glass from north to south and shouted, "The armies of Sagaram and Hansh march with them! We are lost!"

A pall of doom descended upon all who stood there, worse than before. Count Ulanu had sent for reinforcements to complete his conquest, and with all the inevitability of death, they had come.

"Sar Valashu!" Lord Grayam called to me. "Come closer—don't make me shout."

I knelt beside him with my friends to hear what he had to say. Just then he smiled as he saw Liljana and Master Juwain mount the steps to the wall. He beckoned them closer, too, and they joined us.

"You must save yourselves, if you can," he told us. "You must flee the city while you can."

I shook my head sadly; Khaisham was now surrounded by a ring of steel too thick for even Alkaladur to cut through.

"Listen to me!" Lord Grayam called out. "This is not your battle; even so you have fought valiantly and have done all you can do."

I looked from Atara to Kane, and then at Maram, who was biting his lip in fear. Master Juwain and Liljana were so tired that they could hardly hold up their heads. They had seen enough of death during the past day to know that soon, like the coming of night, it would fall upon them as well.

"I should have bid you to leave Khaisham before this," Lord Grayam told us, as if in apology. "But I thought the battle could be won. With your swords, with the firestone that I suspected Prince Maram possessed . . ."

His voice trailed off as a spasm of agony ripped through his body and contorted his face. And then he gasped, "But now you must go."

"Go where?" Maram muttered.

"Into the White Mountains," he said. "To Argattha."

The name of this dreadful city was as welcome to our ears as the thunder of the Count Ulanu's war drums booming out beyond the walls.

"You must," he told us, "try to recover the Lightstone."

"But, sir," I said, "even if we could break out, to simply forsake those who have stood by us in battle—"

"Faithful Valari," he said, cutting me off. His eyes stared up and through me, up at the twilight sky. "Listen to me. The Red Dragon is too strong. The finding of the Lightstone is the only hope for Ea. I see this now. I see . . . so many things. If you forsake your quest, you truly do forsake those who have fought with you here. For why have we fought? For the books? Yes, yes, of course, but what do books hold inside them? A dream. Don't let the dream die. Go to Argattha. For the sake of me, for the sake of my son and all who have fallen here, go. Will you promise me this, Sar Valashu?"

Because a dying man had made a request of me with almost his last breath—and because I thought there was no way we could ever escape the city—I took his hand and told him, "Yes, you have my promise."

"Good." With all the strength that he could manage, he reached inside the pocket of his cloak and pulled out the False Gelstei that we had found in the Library the day before. He gave the gold-colored cup to me and told me, "Take this. Don't let it fall into the enemy's hands."

Then he closed his eyes against another spasm of pain and cried out, "Jonatham! Braham! Captain Varkam!"

Jonatham and Braham, accompanied by a grim, gray-haired knight, came running along the wall. They joined us, kneeling at Lord Grayam's feet.

"Jonatham, Braham," Lord Grayam said. "What I must tell you now, you must not dispute. There is no time. Everyone has noted your valor in rescuing my son's body. Now I must call upon a deeper courage."

"What is it, Lord Librarian?" Jonatham asked, laying his hand on Lord Grayam's feet.

"You are to leave the city tonight. You will—"

"Leave the city? But how? No, no, I couldn't—"

"Don't argue with me!" Lord Grayam interrupted him. He coughed, once, very hard, and more blood flowed out of him. "You and Braham will go into the Library. With horses, at least two of them. Take the Great Index. We can't rescue the books, but at least we should have a record of them so that copies might someday be found and saved. Then go with Sar Valashu and his companions into the hills. From there, they will go . . . where they must go. And you will go to Sarad. For a time: soon Count Ulanu will fall against it and take it as well. He'll take all of Yarkona. And so you must flee to some corner of Ea where the Dragon hasn't yet come. I don't know where. Flee, my knights, and gather books to you that you might start a new Library."

He placed his hands over his belly and moaned bitterly as he shuddered. Then he sighed, "Too late—much too late."

Beyond the wall, the beating of the drums thundered louder.

Lord Grayam drew in a deep breath and said, "Captain Varkam! You will hold the walls as long as you can. Do you understand?"

"Yes, Lord Librarian," the gray-haired knight said.

"All of you, I must tell you how sorry I am that I misjudged, that there just wasn't enough time, and that I, in my pride, didn't see—"

"Ah, Lord Grayam?" Maram said, interrupting him. He alone, of all of us, felt compelled to put need before decorum. "You spoke of fleeing into the hills. But how are we to leave the city?"

Lord Grayam closed his eyes then, and I felt him slipping off into the great emptiness. But then he suddenly looked at me and said, "Long ago, my predecessors built an escape tunnel from the Library to the slopes of Mount Redruth. Only the Lord Librarians have kept this secret. In the crypt, there is a door. It's plastered over, but . . ."

Another spasm ripped through him. His whole body shivered and convulsed, and his gaze seemed to fix onto the great wall surrounding the city of night. So Lord Grayam died. Like many men, he went over to the other side before he was really ready, before he thought it was his time to die.

Liljana, seized with inspiration, took out her blue gelstei and laid her hand on Lord Grayam's head. Her touch lasted only a few moments. But that was enough for her to reach into that land of ice and utter cold—enough, as her grip closed upon the last gleam of Lord Grayam's mind, to freeze her soul. Her eyes suddenly rolled back in her head, showing nothing but white, and I was afraid that she would join Lord Grayam in eternity. Then she shuddered violently as she ripped her hand away and looked at me.

"Oh, Val—I never knew!" she whispered to me.

"Brave woman," I said, taking her cold hand in mine. I smiled and said softly, "Foolish woman."

Now the sun had set, and the sentinels cried out that the armies of Brahamdur, Sagaram, and Hansh were approaching the city's outer walls.

I looked at Liljana and asked, "Could you see anything?"

"I saw where the door is," Liljana suddenly breathed out. "It's in the main crypt. I can find it, I think."

I stood up then, and so did my companions. To Captain Varkam, who was looking at us strangely, I said, "It seems that there may be a way out for us, after all. And yet—"

"Go!" he said to me with great urgency. "This was the Lord Librarian's last command, and it must be obeyed."

He motioned for Lord Grayam's body to be placed on a bier. He told me, "Farewell, Sar Valashu. May you walk always in the light of the One." Then he clasped my hand and turned to look to the Library's last defense.

We sent for our horses and took them down into the gloomy crypt. There we met Jonatham and Braham. They had four horses between them, each of whose saddlebags was packed with their portion of the eighty-four huge volumes of the Great Index. It made a heavy load for the horses, but not nearly so great as the burden that they themselves must bear.

Liljana located a place on the crypt's eastern wall, where the light of the torches through the arches showed most brightly. We brought forth the sledgehammers the Librarians had given us and broke through the veneer of plaster hiding the door. This was a huge slab of steel, untouched by rust despite the centuries since it had been hung there. With a wrenching sound, we opened it. Before us was a tunnel wide enough to drive a cart through—and dark enough to send shudders of doubt through all our hearts.

Our passage through it was like a nightmare. Once the door had locked shut behind us, it seemed that the earth itself had devoured us. The torches we carried sent an oily smoke into the stale air and choked us; the red sandstone through which the tunnel had been carved seemed stained with the blood of all who had died along the Library's walls. We walked down and down through that dank place for what seemed like hours. And then up and up. At last we came to another door, like the first. It opened onto a much larger space that had once been the shaft of a mine. We made our way through it and passed out of its opening, which was overgrown with bushes and trees.

And so we stood on the slope of Mount Redruth beneath the night's first stars. In the air was a sharp coolness as well as a howling coming from the city below us. We could see all of Khaisham in the sheen of the bright half-moon. The Library, rising like a vast salt crystal from Khaisham's highest hill, was ringed by thousands of little lights that must have been torches. Many of these flickered from atop the inner wall; from this sign I knew that it had fallen. The Librarians, no doubt, were making their final defense from behind the Library's immense wooden doors. I wondered how much longer they would stand before Count Ulanu's fire arrows and battering rams.

"You should go now," I said to Jonatham. He stood with Braham by their horses, looking down at his conquered city. I pointed along the curve of the mountain, south toward Sarad. "It won't be long before our escape is discovered. Count Ulanu will surely send pursuit."

"If he does, then they will be slain," Jonatham said with a black certainty. "As we will, all of us. We've entered the Frost Giants' country here, and they'll likely find us before Count Ulanu's men do."

"They may," I said. "But there is always hope."

"No, not always," Jonatham said, taking my hand in his. "But it gladdens my heart that you say that. I shall miss you, Sar Valashu."

"Farewell Jonatham," I said. "May you walk in the light of the One."

Then I clasped Braham's hand, as did my friends, quickly making their farewells. We watched as they led their horses across the trackless slope of the mountain until they vanished behind its contours into the dark.

I stood on the rocky, slanting earth with my hand on Altaru's neck, trying to ease his strained nerves for the journey that we still must make. Maram stood by Iolo near me, as did Atara and Liljana with their horses, and Master Juwain and Kane.

"What are we to do?" Maram said, gazing down at the city.

"There's only one thing to do," I said.

Maram looked at me with horror filling up his face. "But, Val, you can't really be thinking that—"

"I gave my promise to Lord Grayam," I told him.

"But surely that's not a promise you can think to keep!"

Could I keep it, I wondered? I, too, stared down at Khaisham. The thousands of torches had now closed in around the Library like a ring of fire.

"My promise," I said to Maram and the others, "was given from me to Lord Grayam. It doesn't bind any of you."

"But surely it doesn't bind you, either," Master Juwain told me. "You can't promise to do the impossible."

"It can't be impossible. And that is why we must go to Argattha, to find the Lightstone."

"But we don't know that it's even there!" Maram said. "What if Master Aluino's journal was a hoax? What if he was mad, as he thought of the man claiming to be Sartan Odinan?"

I stared at the blazing torches as I relived Lord Grayam's urging that I should enter Argattha. I tried to imagine an invisible cup guarded by dragons and hidden in the darkest of places—the last place on earth that I would ever wish to go. Then I drew Alkaladur and pointed it toward the east. Its blade flared with a silvery light, the brightest I had yet seen.

"It's there," I said, knowing that it must be. "It's still there."

Master Juwain came forward and set his hand on my arm. He said, "Val, there is a great danger here. Danger for us, if we covet the Lightstone as Sartan did. Perhaps it would be best to leave the Lightstone wherever it was that he set it down. It might never be found."

"No," I said, "it will be found—by someone. And soon. This is the time, sir. You said so yourself."

Master Juwain fell silent as he stared up at the stars. There, it was told, the Ieldra poured forth their essence upon the earth in the ethereal radiance of the Golden Band.

Of all my friends, only Kane seemed pleased by the prospects of this desperate venture. The wind off his dark face and rippling white hair carried the scents of hate and madness. A wild look took hold of his face, and he said, "Once Kalkamesh entered Argattha, and so might we."

"But that's madness!" Maram said. "Surely you can see that!"

"Ha—I see that the plan's seeming madness is its very strength. Morjin will continue to seek the Lightstone in every other land but Sakai. He'll seek us there, too, eh? He'd never dream we'd be witless enough to try to enter Argattha."

"*Are* we that witless?" Maram asked.

Liljana patted his hand consolingly and said, "It would be foolish to attempt the impossible. But is it truly that?"

We all looked at Atara, who stared out at Khaisham as from the vantage of the world's highest mountain. And then, in a soft voice that struck terror into me, she said, "No, not impossible—but almost."

From high up on the Library's south wing came a flicker of light, as of a flame brightening a window. I thought of all the Librarians who had died in its defense and the thousands of men, women, and children taking refuge inside. I thought of my father and mother, of my brothers and all my countrymen in far-off Mesh—and of the Lokilani and Lady Nimaiu and even the greedy but sometimes noble Captain Kharald. And, of course, of Alphanderry. I knew then that even if there was only one chance in ten thousand of rescuing the Lightstone out of Argattha, it must be taken. My heart beat out its thundering affirmation of this dreadful decision. There comes a time when a life not willingly risked for the love of others is no longer worth living.

"I will go to Argattha," I said. "Who will come with me?"

Now more flames appeared in the other windows of the south wing, and then in those of the other wings, as well. When it became clear that Count Ulanu's men had fired the Library, Maram called out, "The books! Everyone trapped inside! How can he do this? How, Val, how?"

He fell against me, weeping and clutching at the rings of my mail to keep from falling down in despair. I forced myself to stand like a wall, or else I would have fallen, too—and never to arise again.

"Oh no!" Liljana said, looking at the burning Library. "It can't be!"

Her arms found their way around Atara, who was now sobbing bitterly and silently as she pressed her face against Liljana's chest.

"I should never have used my firestone," Maram gasped out. "All the burning led only to this. I swear I'll never turn fire against men again."

Master Juwain held his head with both hands as he stared down at the horror before us. He seemed unable to move, unable to speak.

"So," Kane said, with death leaping like dark lights in his eyes.

As the fire found the millions of books that the Librarians had collected over the centuries, a great column of flame shot high into the air. It seemed to carry the cries of the damned and the dying up toward the heavens. I smelled the sweet-bitter boil of death in the sudden burning that swept through me like an ocean of bubbling kirax. Fire ravished me. It blazed like starlight in my heart and hands and eyes.

"So," Kane said as I turned to look at him, "I will go with you to Argattha."

I bowed my head to him, once, fiercely, as our hands locked

together. Then I looked at Master Juwain, who said, "I will go, too."

"So will I," Liljana said, gazing at me in awe of what we must do.

"And I," Atara said softly. She stood gazing at me as she fought back her fear, and her deep concern for me filled her lovely heart in its place. In her sudden smile was a blazing certainty that she would never leave my side.

Maram finally pulled away from me and forced himself to stop sobbing. I felt something move inside him, like the shaking of a fire mountain.

"I want to go with you . . ." he began.

He stopped speaking as he drew in a long breath. For a long few moments, he stood looking at me. He blinked at the bitter smoke as if remembering a promise that he had made to himself. He pulled himself up straight, shook out his brown curls, and stood for a moment like a king.

"I will go with you," he told me with steel in his voice. "I'd follow you into hell itself, Val, which is certainly where we are going."

I clasped his hand in mine to seal this troth as our hearts beat as one.

After that, we all looked down to behold the destruction of the Library. There was no desire to utter another word, no need to speak the prayers that would burn forever in our hearts. The fire, fed by many books and bodies, raged high into the sky and seemed to fill all the world, and that was hell enough.

Then we all turned to flee into the darkness that lay before us.

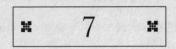

7

AND SO, THAT very night, we went up into the mountains. We turned our horses east and picked our way across the rocky slopes of Mount Redruth. We had no track to follow, only the gleam of my sword and the glimmer of the stars. These points of white and blue grew more vivid as we left Khaisham's glowing sky behind us and climbed higher. Bright Solaru of the Swan constellation gave me hope, as did the brilliant swath of stars called the Sparkling Stairs. They reminded me that there were better places in the One's creation where men did not kill each other with steel and flame.

As the night deepened, it grew cooler, and I surrounded myself in my cloak, which my mother had made of lamb's wool and embroidered with silver. It gave good warmth, as did those of my companions. But not enough to please Kane. He peered at the ghostly white shapes of the greater mountains rising up to the east, and said, "We'll need thicker clothing than this before long."

"But it's still summer," Maram said, walking his horse near him.

"In the deeper mountains, it's already fall," Kane said, pointing ahead of us. "And in the high mountains, winter. Always winter."

His words brought us back to the dangers all about us. These were numerous and deadly. Pursuit by Count Ulanu's men was the least of them. More worrisome, at the moment, was losing our way in the dark and plunging off an unexpected cliff. Certainly there were bears about, as Maram imagined seeing behind every tree. And we all looked for the shapes of the dreaded Frost Giants lying in wait for us, perhaps just behind the next ridge, or the one behind that.

All that night, however, we saw no sign of these fearsome creatures. Nor did we catch sight of the twinkling form of

Flick. Maram supposed that Flick had the good sense not to enter a land guarded by man-eating giants. I wondered if the evil of what had happened in Khaisham had simply driven him away. I was almost ready to say a requiem for him when he suddenly reappeared just before dawn. As the Morning Star showed brightly in the east, he winked into a fiery incandescence that reminded me of the sparks thrown up by the Library's burning. I took this as his own manner of saying a requiem for all of those who had died that night in the hellish flames.

"Flick, my little friend!" Maram cried out when he saw him spinning through the grayness of the twilight. "You've come back to us!"

"Maybe he's been with us all along, and we couldn't see him," Atara said.

Liljana, leaning against her horse, said, "It's strange, isn't it, that Alphanderry did see him just before he died? How can that be?"

We looked at each other in wonder; the world was full of mysteries.

"I don't know, but I'm tired," Maram yawned. "Too tired to think about such things now. I think I'd better lie down before I fall down."

We were all exhausted. As for myself, my body hurt from a dozen bruises gained in battle. And so I led us to a level place in a hollow between two ridges where we set out our sleeping furs for a quick rest. Kane insisted on remaining awake to keep watch over us, and none of us argued with him. I fell off into a sleep troubled with images of Alphanderry hanging from his cross and all the Librarians who had died before my eyes. And it wasn't Morjin who sent these dreams to me, only the demons of war that had fought their way deep into my mind.

We awoke beneath a bright sun to vistas of icy mountains rising up before us. While Liljana went to work on our breakfast, we held council and decided that we had eluded whatever pursuit that Count Ulanu had sent after us—if indeed he had sent anyone at all. Kane thought it possible that the Library had been fired before our escape route through the crypt had been discovered and had collapsed in a smoking ruin to seal it off.

"Very good," Maram said. "Perhaps luck is finally turning our way."

Atara said nothing as she stared out at the great mountains before us. We all knew that we would need much more than luck to cross them.

The smell of bubbling porridge wafted into the air. Liljana stood by her little cauldron stirring the oats with a long wooden spoon. I could tell that she was still unhappy at having had to jettison most of her cookware on our flight across Yarkona. She was unhappy, too, that there hadn't been time to gather the necessary supplies for our journey.

"We've enough food for most of a month, if we stretch it," she told us as we gathered around the little fire to eat. "How far is it to Argattha?"

"If the old maps are right, two hundred and fifty miles, as the raven flies," Master Juwain said. Then his face furrowed as he rubbed his bald head. No one knew very much about Sakai, not even the mapmakers.

"But we," Kane said, "won't be traveling as the raven flies."

We sat discussing our route into Sakai. According to Master Juwain, Sakai was a vast, high plateau entirely ringed by mountains. The White Mountains, he said, rose up like an immense wall from the lake country of Eanna in the northwest and ran for a thousand miles toward the southeast to make up Ea's spine. Somewhere to the east of us, it divided into two great ranges: The Yorgos in the south, and in the north, the Nagarshath, where it was said were the highest mountains on earth. The realm of Sakai lay between them. Master Juwain thought that various spurs of these ranges ran north and south across the plateau, but he wasn't sure.

"At least we know that Skartaru lies along the edge of the Nagarshath," he said. "It's known that the Black Mountain looks out over the Wendrush."

"Then we should follow the line of the Nagarshath until we come to it," I said. I looked at my sword, whose radiance was almost lost in the greater blaze of the sun. It pointed us east and slightly south—straight along the course I imagined the Nagarshath to run.

"Ha, those mountains are said to be impassable," Kane said. "That leaves a journey across the plateau, keeping the mountains to our left. But there, we'll certainly find Morjin's people—or be found by them."

"But what other choice do we have?" Liljana asked.

"None that I can see," Kane said.

We all looked at Atara, who shook her head and told us, "None that I can see, either."

We were silent as we scanned the mountains about us. Maram stared off behind us, still looking for pursuit, while I gazed ahead at the great white peaks rising up like impossibly high merlons directly ahead of us. Trying to show a courage that I didn't feel, I pointed my sword east into their heart. I said, "We'll just have to cut straight across them."

"Ha, straight is it?" Kane laughed out, clapping me on my good shoulder. "So you say—and you a man of the mountains."

That day we had some of the hardest work of our journey. Without any map or track to follow, we had to make our way across the rocky ridges with little more than intuition to guide us. Twice, my sighting of a possible pass through the rising ground before us proved a dead end, and we had to turn back to find another route. It was exhausting to lead the horses up toward the snowline along a slope strewn with boulders and scree; it was even more dispiriting to retreat down these same uncertain steps to seek out another path. Although there was beauty all about us in the gleam of the great mountains and in the sky pilots and other wildflowers that brightened their sides, by the time we made camp that evening, we were all too tired to appreciate it. The thin air cut our throats, and Master Juwain complained of the same dull headache I felt building at the back of my neck. It grew quite cold—and this faint frost of the falling night was only a promise of the ice and bitterness that still lay before us.

Thus for three days we fought our way east. Mostly, the

weather held fair, with the air so thin and dry that it seemed it could never hold the slightest particle of moisture. But then, late on the third afternoon, dark clouds appeared as if from nowhere, and we had a few fierce hours of freezing rain. It cut our eyes with lancets of sleet and stung our lips; it coated the rocks with a glaze of ice, making the footing for both man and beast treacherous. As we could find no shelter from this torment, we sat huddled beneath our cloaks waiting for it to end. And end it did as the clouds finally opened to reveal the frigidity of night. As we could neither retreat nor go forward with any degree of safety, we were forced to spend the night high up on the saddle between two great mountains. There Maram knelt with his flint and steel, trying to get a fire out of the wood that the horses had toted up into this barrenness.

"I'm cold; I'm wet; I'm tired," Maram complained as he struck off another round of sparks into his tinder. His hands shook as he shivered and looked over to where Flick spun about. "Ah, my little friend, perhaps you should help me make this fire."

Then he wondered out loud if Flick might be the seventh told of in Ayondela's prophecy.

It was a strange thought with which to lie against the cold ground and fall off to sleep that night. It made me recall with great clarity Alphanderry's death and the despair that had gripped my heart afterward. And through this dark doorway, Morjin came for me. In my dreams, he sent a werewolf who looked like Alphanderry sniffing through the shadows for the scent of my blood. This demon howled in a rage to show me yet another of my deaths; then it sang sweetly that I should join him in the land from which there is no return. It tried to kill me with the terror of what awaited me. But that night, I had allies watching over me and guarding my soul.

Flick, I somehow knew, spun above my sleeping form like a swirl of stars warding off evil. My mother's love, felt in the deep currents of the earth beneath me, enveloped me like a warm and impenetrable cloak. Inside me shined the sword of valor that my father had given me, and outside, on the ground with my hand resting on the hilt, was the sword called Alkaladur. It quickened the fires of my being so that I was able to strike out and drive the demon away. It cut through the black smoke of the nightmare realm into the clear air through which shined the world's bright stars. And so I was able to awaken beneath the mountains, to find Atara's hand gripping mine and that I was unharmed.

In the morning we made our way down from the saddle between the two mountains into a long, narrow valley. It was a lovely place and heavily wooded, with blue spruce and feather fir and other trees. A sparkling river ran down its center. Its undulating forests hid many birds and animals: bear, marten, elk, and deer. Although we were deep in the White Mountains and it was rather cool, the air held none of the bitterness of the high terrain we had just crossed. And so we decided to make camp by the river and rest that day. Despite our worry about the Frost Giants, Atara went off by herself to hunt, hoping to take a little meat to replace our dwindling stores.

Later that night, over a fine feast of roasted venison, we all sat around the fire discussing the long journey that still lay ahead of us. Maram, looking about the mountains, said, "It's strange that we've come this far and seen no sign of these Frost Giants. Perhaps they don't exist."

"Ha!" Kane laughed out, wiping the meat's bloody juices from his chin. "You might as well hope that bears don't exist."

"I'd rather meet a bear here than a Frost Giant," Maram admitted. "Jonatham told me that they use men's skin for their water bags and make a pudding from our blood. And that they grind our bones to make their bread."

"Perhaps they do—so what? Do you think they're not made of flesh and blood? Do you think steel won't cut them or arrows kill them?"

While Kane and Maram sat debating the terrors of these mysterious creatures, Master Juwain looked up from the book he was reading. "If they do exist, then perhaps they make their dwellings only in the higher mountains. Why else would they be called Frost Giants?"

Here he pointed toward the white peaks of the great massif rising up to the east of the valley.

"Well, then," Maram said, looking about nervously, "we should keep to the valleys, shouldn't we?"

But, of course, we couldn't do that. The cast of the mountains here was from north to south, with the ridgelines and the valleys between them running in those directions. To journey east, as we did, was to have to cut across these great folds in the earth wherever we might find a pass or an unexpected break. And that made a hard journey a nearly impossible one.

The next morning we packed the horses and rode along the river through the sweet-smelling forest. We rode all that day for twenty miles across gradually ascending ground until we came to a little lake at the bottom of a bowl with mountains all around us. And there, just to the south of these blue waters, was the break in the mountain wall that I had been hoping for. It was only a quarter-mile wide and narrowed quickly as its rocky slopes rose toward ridgelines to either side of it. But it seemed to me like a pass, or at least an opening onto other valleys beyond it.

"I don't think it's a pass at all," Maram said, craning back his head. "Why don't we go on and see if we can find a better route?"

Liljana gazed up at the frozen heights before us, and said, "I don't think there are any good routes over these mountains. Have courage, Maram."

Maram cast her a hurt look. "Do you think I lack courage, then?"

"Of course not. I've known few men as valorous as you."

Now Maram fairly beamed. "Is that really true?"

"Of course it is. It's just that sometimes you seem to lose your sense of it."

"It's sense," Maram said, gazing upward again, "that tells me this 'pass' of Val's is just too damn high. Good, common sense: my grandmother, as everyone in Delu knows, was a peasant, and she bequeathed to me her practical ways."

"Ha, practical!" Kane called out. "Well, practical or not, this is our route. Are you coming with us?"

Maram hesitated only a moment as he fought back his sense of impending doom—whether justified or only imagined,

I couldn't know. Then he said, "I am indeed coming with you, my friend, but I must tell you that I don't have a very good feeling about this damned pass."

As it was too late to begin our ascent, we made camp by the lake and settled in early. We ate more venison, sweetened with some pine nuts that Liljana shook out of their cones. We watched the beavers that made their mounded homes on the lake and the geese that swam there, too.

We set out very early, almost at first light. The climb toward the pass was a steep one, with our route following a little stream that wound down from the heights, here cutting through a ravine, there spilling in clear cascades over granite escarpments. We walked the horses higher and higher, leading them by their halters and taking care that they had good footing on the rocky terrain. By late morning, we had climbed beyond the treeline. There the slope leveled out a little but there was no end of it in sight. To our right was a vast wall of mountain, sharp as the blade of a knife. To our left, a huge pyramid of ice and granite—one of the highest that I had ever seen— turned its stark, uncaring face toward us. These great, jagged peaks seemed to bite the sky itself and tear open the entrails of heaven.

Early that afternoon, we reached the snowline, and there it grew much colder. Clouds came up and blocked out the sun. The wind rose, too, and drove little particles of ice against the horses' flanks—and into our faces. It was so frigid that it set us to gasping and nearly stole our breath away. We gathered our cloaks around us, and all of us wished for the warmer clothing of which Kane had spoken a few nights before.

"I'm tired and I'm cold," Maram grumbled as he led Iolo through the snow behind me. Atara and Fire followed him, and then Master Juwain and Liljana with their horses, and finally Kane and his bay. "I can't see our way out of this miserable pass—can you?"

I listened to the sound of my boots breaking through the crusts of snow and the horses' hooves crunching ice against rock. I peered off through the clouds of spindrift whipping through the pass. It seemed to give out onto lower ground only a half mile ahead of us.

"It can't be much farther," I said, turning back to look at Maram.

"It better not be," he said, as he flicked the ice from his mustache. "My feet are getting numb. And so are my fingers."

But when we had covered this slight distance, made much longer and nearly unbearable by the thin and bitter air, we found that our way turned along the back side of the sharp ridgeline on our right. And there another long, white slope lay before us. It led up between two crests to an even higher part of the pass.

"It's too high!" Maram said when he saw this. "We'll have to turn back!"

Atara came up to us then, and so did the others. We all stood staring up at this distant doorway through the mountains. Liljana rubbed her wind-reddened hands together and said, "We can be through it by midafternoon."

"Perhaps," Maram said. "But what will we find on the other side?"

He turned to Atara in hope that she might answer this question. I knew that she was growing weary of everyone always looking to her to read the terrain of the future. And so she smiled at him and said, "Likely we'll find the other side of the mountain."

"But what if this is really no pass at all?" Maram said. "I don't want to spend a night this high up."

"We've wood for a fire," Kane said. "And if the worst befalls us, we can always burrow into the snow. I think we'll survive the night."

"One night, maybe," Maram said.

I took his cold hand in mine and blew on his fingertips to warm them. "We have to take some chances. Or else we'll wander here, and that's the worst chance of all. Now why don't we go on while we still have the strength?"

I led forth, and Altaru and I broke track through the snow for the others. It was very hard work, even worse for the horses, I thought, than for us. Faggots of wood were slung across their backs, weighing them down heavily. I watched the breath steam from Altaru's nostrils as he leaned his neck forward and drove his hooves into the snow. But he made no complaint, nor did any of the other horses. I marveled at their trust in us, marching onward at our behest into a snowy waste that seemed to have no end.

Soon it began to snow. It was not a heavy storm, nor did it feel as if it would be a long one. But the wind caught up the downy flakes and drove them like tiny spears against us. It was hard to see, with bits of ice nearly blinding our eyes. The snow burned my nose and found its way down my neck. It piled up beneath my boots, making the work of walking upward much harder.

And so we continued our ascent for at least an hour. We all suffered from the cold in near silence, except Maram, who made deep growling sounds in his throat as if this noise might simply drive the storm away. As we drew near the pass, the wind suddenly rose and grew more bitter. A cloud of snow whirled about us and tore at our flesh. I began shivering and so did the others. My face burned with the sting of the snow, and my nose felt numb and stiff. My fingers were stiff, too. I could hardly feel them, hardly keep my grip on the ice-encrusted leather of Altaru's halter. I bent forward, into the wind, driving my numbed feet into the snow mounding into drifts all around us. My eyes were nearly frozen shut, and I kept blinking against the biting snow, blinking and blinking as I tried to peer through this blinding white wall ahead to make out the shrouded rock forms at the lip of the pass.

It was there, so close to our much-desired objective, that many great white shapes rose up out of the storm as if from nowhere. At first it seemed that the swirls of snow had formed themselves up into ghostly beings that haunted such high places; in truth, the snowdrifts themselves seemed to come alive with a will of their own. And then, with the whinnying and stamping of the horses, I saw huge, white-furred beasts descending from the walls of rock around us. There were at least twenty of them, and they came for us out of the storm in utter silence, with murderous intent.

"The Frost Giants!" Maram cried out. "Run for your lives!"

But with this new enemy encircling us, there was nowhere to run, nor did any of us have the strength for flight. The Frost Giants, if such they really were, were advancing upon us with a shocking speed. Their footing through the snow seemed sure and stolid. And they were not beasts at all, I saw, but only huge men nearly eight feet tall. Although they were entirely unclothed, their shaggy white hair was so long and thick that it covered them like gowns of fur. Their furry faces were savage, with ice-blue eyes peering out from beneath brow ridges as thick as slabs of granite. There was a keen intelligence in these cold orbs, and death as well. In their hands, they gripped huge clubs: five-foot lengths of oak shod with spiked iron. A blow from one of these would break a horse's back or crumple even plate armor.

"Circle!" I cried out. "Circle the horses!"

I cried out as well, to the Frost Giants, that we were not their enemies, that we wished only to cross their land in peace. But either they didn't understand what I said or didn't care.

"Yes, circle!" Maram shouted. "Quickly!"

We tried to make a wall of the horses; their deadly, kicking hooves, especially Altaru's, might deter even these terrible men. From behind them, we might take up our bows and defend ourselves with a hail of arrows. But the horses were whinnying and stamping, pulling frantically at their halters, and would not cooperate. And in any case, there was no time. The Frost Giants were nearly upon us, raising up their great clubs behind their heads as easily as I might have held a chicken leg.

"Val! Val!" Maram cried out. "Val—my fingers are frozen!"

Mine almost were. I tried to bring forth my bow and string it, but my fingers were too numb. So were Atara's. I saw her behind me attempting to fit an arrow to her bowstring; but she was shivering so badly and her hands were so stiff that she couldn't quite nock it. Kane didn't even bother to try his bow. He drew his sword from its sheath, and a moment later, so did I.

It is strange that compassion can be a force powerful

enough almost to stop the turning of the world. Maram, standing by my side, his frozen fingers fumbling in his pocket, finally managed to draw forth his red crystal. He pointed it at the Frost Giants. His terrified voice wheezed in my ear, "Val—should I burn them?"

Then, as he remembered his vow never again to turn fire against men, his hands shook and he couldn't quite use it. His hesitation saved our lives.

"Hrold!" one of the Frost Giants suddenly called out. "Hrold now!"

The white-furred men halted twenty feet away in a ring around us. Their spiked clubs wavered in the air.

The Frost Giant who had spoken, a vastly thick man with a broken nose and eyes the color of a frozen waterfall, pointed at Maram's crystal and said, "It be a firestone."

The man next to him in the circle peered through the snow at us and said, "Are you sure, Ymiru?"

The being called Ymiru slowly nodded his head. Then his large blue eyes squinted as they fixed on the sword that I held ready at my side. With the moment of my death at hand, Alkaladur began shimmering with a soft, silver light.

"And that be sarastria," he said. His huge, deep voice rumbled out into the pass like thunder. "It must be sarastria."

Sarastria, I thought. Silustria. The Frost Giants spoke familiar words with a strange turning of the tongue, but I could still understand what they said.

"Little man," Ymiru said, pointing his club at me, "how came you to find sarastria?"

It astonished me that this savage-seeming Frost Giant should know anything at all about the silver gelstei—or the firestones. I looked at him and said, "It was acquired on a journey."

"What kind of journey?"

I traded quick looks with Kane and Atara; I was reluctant to tell these strange men of our quest.

"Come!" Ymiru roared out, raising up his club. "Speak now! And speak truthfully or else you and your friends will soon find death."

I had a strange sense that I could trust this giant man—to do exactly as he said. And so I opened my cloak to show him the gold medallion that King Kiritan had placed there. I told him of the great gathering in Tria and of our vows to seek the Lightstone.

"You speak of the Galastei, yes?" Ymiru said. His eyes lit up with a sudden fire, and so did those of his companions. "You speak of the golden cup made by the Galadin and brought down from stars? It be a marvelous substance, this gold galastei, this Stone of Light. Inside it be the secret of making all other galastei—and the secret of making itself."

He went on to say that the Lightstone was the very radiance of the One made manifest—and therefore that which moved the very stars and earth and all that occurred upon it.

He paused to take a deep breath and let it out in a cloud of steam. Then he continued, "You say you've made vows to find the Galastei. But find it where? Surely not in land of the Ymanir!"

This, I gathered, was the name that the Frost Giants gave to themselves. I would learn later that it meant "the Lost People."

"No, not in your land," Kane said from behind me. "We seek only to cross it as quickly as we can."

"So you say. But cross it toward the east? That be the land of Asakai."

At the mention of this name, the Ymanir's hands tightened around their clubs. Their faces grew even more savage and pulled into masks of hate.

I didn't want to tell Ymiru that we proposed to cross Sakai and enter Argattha to seek the Lightstone.

"Perhaps they're really of Asakai," a young-looking man near Ymiru said. "Perhaps they're spies returning home."

"No, Havru," Ymiru said. "They come from Yrakona, I am sure. They're not Morjin's kind."

The giant young man named Havru, whose chin pointed like a spur of rock, shook his club at us and growled out, "It's said that Morjin's kind have the power to seem like other kind. Shouldn't we kill them to be certain?"

Across the circle, a man with a reddish tint to his fur bellowed, "Yes, kill them! Take the galastei, and let's be done!"

Others picked up his cry as they began thumping their clubs into the snow and calling out, "Kill them! Kill them!"

"Hrold! Hrold now!" Ymiru shouted back at them, raising up his club.

Altaru, standing to the left of me, trembled as he shook his head at the falling snow and beat his hoof downward. Any of the Ymanir attacking me, I thought, would find themselves assaulted with the four terrible clubs attached to the ends of his legs.

"Hrold, Askir!" Ymiru said again to the man with the reddish fur.

But then, across the circle from him, a one-eyed giant let loose a tremendous cry and shook his club at us. He shouted, "If they be Morjin's men, I'll break their bones to dust!"

This so alarmed Maram that he cringed and called out to me, "Val! It's as I said! They mean to kill us and eat us! They really do!"

Ymiru turned his face toward Maram, and I could feel in him the same quick rush of emotions that surged through many of the Ymanir: astonishment, insult, horror. Then their mood shifted yet again as Ymiru's lips pulled back in a sad, savage smile. He pointed his club at Maram and called out to his companions: "You may have any of the others you want. But the fat one is mine!"

"Val!"

Ymiru's smile had now been taken up by the young Havru, who said, "But, sir, that be unfair of you. Our rations have been thin, and I'm very hungry. I could get at least ten meals from him."

"Ten?" a sardonic man named Lodur half-shouted. "He's fat enough for twenty, I should think."

"Let's roast him over coals!" another man said.

"No, let's make a soup of him!"

"All right," Havru laughed out wickedly, "but let's save his bones for our bread."

All at once, the twenty Ymanir fell into a long and thunderous laughter. But there was no malice in their huge voices, only a vast amusement. They were only having a joke with Maram, and with us.

"Savages!" Maram shouted at them when he realized this. His face reddened as he wiped the sweat from it. "It's cruel sport you make."

"Cruel?" Ymiru coughed out. "Was it any crueler than your suggestion that we are eaters of men?"

Maram didn't know what to say to this. He looked from Ymiru to me and then back at Ymiru as he stammered out, "Well, I had heard . . . ah, that is to say, the Yarkonans believe that you are killers of men and—"

"Hrold your tongue!" Ymiru said, cutting him off. "We're certainly killers of men: any who serve the Great Beast. And any who would enter our land without our leave."

He motioned to Askir and two other men, who walked around the outside of the circle of the Ymanir and came over to him. While we stood shivering in the driving wind, they gathered in close with each other and conferred in low, rumbling tones.

After a while, Ymiru looked at Maram and said, "You are certainly not of Asakai. No man of Morjin's would hrold a firestone against us and fail to use it. We thank you, little fat man, for your forbearance. We wouldn't have wanted to wind up roasted on your dinner plate."

"Ah, well," Maram said, "thank you for your forbearance in letting us pass through—"

"Hrold your noise!" Ymiru commanded him. His furry hand suddenly tightened around his club. "We have forborne nothing. You have set foot upon Elivagar and cast your eyes upon this sacred land. So by our law, you must be put to death."

Maram's hand shook as he tried to position his gelstei so as to catch what little light filtered through the snow-gray clouds. And then I laid my hand on his shoulder to steady him. I waited on the cold, windy slope, looking up at Ymiru and the grim-faced Ymanir. And so did Kane and my other companions.

"However, these are strange times, and you are a strange people," Ymiru went on in his slow, sad way. "You seek that which we seek, too. Our law be our law. But there be a higher law that speaks of things beyond the commonplace. Our elders are the keepers of it. It is to the Urdahir that we will take you, if you are agreeable."

I saw that it would be hopeless to fight the Ymanir or to try to escape. And it seemed that our fate, in the hands of these giants, was sweeping us along, moving us step by step closer to Argattha. And so I told Ymiru that we would accompany them to the council of their elders.

"Thank you—I wouldn't have wanted your blood on my borkor," Ymiru said, patting his club as he looked at me. Then he asked our names, which we gave, and he told us theirs. "Very good, Sar Valashu Elahad. Now please throw down your weapons and we'll blindfold you. No one except the Ymanir can see the way toward the place we are taking you."

As with my friends, I did not want to be blindfolded, but even less could I surrender my sword and suffer the Ymanir to lay their hands upon it. And so in the end we agreed upon a compromise: while in Elivagar, we would keep our bows unstrung and our swords sheathed.

"Very well, then," Ymiru said to me. "I must tell you that if you break your word, which I have accepted in good faith, the elders will put me to death. And then you and your companions."

And with that, he sent one of his men on ahead to alert these elders, whoever they were. Then Havru removed a roll of red cloth from his pack, and from it the Ymanir fashioned blindfolds—for the six of us as well as our horses. With surprising gentleness, with their huge, hairy hands, they tied them around our eyes. And then they formed a guard around us, and led us off higher into the mountains where the Urdahir would decide our fate.

8

YMIRU APPOINTED HAVRU and four others to be our guides. He himself took my hand in his and began leading me up toward the pass. There was a comforting warmth and great strength in the press of his flesh against mine. With the world plunged into darkness, I suddenly noticed his smell, which was of woodsmoke and wool and cold wind off a frozen lake. Although none of us liked walking blind through the snow, the Ymanir had a friendship with this bitter substance that communicated to us through the sure, gentle pulling of hand against hand. It was remarkable, I thought, that we were led over ice and rocks, and none of us stumbled or tripped. In this way, from guide to guided, a seemingly unbreakable trust was born.

As Maram had feared, the rise toward which we climbed proved not to be the end of the pass. But scarcely a mile farther on, the Ymanir showed us to a hut that they used for sleeping at these frozen heights. There they made a fire for us and later pressed huge bowls of soup into our hands. They gave up their beds to us, and took our boots away to be dried in front of the fire. Their hospitality, I thought, was flawless.

We rested well that night. In the morning, the Ymanir served us porridge mixed with goat's milk, dried berries, and nuts before we set out again. We walked rather slowly for a couple of hours up a steep slope. And then, at the crest of the pass, where the wind blew so fiercely that it nearly ripped the blindfolds from our faces, we began a long descent through what seemed a chute of rock. We walked for a couple more hours, breaking only for a quick lunch. We offered the Ymanir some of the salted pork that we had tucked away in the horses' packs, but this food horrified them. Havru called us Eaters of Beasts; the loathing in his voice suggested that we might as well have been cannibals. Askir explained that although the

Ymanir might borrow milk and wool from their goats, they would never think to take their meat.

Our afternoon's journey took us down a turning track below the snowline, and then up again. Soon it rose in a series of snakelike switchbacks up what seemed to be the slopes of a good-sized mountain. The smells of spruce and dirt gave way to ice as we again crossed onto a snowfield. Frozen crusts crunched beneath our feet. We climbed ever higher. I feared that we might climb too high and fall to cold or sudden stroke of breathlessness. The burning in my lungs told me that I had never been so high in the mountains in all my life.

And then, without warning, we crested yet another pass. The wind shifted and blew strange scents against my face. I heard one of the Ymanir sigh out with anticipation as if he would soon be rejoined with his wife and family. Something very deep stirred in Ymiru, too.

"Sar Valashu," he said to me, "we have come to the place that I have told of. None except the Ymanir have ever looked upon it. And none ever must. And so I ask you, whatever fate befalls you, that you keep this sight to yourself. Do you agree to this?"

With the blindfold still tight around my eyes, I didn't know what I was agreeing to. But I was eager to see again, so I said, "Yes, we are agreed."

Ymiru asked each of my friends also to pledge their silence, and this they did. Then he took my blindfold off. The sun, even at this late hour, pierced my eyelids with such a dazzling white light that I could not open them. I stood toward the south with my hand to my forehead, trying to block some of its intense radiance.

And then, as my eyes slowly adjusted to this new level of illumination, I fought them open, blinking against the stab of the tears there, blinking and blinking at the blinding haze of indistinct forms that was all I could perceive at first. Suddenly my vision cleared. The features of the world came into sharp focus. And I, along with Atara, Maram, and my other friends, drew in a sudden gasp of air almost with one breath. For there, spread out beneath the blue dome of the sky, was the most astonishing sight I had ever beheld.

Far below us, a broad valley opened out between great walls of white-capped mountains. And in its center, built on either side of an ice-blue river, rose a city more marvelous than I had ever dreamed. It filled most of the valley. Although not as large as Tria, it had a splendor that even the Trians might have envied. Many great towers and spires, made of glittering sweeps of living stone, seemed to grow out of the valley's very rock. Some of these were half a mile high and nearly vanished into the sky. Their building stones were of carnelian and violet, azure and aquamarine and a thousand other soft, shifting hues. The city's broad avenues and streets were laid out with precision from east to west and north to south as if to mark the four points of the world. The late-afternoon sun poured down these thoroughfares like rivers of gold. The various palaces and temples caught up its light. But the magnificence of the buildings, I thought, was not in their number nor even their size. Rather, it was their perfect proportions and sparkle that caught the eye and stirred the soul. The houses along even the side streets seemed to cast their colors at each other and reflect those of their neighbors. Their lovely lines and arrangement bespoke an almost seamless blending with the earth—and with each other. It was as if the whole city was a choir of sight, intoning deep and startling harmonies, giving the song of its beauty to the wind and the sky, to the moon and the sun and the stars.

Above the city, on the slope of a mountain to the east, huge and fantastic sculptures gleamed. A few of these were diamond-like figures a mile high; near them, immense but delicate-looking crystals opened beneath the sun like glittering flowers. It seemed like something that only the Galadin themselves could have created. Ymiru saw me staring at it, and told me that this great work was called the Garden of the Gods.

As striking as were these marvels, they paled beneath this place's greatest glory. This was a mountain to the west that overlooked the whole valley. Ymiru said it was the highest mountain in the world. Standing above the lesser peaks to either side, it rose straight into the sky in a great upward thrust of stone and ice. It had an almost perfect symmetry, like that of a pyramid. Although its pointed summit and upper reaches were crowned in pure, white snow, the main body of it appeared to be made of amethyst, emerald, sapphire, and jewels of every color. I could not imagine how it had come to be.

"That is Alumit," Ymiru said as he watched me and my friends staring at it. "We call it the Mountain of the Morning Star."

This name, as he spoke it in his deep voice that rumbled like thunder, stunned me into silence.

"And your city?" Maram asked, "What do you call it?"

"Its name is Alundil," Ymiru told us. "In the old language, this means the 'City of the Stars.'"

As the wind whipped swirls of snow about our legs, I stared down at this fantastic place for quite a while. It was strange, I thought, that all the legends and old wives' tales had told of the Ymanir as only savage and man-eating Frost Giants. And with their fearsome borkors and harsh laws, savage they might truly have been. But they had built the most beautiful creation on earth. And no one, it seemed, except my companions and I, and the Ymanir themselves, had ever beheld it.

Kane gazed down into the valley as if its splendor had swept him away to another world. Then looked at Ymiru and said, "All these years, walking among the other cities of the world, and other mountains—even without wearing a blindfold, I might as well have been."

Maram blinked his eyes, and asked Ymiru, "Did your people make this? How could they have?"

How, indeed, I wondered, staring down at the great sculptures of the Garden of the Gods. How could naked giants with spiked clubs have built a greater glory than had even the ancient architects of Tria during the great golden Age of Law? How could anyone?

"We did—that is who we Ymanir are," Ymiru said. "We are workers of living stone; we are mountain shapers and gardeners of the earth."

He went on to say that the Ymanir's greatest delight was in making things out of things. They especially loved coaxing out of the earth the secret forms hidden there. The Ymanir, he told us, were devoted to discovering how to forge substances of all kinds, and none more so than the gelstei crystals.

"But the secret of their making has been lost to us for most of an age," he said sadly. "At least the making of the greater galastei."

"In other lands," Master Juwain told him, "it has been forgotten how to forge even the lesser gelstei."

"So much has been lost," Ymiru said bitterly. "And that is why the Urdahir, some of them, seek the secret of the ultimate making."

"And what is that?" Maram asked, staring at the jeweled mountain.

"Why, the making of the golden crystal of the Galastei," Ymiru said. "That is why we, too, seek the cup you call the Lightstone. We believe that only the Lightstone itself will ever reveal the secret of how it was created."

With this secret, he told us, the Ymanir could not only reforge the gelstei crystals of old and a new Lightstone, but the very world itself.

That was a strange thought to take with us on our descent to the city. We followed a track that cut through the pass's snowfields and wound down through the treeline of the mountain beneath us. It was nearly dark before we came out of a narrow canyon onto Alundil's heights. Immediately upon setting foot in this enchanting city, with its graceful houses and stands of silver shih trees, I had a strange sense of simultaneously walking down a quiet street and standing a thousand miles high. The sweep of the great spires seemed to draw my soul up toward the stars. In this marvelous place, I was still very much of the earth and on it, never more so—and yet I felt myself suddenly opened like a living crystal that is transparent to other worlds and other realms. Lovely was my home in the Morning Mountains, and magical were the woods of the Lokilani. But in no other place on Ea had I felt myself to be so great and noble a being as I did here.

We proceeded through the streets and onto one of the city's broad avenues, all of which were deserted. Likewise, no fire or light brightened the windows of the houses and buildings that we passed. Maram, somewhat vexed at this strangeness, asked Ymiru if his people had abandoned this part of the city for other districts.

"Yes, for once the Ymanir were a much greater people," he told us. His voice was heavy with a bitter sadness. "Once, we claimed nearly all of the mountains as our home. But when the Great Beast took the Black Mountain, he sent a plague to kill the Ymanir. The survivors were too few to hrold. He drove us off, into the westernmost part of our realm—into Elivagar. He and his Red Priests did dreadful things to our hrome. And thus sacred Sakai became Asakai, the accursed land."

He went on to tell us that, even before Morjin's rise, there had never been enough of his people to fill a city so large as Alundil. And as large as it was, it would grow only larger, for the Ymanir continued to add to it stone by stone and tower by tower as they had for thousands of years.

"I don't understand," Maram said, blowing out his breath into the cold air. "If Alundil is already too big for your people, why build it bigger?"

"Because," Ymiru said, "Alundil is not for us."

The clopping of the horses' hooves against the stone of the street suddenly seemed too loud. Ymiru—and the other Ymanir—suddenly stood as straight and proud as any of the sculptures in the Garden of the Gods.

The look on Maram's face suggested that he was now totally mystified, as were the rest of us. And so Ymiru explained, "Long ago, our scryers looked toward the stars and beheld cities on other worlds. It be our greatest hrope to recreate on earth these visions that they saw."

"But why?" Maram asked.

"Because someday the Star People will come again. They will come to earth and find prepared for them a new hrome."

It was upon hearing this sad history and sad dreams of the future that Ymiru and the others took us to meet with their elders. As Ymiru had said, Alundil was not for the Ymanir, and so his people had built their own town in the foothills east of the valley. This consisted mostly of great, long, stone houses arrayed on winding streets. The Ymanir had applied only a little of their art in raising up these constructions. None were of the marvelous living stone that formed the buildings of the dark city below. Rather, they were made of blocks of granite, cut with great precision and fitted together in sweeping arches that enclosed large spaces. The Ymanir, we soon found, liked open spaces and built their houses accordingly.

They had built their great hall this way, too. We approached this castle-like building along a rising road, lined with many Ymanir who had left their houses to witness the unprecedented arrival of strangers in their valley. Hundreds of these tall, white-furred people stood as straight and silent as the spruce trees that also lined the road. I caught a scent of the deep feelings that rumbled through them: anger, fear, curiosity, hope. There was a great sadness about them, and yet a fierce pride as well.

Ymiru, Havru, and Askir escorted us inside the hall where their elders had gathered—along with many more of the Ymanir. A good two hundred of them were lined up by mats woven of the wonderfully soft goat hair that we had encountered the night before in Ymiru's mountain hut. They faced nine aged men and women who stood near similar mats on a stone dais at the front of the room. We were shown to the place of honor—or inquisition—just below this dais. We joined Ymiru on the floor there as everyone in the room sat down together in the fashion of his people: our legs folded back beneath us, sitting back on our heels with our spines straight and our eyes slightly lowered as we waited for the elders to address us.

This they wasted no time in doing. After asking Ymiru our names, the centermost and most elder of the Urdahir introduced himself as Hrothmar. Then he presented the four women to his left: Audhumla, Yvanu, Ulla, and Halda. The men, to his right, were: Burri, Hramjir, Hramdal, and Yramu. They all turned slightly toward Hrothmar, allowing him to speak on their behalf.

"By now," he said, his gruff old voice carrying out into the hall, "everyone in Elivagar knows of Ymiru's extraordinary audacity in breaking our law by bringing these six strangers to our valley. We are met here to determine if he acted rightly."

Hrothmar paused to catch his breath. With his much-weathered skin about his sad old eyes, few of the Ymanir in the hall had more years than he. And none had greater height or stature, not even the giant guards who stood around the walls of the hall bearing their great borkors at their sides.

"First to speak tonight," he wheezed out, "shall be Burri. He'll speak for the law of the Ymanir."

The man sitting next to him, who had an angry look to his long, lean face, stroked his silver-white beard as he looked down at us. Then he said, "The law, in this matter, is simple: that any Ymanir who discovers strangers entering our land without the Urdahir's permission shall put them to death. This should have been done. It was not. And therefore, also according to the law, Ymiru and all the guard of the South Pass should be put to death."

Ymiru, listening quietly near me, sat up very straight. I hadn't realized the terrible risk that he had taken merely in sparing our lives.

Burri stared at Ymiru and said, "Have you no respect for the law that you break it the first chance that you get?"

Although Ymiru remained silent at this rebuke, Liljana looked at him as if reading his turbid thoughts. And then she surprised everyone when she stood up to answer Burri: "Your law is one of death. But what of life? Should life be made to serve the law, or the law to serve life?"

"The law of the Ymanir," Burri told her, "is made to serve the Ymanir. And so each of us must serve it."

"And this is for the good of your people, yes?"

"It be for my people's life," he growled at her.

Liljana stared out into the immense room, with its stone walls covered with marvelous golden hangings and sweeping arches high overhead. Built into recesses of the columns that supported this great vault were glowstones giving off a soft, white light. The walls themselves, at intervals of ten feet, were set with blocks of hot slate, which radiated a steady heat. And these lesser gelstei were not the only ones visible in the room that night. Many of the Ymanir wore warders about their necks; more than a few sported dragon bones, and at least one old woman rolled a music marble between her long, furry hands. Not even in Tria had I seen so many surviving works of the ancient alchemists. From what Ymiru had said, I thought that these gelstei might not be so ancient. For the Ymanir had surely preserved the art of forging them. They had as much pride in this, I sensed, as they did sadness in being slaughtered by the Red Dragon and driven into this lost corner of their ancient realm. They were a strange people and a great one; I could not blame them for savagely enforcing laws that preserved what little they had left.

Liljana's round face fell soft and kind as she gathered in all her compassion and looked back up at Burri. She said, "The lowest law is the law of survival, and even the beasts know this. But a human being knows much more: that she may not live at the sacrifice of her people."

"Just so," Burri growled again.

"And so each of us must obey the law of her people."

"Just so, just so."

"And a people," Liljana went on, smiling at him, "may not live at the sacrifice of their world. And so any people's law must always give way before the higher law."

Burri, not liking to be swayed by Liljana's relentless calm, suddenly lost his temper and thundered down at her: "And how do you know of the Ymanir's higher law?"

"I know," she said, "because the higher law is the same for all peoples. It is just the Law of the One."

Burri suddenly stood up to his full height of eight feet. His hands opened and closed as if they longed to grip a borkor. He turned toward the other elders and said, "We all knew that Ymiru would invoke the higher law. And so he has, through this little woman. But what could possibly persuade us of the need? The fact that two of the strangers bear the great galastei? That they are seekers of the Galastei? The Red Dragon's priests are seekers of the same and have come to us with firestones in their hands—to burn us. And so no one has ever objected to sending them to their fate."

Liljana waited for him to finish speaking and said simply, "We are not the Red Dragon's priests."

"But how do we know this?" Burri said, looking out at the hundreds of Ymanir in the hall. "The Red Dragon has set clever traps for us before. Who among us be more clever than he? No, we Ymanir are clever with our hands, but not in this way. And so we've made our law. And so we should use it."

"Before hearing what we have to say?" Liljana asked him.

"We've all heard the cleverness of your words, little woman. Must we hear more?"

He glanced at the guards along the walls and by the door, and called for the elders to decide our fate then and there. But Hrothmar held up his hand for silence as he turned to me and said, "Others have spoken for the law; will you speak for your people, Sar Valashu?"

"Yes," I said, standing before the elders. "I will speak for us."

And so I did. While the glowstones shined on sempiternally through the night, I told the Ymanir a tale such as they had never heard before. I began it six long ages past, when Aryu had killed Elahad and had stolen the Lightstone. Its history, much of it unknown to the Ymanir, I then recounted, much as King Kiritan had when he had gathered the thousands of knights in his hall and called the great quest. My part in this, and my friends', I explained with as much candor as I could. I told of the black arrow and the kirax that had poisoned my blood; I even told them of Ayondela Kirriland's prophecy and pointed out the scar that had saved us from the Lokilani's arrows. The hundreds of men and women in the room fell into a deep silence as I went on with the story of our long journey that had taken us across most of Ea to the Library at Khaisham. What we had found there, however, I did not tell. It would be very dangerous, I thought, to announce the Lightstone's hiding place to so many people.

"Your story," Burri said, shaking his head when I had finished, "be too fantastic to be true."

"It be too fantastic not to be true," Yvanu countered. She was the youngest of the Urdahir and a beautiful woman, whose long white fur about her head and neck had been twisted into long braids.

All the elders were now staring at me. Still shaking his head, Burri said to me, "How will we ever know if you speak the truth?"

"You will know," I said softly. "If you listen, you will know."

"But where are the proofs of your story? Let us see the proofs."

I looked at each of my friends then, and they brought forth their gelstei. The sudden sight of Maram's firestone and Atara's crystal sphere, no less Liljana's little blue whale, Master Juwain's varistei, Kane's black stone, and my shining sword, stunned everyone in the room. Nowhere on Ea are any people so in awe of the gelstei as are the Ymanir.

Then I reached into the pocket of my tunic and drew forth the False Gelstei that we had found in the Library. I walked up to the dais and set it into Burri's outstretched hand.

"In ages past," he murmured, looking at the cup in amazement, "it is said that the Ymanir made many such cups. Perhaps even this very one."

"If that is so, then it would be fitting that you keep it, for your people."

Burri's icy blue eyes froze into mine. "You can't buy our mercy."

I felt my spine stiffen with pride; I felt my father in me as words that he would have spoken formed themselves upon my lips: "In my land, when a gift is given, we usually just say 'thank you.' And it is not your mercy that we seek—only justice."

So saying, I turned and sat back down with my friends.

"Then justice you shall surely have!" Burri half-shouted at me. He looked at Hrothmar and the other elders as he said, "There be much of the stranger's story for which we can never have proofs. His claim of descent from this Elahad. This twinkling Timpum being that only the strangers can see.

Why should we believe him? Why shouldn't we do what we must do?"

I looked straight into Burri's hard eyes as I said, "Because all that I have told tonight is true."

Burri opened his mouth as if to gainsay me, but again Hrothmar held up his hand for silence. And then he looked at me and said, "I believe all that you have told is true. But you have not told all that is true."

This wise old man needed no truth stone to discern the part of my story that I had left incomplete. The two hundred Ymanir in the hall waited for him to say more.

"Sar Valashu, you have told that you and your companions have sought the Lightstone across the length of Ea. But you have not told why you entered our land to seek it."

No, I thought, I hadn't. But I saw that I finally must. And so I took a deep breath and told them about Master Aluino's journal. Then I admitted that my friends and I had vowed to journey into Sakai and enter the underground city of Argattha.

For a long time, no one in the hall spoke. No one even moved. I felt the great hearts of the hundreds of Ymanir beating out a great thunder of astonishment.

At last, Hrothmar found his voice and spoke for all his people, even Burri: "Even the bravest of the Ymanir seldom go anymore into Asakai, where once we went so freely. Either you and your companions are mad or you are possessed of a great courage. And I do not believe you are mad."

A roar of voices cascaded through the room like a suddenly unleashed flood. Hrothmar let his people speak for quite a while. Then he held up his hand for silence.

"The strangers have brought us the greatest chance that we Ymanir have ever had," he said in his grave, deep voice. "And the greatest peril, too. How are we to decide their fate—and our own?"

He paused to rub his tired eyes. Then he said, "Let us not try to make this decision tonight. Let us reflect and sleep and dream. And let us all gather before first light in the great square, that we might call upon the wisdom of the Galadin to help us."

He dismissed the assemblage and stood, as did everyone else. Then the men who had guarded the hall escorted us to Ymiru's house at the edge of the town, where we had been offered quarters. Compared with the other Ymanir houses on the wooded slopes nearby, it was a small affair of stacked stone and rough-hewn beams—but quite large enough to accommodate us.

As we were settling in for the night, Maram looked at Ymiru and said, "How can I sleep when tomorrow will come all too soon? That Burri gave us a bad enough time today."

Ymiru's eyes fell sad, and he surprised us, saying, "Burri be a good man. But he has many sorrows."

He explained that once, years ago, he and Burri, along with others in the hall, had lived in the same village in the East Reach near Sakai. And then one day, Morjin had sent a battalion to annihilate it.

"We were too few to hrold," he told us. He took a sip of a bitter tea that he had made for us. "I lost my wife and sons in the attack; Burri lost almost his whole family. And the Ymanir lost part of Elivagar. Burri has vowed that we won't lose any more."

Ymiru's sorrow then became my own as a hard lump formed up in my throat, and I bowed my head to him.

After that he fell into a deep silence from which he could not be roused. He brought out a song stone, a little sphere of swirling hues; he sat listening to the voice of his dead wife long after Maram had finally gone to sleep.

It was cold the next morning when we gathered at the appointed hour in Alundil's great square. The city's empty towers and buildings were even darker than the sky, which was hung with many stars. Ten thousand men, women, and children crowded shoulder-to-shoulder facing a great spire to the west of the square. At the head of them were Hrothmar and Burri and the others of Urdahir. We stood with Ymiru near them, ringed by thirty Ymanir gripping borkors in their massive hands. The sharp wind falling down from the icy mountains around us seemed not to touch them. But it pierced us nearly to the bone. I stood between Atara and Master Juwain, shivering as they did, waiting with them and our other companions, for what we didn't know.

"Why are we meeting here?" Maram asked for the tenth time.

And for the tenth time, Ymiru answered him, saying, "You will see, little man, you will see."

Now many of the Ymanir behind us had turned to look out above the spire to the east of the square. There, above the Garden of the Gods, above the icy eastern mountains, the sky was beginning to lighten with the rising of the sun. There, too, the Morning Star shined, brightest of all the heavens' lights. It cast its radiance upon us, touching Alundil's houses and spires, illuminating the faces of all who gazed upon it. Through the clear air and straight across the valley streaked this silver light, where it fell upon the shimmering face of Alumit. It was still too dark to make out the colors of this great mountain that seemed to overlook the whole of the world. I wondered yet again how it had come to be. Ymiru had told us that his ancestors had raised up the sculptures of the Garden of the Gods; but it seemed that the building of an entire mountain had been beyond even the ancient Ymanir. Ymiru believed that once, long ago, the Galadin had come to earth to work this miracle. As he believed that someday they would come again.

As the wind quickened and our breaths steamed out into the air, the eastern sky grew even brighter. The rising of the sun stole the stars' light one by one until only the Morning Star remained shining. Then it, too, disappeared into the blue-white glister at the edge of the world. We waited for the sun to crest the mountains behind us. Ahead of us, to the west, Alumit's great white peak caught the sun's first rays before the valley below it did. Its pointed crown of ice and snow began glowing a deep red. Soon this fire fell down the slopes of the mountain and drew forth its colors. Again I marveled at the crystals from which it was wrought, the sparkling blues that seemed to pour forth from sapphire, the reds of ruby and a deep, vivid, emerald green.

At last the sun broke over the flaming ridgeline to the east. The air warmed, slightly, as the morning grew brighter. And

still we waited, facing this great Mountain of the Morning
Star. And then, to the thunder of ten thousand hearts and the
rising of the wind, the colors of the mountain began to change.
Slowly its jewel-like hues deepened and grew even more
splendid. They seemed to flow into each other, red into yellow,
orange into green, miraculously transforming into a single
color like nothing I had ever dreamed. It was not a blending or
a tessellation of colors, but one solid color—though perhaps
not so solid at all, for in staring at it, I seemed to fall into
it and become aware of infinite depths. How could this be, I
wondered? How could there exist in the world an entirely new
color of the spectrum that no one ever saw? It was as different
from red or green as those colors are from violet or blue. And
yet I could only describe it to myself in terms of the more
common colors, for that was the only way I could make sense
of such an amazing thing: it had all the fire of red, the brightness and expansiveness of yellow, the deep peace of the purest
cobalt blue.

"How is this possible?" I heard Maram whisper behind me.
"Oh, my Lord, how can this be?"

I shook my head as I stared at the great mountain, now
wholly shimmering with a single hue, at once like living gold
and cosmic scarlet—like the secret blue inside blue that people do not usually see.

"What is it?" Maram gasped, directing his words at Ymiru.
"Tell me before I fall mad."

"It be glorre," Ymiru said to him. "It be the color of the
angels."

Glorre, I thought, glorre—it was so beautiful that I wanted
to drink this color into my deepest depths; it was almost too
real to be real. And yet it was real, the truest and loveliest
thing I had ever beheld. I melted into it; I felt it washing
through my entire being, carrying into every part of me the
clear, sweet, numinous taste of the One that is just the essence
of all things.

"But yesterday," Maram gasped out, "the mountain didn't
appear so!"

"No, it did not," Ymiru agreed. "It only takes on this color once each day, in the light of the Morning Star—with the rising of the sun."

Atara stared at Alumit as intensely as she ever had her scryer's sphere. Then Master Juwain asked, "Has it always taken on this color?"

"No, only for the last twenty years," Ymiru said. "Ever since the earth entered the Golden Band."

"I see," Master Juwain said, rubbing his bald head. "Yes, I see."

Liljana looked upon the mountain in awed silence while Kane stood stricken beside her. His fathomless eyes drank in the glorre of the mountain. He didn't move; he seemed not even to breathe. If one of the Ymanir had fallen on him with a club just then, I did not think that he would have drawn his sword to defend himself.

"The mountain speaks to those who listen," Ymiru said softly. "As we must listen now."

The silence that then descended upon the square was a strange and beautiful thing. We stood with the ten thousand Ymanir looking up at the sacred Alumit to the west, and not even a single child fidgeted or called for his mother to take him home. I tried to listen with the same concentration as did they. As my eyes drank in this mountain of a numinous hue seen only in the stars, I became aware of voices singing as from far away. Far but almost impossibly near: every building in the city seemed suddenly to vibrate with these sweet sounds, which I felt resonating inside me. It was like the ringing of bells and gentle laughter carried along the wind. The music reminded me of that which Alphanderry had sung in the Kul Moroth. I tried to understand the words that formed up in my mind, breaking like the crest of a wave always just beyond my reach. And yet I knew that I could always keep them within me, in my heart and hands, if only I had the courage to hold on to them.

Others, however, were more gifted at such apprehension. Liljana stood with her gelstei pressed to her forehead over her third eye. The little blue whale seemed to have deepened to the color of glorre. Liljana's eyes, wide open, flicked about with the little movements of one who is deep in dream.

"What does she see?" Maram whispered to me.

"You might better ask yourself," Ymiru told him, "what she hears."

We soon had our answer. As the sun rose still higher, Liljana's hand fell down to her side. She smiled at Master Juwain in her peaceable way, and then turned to Atara and me. "They're waiting for us, you know. On many, many worlds, the Star People are waiting for us to complete the quest."

The nine elders of the Urdahir, led by Hrothmar, turned our way. The guards around us pulled aside to allow him room to step forward.

"They are waiting," he told us. "As are the Elijin and Galadin themselves. We feared that it would be so."

He sighed as he pulled at the white fur of his chin and looked at me. "Sar Valashu, we believe that you and your friends must try to enter Argattha and recover the Lightstone. And we must help you."

Audhumla and Yvanu, standing just behind him, smiled as he said this; Hramjir and Hramdal nodded their massive heads, while even Burri seemed to have been moved by the wonder of what he had just heard.

"We would welcome," I told them, "any help you have to give us."

"Very good," Hrothmar's huge voice rumbled out. He looked from Atara to Liljana, and then at Kane, Maram, Master Juwain, and me. "The prophecy you told us spoke of the seven brothers and sisters with the seven stones of the greater galastei. And seven you were until you lost the minstrel in Yrakona. Therefore, you need one more to complete your company. And so we must ask that we send one of our people with you to Argattha."

I knew from the set of his hard face that there could be no disputing this demand. I looked toward the edge of the square at the guards, with their fearsome borkors. Either we accepted one of these giants into our company, I thought, or we must remain here forever.

"Who would you send with us?" I asked him.

He turned to Ymiru and said, "I have seen in you a desire to make this journey. It would be fitting, would it not, that after breaking the lower law, you should fulfill the higher?"

"Yes," Ymiru said, "it would."

"Will you show the little people the way through Asakai?"

"Yes, I will."

Hrothmar looked at me. "Well, Sar Valashu—will you take Ymiru into your company?"

I nodded my head to Ymiru. "Gladly," I said. Then I reached out to grasp Ymiru's huge hand with mine.

Now, as the sun rose still higher and the glorre of Alumit began to break apart into its usual, brilliant colors, the thousands of people in the square all turned their attention on Ymiru and the nine elders—and us.

"But we've still only six gelstei," Maram pointed out. "How can Ymiru come with us without a gelstei?"

Hrothmar's sudden grin seemed bigger than the sky. I noticed then that he was holding a small, jeweled box in his hand next to his furry hip. He lifted it up and said to us, "You have found six of the galastei on your journey; now we would like to give you the seventh."

And with that, he opened the box. He pulled out a large, square-cut stone, clear and bright and purple as wine.

"This be a lilastei," he said, handing it to Ymiru. "It be the last one remaining to our people. Take it with our blessing. For with you goes the hope of our people."

Ymiru held the gelstei up to the sun. Its bright rays passed through it and fell upon the ground. The stone there seemed to soften in the violet light.

"Thank you," Ymiru said.

Maram came forward then and took Ymiru's free hand. "This is a lucky day for us. With you by our side, we'll be more like seventeen than seven."

Atara was the next to welcome Ymiru into our company, followed by Liljana and Master Juwain. And then Kane stepped up to him. He clasped hands with Ymiru, fiercely, like a tiger testing the strength of a bear. He said nothing to him. But the fire of fellowship brightening his face said more than words ever could.

Hrothmar swept his hand toward the seven of us and said, "Your courage in undertaking this journey cannot be questioned. But we must ask you to find an even greater courage within yourselves: that should fate fall against you, you will seek death before revealing to the Beast the secrets of Alundil."

Ymiru agreed to this grim demand with a bow of his head. As did Master Juwain, Liljana, and I. Atara smiled with a chilling acceptance of what must be. And Maram, his face flushed with fear, looked at Hrothmar and said, "Set your mind at ease. I'll gladly seek death before torture."

Hrothmar turned to Kane. "And you, keeper of the black stone?"

Kane looked toward the east in the direction that we soon must travel. In a voice burning with defiance, he said, "No torture of Morjin's will ever make me speak."

So great was the will that steeled his being that Hrothmar did not question him further.

"Very good," Hrothmar said. Then he embraced us one by one and gave us his blessing.

Hramjir, with his one arm, did likewise as well as he could, followed by Audhumla, Yvanu, and the other Urdahir. Burri was the last to approach us. After wrapping me up in a mound of living fur, he took out the cup that I had given him. He looked down at me and said, "Thank you for your gift, Sar Valashu. We have lost our last lilastei only to gain one of the greatest of the silver galastei."

Then he turned to Ymiru and told him, "I was wrong about the little people. And about you." He embraced Ymiru with an unexpected tenderness. Then he shocked us all, saying, "I'm sorry, my son."

From the way these two fierce giants looked at each other, I knew that even the hardest ice could melt and be broken.

To direct my attention elsewhere, Burri pointed above the square toward Alumit. There, limned against the last patch of glorre to light up the mountain, Flick danced ecstatically through the air, whirling and diving, describing incendiary arcs. His being blazed with silver, scarlet, and gold—and now, too, with glorre. I must have been blind, I thought, never to have beheld this dazzling color within him. As others were now beholding it as well. At least a hundred of the Ymanir nearby had their long fingers aimed at him, and their large eyes seemed suddenly larger with wonder. And Burri, perhaps, held the most wonder of all.

"I think you did tell one lie, Sar Valashu," he said to me. "You told that the Timpum twinkled. But these lights—they be a glorious thing."

Glorious indeed, I thought, watching Flick spin beneath the shining mountain that the Galadin had made. As Burri and the other elders began wishing us well on our journey, it gave me hope to enter another mountain whose faces were as hard as iron and whose color was as black as death.

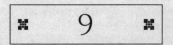

IT TOOK US four days to set out from Alundil. Much of this was spent in gathering supplies for our journey: rations such as cheeses and dried fruit, pine nuts and potatoes and the Ymanir version of the inevitable battle biscuits. To Maram's delight, Ymiru laid in a few small casks of a fermented goat's milk called kalvaas. I thought it a foul, rancid-smelling brew, but Maram announced that drinking it gave him visions of the angels or beautiful women—to him, it seemed, the same thing.

"Now, take these Ymanir women," he said to me one night after we had worked very hard to reshoe the horses. "Now, it's true, they are, ah, rather large. But they have a certain comeliness of form and face, don't you think? And—oh my Lord!— they would keep a man warm at night."

As it happened, the Ymanir women worked very hard to keep us all warm on our journey. It took Hrothmar's daughters— along with Audhumla, Yvanu, Ulla, and others—most of four days to make for us long coats that covered us from head to ankle. They were wonderfully soft and thick, woven from the long fur that the Ymanir women had sheared from their own bodies. Their whiteness, like that of snow, would help hide us against the frozen slopes of the mountains to the east.

The Ymanir men were equally clever at the making of things. They filled Atara's empty quivers with arrows, a few of which were tipped with diamond points for piercing the hardest armor. One of their smiths presented Liljana with a new set of cookware, forged from a very light but very strong goldish metal called galte. Burri himself, on this last night of our stay in Alundil, brought Ymiru a map that one of their ancestors had fashioned generations before. He kept this gift wrapped in brown paper and string, and admonished Ymiru not to reveal its secrets to us until we were well away from the city.

"For the time, this be for your eyes only," he said to Ymiru. "And for your hands: only the fathers and sons of our line have ever touched this."

After Burri had gone, we asked Ymiru why he hadn't told us outright that he was his father. But Ymiru was not very good at bringing forth memories and sadnesses from the gloom inside him. It took much prodding for him to confess one of the reasons that the Urdahir had chosen him to show us the way toward Argattha: when he was younger he had led raids into Sakai in a fierce effort to beat back the encroachments of the Red Dragon's armies. Although he and the other Ymanir had killed many with their borkors, in the end they were too few, and much of the East Reach had been lost.

"The Dragon grows ever stronger while we weaken," he told us. "Burri and Hrothmar, all of the Urdahir, know that we can hrold Elivagar for another generation, perhaps two—but not forever. And so they were willing to take the dreadful chance of sending me with you to Argattha."

Evil omens, he said, were everywhere: in the stars, in the fall of Yarkona, in the rumor of a fire-breathing dragon that Morjin held ready to unleash upon the world.

"Elivagar might be the last place on Ea to fall," he said to us. "But fall it finally will. And so the Star People will never come."

"No, don't speak so," I told him. "There is always hope."

"Hrope," he said bitterly. "I have had none since the Beast took my children from me. And now—"

I gripped his massive forearm, wondering if he could feel the incredible strength there that I did.

"And now, tomorrow, the seven of us will leave for Argattha. Be there really any hrope in this quest? I suppose we must at least act as if there be."

Ymiru's sudden melancholy, which fell upon him like an ice fog, seemed to evaporate the following morning when the elders and many of the Ymanir again gathered in the great square to wish us farewell. He had girded himself for our journey, strapping onto his back a huge pack and taking into his hand the great borkor that had felled many of his enemies. As well, he had taken on the task of leading the thirty Ymanir guards who would escort us from Alundil; now he was all business and bluff good cheer, checking the guards' loads, calling out commands in his thundering voice. His new mood, that sunny morning, was that of his people. They swarmed around us, cheering and calling out encouragements. When it came time for us to set out, they formed up on either side of us like living mountains of fur. Down one of Alundil's broad avenues, as through a valley, we passed between them as they cast sprigs of laurel at us and sang out their prayers.

We left Alundil by way of a great road leading through the valley to the south of the city. Here, along the banks of the blue Voluspa, were many fields planted with barley, rye, potatoes, and other hardy crops. I rode on top of Altaru, leading the line of my friends on their mounts. And the Ymanir led us. With Ymiru at their head, our guard marched along with huge strides, matching the pace of our horses. For a moment, I wished that these thirty giants might accompany us all the way to Argattha, where they might simply batter down its gates with their huge clubs.

Some miles outside of the city, it came time for our eyes to be bound again so that if by ill fate we were captured, we might tell of Alundil's existence but not the way into it. Thus we walked blind as bats for the rest of the day. With the negation of this most vital of the senses, I became more aware of my others. The road led up a winding way through a forest into the mountains. I felt this steep gradient through the angle of my feet as I felt the air growing colder and colder with every yard higher we climbed. The wind on my face carried scents of spruce, feather fir, and new flowers that I had never smelled before. I listened to the sweet *cheer-lee churr* of what sounded like a bluebird and to the bellows and whistles of an elk. And then my senses drove deeper, and I dwelled on the pull of Ymiru's hand against mine as he guided me along and the rushing of the breath from his lips.

We made camp that night by a little river, where it pooled just beneath a waterfall. The next day we set out early and spent most of the morning climbing over a snow-steeped pass. There were turnings and twistings to our route—and risings and fallings, too. But mostly risings: we climbed beneath a bright sun into cold air that grew thinner and thinner as the mountain beneath us thrust itself up into the sky. We plowed through snowdrifts up to our thighs; in places, we slipped upon ice-glazed rocks. But Ymiru's guidance, and that of the Ymanir who had my other companions' hands, proved steady and true. That night we found shelter in one of the stone huts that the Ymanir had built through the high country of their land.

On our third day out from Alundil, after making our way over another pass, Ymiru finally called for our blindfolds to be removed. As on our approach to Alundil, the sudden touch of the afternoon sun dazzled our eyes. It was quite a few moments before our sight returned to us. When I again managed to make out the world's forms, I saw that a high valley lay below us. All around us were sculpted white peaks as far as the eye could see.

We said good-bye to our escort there on that cold mountain. With the hour fallen so late, we hastened our descent down its side. Even so, we were forced to make camp fairly high up, barely within the shelter of the trees that blanketed the mountain's lower slopes. When the wind rose later that night and it grew cold, we had a good, crackling fire to warm us—as well as the thick coats that Hrothmar's daughters had made for us.

"Well, this isn't so bad," Maram whispered to me, drawing his white coat around himself. "Such softness—I wonder if the Ymanir women are so soft. Now, that is something I would like to live to discover."

He must have thought that Ymiru, lying on the bare ground between Kane and Liljana with only his own fur to cover him, was asleep. But it seemed that he was only deep in thought. And his hearing, as Maram discovered to his embarrassment, was very keen. He turned about, facing the fire—and Maram. Then he laughed and said, "And just what would you do with one of our women, little man?"

"Little? I confess that there aren't any yet who have found me so."

"No? Are you considering the size of your mouth? Or perhaps you speak of your head, which seems swollen with unattainable dreams?"

"Ah, well, my head," Maram muttered. He shot me a quick, knowing look as if giving thanks that Lord Harsha hadn't cut it off. "Let's just say I'm speaking of the size of my, ah, soul."

"Your soul, is it? Now that be a great and glorious thing, I'm sure. Even a little man can have a great soul."

"Just so, just so."

"It must be your plan, then, to find a willing woman and fill her with this magnificent, questing soul of yours?"

"Ah, you do understand."

"I do indeed," Ymiru said, letting loose a laugh that shook the side of the mountain. "Now, that would be something I would like to live to see."

We all laughed with Ymiru and Maram, and felt the better for it. Since Alphanderry's death many days before, we'd had little enough opportunity for laughter and even less inclination. In truth, making jokes again around a campfire made us

miss his mirthful ways terribly and seemed almost to mock
his memory. But it would have been worse, I thought, if we
had kept to our mournful mood forever. Alphanderry, of all
people, would not have wanted it so. He would have wished
upon us music and song, dancing and friendship and laughter.
I knew that the only way we could ever really honor his death
was to live our lives more deeply and take his spirit into us.

The coming of Ymiru into our company made this easier in
some ways and more difficult in others. He had a wit to match
Alphanderry's and a song in his heart—but the melodies that
sounded there were less often light and sweet than complex,
dark and deep. His quiet glooms and occasional enthusiasms
reminded us that he could never simply replace Alphanderry as
the seventh of our company. He was his own person, as brood-
ing and mysterious as Alphanderry was cheerful and open. Although we already appreciated his thoughtfulness and courage,
no less his steadiness and strength, he would have to find his
way toward us, and we toward him.

After breakfast the following morning we crossed a high
valley peopled with only a few dozen Ymanir families. The
afternoon found us working our way over a low ridgeline into
a wild country broken with many tors. The air grew cold as we
gradually gained elevation. The horses, driving their newly
shod hooves against the icy rocks and patches of snow, moved
steadily forward, bearing the six of us on their backs as Ymiru
walked a few paces ahead of them. Of all the horses, I
thought, only Altaru knew how much I worried over the finding of grass for them in the even more forbidding land into
which we were headed.

We made camp well before sunset by a stream that flowed
out from between two good-sized hills. The faces of these rocky
heaps were jacketed with slabs of sandstone, growing out of
the earth at a steep angle like huge flatirons. After the work of
gathering water, making a fire and preparing dinner had been
done, Ymiru sat by the fire playing with some chips of sandstone that he had found. Then, from a pouch on the great
black belt that he wore, he took out the gelstei Hrothmar had
given him. He held the flat, purple crystal over the sandstone

chips in various positions, turning it this way and that. His ice-blue eyes were afire with concentration.

"May I ask what you're doing?" Maram said. He held a mug of kalvaas in his hand and sat nearby looking on.

When Ymiru didn't answer him, Atara came close and said, "That should be obvious."

"Well, it's not obvious to me."

Now Liljana moved closer, and so did Kane. And Atara said, "You might say he's trying to make a silk purse out of a sow's ear."

Ymiru's faint, curving smile suggested that he had heard Atara's words as from far away.

"Trying?" Maram said. "But he's a Frost Giant! Don't they all know how to use these stones?"

Maram then began a long speech—made much longer by the quantity of kalvaas that he drank—about the wonders of Alundil. After he went on and on extolling the great, crystalline sculptures of the Garden of the Gods, which could only have been formed through the power of the purple gelstei, Ymiru had finally had enough. He held up his great hand for silence. Then he said to Maram, "The Garden of the Gods was made long ago, with knowledge that has been lost to us. And with much greater galastei than this one."

As he looked at the gleaming stone in his hand, Master Juwain came over and said, "It is told that the purple crystals sing with the deeper vibrations of the earth. Thus, in many ways, they are the hardest to use."

"And who tells this?"

"My Brotherhood's alchemists."

"Have they worked with many of the lilastei, then?"

Master Juwain shook his head. "Not for three thousand years. The purple stones have been lost to us, too. The alchemists' knowledge comes from books."

"So does mine," Ymiru said, fingering his crystal. "And from my elders' teachings. Many of my people are instructed in the ways of the lilastei, should the Ymanir ever find the secret of making more of them."

And with that, he bent over to direct his attention to the

task at hand, trying to unlock the secrets of his violet-colored crystal.

After a while, Liljana and Atara went to work on cleaning the pots and dishes while Maram slipped off into a drunken doze. And I overheard Atara say to her: "Why should we do all the drudgery while he sleeps?"

And Liljana said to her, "But my dear, I like cleaning. Besides, he needs his rest more than I do, and he is so very grateful for his sleep."

I smiled at this because I realized that Liljana liked to use people's gratitude and guilt as levers by which she might move them to her deeper purposes. I remembered a phrase of my grandfather's: She stoops to conquer. I resolved then to help with the dishes and other such tasks when I could, out of self-defense no less than fairness.

But that night, I did little more than to stand up to cover the horses with the white blankets that the Ymanir women had woven for them. Kane stood because he hated sitting; he walked about the perimeter of our camp, staring off into the darkness to look for enemies that he was unlikely to find within the safety of the Ymanir's land.

And then, just as I was feeding Altaru a chunk of carrot that I had saved from my soup, I heard Master Juwain cry out with delight: "Do you see? He's done it after all! Val, Kane, Liljana—come here and look!"

As Maram awoke with a loud, breaking snore, we all gathered around Ymiru. I looked down at the ground beneath his purple gelstei. Where only a few moments before a pile of sandstone chips had been, now three long, clear, quartz crystals grew out of a fused mass of stone.

"What is it?" Maram asked. He struggled to sit up as he peered at Ymiru's work through his bleary eyes. "What is this—sleight of hand?"

He looked at Ymiru as he might a street magician who has been given a bauble to play with. I did not think that he would ever be willing to lend Ymiru a gold coin for fear that Ymiru would return to him only a lump of lead.

"There's your silk purse," Atara said, pointing at the newly-formed quartz crystals. "It's good work—they're lovely, Ymiru."

"So small," he said, holding the crystals up to the light of the fire. "And stived with flaws. But it be a beginning."

Master Juwain had his own crystal in his hand as he looked at Ymiru approvingly. He couldn't have helped noticing, I thought, that just as Ymiru's knowledge and will had brought out the power of the purple stone, the stone had also brought out his power and exalted him.

"It is a beginning," Master Juwain said, to Ymiru and to all of us. "Or, I should say, a completion. Now, for perhaps the first time since the Age of Law, seven of the greater gelstei have been brought together."

He explained that the seven greater gelstei were each emanations of the gold gelstei and held something of its virtue. Used together, they were much more powerful than all of the stones used separately. They were like the fingers of a hand gripping the cup of fate that is also called the Lightstone.

"And as with the gelstei, so with us," he said, looking at Ymiru. "For we are only emanations of the One. Each of us—all have some seeds of the great gifts. It's the gelstei's purpose to quicken these gifts."

Maram let loose a loud belch and said, "You seem happy, sir."

"I am happy, Brother Maram. Do you see? It's as I've always said—there is only one pattern to everything, a single tapestry. And we are its threads."

Maram, still trying to wake up, rubbed his eyes and said, "I don't quite understand."

"One pattern," Master Juwain said to him again. "And the Lightstone holds the secret of its making. *Its making.* And I've sought just the opposite. All my life, looking for the knowledge to cut through and understand, the way to unravel the tapestry—all my life. And now, when perhaps there is not much left of it, I see that I was misguided."

He turned to look at Liljana and Atara, and then at Kane and me. He said, "We've been seeking to quicken our gifts and use the gelstei in order to find the Lightstone. But perhaps we should seek the Lightstone in order to quicken our gifts."

He went on to tell us that our work with the gelstei had great merit, as did our lives, even if we failed in our quest. "Alphanderry said it best," he reminded us. "Do you remember his words?"

We are the songs that sing the world into life, I thought. And then I said them aloud for all to hear.

I sat staring up at the stars, wondering if Alphanderry's music had ever found its way toward these eternal lights. And then Kane's gruff voice brought me back to earth: "Our lives are our lives, and we shouldn't give them up too easily. So, I'll sing better when we hold the Lightstone in our hands."

I fell off to sleep that night holding the hilt of Alkaladur in my hand. I prayed for the thousandth time that I might never again use this sword to take others' lives, but only to find my way through to the Lightstone.

The next day we had our first sight of Sakai. After a breakfast of fried eggs and toasted rye bread, we set out and soon pushed our way between the two hills where we had encamped. A line of low mountains lay ahead of us. We found a pass cutting through this chain, and spent the rest of the day working our way over it. And when we came out on the other side, we found that we had come to the end of the Ymanir's country.

By chance, it seemed, Ymiru had led us to the exact spot on earth that we had first sought. For here was the great hinge in the White Mountains. To our right, toward the south, the line of mountains that we had just crossed quickly gained elevation as they built toward a wall of white peaks running off into the distance. These were the mountains of the Yorgos range, and most of Elivagar was spread across their ridges and valleys. To our left, toward the south and east, rose the rocky masses of the Nagarshath. It chilled me merely to look up the unbroken chain of these vast upthrustings of the earth, with their jagged, white, ice-frozen crests. There was no way, I thought, that either man or beast could survive in such great heights. Surely our only hope, as we had discussed, was to pass through Sakai by way of the broad plateau opening out straight ahead of us between the two mountain ranges.

"So that is Sakai," Maram said as we stood by the horses on the side of the mountain. "Well, I don't like the look of it."

Neither did I. The land below was windswept and sere, its brown grasses and patches of bare earth already showing occasional shags of snow. It went on and on toward the gray haze of the horizon. I thought I could make out, off in the distance, outcroppings of dark rock marking the face of this forbidding plateau. It did not seem a place where people would live. And yet I knew that when we went down into it, we would likely find nomads herding their flocks—or the Red Dragon's cavalry riding the borders of his dreadful realm.

"So," Kane said as the wind whipped up his snowy hair. "So."

Atara stood near me, staring down into Sakai as if she had seen it before in her crystal sphere.

Maram looked at Ymiru doubtfully. "You said that you've led raids down into that?"

"No, not here," Ymiru said. "Our battles with the Beast's armies were almost a hundred miles to the south."

"But you still propose to lead us across it?"

"No," Ymiru said, "I don't."

We all looked at him in surprise, even as did Maram, who said, "But you were to lead us through Sakai. Has seeing it changed your mind?"

"I will lead you through Sakai." Ymiru's hard blue eyes looked to the left as he pointed at the mountains of the Nagarshath. "That, too, be Sakai."

Although the wind was burning Maram's face bright red, for a moment the color drained from his cheeks. "But there's no way through those mountains!"

"No, there be a way," Ymiru said. The coldness of his eyes made me want to shiver. "An ancient way—we call it the Wailing Way."

He told us that long ago his ancestors had built a system of roads, tunnels, and bridges through the Nagarshath in order to help them fight their wars against Morjin. There, along the icy peaks of these mountains, the wind wailed almost continually. There, too, the mothers of the Ymanir had wailed for many hundreds of years to see so many of their sons and daughters slain.

"It took the Beast a long, long time to drive us from the Nagarshath," Ymiru told us. "But the mountains were too vast, and we were too few to defend them. So in the end we had to retreat to Elivagar."

"But surely, then," Maram said, "the Red Dragon's men now guard this Wailing Way of yours."

"No, they would have no reason to—none of my people has been that way for a thousand years."

"You haven't either?"

"No, I haven't."

"Then how do you know it still exists?"

"It must still exist. You've seen how my people build things."

"But what if the Red Dragon has destroyed it?"

"It is my hrope that he has not," Ymiru said. "You see, it was a secret way, and it may be that his men never found it."

We all stood wondering if Ymiru could find his way through these terrible mountains and so lead us to Argattha through Sakai's back door. In answer, he took off his pack and removed the paper-wrapped package that Burri had given him. It took him only a moment to open it and take out his father's map.

"What is that?" Maram said, crowding close to look at it.

Ymiru held in his hands what seemed a pair of lacquered boards, square in shape and inlaid with various dark woods. With great care, Ymiru pulled away the top board, which was set neatly against the bottom board's rune-carved frame so as to protect its interior surface. This was a smaller square within a square, wrought of a reddish brown substance that looked much like clay. Indeed, Ymiru called it living clay, and said that his great-grandfather had crafted it nearly ninety years before.

"This be one thing my people haven't lost," Ymiru said. "Almost every Ymanir family has such a map."

Maram reached out his finger to run it over the clay's

smooth, unbroken surface. And then Ymiru's great voice suddenly bellowed out and froze him motionless: "Don't touch that! You'll ruin the map!"

Maram jerked back his hand as if from a heated iron. He said, "I don't understand how you can call this a map."

"Watch, little man. If I be steady of hand and clear of mind, you'll see something you've never seen."

As Ymiru oriented his father's map toward the mountains of the Nagarshath, we all gathered in as close as we could. We watched as Ymiru closed his eyes and slowly shifted the position of his furry feet about the ground. He seemed to draw strength from it and something else. Almost as slowly as the turning of the earth, he rotated the clay-laden board, apparently seeking to position it along lines that only he could apprehend.

And then without warning, the map's living clay began moving about as if being molded by invisible hands. In places, fissures and furrows marked its rippling surface even as bits of clay formed themselves into ridges and crests, and thrust upward in long, jagged lines that looked like miniature mountain ranges. It took very little time for this transformation to occur. But when it was completed, as I saw to my amazement, Ymiru held in his hands an exact replica of the mountains that lay before us.

"This be a map of the nearer mountains of the Nagarshath," Ymiru said, opening his eyes. He pointed down with his chin. "Do you see the valley behind the front range?"

Of course, we could all make out the deep groove in the clay behind the map's front mountains. But when I looked out at the world, through the cold air that hung heavy beneath the blue sky, all I could see was a vast, white wall of rocky peaks edging Sakai's umber plateau. If a valley lay beyond these very real mountains, the map could see it but I couldn't.

"If the map is true," Master Juwain said, pointing his finger at the gleaming clay, "then it seems the valley runs for many miles."

"The map be true," Ymiru said, looking down at it proudly. "And the valley be eighty miles long. It will take us a third of the way to Argattha."

"But what is the magic of this map?" Maram asked him. "I've never heard of such a thing."

Ymiru smiled as he looked out upon Sakai. And then to Maram, he said, "The world be a great and glorious place. And through it, along its valleys and rivers and within its hills, pulse the currents of the earth—much as your blood pulses through your big nose and follows its contours. The living clay resonates with these currents. And so it hrolds within its form the forms of the earth."

Master Juwain's clear gray eyes fixed on the map. And then he said, "But not all the earth, it seems."

"No, there be a limit to what the map can model," Ymiru said. "It will show the terrain ahead to a distance of a hundred miles but no more."

"Then," I said, pointing at the edge of the map, "there is no way for us to know what lies beyond this valley."

"No, not until we've covered some further distance," Ymiru said. "But it be my hrope that we'll find other valleys paralleling this one. The line of Nagarshath runs toward Argattha, and so must its valleys."

"And this Wailing Way of yours?" Kane asked him. "Does it follow the Nagarshath's valleys, too?"

"It be said that it does."

"Do you think you can find it?"

Ymiru looked at the map as he nodded his head. "That be my hrope."

With his marvelous map revealing a possible way through the mountains, it seemed that we might not have to brave Sakai's plateau after all. But I was reluctant to commit to this new course. At least on the plateau below us, there would be abundant grass for the horses.

"There be grass in the mountains' valleys, I think," Ymiru said. "At least the lower valleys."

As he pointed out, the horses' packs were still full of the oats that we had gathered for our journey. "And if the worst befalls and the horses starve, you can always eat them and continue the journey afoot."

Just then Altaru nickered nervously, and I looked at Ymiru

as if he had suggested eating my own brother. Ymiru, who had watched in horror as we savored the taste of our salted pork, could not quite understand the different kind of love that we held for our horses.

"Come, Val," Kane said to me. "There are risks in whatever path that we take."

We held council then, and Kane, Master Juwain, Liljana, and Ymiru all agreed that the greater risk was in riding straight across Sakai's plateau with barely a rock for cover. But Maram declared that the mountains' freezing heights would likely kill us, whereas we might get lucky and encounter none of the enemy on the lower route. Atara remained silent, staring into the darkening land before us. Because I sensed in her a great disquiet, I asked the others if I might have some time alone with her.

"Of course you may," Liljana told us. "It's nearly dusk, and we should be making camp. Why don't we put off our decision until morning?"

She and Maram took the reins of Fire and Altaru, and moved off with the others to make camp near a stream that we had passed a quarter mile back. Atara and I walked on a hundred yards to a shelf of earth dusted with snow. Against the fall of night, its whiteness was quickly dying to various shades of gray. Although it was too cold to remain ungloved, Atara stood rolling her crystal sphere between her naked hands.

"What is it," I asked her, "that you don't want to tell our friends?"

Her eyes flicked down toward her crystal, but she said nothing.

"I think you see more than you say, Atara."

"And what about you?" she said, looking at me. "I don't think you've told us very much of your dreams."

Now it was my turn to seek refuge in silence.

"He sees you, doesn't he?" she asked.

"In a way," I said. "But it is more as if he can smell the taint of the kirax in me. He knows that I am still alive."

"He is still seeking you, then?"

"Yes, seeking—but not quite finding. Not as he would like."

"He mustn't find you," she said.

There was a new fear in her voice when she spoke of Morjin and a new tenderness in her fingers as she reached out and stroked my hand. I pointed at her sphere of white gelstei and then at the land of Sakai. I asked, "Have you seen him then? In your crystal? Or down there?"

"I've seen many things," she said evasively.

I waited for her to say more but she fell into a deep silence.

"Tell me, Atara," I whispered.

She shook her head and whispered back, "You're not like Master Juwain. You don't need to know everything about everything."

"Is it that bad then? Is it any worse than what I've seen?"

I told her about the thousands of deaths I had died in my dreams. This touched something raw inside her. I felt her seize up as if I had stuck my finger into an open wound.

"What is it?" I asked her. Her whole body shook as if suddenly stricken with the night's falling cold. I put my arms around her and held her against me. "Please tell me."

"No, I can't, I shouldn't—I shouldn't have to," she whispered.

And then she was kissing my hands and eyes, touching the scar on my forehead, kissing that, holding me tightly before breaking away a moment later. Then she collapsed to her knees and threw her arms around my legs as she buried her face against my thighs and shook even more violently.

"Atara," I called to her as I stroked her hair, "Atara, Atara."

A little later, with the night's wind cooling her grief, she managed to stand again and look at me. And she told me, "Almost every time I see Morjin, I see you. I see your death."

The wind off the icy peaks around us suddenly chilled me to the bone. I smiled grimly at her and asked, "You said almost every time?"

"Almost, yes. There are other branchings, you see, so few other branchings of your life."

"Please tell me, then."

She took a deep breath and looked at me. "I've seen you kneeling to Morjin—and living."

"That will never be."

"I've seen you turning away from Argattha, too. And going far away from him. With me, Val. Hiding."

"That can't ever be," I said softly.

I held her tightly as her heart beat against mine. I felt both her terror for what might be and her desire for what she wanted to be. And I said, "If you've seen your death, in Argattha or along the way, you should tell me. So that I might fight against it and make my own fate."

"You don't understand," she said, shaking her head.

She went on to tell me something of the gift with which she had been touched. She tried to describe how a scryer's vision was like ascending the branches of an infinite tree. Each moment of time, she said, was like a magical seed quivering with possibilities. Just as a woman lay waiting to blossom inside a child, the whole tree of life was inside the seed. Every leaf, twig, or flower that could ever be was there. A scryer opened it with her warmth and will, with her passion for truth and her tears. To move from the present to the future, as a scryer does, was to find an eternal golden stem breaking out of the seed and dividing into two or ten branches, and each one of these dividing again and again, ten into ten thousand, ten thousand into trillions upon trillions of branches shimmering always just beyond her reach. The tree grew ever higher toward the sun, branching out into infinite possibilities. And the higher the scryer climbed, the brighter became this sun until it grew impossibly bright, as if all the light in the universe were pulling her toward a single, golden moment at the end of time that could never quite be.

"It sounds glorious," I said to her.

"You still don't understand," she said sadly. "Morjin, and his lord, Angra Mainyu—they are poisoning this tree. Darkening even the sun. The higher I climb, the more withered branches and dead leaves."

The wind in my face seemed to carry the dark scents of the land that lay before us. It made me wonder what I would find in the realm of Sakai.

"But there must be a branch that is whole," I said to her. "Leaves that even he cannot touch."

"There might be," she agreed. She put her crystal in her pocket and grasped my hands. "But I'm afraid to look, Val."

"You, afraid?"

She nodded her head. The light of the first stars seemed to catch in her hair. Then she told me that the tree of life grew out of a strange, dark land inside her. "There be dragons there," she said, looking at me sharply.

My heart ached with a fierce desire to slay this particular dragon.

"A scryer," she said, "a true scryer must never turn back from ascending the tree. But the heights bring her too close to the sun. To the light. After a while, it burns and blinds—blinds her to the things of the world. Her world grows ever brighter. And so she lives more for her visions than for other people. Living thus, she dies a little and grows ugly in her soul. Old, ugly, shriveled. And that is why people grow to hate her."

"Do you think I could ever hate you?"

"I'd want to die if you did," she said.

I thought of Ymiru's living clay that modeled Ea's landscapes, and I wished that I had a map of her interior world. In the gloom of dusk I found her eyes as I took a deep breath and said, "There must be a way."

There must be a way that she could stand beneath this brilliant, inner sun and return in all her beauty bearing its light in her hands.

"Atara," I whispered.

I knew that for me, too, there was a way that the *valarda* could not only open others' hearts to me, but mine to them.

"Atara," I said again.

What is it to love a woman? It is just love, as all love is: warm and soft as the down of a quilt yet hard and flawless like a diamond whose sheen can never be dimmed. It is sweeter than honey, more quenching of thirst than the coolest mountain stream. But it is also a song of praise and exaltation of life's wild joy. It makes a man want to fight to the death protecting his beloved just so this one bit of brightness and beauty, like a perfect rose, will remain among the living when he has gone on. Through the hands and eyes it sings, calling and calling—calling her to open up the bright petals of her soul and be a glory to the earth.

I touched the tears gathering at the corner of Atara's eye and then wiped away my own. I looked at her a long time as she looked at me. She grasped my hand and pressed it against her wet cheek. At last she smiled and said, "Thank you."

Then she took the white gelstei out of her pocket. She held it so that its polished curves caught the faint light raining down from the sky. Inside it were stars, an infinitude of stars. For a moment, her eyes were full of them as they seemed to grow almost as big as her crystal sphere. And then she disappeared into it as if plunging through an icy lake into a deeper world.

I waited there on the cold snow for her to return to me; I waited a long time. The constellations wheeled slowly about the heavens. The wind fell down from the sky with a keening that cut right through me. It sent icy shivers along my veins and set my heart to beating like a great red drum.

"Atara," I whispered. But she didn't hear me.

Somewhere behind me, a raven cawed and the wind shook the needles of a tree. These sounds of the earth seemed a million miles away.

"Atara," I said again, "please come back."

At last she did. With a great effort, she tore her gaze from her crystal to stare at me. There was death all over her beautiful face, now tightening with a deep anguish. Something worse than death haunted her and set her whole body to trembling. She shook so badly that her fingers opened and the gelstei fell down into the snow.

"Oh, Val!" she sobbed out.

Then she fell weeping against me and I had to hold her up to keep her from collapsing altogether. I was afraid that I would have to carry her back to our camp. But she was Atara Ars Narmada of the Manslayer Society, after all, and it wasn't in her to allow herself such weakness for very long. After a few moments, she gathered up her dignity and stood away from me. She dried her tears with the edge of her cloak. Then she bent to retrieve her scryer's sphere from the snow.

I waited for her to tell me what she had beheld inside it. But all she said was "Do you see? Do you see?"

I saw only that she had been stricken by some terrible vision and was afraid that she was now mutilated in her soul. Whatever this affliction was, I wanted to share it with her.

"Tell me what you saw, then."

"No . . . I never will."

"But you must."

"No, I must not."

"Please, tell me."

She stared out at the snow-white contours of the mountains around us. Then she looked at me and said, "It's so hard to make you understand. To make you see. Just talking about this one thing can change . . . everything. There are so many paths, so many futures. But only one that can ever be. We can choose which one. In the end, we always choose. I can, Val. That's what makes this seeing so hard. I blink my eyes just one time, and the world isn't the same. Master Juwain once said that if he had a lever long enough and a place to stand, he could move the world. Well, I've been given this gift, this incredible lever of mine. Shouldn't I want to use it to preserve what is most precious to me and save your life? And yet, how should I use it if in saving you, you are lost? And the world along with you?"

She had told me almost too much; more than this I did not wish to hear. And so I gave voice to what my soul whispered to be true: "There must be a way."

"A way," she said, her voice dying into the bitterness of the wind.

If there was a way she would never tell it to me for fear of what might befall. And yet, I knew that she had found some gleam of hope in the dragon-blackened tree inside her. Her eyes screamed this to me; her pounding heart could not deny it. But it was a terrible hope that was tearing her apart.

"Do you see?" she asked me. "Do you see why scryers are stoned and driven off to live in the ruins of ancient towers?"

"That is not what I see, Atara."

She stood before me with a new awareness of life: prouder, deeper, fiercer, more tender, more passionate and devoted to truth—and this was a beauty of a wholly different order. This was her grace, to transform the terrible into a splendor that shined forth from deep inside her. And she, who could see so much, could not see this. And so I showed her this beautiful woman.

"Valashu," she said to me.

What is it to love a woman? It is this: that if she hurts, you hurt even more to see her in pain. It is your heart stripped of protective tissues and utterly exposed: soft, raw, impossibly tender; if a feather brushed against it, it would be the greatest of agonies. And yet also the greatest of joys, for this, too, is love: that through its fiery alchemy, what was once two miraculously becomes one.

We gazed at each other through the darkness, locking eyes as we called to each other—calling and calling. My heart, fed with fire, swelled like the sun. Suddenly it broke open in a blaze of light. It broke her open, too. She reached out to me, and we closed the distance between ourselves like two warriors rushing to battle. She flew into my arms, and I into hers. Our mouths met in a fury to breathe in and taste each other's souls; in our haste and artlessness, we bruised our lips with our teeth, bit, drew blood. We were like wild animals, clawing and pulling at each other, and yet like angels, too. In the heat of her body was a fierce desire that I tear her open to reveal the beautiful woman she really was. And that I should join her in that secret place inside her. She called me to fill her with light, with love, with burning raindrops of life. Only then could she feel all of the One's glory pouring itself out through her, as well. Only then could we both drive back death.

Valashu.

I felt her hand against my chest, pressing the cold rings of my armor against my heart. She suddenly pulled her lips away from mine. She fought herself away from me, and stood back a few paces, trembling and sweating and gasping for breath.

"No!" she sobbed out. "This can't be!"

I teetered on top of the snow, sweating and trembling, too, stunned to find myself standing alone. There was a terrible pressure inside me that made me want to scream.

"Don't you see?" she said to me as her hands covered her belly. Her eyes, fixed on the emptiness of the night, suddenly found mine. "Our son, our beautiful son—I can't see him!"

I didn't know what she meant; I didn't want to know what she meant.

"I'm sorry," she said, taking my hands in hers. "But this can't be, not yet. Maybe not ever."

"I know that there is hope," I said to her. "I know that there is a way."

She drew herself up to her full height and gazed at me as from far away. Then she asked me, "And how do you know this?"

"Because," I said, "I love you."

It was a foolish thing to say. What did love have to do with overcoming the world's evil and making things come out all right? My wild words were sheer foolishness, and we both knew this. But it made her weep all the same.

"If there is a way," she said, pressing her hand against the side of her face, "you'll have to find it. I'm sorry, Val."

I stood looking out at the ghost-white peaks of the Nagarshath range before us. I said to her, "But what about our route to Argattha, then?"

"I'm sorry, but you'll have to find that way as well."

She leaned forward and kissed me, once, on my lips with great tenderness. I felt in her a sadness that seemed to touch all things, the rocks and frozen needles on the evergreens no less than Atara and me. And yet something lit up her face with all the radiance of the heavens. I couldn't help thinking of the words that Maram had called out in Anjo some months before: Her eyes are windows to the stars. He had forgotten the lines of his poem even more quickly than he had Duke Rezu's niece. But I hadn't. Neither had I forgotten the verse that he had recited the night of the feast in my father's hall:

Star of my soul, how you shimmer
Beyond the deep blue sky
Whirling and whirling—you and I whisperlessly
Spinning sparks of joy into the night.

Even as Flick appeared and sent his own sparks spinning into the darkness, I was overwhelmed with a strange sense that Atara and I had once come from this nameless star. In truth, whenever she looked at me it seemed that we returned there. As we did now. For ages and ages, it seemed, we stood on the cold snow beneath the ancient constellations as the world turned and the stars whirled. Almost forever, I looked into her eyes. What was there? Only light. How, I wondered, could I ever hold it? Could I drink in the sea and all the oceans of stars?

Wordlessly, she reached out her hand and grasped mine. Her touch was like lightning splitting me open. All of her incredible sadness came flooding into me; but all of her wild joy of life came too. In the clasp of her fingers against mine there was no assurance of fulfillment in marriage or even victory, but only a promise that we would always be kind to each other and that we wouldn't fail each other. And that we would always remind each other where we had come from and who we were meant to be. It was the most sacred vow I had ever made, and I knew that both Atara and I would keep it, even unto our deaths.

Then she took her arm in mine to walk back toward our camp. One last time I gazed out at the frozen land to the east that the Ymanir had named the Wailing Way. I knew then that it was our way and that we must somehow cross over the Nagarshath's greatest mountains if we were to reach Argattha.

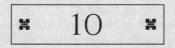

10

AND SO WE went into Sakai. It was the work of the next day to fight our way over the nearest pass in this towering front range. We had a bad time of it. Atara slipped on an ice-glazed rock and nearly broke her leg. The horses suffered grievously in the thin air, panting and sweating until their fur froze in the cold. We put blankets over them to ease their shivering, but it didn't seem to help very much. When the wind rose to a screaming howl as we crested the pass, whipping up flurries of snow, it seemed that our great, white coats didn't help us much, either.

"I'm cold, I'm tired," Maram complained as he drove himself into the wind and pulled at Iolo's reins. To either side of us were towers of rock and clouds of snow; beneath the powder at our feet was a mat of old snow made hard as ice by a season of melting and refreezing. "In fact, I'm very cold. I'm so cold that I'm . . . frozen! Oh, no, my fingers—I can't feel them!"

I hastened to his side and helped him pull off his mittens. The tips of his fingers were hard and white. I placed them between my hands and blew on them to warm them. Then Master Juwain came over to take a look.

"I was afraid of this," Master Juwain said, gently pressing his knotty fingers against Maram's.

Dread cut through Maram like a shark's fin breaking cold waters. "Is there anything you can do? Never to touch a woman again, never to feel—"

"I think," Master Juwain said, "we can save the arm."

He winked as he said this to reassure Maram. He told me to keep working on Maram's fingers until I had completely thawed them; he told Maram to keep his hands in his pockets close to his body until we made camp that night and he could heal Maram's savaged flesh with his varistei.

"All right," Maram said. "But I've had enough of Sakai already."

So had I. So, I thought, had all of us—except perhaps Ymiru, who consented to take Iolo's reins and lead the descent down into the valley that his map had showed. Here, in this windy groove in the earth tens of miles long, we found a few stunted dead trees that provided us wood for a fire. There was a little grass for the horses, too, and water that ran down its center in a little brown stream. The valley seemed too high to shelter much life beyond some marmots and a few rock goats. Blessedly, we seemed the only people to have set foot here for a thousand years.

Our camp that night was a cold one. Master Juwain, his green crystal in hand, accomplished the minor miracle of fully restoring Maram to himself. Maram vowed to exercise more caution on the long journey that still lay ahead of us. I knew that he would. No man, I thought, had a greater fondness for his various appendages.

For the next four days we worked our way down the valley. I didn't like it that we had so little cover here. But there seemed no one to see us, except a few vultures circling on the mountain thermals high above us. We made good time and good distance. The horses held steady and so did we. By the afternoon of our fifth day in Sakai, with the valley abruptly coming to an end in a great massif that blocked our way, we were all gathering our strength for yet another foray into the grim, mountain heights.

Ymiru's map showed a pass off to our right, hidden by a great buttress of the massif ahead of us. We climbed up the rocky slope at the valley's very end, praying that the map proved true. And so it did. After an hour of hard, panting work, we came upon a break in the massif, the highest pass yet that we had tried to cross. Master Juwain took his first look at this huge saddle of snow and ice, and thought it was too high to cross. And so, for a moment, did I. And then I noticed a cleft cut straight through the very center of the pass. It looked much like the Telemesh Gate connecting Mesh to Ishka.

"It seems," Kane said to Ymiru, looking at him strangely, "that your people once used firestones against the earth."

As Ymiru stared up at the pass, I sensed some deep, dark thing devouring his insides. There was great doubt in him, and great sadness, too.

"Yes, we used firestones," he said, pointing upward. "Thus we made the Wailing Way."

Liljana shifted about uneasily, as if trying to gain respite from the fierce wind pounding against the shawl she had wrapped around her head. I felt within her the same dread that crept into my spine: that here it wasn't just the wind that wailed but the very earth itself.

If ever there had been road leading up to the pass, the relentless work of the seasons had long since obliterated it. But the cleft through the pass itself remained much as the Ymanir's firestones had burned it long ago. And on the other side, below some of the deepest snowfields we had plowed through yet, we found an ancient track leading down from the heights.

We followed this band of packed earth and stone for many miles, all that afternoon and for the next ten days. It wound its way toward the southeast through the furrows between great ice-capped prominences. In places, where it led across a mountain's slope, it was cunningly cut so as to be hidden behind rock and ridgeline from the vantage of the valleys farther below. In other places it disappeared altogether, and there Ymiru had to trust his instinct, following the logic of the land around pinnacles, across basins, until he found the track again. It was a high road, this Wailing Way that the Ymanir had built. In most of the valleys through which it ran, we could find only a little grass for the horses; a few were altogether barren and seemed nothing more than chutes of rocky earth.

This starkness of Sakai appalled us all. But it was nothing against the much deeper ugliness that had been worked into the land by the hand of man. The few tunnels—through icy ridges too high to cross—seemed like holes cut through the flesh of the earth into her very bones. And worse, by far, were the open pits scooped out of the high meadows, sometimes out of the sides of the mountains themselves. They were like sores in the

earth that hadn't healed after even thousands of years. Something in their making, perhaps the piles of slag torn up from
the ground, seemed to have poisoned the earth currents that
Ymiru had spoken of, for near them nothing would grow.

"This must be the work of the Beast," Ymiru explained to
us, pointing at a circular pock in the valley far below us. "It be
told that his men have dug such pits all across Sakai."

"But why?" Maram asked him. "Are there diamonds here?
Gold?"

I had my sword drawn and pointing east to see if the
Lightstone still lay in that direction. In the flash of sunlight
off its silvery surface, a sudden thought flashed through my
mind.

"The Red Dragon does seek gold," I said. "The true gold,
from which he hopes to forge another Lightstone."

Ymiru looked at me strangely. "So it be, so it be."

This mark of the Beast disturbed me, and all of us, for if
Morjin's men had once come here, they might come again. I
felt his presence all around me, in the jagged knifeblades of
the ridgelines, in the pinnacles' icy spears, and most of all, in
the bitter wind. As promised, it swept across the Nagarshath
as through a dragon's teeth and wailed without relief. It bit at
my bones; it carried in its icy gusts whispers of torment and
death. As we drew closer to Morjin and the seat of his power
on earth, it seemed that he was seeking me even as I sought
the Lightstone, calling me as always to surrender up my will
and dreams and kneel before him.

I doubted that he could perceive my actual physical presence in these terrible mountains he claimed as his own. But
the kirax still poisoned my blood and connected us in ways
that chilled me with a growing dread. I knew that he could
sense my soul. The howling wind told me this, as did the
silent screaming of my lungs. In the icy wastes through which
we passed for many days, he sent illusions to confuse and
break me. In many of these, I saw myself chained to the face
of some rock and being tortured with fire and steel; in others,
the frozen ground beneath me suddenly gave way, and I found
myself plunging into a black and bottomless abyss.

But the hardest illusion for me to bear was the one in which I had regained the Lightstone and used it to restore the tormented lands of Ea. The imagined pleasure of touching this golden cup nearly overwhelmed me. It seduced me into covetousness and pride, and made me want to possess the Lightstone for myself alone and never suffer another even to behold it. So great was the greed for the golden light that Morjin aroused in me that I made for myself illusions of my own. In the dazzling whiteness of Sakai's snows, in the glare and glister of the sun off glacier ice, I began seeing the Lightstone everywhere: on rocky ledges, half-buried in frozen drifts or even floating in the air. It was there, in the blinding fastness of the White Mountains, that I began the fiercest battle yet for my sanity and my very soul.

I drew great strength to join it from my friends, particularly Atará. Her smiles, even in the harshest of circumstances, were a wonder and an inspiration to me. But in the end, one must journey far out into the icy wastes of despair to face one's demons alone. At least I had a mighty weapon with which to fight. Alkaladur's silustria, like a perfect mirror, threw Morjin's deceits back at him and shielded me from his hideous golden eyes and the worst of his hate. And more, as I attuned to it, it helped me cut through all illusion to see the world as it really is. My whole being began opening to the numinous and the true: in the stark, snowy landscapes of the White Mountains and in the shimmering stars above them, but also within myself. For there shined the bright sword of my soul. I saw that it was indeed possible to polish it more brilliantly than even the silustria itself. And with every bit of rust that I rubbed from it, as I cleansed myself of pride and fear, I felt this sword gleaming brighter and brighter and pointing me on toward my fate.

One night, just past the ides of Ioj, we made camp at the foot of a glacier. Maram got a fire going out of the last of our wood, and there Ymiru sat with a huge chunk of ice between his legs as he chiseled it with his knife. He worked with a fierce concentration. It was as if he were trying to bring forth the image of some perfect thing that he longed to create. He would not tell us what this was. He did not speak to us, for he had fallen deep into one of his glooms. He was, I thought, a man who held on to the dark side of his feelings, afraid that if the demons of his melancholy were driven from him, the angels of his ecstasies would be, too.

"What is it you're carving there?" Maram asked, sidling closer. "It almost looks like Val's mother."

It looked like, I thought, the great carving of the Galadin queen I had seen passing through the Ashtoreth Gate on our entrance to Tria.

But Ymiru didn't answer him. He just set his sculpture down into the snow and then took up a flaming brand from the fire. He held it so that it melted the ice of the sculpture's surface. Then he brought out his purple gelstei, positioning it in front of the sculpture's face.

"What are you doing?" Maram asked him.

None of us knew. But we all gathered around to watch.

And then, as the starlight flickered off the blade of my drawn sword, a sudden thought came to me: "He's trying to turn his carving to stone."

"Turn ice to stone?" Maram said. "Impossible!"

Ymiru suddenly looked up from his work, staring at me in amazement. "How did you know that?" he asked me.

How did I know, I wondered? I looked down at the star-sparkled length of my sword. Its silustria gave me to know many things from the slightest hint.

"It be impossible to turn ice to stone, truly," Ymiru said. "But to turn water to stone—this be one of the powers of the lilastei."

"But how?" Maram asked.

Ymiru ran his finger over the sculpture's dripping surface. "When water falls cold, it wants to turn to ice. This be its natural crystallization. But there be another, too, and that is the clear stone called shatar. The purple galastei makes water want to freeze into this stone. And stone it truly be: shatar be as hard as quartz and never thaws."

As he moved to put away his violet stone, Maram said, "What are you doing? Aren't you going to show us this shatar of yours?"

"No," Ymiru said, "I can't make the lilastei make the water want to freeze this way. I haven't the power."

"Perhaps not yet."

Ymiru said nothing as he stared at his sculpture's wet face, now freezing in the wind like that of a spurned lover.

"But what else can the lilastei do?" Maram asked. "You've told us so little about them, or your people."

The silence into which Ymiru now fell seemed greater than the expanse of all the mountains of the Nagarshath. He looked east, along the line toward which my gleaming sword pointed.

"The lilastei," I gasped as images flooded into my mind, "can mold rock, as the firestones can burn it. That was how the Ymanir made Argattha."

Everyone looked at me in astonishment. And Ymiru thundered at me, "Who told you that?"

I felt Alkaladur's bright blade almost humming in the starlight. I said, "Is it true, Ymiru?"

Ymiru suddenly slumped back, his great chest deflating like a bellows emptied of air. And then he sighed out, "Yes, it be true."

"But how?" Maram asked. "How can it be?"

Ymiru rubbed his broken nose for a few moments and sighed again. "How? How, you ask? You see, there was a time when we Ymanir thought that Morjin was our friend."

The story he now told us was a sad one. Long, long ago, he said, during Morjin's first rise at the end of the Age of Swords, he had gone to Sakai to win the Ymanir to his cause. At this time his evil deeds were mostly unknown. Morjin was fair of form and graceful with his words; he flattered the ancient Ymanir and brought them gifts: diamonds and gold, but greatest of all, the purple gelstei.

"It was the Beast," Ymiru said, "who gave us the first lilastei and taught us to use them. It was he who suggested that we seek beneath Skartaru for the true gold that we might use it to forge a new Lightstone."

Toward this end, Morjin had called his Red Priests into Sakai to aid in the excavations beneath Skartaru that would come to be the city called Argattha. They remained as counselors when Morjin went off to conquer Alonia and eventually be defeated at the Sarburn. It was they who poisoned the ancient Ymaniris' minds and seduced them into believing terrible lies: that Morjin only wished to unite Ea under one banner to bring peace to its torn lands; that his fall had been brought by treachery and the evil of his enemies. And so, when Morjin had been imprisoned on Damoom for all the Age of Law, Ymiru's ancestors had worked hard and long to prepare Argattha for Morjin's return.

"We built a city fit for kings," Ymiru said. "Argattha was a great and glorious place, as we may yet live to see."

Maram, sipping a mug of kalvaas as he listened to Ymiru speak, said, "I don't care what we see there—I just want to live to come back out."

"Tell us," Kane said, watching Ymiru with his dark eyes, "what happened when the Lord of Lies did return."

"That be easy to tell," Ymiru said sadly. "Easy, but the hardest of tales: in the time that followed Morjin's second coming to Argattha, we discovered that the Lord of Light, as he called himself, was really the Lord of Lies. He had taken back the Lightstone then, but he kept us digging beneath Skartaru all the same. He used the cup to try to bend us to his will and make us slaves. But no one will rule the Ymanir—not even other Ymanir. And so began our war with the Beast that has lasted until this day."

After he had finished speaking, Atara sat listening to the wind as she stared into her white crystal. Master Juwain gripped his old book and looked at Liljana, who had taken out her blue whale. Kane crouched near Ymiru and looked like a tiger ready to spring.

Maram was nearly drunk, but he had a clear enough wit to appreciate that as far as we were concerned, Ymiru's story might not be wholly tragic. He asked, "If your people made Argattha, did they keep any maps of it?"

"No," Ymiru said, "all such perished in the wars."

"Too bad. I had hoped that there might be another way into the city other than through one of its gates."

For a hundred miles, at least, we had discussed the problem of entering Argattha and finding our way to Morjin's throne room. I had thought that our knowledge of the city was scarcely more than anyone's: that Argattha had been built up through the black mountain on seven levels, with Morjin's palace and throne room at the highest. And that five gates, named in mockery of Tria's, opened upon its streets. Each gate, it was said, was guarded by ferocious dogs and a company of Morjin's men. And perhaps, as Kane suggested, by the mind-reading Grays as well.

"There be another way into Argattha," Ymiru said. "A dark way, an ancient way."

We all looked at him, waiting for him to say more.

"When Morjin came to Argattha with the Lightstone," he explained, "he feared that his enemies would assault the mountain and trap him inside. And so my people built escape tunnels for him. Secret tunnels, and the knowledge of all of them has been lost to us—except one."

"Do you know where this tunnel is?" Maram asked.

"No, I don't know. But I know where it might be found."

Maram's face brightened as Ymiru brought out his map and oriented it toward the east. For quite a few days now, we had used it to set our course on the greatest of the mountains to show through the clay along the map's eastern edge. This was Skartaru, whose shape was famous across Ea: as seen from the east, from across the Wendrush, its twin peaks thrust like the points of pyramids high into the sky. And now, as Ymiru told us of a secret way into this dread mountain, we studied the model of it in the map that he held in his huge, furry hands.

"I can't see anything here," Maram said, peering at the living clay in the fire's flickering light.

"No, the scale be much too small," Ymiru said. "The map shows only the mountain's greater features."

"Then how do you hope to find this tunnel of yours?"

"Because there be a verse. Words that have survived where paper or clay have not."

"What is it, then?"

Ymiru cleared his throat, and then recited for us six ancient lines:

> *Beneath the Diamond's icy walls,*
> *Where brightest sunlight never falls;*
> *Beside the Ogre's knobby knee:*
> *The cave that leads to liberty.*
> *The rock there marked with iron ore*
> *Which points the way to Morjin's door.*

We sat there listening to the wind shriek across the high mountains around us. It seemed to carry the whisperings of the frozen rocks and echoes ten thousand years old.

"So," Kane said, pointing his finger at Ymiru's map, "this Diamond that the verse tells of must be Skartaru's north face."

The black mountain's north face, I saw, was indeed shaped like a standing diamond three miles high, with great buttresses on either side seeming to hold it up.

"That is confirmed by the verse's next line," Master Juwain said.

"But what about the Ogre?" Liljana asked, looking at the map's dark clay. "I don't see any such formations beneath the north face."

"No, the scale be too small," Ymiru said. "And so we can deduce that this Ogre rock formation will be rather small, in relation to the rest of the mountain. We won't be able to find the cave until we stand beneath it."

"We won't find anything," Kane said, "if the verse doesn't tell true."

Maram took another swig of his kalvaas, then asked Ymiru, "This matter of the verse, ah, your people making escape tunnels, making Argattha itself—why didn't you tell us all this before now?"

"I didn't want to arouse false hrope."

I sat beneath the stars of the bright Owl constellation, which I could see reflected in the silver of my sword. Then I looked up and said, "Isn't there another reason, Ymiru?"

Ymiru looked straight at me then, but seemed not to see me. His great heart was booming like a drum.

"The ancient Ymanir," I said to him, "sought the true gold beneath Skartaru, but they also sought something else, didn't they?"

"Yes," he finally said, as everyone stared at him. "You see, beneath the White Mountains, the earth currents are very strong—the strongest on all of Ea. And they touch the currents of other worlds."

Kane's gaze seemed to flare up in the firelight and fall upon Ymiru with great heat. I remembered him telling us how the telluric currents of all worlds were interconnected.

"My ancestors believed," Ymiru said, "that if they could open the currents beneath Skartaru, they might open doors to other worlds. The worlds of the Galadin. They built Argattha to welcome them to Ea."

"And who," I asked him, "suggested to the ancient Ymanir that such doors might be opened?"

"Morjin did."

If my sword had shattered into a thousand pieces just then, I would have been able to see the whole of it from a single glittering shard. I said to Ymiru, "Seeking the true gold was never Morjin's real purpose either, was it?"

"No," Ymiru whispered. As the wind cut at us with icy knives, we waited for him to say more. Then he looked down at his map and told us, "Morjin wanted to open a door to the Dark World where the Baaloch, Angra Mainyu, is imprisoned. And he came close, we believe, so very close."

I could hardly bear Kane's presence just then, so deep and dark was the well of hate that opened inside him.

He knows, I thought. Somehow, he knows.

"And what, do you believe," Kane growled at Ymiru, "kept Morjin from opening this door?"

"Kalkamesh did," Ymiru said. "And Sartan Odinan. When they took the Lightstone out of the dungeon where it was kept, they took away Morjin's greatest chance of freeing the Baaloch."

"How so?" Master Juwain asked.

"Because the Lightstone," Ymiru said, "is attuned to the galastei and all things of power, but especially to the telluric currents. With it, Morjin almost certainly would have been able to see exactly where in the earth beneath Skartaru he must send his slaves to dig."

All this time, even as Atara stared silently into her crystal, Liljana had been nearly as quiet. But now she fingered her blue gelstei and turned to Ymiru. "When I stood beneath Alumit and its colors changed, I thought I heard the voices of the Galadin. Speaking to me, speaking to everyone. There was a warning about Angra Mainyu, I think. A warning told of in a great prophecy."

Now Atara finally looked up from her gleaming sphere as she waited for Ymiru to speak.

"Yes, there be a great, great prophecy," he said. "An old prophecy—ages old. The elders know of this. They have heard Galadin speak of it."

He went on to tell us what the Urdahir had gleaned from the otherworldly voices that poured out of Alumit's singular color. He said that ages ago, when the Star People discovered Ea, their greatest scryer, Midori Hastar, had prophesied two paths for this sparkling new world: either it would give birth to the Cosmic Maitreya who would lead all worlds everywhere to a glorious destiny, or else it would descend into the darkest of worlds and bring forth a dark angel who would free the Baaloch, thus loosing upon the entire universe a great evil and possibly destroying it.

"The Galadin," Ymiru told us, "took a terrible chance in sending the Lightstone to Ea. And the dice they shook six ages ago are tumbling still."

I felt my heart beating in rhythm with Ymiru's and with the deeper pulsing of the earth. My sword gleamed in my hand as the distant stars called to me. I saw in their shimmering lights a grand design that had long awaited completion. Some great event, I sensed, had been coming for untold years, set into motion ages of ages ago with the force of whole worlds tumbling through space. I knew then that I, and my friends, must face Morjin in Argattha. For that, too, was one of the virtues of the silver gelstei, that it let me see the way that my fate was aligned with the much greater fate of the world and the whole universe itself.

"You should have told us," Atara said to Ymiru. "You should have told us before this."

"I'm sorry, I should have. But I didn't want to crush your hrope."

Maram was now drunk on the potent kalvaas—but not quite drunk enough to suit him. He took another swallow of it, belched and sighed out, "Ah, to think we've come this far for nothing."

"What do you mean, little man?"

"Well, surely in light of what you've told us, the risk of entering Argattha is too great. If we should find the Lightstone, and Morjin finds us, then . . . well, I don't like to think about then."

"I can't see that," Atara said, squeezing her white gelstei in her hand. "We've known for many miles that we were taking a great risk."

Master Juwain nodded his lumpy head, agreeing with her. To Maram, and all of us, he said, "The Galadin, in their wisdom, sent the Lightstone to Ea, hoping for the best. So we should hope, too."

"So we should," Liljana added. "It's not upon us to weigh this risk down to the last grain. Only to take it."

Maram took yet another pull of his drink. He looked at me and asked, "Does that mean we are still going to Argattha?"

"Ha!" Kane said, clapping him on the back, "it means just that."

"Does it, Val?" Maram asked me.

"Yes," I said, with my heart pounding wildly, "it does."

With the exception of Ymiru, who insisted on staying awake to take the first watch, we all retired to our furs. But I, at least, could not sleep. Great things had been told that night. Great things we soon must do—and try to keep from being done. Far beneath Skartaru's pointed summit, in the bowels of the earth, Morjin labored long and deep to free the Dark Lord from his prison on the world of Damoom. And now we must labor to find the door into Argattha. What we would find on the other side, I thought, not even the Galadin themselves could know.

■ **11** ■

WE WERE ALL quiet when we set out the next morning. Our breath steamed out into the bitter air, and our boots crunched against the cold, squeaking snow. It was enough, I thought, to avoid tripping and tumbling down some steep slope, enough merely to keep placing one foot ahead of the other and continue plowing through Sakai's frozen wastes. But I couldn't help thinking of Angra Mainyu, this great, fallen Galadin whose dreadful face could darken whole worlds. I knew that somehow, through Morjin, he, too, sensed my defiance and trembled to crush me in his wrath.

And so for two days we worked our way closer to Argattha. Our approach led us through a wild, broken country where we lost the thread of our road. Finally, following Ymiru's map and the lines of the land, we came to a great gorge running for forty miles to either side of us, north and south. It was hundreds of feet wide and very deep: standing at the lip of it, we looked down and saw a little river winding its way past layers of rock far below. Ymiru had hoped to find a bridge here, but it seemed that the only way across the gorge was to fly.

"I can't see any way down it," Atara said, peering over the edge.

Liljana looked up and down the gorge and then at the map, which Ymiru held out before him. She said, "It would be hard work to walk around this. I should think it would add a hundred miles to our journey."

"That's too far," Master Juwain said. "The horses would starve."

As we stood with the horses on the narrow shelf of land above the gorge, I felt Altaru's belly rumbling with hunger— as I did my own. We had run out of oats for the horses and had little enough food for ourselves.

"Perhaps the bridge you seek is farther up the gorge," Liljana said to Ymiru. Then she looked toward the right and said, "Or perhaps that way."

"I had thought the bridge would be right here," Ymiru said. He walked away from us, along the ragged lip of the gorge, looking down at the rocks below for any sign of a fallen bridge. Then he sat down on a rock and bent his head low as he stared down at the ground in silence.

"Seeking," Kane said, "for nonexistent bridges up and down this gorge would be as futile as trying to walk around it."

"Then we will have to turn back," Maram said.

"Turn back?" Kane said to him. "To what?"

After a while, I gave Altaru's reins to Atara, and went over to Ymiru where he sat fifty yards away, now staring down into the gorge as if he were contemplating throwing himself into it.

"I was sure the bridge would be here," he said, not even bothering to look up at me. "Now I've put us in a horrible spot."

"You can't blame yourself," I said, sitting down beside him.

"But, Val, what are we to do?" He pointed at the gorge. "Walk across this on air? You might as well put your hropes into old wives' legends."

Something sparked in me as he said this. And so I asked him, "What legends are these?"

He finally looked up at me and said, "There are stories told that the ancients built invisible bridges. But no one believes them."

"Perhaps you should." I said, gazing at the sun-filled spaces of the gorge. "What else is there to do?"

"Nothing," he said. "There be nothing to do."

"Are you sure?"

He smiled at me sadly and said, "That be what I love about you, Val—you never give up hrope."

"That's because there always is hope."

"In you, perhaps, but not in me."

Inside him, I sensed, was a whole, dark, turbid ocean of self-doubt and despair. But there, too, was the sacred spark: the ineffable flame that could never be quenched so long as life was in life. And in Ymiru this flame burned much brighter than it did in other men. How was it that he, who could feel so much, couldn't feel this?

"Ymiru," I said, grasping his huge hand. It was much warmer than mine, and yet as my heart opened to him, I felt a knifelike heat passing from me into him. "You've led us this far. Now take us the rest of the way toward Argattha, or else the work of your father and all your grandfathers will have been in vain."

His face suddenly lit up as he squeezed my hand almost hard enough to break it. He looked across the gorge and said, "But even if there were such a bridge here, how would I ever find it?"

"Your people are builders," I said to him. "If *you* were to build a bridge across this ditch, where would you put it?"

A fire seemed to flare up inside him then. He gathered up a great handful of stones and leaped to his feet. His hard eyes darted this way and that, measuring distances, assessing the lay of the great, columnar buttresses of rock along the length of the gorge. He began walking along it with great strides and great vigor. Here and there, he paused a moment to hurl a stone far out into the gorge and watch it plunge through the air down towards the river below.

"What is he doing?" Master Juwain asked as Ymiru came up to the place where he and the others waited with the horses.

Ymiru cast another stone arcing out into space, and Maram said, "No doubt he's calculating how long it will take us to fall to the bottom if we're foolish enough to try to climb down this wall. Ah, we're not that foolish, are we, Val?"

At that moment, one of Ymiru's stones made a tinking sound and seemed to bounce up into the air before continuing its fall into the gorge. As Maram watched dumbfounded—along with Kane and the others—Ymiru threw another stone slightly to the right and achieved the same effect. Then he flung all the remaining stones in his hand out into space, and many of them bounced and skittered along what could only be the unseen span of one of the bridges told of in the Ymanir's old wives' tales.

"I suppose I'll have to pay more attention to old wives," Maram said after Ymiru had explained things to him. "Invisible bridges indeed! I suppose it's made of frozen air?"

Ymiru, looking out at the gorge with a happy smile, said, "Our elders have long sought the making of a crystal they called glisse. It be as invisible as air. This bridge, I'm sure, be made of it."

It seemed a miracle that the gorge should be spanned by a crystalline substance no one could see. All that remained was for us to cross over it.

"Perhaps," Master Juwain said to Maram, "you should lead the way."

"I? I? Are you mad, sir?"

"But didn't you tell us, after your little escapade at Duke Rezu's castle, that you're unafraid of heights?"

"Ah, well, I was speaking of the heights of love, not this."

Ymiru stepped forward and laid his hand on Maram's shoulder. He said, "Don't worry, little man. I think you're going to love walking on air."

As we made ready to cross the gorge, we found that the horses would not step close to its edge; surely, I knew, they would balk at setting their hooves down on seemingly empty space. And so in the end, we had to blindfold them. We found some strips of cloth and bound them over their eyes.

"You'd do better to blindfold me," Maram muttered as he fixed the cloth around Iolo. "We're not really going to step out onto this glisse, are we, Val?"

"We are," I said, "unless you first discover a way to fly."

Ymiru, who was the only one of us freed from the burden of leading a horse, borrowed Kane's bow so that he could feel the way ahead of him. He stepped to the very edge of the gorge. Slowly, he brought the tip of the bow down through the air until it touched the invisible bridge. And then, as we all held our breaths, he stepped out into space onto it.

"It be true!" he shouted. "The old tales be true!"

In all my life, I had seen nothing stranger than this great, furry man seeming to stand on air. And now it was our turn to join him there.

And so, as Ymiru led forth, tapping the bow ahead of him like a blind man, we followed him one by one out onto the invisible bridge. With Maram and Iolo right behind him, we kept as straight a line as we could. Our lives depended on this discipline and exactitude. Ymiru discovered that the bridge wasn't very wide: little more than the width of a couple of horses. And it had no rails that we could grasp on to or keep us from slipping over its edge. It was, quite simply, just a huge span of some flawlessly clear crystal that had stood here for perhaps a thousand years.

For the first half of our crossing, we walked up a gradually curving slope. The horses' hooves clopped against the unseen glisse as they might any stone. We tried not to look down at what our boots were touching, for beneath the bridge, straight down hundreds of feet, were many rocks and boulders that had fallen into the gorge and piled up along the river's banks. It was all too easy to imagine our broken bodies dashed upon them. The wind—the icy, merciless wind of the Wailing Way—howled through the gorge and cut at us like some great battle-axe, threatening to drive us over the edge. It set the bridge swaying through space with a sickening motion that recalled the pitching and rolling of Captain Kharald's ship.

"Oh," Maram gasped ahead of me as he clutched his belly with his free hand, "this is too much!"

"Steady!" I called out to him. "We're almost across."

In truth, we were just cresting the highest part of the bridge, with the river directly below us.

"Perhaps," Maram groaned, "I shouldn't have drunk that kalvaas before trying this."

My anger as he said this was an almost palpable thing. It seemed to reach out from me unbidden, like an invisible hand,

and slap him across the face. "But you'll wreck your balance!" I called to him.

"I only had a nip," he called back. "Besides, I thought I needed courage more than coordination."

It seemed, as I watched him stepping daintily behind Ymiru, that he had coordination enough to complete the crossing. He moved quite carefully, with a keen awareness of what lay beneath him. And then, as he grabbed at his churning belly yet again and the wind hit the bridge with a tremendous gust at the same moment, his foot slipped on the glisse as against ice. He lost his balance—as the rest of us nearly did, too. He grabbed at Iolo's reins to steady himself, but just then Alphanderry's spirited horse stamped and whinnied and shook his head. This was enough to further throw Maram off his center. With a great cry and terror in his eyes, his arms and legs flailing like windmills, he began his plunge into space.

He surely would have died if Ymiru hadn't moved very quickly to grab him. I watched in disbelief as Ymiru's great hand shot out and locked on to Maram's hand. For a moment, he held him dangling and kicking in mid-air. Maram, despite what Ymiru liked to call him, was no little man. He must have weighed in at a good eighteen stone. And yet Ymiru hauled him back onto the bridge as easily as he might a sack of potatoes.

"Thank you!" Maram gasped, falling against Ymiru and grabbing on to him. "Thank you, thank you!"

Almost as quickly, Ymiru had moved to grasp Iolo's reins with his other hand and steady him. Now he pressed these leather straps into Maram's hand and told him, "Here, take your hrorse."

Maram did as he was bade, and he stroked Iolo's trembling side to calm him—and himself. Then he gathered up the best of his courage and turned to Ymiru. "Thank you, big man. But I'm afraid we both missed a great chance."

"And what be that?"

"To see if I could really fly."

We completed the rest of the crossing without further incident. When we reached the far side of the gorge, Maram let loose a great shout of triumph and insisted on drinking a little kalvaas to celebrate. My nerves were so frayed that I agreed to this indulgence. Maram smiled, glad to be forgiven his foolishness, and passed me his cup. The disgusting brew was just as greasy and rancid as it always was. But at that moment, with our feet firmly planted on ground that we could see, it tasted almost like nectar.

That was the last great obstacle we faced along the Wailing Way. Five days later, after traversing a good part of the Nagarshath to the south of the headwaters of the Blood River, we came out around the curve of a mountain through some foothills to behold the great, golden grasslands of the Wendrush. To the east of us, as far as the eye could see, was a rolling plain opening out beneath a cloudless blue sky. There antelope gathered in great herds and lions hunted them. There, too, the tribes of the Sarni rode freely over the wind-rippled grass, hunting the antelope—and each other. Many times before, facing west from the kel keeps of Mesh's mountains, I had lost myself in the vast sweeps of this country. And now I wondered what it would be like to ride across it, five hundred miles, toward Vashkel and Urkel and the other mountains I knew so well.

"That way be your hrome," Ymiru said as we gathered on the side of a great hill. Then he turned and pointed to the south of us, where the easternmost mountains of the Nagarshath edged the grasslands. "And that be Skartaru."

The sight of this grim, black mountain struck an icy dread deep into my bones. If Alumit had been made by the Galadin, Skartaru might have been carved by the Baaloch himself. It was a great mound of basalt, cut with sharp ridges and points like the blades of knives. Snow and glaciers froze its upper slopes; sheer walls of rock formed its lower ones. I marveled at Ymiru's feat of navigation, for he had brought us out on the side of a mountain just to the north and east of it. From this vantage, we had a good look at two of its faces. The famed east face was shaped like an almost perfect triangle, save that near its higher reaches, a notch seemed to have been cut from it between its two great peaks. Far beneath the higher and nearer of these—a great pointed horn of black rock three miles high—a road led out of one of Argattha's gates and sliced across the Wendrush. Along this road, I thought, the ancient Valari had been crucified after the Battle of Tarshid, when my people had tried to wrest the Lightstone from Morjin by force of arms. And a thousand feet above the gate, on the east face's sunbaked rock, Morjin had crucified the great Kalkamesh for taking the Lightstone from him.

I stared at this glowing black sheet, and almost unbidden, the ancient words formed upon my lips:

> The lightning flashed, struck stone, burned white—
> The prince looked up into the light;
> Upon Skartaru nailed to stone
> He saw the warrior all alone.

"It doesn't seem possible," I whispered to the wind.

"What doesn't?" Maram asked me. "That Kalkamesh could have survived such torture?"

"Yes, that," I said. "And that Telemesh could have climbed that wall at night and brought Kalkamesh down."

I was not the only one struck with the marvel of this great feat. Liljana and Atara stared at the mountain's east face, while Ymiru pointed his furry finger at it and Master Juwain shook his head. And as for Kane, sometimes I could sense the swell of the passions and hates that streamed inside him. But now there was only a burning, bottomless abyss.

"Skartaru," he growled. "The Black Mountain."

He looked away from its east face and pointed at the darker north one. "There's the Diamond," he said.

A few miles from where we stood, across some grassy buttes where the plains came up against the mountains, we had a good view of the long-sought Skartaru's north face. As shown by Ymiru's map, this was a towering diamond of black rock, at least three miles high, framed on either side by enormous, humped buttresses. We looked between them for the rock formation told of as the Ogre. But either we were too far away or lacked the proper angle for viewing, because we couldn't discern it.

"It be there, I'm sure," Ymiru said. "But we've got to get closer."

So began the final leg of our journey toward Argattha. Rather than risking the exposure of riding straight across the mounded grasslands before us, we kept close to the mountains, hugging their curve through their foothills. This route took us over wooded slopes and around rocky ridges, past the mouth of a small canyon giving out onto the Wendrush's plain. Through the land of our enemies we walked for the rest of the day.

Here, so close to Argattha, every flight of a bird and every sound was a call to grip our weapons more tightly. Atara, who had the best eyes of any of us, kept a tense vigil, watching the ridgelines above us, peering far out on the plains of the Wendrush for signs of the Zayak warriors who had made alliance with Morjin. Kane brought up the rear of our company, and he seemed able to sense danger through every pore of his skin. And yet despite Skartaru's looming presence and the dread that crushed down upon us like immense black boulders from its heights, our luck held good. We reached a little canyon to the north of the mountain without sighting anyone. Here, in this grassy hollow where only a single ridge blocked the way toward Skartaru's north face, we came to the moment that I had been dreading almost more than entering the mountain. For here we decided that we must set the horses free.

"Perhaps one of us should remain with them," Maram said, looking about the canyon.

Actually, it was more of a great bowl scooped out of the side of the mountain to the west, with ridges framing it to the north and south. Some trees carpeted these ridges, but in between was a half mile of good grass.

"Hmmph," Atara said to Maram, "has coming so close to Argattha made you forget the prophecy?"

"I know, I know," he said, "the seven of us must go forth . . . to where we must go. But what will happen to the horses? And what will happen to us should our quest prove a success and we return to find the horses gone?"

He suggested that we should perhaps hobble the horses or even picket them so that they remained in the valley.

"No, there are wolves and lions about," I said, looking down into the plain. "If we tie the horses, they'd be unable to run or defend themselves. And if we don't return . . ."

Maram watched my face for sign of despair, and then asked, "But what are we to do?"

I moved quickly to ungird Altaru's saddle and remove his harness. When he was free of these encumbrances and naked as an animal should be, I faced him stroking his neck and looking into his eyes. In these large brown orbs was something deep and ancient that brought a mist to mine. I stood there breathing my love for him into his nostrils, while he gave voice to the covenant of friendship that had always been between us.

"Stay with the other horses," I told him as he nickered softly. "Don't let them leave this valley—do you understand?"

He nickered again, this time louder, and I was seized with a strange sense that somehow he did understand.

It took Atara and the others only a few moments to loose their horses, too. We hid the saddles and tack in some bushes beneath the nearby trees. After taking up our weapons and some supplies, we turned to leave the horses grazing on the canyon's brown grass.

We might have done well to wait for night and approach Skartaru under the cover of darkness. But we needed to find the Ogre and the cave leading into Argattha, and for this we needed light. And so in the day's last hours, we crossed the ridge to the south and then made our way across the narrow canyon cutting beneath the mountain's north face. Now Skartaru loomed so huge above us that it blocked the sun and most of the sky. Its black rock seemed the whole of the world; looking at this stark and terrible face, I could almost feel Kalkamesh's blood running down its jags and cracks, even as the cries of those still trapped inside the underground city sounded from inside it.

We walked almost straight up a rocky slope toward the base of the Diamond. We expected to be caught at any moment. But except for a few deer keeping a watch for lions, the valley seemed empty of anyone except us.

"Look!" Ymiru said in a low voice that broke into the air like thunder. He pointed at a great hump of rock five hundred feet high swelling out the Diamond's dark wall. "Does that look like an Ogre to anyone?"

"Almost," Liljana said. "But it's hard to tell from this vantage."

We changed the course of our hike slightly toward the west. After a couple of hundred yards, we came to the very bottom of the Diamond's lower point, in a hollow pressed between the north face's two immense buttresses. And there, jutting out of this dread face, the hump of rock did indeed look like an ogre kneeling down on one knee.

We rushed up to this knoblike prominence, looking for the cave told of in Ymiru's verse. But no cave, to either side of it, could we find. The black rock of the Diamond was scarred with many cracks, but otherwise unmarked.

"But it must be here!" Ymiru said, pounding the rock with his great fist.

Maram leaned back against what must have been the Ogre's knee and sighed, "Well, who's ready to try one of Argattha's gates?"

Liljana fixed her gaze upon the mountain's rock; then she spoke to both of them, saying, "Don't you give up so soon. Don't you remember the verse's last two lines?"

Even as she said this, Atara, standing back from the wall, descried a vein of red running through the black rock. Now we all stood back as she pointed at it. It was surely iron ore, I thought, and it ran in jagged bands that pointed like an arrow straight toward the base of the wall just to the right of the Ogre's knee.

"But there be no cave there!" Ymiru said. "There be nothing but rock."

"Only rock," Kane muttered. Then he stepped back toward the wall and began moving his hands over it. "And smooth rock at that, eh? Ymiru, come look at this! Tell me if you've ever seen a mountain's rock so smooth."

Ymiru joined him there, as did the rest of us. Then Ymiru said, "It looks like the rock that the ancients cut through the passes of the Wailing Way."

"So, cut with firestones," Kane said. "Melted out of the mountains—as this mountain has been melted down over the cave."

He told us then that Morjin, perhaps after making other escape tunnels from Argattha, must have sealed off this one.

"But why?" Maram asked. "Just to confound us, no doubt."

"Who knows why?" Kane said, rapping his knuckles against the wall. "Maybe too many knew about this. But I'd wager our lives that we'll find the cave behind this rock."

We all looked at each other in the grim certainty that we were wagering our lives here. And then Ymiru, after first casting quick glances up and down the valley, began tapping his borkor at various points along the wall. When he reached the place beneath the bands of iron ore, the reverberations from the rock sounded slightly hollow.

"There be something behind here," he said.

Now he raised his iron-shod club straight back and struck the wall a tremendous blow. The rock rang as if hammered by a god. Chips of black basalt sprayed out into the air. But if Ymiru had hoped to break through to the hidden cave, he failed.

Thrice more he wielded his club, before turning to Kane and saying, "The rock be too thick. And I haven't the right tools to mine into it."

"No, you don't," Kane said. Then he looked at Maram. "But he does."

Maram drew forth his firestone and stood looking up at the sky. "There's not much light here, and I've never burned rock like this, but . . ."

He pointed his red crystal at the wall and told us, "Stand back now!"

We did as he bade us. A moment later, a wisp of flame flickered out from his crystal and licked the wall. But it scarcely heated up the rock there.

"It's too dark here," Maram muttered. "There's too little light."

And Kane told him, "I think it's not only light that fires your stone."

Maram nodded his head and closed his eyes as he searched inside himself. And then, as his gelstei began glowing bright red, he looked straight at the wall, concentrating on the exact spot that he wished to open. At that moment, a great bolt of lightning shot from his crystal and burned into the rock, which vaporized in a tremendous blast. Fire flew back into Maram's face, scorching it lobster-red and singeing his beard and eyebrows. Lava ran down from the wall in thick, glowing streams. Maram had to be careful that it didn't engulf his feet and melt away his flesh into a hellishly hot soup.

"Be careful with that stone or you'll kill us all!" Kane shouted at him. He looked at the shallow hole that Maram had melted in the rock. "Here, now! Here, now!"

He took out his black gelstei and held it facing Maram's firestone. He nodded at him and said, "All right."

For the next half-hour, he and Maram worked together to open the way into the mountain. At times, when the red crystal flared too brightly and great sheets of flame fell out against the rock, Kane used his black gelstei to damp the fury of the firestone. At other times he had to desist altogether, for all Maram's efforts sufficed only in coaxing from his stone a dull red glow. Little by little, however, Maram melted away layers of rock and cut deeper into the face of Skartaru.

All this time, Atara and I had been keeping watch. Now she nudged me gently and pointed down the valley out toward the plain. "Val, look!"

I squinted and strained my eyes to see some twenty men on horses riding straight toward the canyon.

"Do you think they saw us?" Liljana asked Atara, looking toward the riders, too.

"They saw something. Probably the flashes of the firestone."

Ymiru approached the hole that Maram had made in the wall, and rammed his club against the still-glowing rock there. But he failed to break through. He said, "It still be too thick."

"Get down!" I said to him, waving my hand toward the ground. The men were approaching the mouth of the canyon. "Get down, Ymiru—they mustn't see you!"

I pointed at a nearby rock formation to our left and told him to hide behind it. Then I nodded at some trees to our right, and told Liljana, Master Juwain and Atara to wait there.

"So, Val," Kane said, looking down the canyon. "So."

"Oh, no!" Maram said, hurrying down from the scorched wall over to where I stood. "Val—shouldn't we flee?"

"No, they might already have seen us," I said. "They would catch us wherever we ran. Or give the alarm."

"But what are we to do, then?"

I smiled at him and said, "Bluff it out."

And so, there beneath Skartaru's dark face, with the Ogre's grim, black eyes staring down at us, we waited as the twenty riders drew closer. Maram, who was clever enough at need, busied himself gathering wood as if for a fire. Kane sat back against a rock and began whittling a long pole with his knife. And I gathered some round stones and set them in a circle as for a firepit.

Soon we saw that the riders were wearing the livery of Morjin: their surcoats showed blazing red dragons against a bright yellow field. They had sabers girded at their sides and bore long lances pointing at us. At a quick pace, they urged their snorting mounts up the rocky slope straight toward the place where we sat.

"Who are you?" their leader called out to us. He was a thickset man with long yellow hair that spilled out from beneath his iron helm. His drooping mustaches couldn't hide the scars cut into his long, truculent face. "Stand up and identify yourselves!"

After grabbing up a stone in either hand, I did as he bade us, and so did Maram and Kane. We gave the scowling captain names and stories that we had made up on the spot. He glowered at us as if he didn't like our look and said, "Three more vagabonds come to sell their swords to the highest bidder. Well, you've come to the right place—show us your passes!"

"Passes?" Maram asked him.

"Of course—you're in Sakai now. How did you come this far without being given a pass?"

Now he gripped his lance more tightly as he looked at us

suspiciously. He told us that no one was permitted to move about Sakai without the proper scroll signed by an officer of the border guard—or without one of the seals of the kingdom which the Red Priests bestowed upon the especially privileged.

So saying, he touched the heavy gold disk that hung on a chain from his neck. It was hard to tell across a distance of twenty feet, but it seemed embossed with a coiled, firebreathing dragon.

"Oh, that," Maram said with a nonchalance that I knew he didn't feel. "We didn't know you called them passes."

And with that he opened his cloak to show the captain the gift that King Kiritan had given him. I did the same, and so did Kane.

Our medallions, cast with the Cup of Heaven at their centers, gleamed in day's last light. For a moment, I thought that this mistrustful captain might let us go. And then, as he spurred his horse forward, he called out, "Let me see those!"

We waited for him and three of his men to come closer, and then Kane growled out, "I'll let you see this!"

And with that, he cast the pole that he had been whittling straight through the captain's eye, killing him instantly. I hurled the two stones in my hands at two of the knights bearing down on us, and managed to strike one of them full in his face, knocking him off his horse. And then, at the call of one of the captain's lieutenants, the remaining knights whipped up their horses and thundered down upon us, and the battle began.

The knights clearly intended to make quick work of us. Their lieutenant, a young man with a dark, vulpine look that reminded me of Count Ulanu, pointed his sword at us and said, "Take them alive! Lord Morjin will want to question them!"

But it was not so easy for anyone to take Kane this way—or to kill him. With a lightning-quick motion, he reached back the hand holding his knife and whipped it forward. The knife spun through space, and its sharp point tore straight into the lieutenant's mouth, which he hadn't had time to close. At the same moment, from the right, an arrow hissed out from behind a tree as Atara found her mark and killed another of Morjin's men. Three more arrows followed in a quick, sizzling succession before the knights even realized that a hidden archer was firing upon them.

And then, from the left, with a great, thundering war cry that shook even me to my bones, Ymiru arose from behind his rock. His face contorted with a ferocious look as he raised his huge club above his head.

"The Yamanish!" a knight cried. "The Yamanish are upon us!"

Ymiru stood as high as the knights upon their horses; with four quick, savage blows, he knocked four of them off them. None got up.

And then the remaining nine knights, who had given up all thought of capturing us, fell upon Kane, Maram, and me. They tried to kill us with their lances and maces. And we tried to kill them. Kane drew his sword; I drew Alkaladur and cut one of the knights off his mount. Ymiru swung his club against the side of a knight's neck, and struck his head clean off. Blood sprayed the air as more arrows hissed out. Horses flailed their hooves against the earth, reared and screamed. I heard Maram call out the name of his father as he met a flashing saber with his sword and then managed a clean thrust through the belly of one of the knights—just in time to keep him from skewering me with his lance. And Kane, as always, fought like an angel of death in the thickest part of the battle, growling as horses knocked against him, grabbing their bits and tearing them from their mouths, parrying the blows of the knights, cutting and thrusting and snarling out his hate.

And then, miraculously, it was over. The agony of the men I had killed came flooding into me as I stared at the bodies of the nineteen dead knights and fought to keep myself from falling down and joining them.

"Look!" Ymiru called out. "One of them is getting away!"

Indeed, one of the knights, in the blood of the battle, had turned his horse around and was now galloping straight toward the mouth of the canyon.

Atara came out from behind her tree then to get a better angle upon him. She pulled back the string of her great bow, sighting one of her diamond-tipped arrows on the red dragon of the surcoat covering the knight's back. It was a long shot that she trembled to make—made even longer with every second that she hesitated loosing her arrow.

"Shoot, damn it!" Kane shouted. "Shoot now, I say, or all is lost!"

Atara finally let fly the arrow. It split the air in an invisible whining and drove straight through the knight's surcoat and armor, burying itself in his back. He remained in his saddle for only a few strides of his bounding horse before plunging off to crash against the rocky ground.

Now Kane went about the mountain's slope with his sword, making sure that none of Morjin's men remained alive. And then Master Juwain noticed that some of the blood dripping from his white hair was not the enemy's but his own. It seemed that one of the knights had sliced off his ear.

"Oh, Lord!" Maram said.

None of us had ever seen Kane wounded. But as always, he made no complaint, not even when Maram set a brand afire and Master Juwain used it to cauterize the bloody hole at the side of his head.

"That was close," he said as Master Juwain fixed a bandage over what remained of his ear. "The closest yet, eh?"

All the rest of us were untouched. But I was still shaking from the deaths I had meted out, and Maram stood staring at his bloody sword, not quite daring to believe that he had used it to kill two armored knights.

"You did well, Maram," Kane said to him. "Very well. Now let's get back to work before anyone else comes, eh?"

Maram cleaned his sword and sheathed it. He took out his red crystal. But he was not quite ready to use it. He walked off a way, up a slight rise, and stood staring down at the carnage that we had made.

After a while, after the shooting pains were gone from my chest and I could breathe again, I went over to him and said, "You did do well, you know. You saved my life."

"I did, didn't I?" he said as he smiled brightly. And then the horror returned to his face as his eyes fell upon the bodies of the slain. "Kane was right, I think. That was the closest yet."

He turned to look at the dark hole that he had burned in Skartaru's dark north face. "And yet I think that perhaps worse awaits us inside there."

"Perhaps," I said.

"Perhaps it's the end of the road, for all of us."

"Don't worry," I said to him, grasping his hand. "I won't let you die."

"Ah, death," he said, smiling sadly. "I must die someday. It seems strange, but I know it's true."

I squeezed his hand harder, trying not to think of the lines of the poem that had haunted me ever since I had killed Raldu in the forest beneath my father's castle.

"And when I do die, Val," he said, "if I could choose, I'd rather have it come fighting beside you."

"Maram, listen to me, you mustn't speak—"

"No, I must speak of this, now, because I might not have another chance," he told me. Then he looked straight into my eyes. "Ever since we set out from Mesh, you've shown me a realm I never dreamed. I . . . I was born the prince of a great kingdom. But it's you who have made me noble."

He clasped me to him then and hugged me as hard as he could. And then, as he dried his eyes and I did mine, he took a step back and said, "Now let's finish this nasty business and get out of here, if we can."

There was a man whom Maram wished to be. That man now gathered up all of his bravura and stood up straight and tall. Then he gripped his red crystal and marched up to Skartaru's darkening face without hesitation.

As before, with Kane's help, he used his firestone to melt the mountain's black rock. He stood there, by the base of the Ogre's knee, for most of an hour, working flame against the wall. At last, in the failing light, he broke through to the hidden cave spoken of in the ancient verse. And then he smiled proudly to show us that the door to Argattha had been opened.

For a long moment I stared into this black, glowing gash in the earth. Screams rang out from somewhere deep inside it—or perhaps I was only hearing the long, dark roar of my soul. I could not bear to see Atara or my other friends go down into this hellish hole. An overwhelming urge to turn about and run away as quickly as I could seized my whole body and being. But Maram had spoken to me of nobility; how could I just slink away like a frightened beast? And so I drew in a deep breath of air, and clasped my hand around the hilt of my sword. And then I led the way down into the darkness.

12

WE SPENT SOME time in gathering up the knights' horses and divesting them of their saddles and tack, which we piled up inside the cave. We dragged the dead knights inside, as well, and covered them with stones; it wouldn't do for the vultures or other animals to find them and so alert another patrol as to what had happened here. After driving off the horses, out toward the Wendrush, we made our final preparations for entering Argattha. Ymiru unpacked some torches, which he had anticipated needing as far back as Alundil. He also brought out and donned his disguise for making his way through the city: a great, black, cowled robe that covered him from head to foot. A veil, built into the cowl, hid his face, while he had a huge pair of boots and black gloves to pull on over his furry feet and hands. Thus did the very tall Saryaks of Uskudar dress.

"And if we are stopped," Kane said, holding up one of the knights' medallions, "we must hope that these will win our way through."

At his bidding, we each put on a medallion and hid away our own. And so we would go forth into the city, dressed in our mail and tattered tunics, looking for all the world like vagabonds come to sell our swords, as the knights' captain had suggested.

Our final preparations having been completed, Ymiru heaved a few great boulders over the cut into the mountain that Maram had made so that any passersby would not notice it. Then, sealed inside the cave with the bodies of the men we had slain and praying that we would return back through this mausoleum before they began to rot, we lit the torches. Their acrid smoke filled the black cavity around us. Their flickering yellow flames gave enough light to show the cave's curving roof and black walls—and the tunnel at its far end: black and rectangular and opening like a gate into hell.

Holding a torch in one hand and my father's shield in my other, I led forth into it. Ymiru had told us all that he knew about this secret passage: that it wound its way beneath Argattha's first level, long since abandoned by Morjin and the city's other denizens. Ymiru thought that the tunnel might give out in the old throne room or onto stairs leading to it. And from there we could make our way up to the second level where people lived, and so up to the higher levels until we came to Morjin's new throne room on the seventh and highest level of the city.

In the dark tunnel, it was cold and close. Although it had been cut high enough for Ymiru to walk without stooping— barely—it was so narrow that we had to walk in single file. I moved forward slowly, not knowing what my torch would show in the curving, black passage ahead of me. Its walls, of greasy-looking basalt, seemed to press upon me from either side and crush the breath from my chest. The air was stale and smelled bad, having pocketed here for perhaps a thousand years. In its cloying moistness were the scents of decay, suffering, and death.

Ymiru walked behind me, awkward in his new boots. Maram kept close to him, followed by Master Juwain, Liljana, Atara, and finally Kane. Their dread of this dark place was like a scent of its own that I could no more avoid than the torches' oily smoke. I smelled Maram's nervous sweat and the rancidness of the kalvaas in his mustache and beard. Atara was fighting hard to keep her spirit from being crushed away in the chilling gloom. And I sensed some dark thing eating at Kane's insides, which dwelled even deeper than his hate.

We marched on into the gloom, stepping over broken boulders and the occasional crack through the tunnel's floor. The rock here, I thought, seemed to hold shrieks and screams ages old. Moisture clung to the tunnel's walls as if blood had been sweated and tortured from them. The slick floor ran with a trickle of water and other liquids that must have seeped down from the levels of the city above us. In places it pooled inches deep: a foul-smelling effluvia of metallic sludges, rotting garbage and human waste. As Ymiru slogged along, he admitted that he was very glad for his boots—as were we all.

We came to a place where the tunnel divided. Each fork, the right and the left, looked equally ominous. I turned to Ymiru and asked, "Do both these lead to the old throne room?"

"I don't know," he told me, shaking his head. He patted the pack on his back, where he had stowed his father's map. "I wish the living clay showed earth forms so small as these."

I called for Atara to come up, and Ymiru pressed himself flat against the tunnel's wall to allow her room to squeeze by. She stood next to me at the fork in the tunnel, looking right and looking left.

I asked her, "Which way, Atara?"

She brought out her scryer's crystal and held it before her. And then without hesitation, she said, "Right."

We resumed our journey through the dark, and after a few minutes of slogging along, I nearly tripped into a black chasm running across the tunnel's rock. As the chasm was some yards across, I needed a running jump to clear it, as did Ymiru and Maram. And Master Juwain needed more than this. When it came his turn to make the leap, he fell short, and only Maram, grabbing on to his arm, kept him from falling back into the blackness.

"Thank you," Master Juwain gasped out. He stood with Maram at the chasm's edge, not daring to look back at it.

"You're welcome," Maram said. Then he smiled as if re-membering how Ymiru had saved him. "Don't worry—I wouldn't let you die."

When the others had each crossed the chasm and we stood safely on the other side, we set out again. We walked as quietly as we could though the stifling darkness. We came to other branchings in the tunnel and other cracks through it—one so wide that it had been spanned by a narrow stone bridge. This arch seemed so worn and old that I feared it might crumble at the first footfall. After we had all crossed over it, Maram stood holding his hand out as if to feel the air.

"It's warm," he said. "Ah, it's almost hot."

I crowded close to him, letting this upwelling of hot air blow across my face. In its searing jets, I thought I heard the sound of beating iron, cracking whips and men crying out in pain.

"What lies beneath here?" I asked Ymiru.

"Only the mines, I think."

"And how many levels are there to these?"

"To the mines there be no levels," he said. He told us that the mines beneath Argattha had been tunneled like the twist-ings of a man's bowels, leading far down into the earth.

"But how far, then?"

"I don't know, Val," he said. "There be seven levels to the city, and each them five hundred feet thick. It be said that the mines ran twice as deep as all the levels were high, together. And that was more than two thousand years ago."

How far, I wondered? How far had Morjin come toward finding the dark currents in the earth that he sought and free-ing the Lord of Death known as Angra Mainyu?

I led off again, holding high the blazing torch. Soon the foul smell began to work at me and burn like a poison in my blood; the distant drip of water beat at my head like a relent-less hammer. Although my torch gave little enough light, it was enough to warn away the rats that jumped out of the dark-ness in their panic to flee from us. Some of these were nearly as big as cats; their glowing red eyes were like hot coals as they scurried along with their claws scraping against rock.

The tunnel wound mostly toward the south, across more chasms, into the middle of the mountain. After about a mile, we came to another forking where the tunnel curved off toward the right and the left as if cut along the lines of a circle. I was reluctant to go forward in either direction. Even Atara, when she came forward, seemed unable to decide which way to go.

"I don't know," she said to me, shaking her head. "You choose."

"Very well, then," I said. "We'll go right."

And so we did. But after a hundred yards, we came to another node. Again, I led toward the right and we moved off, circling that way.

So it went, the nodes coming one after another, the tunnel turning sharply west and then north, and then curving back south again. Thrice we came to dead ends and had to retrace our steps. Soon it became apparent that we had entered a labyrinth—and that we were lost within it.

"This is too much," Maram said as we gathered in the space of one of the nodes. A hungry rat lunged at him, trying to bite a chunk out of his leg. He kicked it squealing away from him and muttered, "This is like hell."

Liljana, who was having a hard time breathing in the fetid air, turned to Ymiru and said, "You didn't tell us we'd find a labyrinth here."

"I didn't know," Ymiru said. "Morjin must have had it built to confound assassins or anyone pursuing him out of the city."

Kane, who had tired of standing still, shook his torch at the corridor off to the left and said, "Let's walk then, eh? What else is there to do?"

And so we walked, as he had said. For a long time we made our way through the labyrinth's curves, which ate through the bare rock like dark, twisting worms. After a while we grew very tired. Liljana's torch, its oil all burned, was the first to sputter out. Then, as we sucked in the greasy, stifling air, over the next half-hour, the other torches flickered out one by one; after a while, only a single torch remained afire. I took it to lead the way while Ymiru and the others followed this sickly yellow light.

At last we came to a large, circular chamber at what I guessed to be the labyrinth's very center. There our last torch died, and much of our hope with it as we huddled together in the utter blackness.

"Ah, this is the end," Maram muttered, "surely the end."

I reached out through the gloom and grasped his hand. Through his cold skin, I felt him shuddering.

And then, at last, I drew my sword. It glowed with a soft, silver light. It was not enough to fill the chamber and illumine its dark walls, but it brightened our spirits all the same.

When I pointed my sword upward, its sheen deepened, slightly. It was strange to think that the Lightstone might be so close, somewhere above us through half a mile of rock in Morjin's throne room. Morjin, I thought, was near there, too. I could almost feel our hearts beating with the same poisoned blood and sense his mind seeking mine. This connection that he had made between us with a bit of kirax suddenly darkened my soul. For a single moment, I allowed my dread of him to take hold of me and split me open. And through this dark crack in my being, beasts and demons came for me.

"What!" I called out.

Black, birdlike things with razor talons and the faces of those I had slain fell at me out of the air. I cut at them with my sword, and its touch caused them to burst into flame and scream so pitifully that I thought I was screaming myself. And then a huge shape lunged through the chamber's doorway. It had great, golden eyes, scales as red as rust and hooked claws that sought to tear me apart. Through its slashing white teeth, it breathed fire at me, as the dragons of old were said to do. I swung my sword against its writhing neck, and watched in horror as my bright blade shattered into a hundred glittering shards. And then the fire caught me up in its incredible heat and began burning through my mail, melting the steel into a glowing lava that ate into my heart, burning and burning and . . .

"Val!" someone called to me.

A sudden shimmering radiance poured out into the chamber. It was Flick, I saw, spinning about in swirls of silver and iridescent blue. Once again, he had returned to us. And beneath his reassuring form, Master Juwain stood in front of me with his varistei pointing at my chest. It flared a deep and bright green. I felt its healing touch, like cool waters, quench the evil fire inside me. And then my mind cleared as I slowly shook my head.

Kane, his sword drawn, stood next to him looking at me intently. I remembered that in my madness, I had swung my sword at him—and at my other friends. Only Kane's great skill in parrying my wild slashes, it seemed, had saved them from being hacked in half.

"Val, what happened?" Master Juwain asked me.

"That . . . is hard to say, sir." I looked at Alkaladur's bright blade. "When my sword first flared, there was a moment of hope. And I saw it leading us to the Lightstone. But there the Red Dragon waited, too—always watching and waiting. And my hope turned into despair."

Master Juwain nodded his head gravely and said, "There is a great danger for you here—and for all of us. Danger beyond death or even capture and torment. This turning that you have told of: it seems that the Lord of Lies has a great talent for poisoning even the strongest of trees and twisting good into evil."

He went on to ask me if I had been practicing the exercises he had taught me, particularly the light meditations.

"Yes, sir, all the time," I said. "And my sword has helped me. The silustria has. It has shielded me all through the Nagarshath. And so I began to think that the battle against the Dragon's lies had been won."

"That battle can never be won," Master Juwain told me. "And it is lost most surely the moment we think that it is won."

Kane tapped his sword against mine, and its steel rang throughout the semi-lit chamber. "There are battles to be fought, but not with each other, eh? Are you ready to lead us out of here, Val?"

His deep eyes searched in mine for faith, and Master Juwain and the others looked at me in this way, too. And suddenly I knew that there was a way out. In my connection to the dark corridors of Morjin's mind, I became aware of a twisted logic that ordered its turnings. It was the logic of his life and all the works of his hand, this labyrinth among them. For hours upon hours, I had wandered through part of it. Its curved passages and nodes were recorded inside me as if my blood were a liquid, living clay. And now, as I gazed at the bright, silver crystal of my sword and my mind opened, in a flash of light, I saw the whole of the labyrinth from this chamber at its very center.

"Come," I said, leading forth toward the doorway. "We've only a little farther to go."

We lined up as before, with Ymiru just behind me. He shuffled along the winding corridors, keeping his eyes fixed on my glowing sword. He and Liljana were unable to see Flick and thus were blind to this strange being's dancing lights. But the others perceived him well enough, and marveled that he had now fallen into a steady, flaming spiral just above my head. His presence gave them strength to move with more hope through the turnings of the labyrinth.

At last, after circling east and north and then abruptly reversing our direction through a black tube of rock, we came to a break in the curving wall that opened upon a new passage. As this led straight toward the south, I knew that we had finally found our way out of the labyrinth's south end.

"Are you sure this way be south?" Ymiru asked me. "I admit I've been turned around for quite a while."

"Val has a sense of direction," Maram said from behind him. "He never gets turned around."

Not never, I thought, remembering the disappearing moon of the Black Bog. But now, it seemed, I had led us true. For after a hundred yards, the tunnel suddenly gave out onto a set of stairs.

"Saved!" Maram cried out. "These must lead up to the first level!"

"Quiet now!" Kane hissed at him. "We don't know what we'll find there!"

The stairs wound up through the rock, spiraling left, like those in my father's castle. Ymiru had said that the distance between the levels of Argattha was five hundred feet. But Morjin had built his escape tunnel just beneath the first level, it seemed, and so we did not have to climb nearly so far. After a few minutes, the stairs gave out onto a short corridor that led through an open doorway into a huge hall.

"The old throne room," Ymiru murmured out to me.

I remembered him telling us how Morjin had come to Argattha near the end of the Age of Law to find a whole underground city prepared for his rule. After two hundred years, however, he had finally moved into a sort of palace hollowed out of Argattha's uppermost level. There, in the new throne room, in the year 82 of the Age of the Dragon, if Master Aluino's journal proved true, as we prayed, Sartan Odinan had dropped the Lightstone. Just as we also prayed that the old throne room really had been deserted.

I was the first to step into it, and I saw at once that it was dimly lit by the few ancient glowstones still set into its steeply rising walls. Great columns of rock, many now broken into cracked wheels of basalt, supported the curving ceiling three hundred feet above us. The sheer vastness of this place, carved from the heart of the mountain, struck me with awe. There was terror there, too—and not only mine. For just as Ymiru and the others joined me a few feet beyond the doorway, I saw that we were not alone. At the south end of the hall, off to the left, a small, ragged figure was struggling mightily against the chain and shackle locked around his ankle.

"Look!" Atara said to me. "It's a child."

I started straight for him, but Kane suddenly laid his hand on my shoulder and said, "Be careful—this might be a trap!"

The child, if that he really was, saw us almost immediately. And now he lunged against his chain as his eyes leaped with terror.

"It's all right," I whispered, "we won't hurt you!"

Again, I started across the rubble-strewn floor, fighting the child's scent of fear and the overpowering foulness of the air.

This stank of cinnamon and sweat, of burning pitch and heated rock and evil as old as the mountain itself.

"Who are you?" I said to him, crossing the distance between us cautiously. "Who chained you here?"

I saw that he was indeed a child, a boy, about nine years old. Greasy rags barely covered his skinny body. His hair was black and hung about his dirty face in tangles. He had the dark skin and almond eyes of the Sung and some Hesperuks—and yet he clearly belonged to Morjin. For upon his forehead was tattooed the sign of his slavery: a red dragon coiled as if burned deep into his flesh.

"Look!" Kane said to me as he came running up to my side. He pointed at the far end of the room toward the north. There, between two great pillars, stood a pyramid of human skulls perhaps twenty feet high. Their curving bones and empty eye hollows gleamed a ghastly yellow in the glowstones' dim light.

"Oh, I don't like this place!" Maram said. "Let's get out of here."

He looked toward a great, open portal along the west wall opposite the stairs by which we had entered the hall. The doors of both of these openings had long since been torn off their hinges. What use, I wondered, did Morjin now make of this foul chamber? A dungeon for the torture and execution of his enemies? But how could a child be anyone's enemy, even Morjin's?

"What is your name?" I said to the terrified boy, laying my hand on his head. "Where is your mother? Your father?"

He jumped at my touch. He knocked my hand away and looked frantically toward the portal, where once a great iron gate had been.

"He's coming!" he said to me in a sweet voice made bitter by bondage.

"Who is coming?" I asked him.

I looked down at the boy's bare leg. So hard had he lunged against the shackle there that its iron had torn him bloody. There were bite marks about the ankle, as well. I did not want to admit what I knew to be true: that this poor boy, like a trapped animal, had tried to gnaw off his own leg.

"Who is it?" I asked him again.

He looked at me as if trying to decide who I might be. And then, as deep courage pushed away some of his fear, he said, "It's the Dragon."

"Morjin, here?" Kane snarled, shaking his sword at the air.

The boy pulled to the limit of the chain attached to a bolt in the floor. He fell to his knee and crunched down upon some bones there. All about him, I saw, were piles of rat skulls and their skeletons. His torn tunic was stained with the guts and gore of rats, which it seemed he had eaten.

"It's the Dragon," the boy said again. "Can't you hear him?"

The vast hall rumbled with distant sounds of the other parts of the city. Water trickled and iron beat against stone; the stone itself seemed to beat like a great, black heart with rhythms as old as time.

"Listen, Rat Boy," Maram said, coming up close to him. "You've been here too long and must be hearing things that aren't—"

"No, it's the Dragon! We've got to get out of here!"

Now he stretched out his thin hand as if beckoning toward the rat leavings littered across the floor. And there, among these gnawed white bones, just beyond his reach, lay a black, iron key.

"Every abomination," Kane muttered as I bent to pick up the key. "Every degradation of the spirit."

I turned to see if the key would indeed fit the locked shackle. As I bent low, Atara stroked the boy's trembling head and asked him, "Was it the Dragon who locked you here?"

"No, it was Morjin. Lord Morjin."

"And you think he's coming back here?"

"No! I told you—it's the Dragon who's coming!"

Now Liljana and Master Juwain both drew out their gelstei. Liljana was fingering her blue whale, clearly contemplating entering the boy's mind to see where it had cracked. And Master Juwain wanted only to heal him of his delusions and terror.

I pushed the key through the hole in the lock. It slipped in with a loud click. The boy's heart was now beating even more rapidly than my own: doom, doom, doom.

"Quick!" the boy said to me. "We've got to run!"

Now the smells of cinnamon and burning pitch suddenly grew overpowering as a blast of hot air blew into the room. From the dark corridor beyond the hall's open portal came a loud, rhythmic, thumping sound.

"Quick, Val!" Maram said. "Back to the stairs! Something is coming."

I turned the key, screeching metal against metal, right and then left. I jiggled it in the lock as the boy pulled with all his might against the chain. The sweaty cinnamon smell grew much stronger. And now the thunder of shaken stone filled the hall.

The shackle's lock suddenly snapped open just as Atara sighted an arrow on the opening of the portal. And then there, in that dark, huge rectangular space, a great shape appeared. It stood fifteen feet high and was perhaps thrice that long. Scales, red like rusted iron, covered the whole length of its long, sinuous body nearly down to the knotted tip of its tail. At the end of its great hind legs, claws as sharp as steel cut grooves into the rock of the floor. Its leathery wings were folded back along its sides like a cat's ears before a battle. Its great, golden eyes fixed on the boy with a malign intelligence. As I pulled the shackle from his leg, they fixed on me.

"Oh, no!" Maram said, fumbling for his firestone. "It can't be!"

But it was, as the boy had tried to tell us, a dragon—and a female at that. And she was clearly angry that we had just robbed her of her feast.

"Liljana! Master Juwain!" I shouted. "Take the boy back to the stairs!"

Liljana grabbed the boy's hand and started running toward the stairs with Master Juwain close behind him. And then, just as the dragon sprang forward, Atara loosed her arrow at one of the dragon's eyes. But the dragon turned her head just in time so that the arrow glanced off her hard scales.

Her great jaws now opened to show sharp white teeth as long as knives. I sensed that the dragon longed to charge Atara and bite her in two. And so I stepped forward, pointing my sword at the dragon as I raised up my shield. It was good for me that I still had my father's shield.

"Val, the fire!" Maram called to me. I thought, for a moment, that he must be speaking of his gelstei. "The fire, beware!"

Suddenly, as the dragon seemed to quiver and cough, all at once, a great breath of flame shot from her mouth. It fell in an orange stream against my shield. Some of the flame spilled over my shield's rim and scorched my face. I rushed forward then to strike the dragon dead before she could draw breath and summon her fire again.

As did Ymiru and Kane. Kane closed in toward the dragon's side and thrust his sword at the dragon's belly. It struck sparks against the scales there, and glanced off her, as did the second arrow that Atara fired at the dragon's eyes. Ymiru had greater success swinging his borkor at the dragon's still-open mouth. With tremendous force, it cracked into the jaw, breaking off two huge teeth and shaking the dragon to her bones. But then the dragon used her great, knotty head like a club of her own, swinging it sideways into Ymiru's chest, cracking ribs and knocking him off his feet. Her tail suddenly lashed out at Kane; if he hadn't been quick to duck beneath its terrible sweep, the mace-like spikes at the tip would have taken off his head.

The dragon having been distracted, I worked in close to her huge, heaving body. I thrust my sword straight at her chest. But Alkaladur's gleaming silustria, which had split open even plate armor, failed to pierce the dragon deeply. It drove between two of the thick scales to a distance of perhaps an inch. It was enough only to wound the dragon—as a bloodbird might peck at me.

"Val, she's too strong!" Atara called to me. "Back to the stairs!"

Maram wasted no time in heeding her call to retreat. Gripping his gelstei, which had failed to produce the slightest spark, he turned to run back toward the narrow opening to the east. While Kane helped Ymiru regain his feet, I stood before them, covering them with my shield. The dragon, dripping blood from her battered mouth, regarded Ymiru with wariness and hate. Then she suddenly opened her jaws again to burn us.

This time I saw that her breath was not really of fire. Rather, as she coughed and heaved, she spit out a stream of a reddish and jellylike substance. Upon touching the air, it burst into flame. It clung to my shield with all the stickiness of honey. It burned into the steel there, etching it as might a blazing acid.

"Retreat, Val!" Kane shouted at me.

He and Ymiru, following Atara, bolted toward the stairs. I backed away from the dragon as quickly as I could. Once more, the dragon aimed a fiery blast at us. I caught it again on my shield, and then turned to run back toward the stairs before the dragon could summon up more of this evil red liquid. I reached the doorway and bounded down the stairs just as another stream of fire poured through. Some drops of the jelly stuck to my mail and burned into my back. But at least my friends and I were safe. There was no way the dragon could force her huge body through the narrow doorway.

But there was no way either that we could go forward. It seemed that we were trapped in the deeps of Argattha.

THAT WAS CLOSE!" Maram gasped as we gathered in the winding stairwell just below the corridor leading to the dragon's hall. When I peeked over the top stair into the corridor, I could see the dragon's golden eyes looking back at me through the doorway. "Are you all right, Val?"

I was not quite all right. The dragon's fire had burned holes clean through my armor. This I now removed so that Master Juwain could tend the seared flesh along my back.

"A dragon!" Maram marveled, not quite daring to look into the corridor. "I never really believed the old stories."

He and Atara stood just beneath me on the steps. And beneath them were Kane and Ymiru, and then Liljana, who had her arms wrapped around the boy that we had found.

As Master Juwain held his crystal above my back, I looked down the stairs at the boy and asked him, "Do you have a name?"

This time he answered me, looking me straight in the eyes as he said, "I'm called Daj."

"Just 'Daj'?" I asked him.

His face tightened with old hurts as if he didn't want to tell me anything more about his name. And so I asked him what land he hailed from. But this, too, it seemed, touched upon terrible memories.

"Well, Daj, please tell us how you came to be chained up there."

"Lord Morjin put me there," he said.

"But why?"

"Because I wouldn't do what he wanted me to."

"And what was that?"

But Daj didn't want to answer this question either. A deep loathing fell over him as his little body began to shudder.

"Are you a slave?" Atara asked him, looking at his tattooed forehead.

"Yes," he said, pressing back into Liljana. "But I escaped."

The story he now told us was a terrible one. A couple of years before, after watching his family be slaughtered by Morjin's men and being enslaved in some distant land that he wouldn't name, he had been brought in chains to Argattha. And there—in the city above us—Morjin had taken this handsome boy as his body servant. For a slave, it had been a relatively easy life, tending to Morjin's needs in the luxury of the private rooms of his palace. But Daj had hated it. Somehow he had found a way to displease his master. And so Morjin had consigned him to the mines far below Argattha's first level.

There, in tunnels so narrow that only young boys slight of body could squeeze through, Daj was given a pick and told to hack away at the veins of goldish ore running through the earth. His life became one of bleeding hands and gashed knees, of whips and curses and the terror of despair. He had slept with the corpses of the many other boys who had died around him; some of the other starved boys, he said, had been forced to eat from these bodies. And somehow, the brave and clever Daj had contrived a way to escape from this living hell.

"I found a way from the mines up to the first level," he told us, pointing up toward the top of the stairs. "That's where the dragon is kept. And so no one usually goes there."

For some months, he told us, he had survived by wandering the first level's abandoned streets and alleys; he had captured rats for food and ripped them apart with his hands and teeth. When the dragon drew near, he hid in crumbling, ancient apartments or even in cracks in the earth. But finally, his dread of the dragon—and his hunger—had grown too great. And so he had tried to steal up into the second level of the city.

"They captured me there," he said. Then he pointed at his forehead. "The mark gave me away. Lord Morjin himself came to see me taken back down to the first level and chained in the great hall. He gave me to the dragon. Just like he's given all the others."

I thought of the pyramid of skulls in the hall above us and shuddered.

Maram, moved to great pity by Daj's story, began weeping uncontrollably. But he seemed to realize that his tears might only inflame the boy's grief. So instead he forced out a brave laughter as if trying to inspirit him. He said, "Oh, you poor lad—how old are you?"

"Older than you."

Maram looked at him as if he had fallen mad. "How can you say that?"

"You laugh and cry like a little boy, but I haven't laughed for years, and I don't cry anymore. So you tell me, who is older?"

None of us knew what to say to this. So I turned to Daj and asked him, "How long were you chained there?"

"I don't know—a long time."

"But why did the dragon take so long in coming?"

"She did come, all the time," he said. "She brought me rats to eat. I think she wanted to fatten me up before she ate me."

After Master Juwain had finished with his crystal, he rubbed an ointment into my cooked skin, and then I put my armor back on with much wincing and pain. And then I looked down the dim stairwell at Daj and asked him, "How is it that the Lord of Lies and his men could have chained you without the dragon adding their skulls to her stack? Have they enslaved it, too?"

"In a way," Daj told me. "Lord Morjin said not all his chains are iron."

"Of what be this particular chain made?" Ymiru asked him.

Daj looked up at Ymiru in wonder at his great height; it seemed that he was trying to peer beneath Ymiru's cowled robe and get a better look at him.

"I heard Lord Morjin tell a priest something about that," Daj explained. "He said that long ago, he brought dragons here from somewhere else."

"From where?" Kane asked him sharply.

"I don't know—somewhere."

"You said dragons. How many were there?"

"Two of them, I think. A dragon king and his queen. But Lord Morjin poisoned the king; he took the eggs from the queen. A dragon queen lays only a single clutch of eggs, you know."

He paused to let Liljana pick a few lice from his head before continuing. But I had already guessed what he would say.

"Lord Morjin keeps the eggs in his chambers," he told us. "They won't hatch if they're kept cold. And that's why the dragon won't touch Lord Morjin. Because if she does, she knows the eggs will be destroyed."

Morjin, I suddenly knew, was keeping the dragon bound for his final war of conquest of the world.

Master Juwain rubbed his head as he smiled at Daj. "I see, I see. But you said that Morjin took the eggs long ago. They can't still be viable?"

"What does that mean?"

"Still alive and capable of hatching."

"Oh, well, dragons live forever—like Lord Morjin. And so do their eggs."

It was strange to think that the terrible, fire-spewing creature above us could so love her eggs that she was held in thrall by fear of their being destroyed. And what Daj told us next was stranger still: "The dragon is making a pyramid of the skulls of all the men she's killed. Because of Lord Morjin, she hates all men. But she hates Lord Morjin most of all. She's saving the very top place on the pyramid for his skull."

We all fell quiet for a moment as we listened to the dragon thundering about the chamber above us. And then Master Juwain asked Daj, "But how could you possibly know that?"

"Because I heard the dragon say this."

"The dragon talks to you?"

"Not with words, not like you do." Daj pressed his finger into his ratty hair above his ear. "But I heard her inside here."

"Are you a mindspeaker then?"

"What's that?"

Master Juwain looked at Liljana, who continued stroking Daj's hair as she tried to explain something about her powers that her blue gelstei quickened.

"I don't know anything about that," Daj said. "The only one I ever heard speak that way was the dragon."

"So it is with dragons," Kane told us. "It's said they have this power."

I looked at him in amazement. "But what do you know about dragons?"

"Very little, I think. It's said that they're stronger in their minds than men and darker in their hearts."

"But where did you hear that?" Master Juwain asked him. "It's known that the ancient accounts of this matter were fabricated."

Kane pointed up the steps and said to him, "Was this beast fabricated then? She came from somewhere, as the boy said."

"But where?" I asked.

Kane's face was as hard as iron as he looked at me. "It's said that dragons live on the world of Charoth and nowhere else."

"But Charoth is a Dark World, isn't it?"

"That it is. Morjin must have opened a gateway to it. He must be very close to opening a gate to Damoom and freeing the Dark One himself."

I risked another peek above the top of the stairs. It seemed more important than ever that we get past the dragon and complete our quest.

"What do you see, Val?" Maram called to me.

The dragon, it seemed, had given up staring through the doorway into the corridor above the stairs. But I sensed that she was still waiting for us in the hall. And so, as lightly as I could, I stole along the corridor until I came to the doorway. I looked out of it to see the dragon coiled around her skull pyramid as if guarding a treasure. Her golden eyes were lit up and fixed on the doorway; I thought that she was daring us to make a dash across the hall for the great portal that opened upon Argatha's abandoned first level.

"She's guarding the portal," I said when I returned to the others. I looked into the stairwell at Daj. "Is there another way out of the hall?"

"Only these stairs," he told us.

"What will we find beyond the portal?"

"Well, there's a big passage to a street, and then a lot of streets, like a maze almost—they lead mostly east toward the old gates in the city. They're all closed now, so the dragon can't escape."

"But you said that there is a way up to the second level?"

"Yes, that's right—there are some stairs about a mile from here. But they're too narrow for the dragon to use."

"Could you find these stairs again?"

"I think so."

Maram looked at me in horror of what he knew I was planning. He said, "You're not thinking of just running for these stairs, are you?"

"Not just running," I said.

"But shouldn't we wait for the dragon to leave? Or, ah, to go away?"

Upon questioning Daj further, we determined that the dragon never slept. And as for waiting, it seemed, the dragon could wait much longer than we. We had very little food, less water, and no time.

"The dragon," Liljana unexpectedly announced, "is waiting for something. I think the Red Priests are due to bring another here. What will they think when they find the boy gone and his shackles unlocked?"

"But how do you know that?" Kane asked her.

"I know," she said, tapping her blue stone against her head, "because the dragon is in my mind."

"So," Kane murmured as he rubbed his bandaged ear.

Liljana's face suddenly contorted as she shook her head violently back and forth. She gasped out, "She's trying . . . to make a ghul of me!"

Kane waited for her to regain control of herself and then snarled out, "Perhaps you should try to go into her mind. And make a ghul of her."

This suggested an elaboration on the desperate plan that I was considering: We would all rush out into the hall. And then, while Liljana used her blue gelstei to engage the dragon's mind, Atara would shoot arrows into her eyes. This would allow me to steal in close and try once more to cut through the dragon's iron hide.

Master Juwain, his green crystal in hand, looked at me and said, "I shouldn't be telling you how to kill anything, not even a dragon. But the place in the chest that you stabbed—that's not where her heart is, I'm sure. If my stone tells true, you'll find it beating three feet farther down, just where the scales darken, closer to the curve of her belly."

Ymiru had his purple gelstei in hand as he listened to Master Juwain tell us this, and he slowly nodded his great head.

But Maram remained horrified by what we were about to do. He shot me a quick look and said, "But what of the dragon's fire, Val?"

"What of your own fire?" I countered, looking at Maram's red crystal.

"Well, what of it? There's no sun in this accursed city to light it."

"But didn't you once tell me that you thought the firestone might be able to hold the sun's light and not just focus it?"

"Ah, perhaps, one bolt of flame, no more—if only I could find it."

"Find it, then," I said, smiling at him.

Kane, standing below me on the stairs, caught my glance and said, "This red jelly that bursts into flame—it's very much like the relb, eh?"

I remembered the story of the Sarni, with Morjin's help, painting the Long Wall with relb and watching as the rising sun set it aflame and melted a breach in the stone for their armies to ravage Alonia.

"And the relb," Kane went on, gripping his black stone, "was a forerunner of the firestones, was it not?"

"That it was," I said, smiling at him as well. The flash of his white long teeth gave me hope that we really might win the coming battle.

Atara squeezed her crystal sphere as her haunted eyes found mine. Her face was white as she said, "I see one terrible chance, Val."

I smiled at her, too, although it tore my heart open to do so. And I said, "Then one chance will have to be enough."

I turned to take council with the others. And there, in the dim, curving confines of the stairwell, smelling of sweat and fear and the burning reek of relb, we decided that if we weren't to abandon the quest, we would have to fight the dragon.

"But what about the boy?" Maram asked, looking at Daj. "We can't take him with us, can we?"

Of course we couldn't. But how could we abandon him to certain recapture, or starvation and death?

In the end, it was Daj who decided the question for us. Despite his words to Maram earlier, he was still only a boy. He gripped Liljana's tunic, pressing himself into her soft body.

"Don't leave me here!" he said. "Please take me with you!"

Atara looked at me and said, "His fate is tied to ours now. The moment you turned the key in the lock, it was so."

"All right," I said, bowing my head to Daj, "you can come with us, then. But you must be brave, as we know you can be. Very, very brave."

And with that, I turned to lead the way into the corridor. Very quietly, we walked in file through it to the doorway of the hall. As I had feared, the dragon remained coiled around her skulls, watching us—watching us break into a run as we made for the portal across the hall. She sprang up from the skulls with a frightening speed. She bounded straight toward us to cut us off. Her great hind claws tore at the floor as she thundered closer. So quick were her bunching, explosive motions that I knew we had no hope of outrunning her.

Her first fire fell upon my shield just as Ymiru broke from our formation to grab up a great slab of fallen rock. He used this as a shield of his own, holding the immense weight in front of him in order to work in close to the dragon. The dragon turned her fire upon him. The flaming relb blasted against the slab and began burning the stone into lava. And then Atara pulled back the string of her bow and loosed an arrow at the dragon's eye.

As before, however, the dragon sensed her intention just as the bowstring twanged. She turned her head at the last instant, and the arrow skittered off her iron scales. She trembled to leap at us, to rend us with her great teeth and claws, to stomp us into a bloody pulp. But just then Liljana, holding her blue whale against her head, engaged the dragon's mind. I felt a smoldering malice burning into Liljana as she froze in her tracks.

And in that moment, I dashed forward. So did Ymiru, who cast down his rock shield. I ran straight in beneath the dragon's long, twisting neck, where her huge chest gave way to her belly. I saw the place on the curve of her heaving body where the scales darkened, even as Master Juwain had said. And there I thrust my sword. This time it penetrated to a distance of perhaps two inches. The dragon roared out her pain and wrath, and kicked her claws into my shield, sending me flying. I hit the floor backward; the force of the fall bruised my back and knocked the breath from me. I lay there gasping for air, watching in puzzlement and horror as Ymiru worked in still closer to the dragon with his gelstei in hand.

"Ymiru—what are you doing?" Kane called to him.

As Atara fired off another arrow, to no effect, Ymiru brought his flaring purple crystal up to the place on the dragon's belly where I had stabbed her. The scale there seemed to darken to a pitted, reddish black. And then Liljana, still staring at the dragon, cried out in pain. I could almost feel her connection with the dragon's mind break like snapped wood. The dragon, finally unbound, turned about in a snarling, spitting rage and bit out at Ymiru. Her jaws closed about Ymiru's arm, and she tore it clean off, swallowing it whole. A fount of blood sprayed the air. Ymiru cried out as he gripped his gelstei in his remaining hand and tried to move backward, away from the dragon. But the dragon was too quick and Ymiru was in too much pain. Again the dragon's jaws opened. I was sure that she was about to rend Ymiru into meat or burn him. And then Atara shot off still another arrow.

This time it drove straight into the dragon's mouth. But not quite straight enough: the shaft stuck out from between two of the dragon's teeth like a long, feathered toothpick. The dragon, turning her attention from the quickly retreating Ymiru, shook her head furiously in a futile effort to dislodge it. Blood as red as Ymiru's leaked from her wounded gums. She gazed hatefully at Atara as she opened her jaws again to spit fire at her.

"Atara!" I cried as I sprang to my feet. "Atara!"

I raced across the few feet separating us just in time to take the full blast of the dragon's fury upon my shield. It was a great gout of flaming relb that the dragon spewed at me. It melted huge holes in the steel of the shield and burned straight through to the leather straps covering my forearm. I had to take it off and cast it from me lest I lose an arm as had Ymiru. Once again—and for the last time—my father's shield had saved my life.

But now there was nothing except air between me and the dragon. She glared at me with her ancient glowing eyes in her promise to burn me. I had hoped that Kane might keep me from this fate. All this time, he had stood with his black gelstei in hand trying in vain to steal the dragon's fire. And so, to my astonishment, it was Maram who saved me—with help from Daj. Quick as a bounding rat, the agile boy broke from behind Liljana and dashed across the room. He scooped up a large stone and hurled it at the pyramid of skulls, knocking a couple of them from the top. This drew the dragon's attention and all her wrath toward him. And in that moment, Maram moved.

He stood away from the others and pointed his firestone at the dragon. A tremendous blast of flame, like a lightning bolt, leaped out from the crystal even as Maram let out a great cry of agony. I saw the firestone crack in his seared hands. And the flame drove straight into the dragon's neck, wounding her terribly. She let out a great roar of anguish. In a few quick bounds, she sprang toward the part of the room where Daj had been chained. There she backed into the corner, roaring and stinking of burnt blood, dropping her huge head low to the floor as she shook and glowered and waited for me.

"Val, no!" Atara said, laying her hand upon my shoulder as I started forward. "She'll burn you!"

I shook off her hand, wondering how I could get at the dragon's belly, now pressed down against the hall's hard floor. The dragon, I sensed, was shocked and very weak.

"I've seen you dead here!" she said to me.

She grasped my hand and pulled at it even as Kane bellowed out, "Run, damn it! All of you run for the portal!"

At the opposite end of the room, Daj heaved a last stone into the stack of skulls, shattering one of them. And then he bolted for the portal. So did Atara, Kane, Maram, and I. Liljana and Master Juwain, who had just finished wrapping a cord around Ymiru's severed arm, followed quickly after us.

We raced through it and out into a corridor leading to a dimly lit street. This great tunnel—fifty feet wide and thirty feet high—opened through the black rock ahead of us. Once, perhaps, there had been stalls here selling food and water, silks and jewels. But now it was empty save for a few broken rocks, dead rats and heaps of steaming dragon dung. We made our way east past the rotted-out doorways of ancient rooms and apartments. Smaller streets, every sixty yards or so, gave out onto what I took to be one of this level's great boulevards. Just after the place where it bent sharply toward the north, Daj led us to the left onto one of these side streets. We hurried as quickly as we could, but Ymiru could not run very fast missing one arm and clutching his great war club in his remaining hand.

"Here," Master Juwain said, calling for a halt. He gathered us up close to a dark doorway in the side of the street. "Ymiru, let me see your arm."

Master Juwain pulled aside Ymiru's robe to look at his arm, bitten off at the elbow. The cord tied above it had stopped the spurting, but a good deal of blood still leaked from the raw, red stump. Master Juwain brought out his emerald crystal then. He summoned from it a green fire that cauterized the wound without burning and set the exposed and ragged flesh to healing. The sweet flame filled Ymiru like an elixir and took away his pain and shock.

"The arm will grow back, won't it?" Maram asked Master Juwain.

"No, I'm afraid not," he said. "The varistei hasn't that power."

As Kane rubbed the bandage over his missing ear, Ymiru looked at him sadly as if to find confirmation of his gloomy view of the world. But he had no pity for himself. He looked down as Master Juwain bandaged the stump and arranged the torn robe over it. Then he said, "The dragon took my arm from me, but at least he didn't take this."

He opened his robe to show us his purple gelstei tucked away. "And if the dragon comes for us again, this might prove her death."

"Will the dragon follow us?" Maram asked.

Daj, who was growing more impatient by the moment, pulled at my hand and said, "The dragon is very strong. She'll come soon—let's go!"

Liljana looked at me as she nodded her head. "She'll come, Val."

I knew she would. I turned to Daj and said, "Take us out of here, then."

Daj led forth just ahead of me; Maram puffed and panted behind me followed by Liljana, Kane, Master Juwain, and Ymiru. Atara insisted on bringing up the rear. If the dragon caught us here on the open streets, she said, she still might be able to stop her with a few well-placed arrows.

And so we made our way through dark tunnels of rock that twisted through the earth. We passed by scoops in the mountain's basalt where once people had burrowed like moles. Daj led us through a snarl of streets almost as complex as the labyrinth. I had hoped that if the dragon did pursue us, we might lose her in this maze. But the dragon, I sensed, could track us by the scent of our sweat no less than of our minds. And since she had been imprisoned here untold years, perhaps no one or nothing knew the streets of Argattha's first level so well.

It was just as we had turned onto a narrow street that we heard the drumming of the dragon's footfalls behind us. Daj took a quick look behind him and called out, "Run! Faster now! The stairs are close!"

We ran as fast as we could. My boots slapped against dark, dirty stone as Maram wheezed along behind me. Farther back, Master Juwain was working very hard to keep up, while Ymiru's breath broke upon the fetid air in great gasps. His strength amazed me. He seemed to have shaken off the shock of his terrible wound. As had the dragon.

She was drawing closer now, gaining upon us with frightening speed. Her great body, no doubt filling most of the narrow tunnel, seemed to push the air ahead of her. Her thick cinnamon scent carried to us and stirred up a thrill of fear. And the sound of her clawed feet echoed down the twisting tube of rock like the pounding of hammers.

"Quick!" Daj shouted as his feet flew across the rock. "We're almost there!"

He led us onto a long, winding street that seemed not to have any outlet. If we were caught here, I thought, it would be the end. And then, to the drumming of the dragon's feet and the growing stink of relb, as I had begun to fear that Daj had forgotten the way toward the stairs, he ran down the street's final turning and through a portal into an immense open space. This, it seemed, had once been a great hall or perhaps an open square where people had gathered. Long ago, it seemed, the mountain had moved, opening a huge rent through the rock here. A chasm thirty feet wide ran almost straight through the center of this cavernous square. It would have blocked our way if not for the narrow stone bridge that led across it.

"Come on!" Daj shouted to us as he made for the bridge.

On the other side of it was a huge shelf of rock about as large as the dragon's hall. And at the far end of the chamber, two hundred yards away, loomed a large portal.

"Val!" Maram shouted, "she's coming!"

Even as he said this, the chamber shook with the dragon's terrible cry.

"Run!" I called.

Daj was the first across the crumbling old bridge, followed by me, Maram, and Liljana. But just as Kane set foot upon it, Atara's bowstring cracked, and I turned to see the dragon thunder into the chamber. She drove her great, scaled body bounding toward us as she hissed and growled. I could feel the poisonous relb building in her throat, as with a burning gout of hate. There was no time, I saw, for anyone else after Kane to cross the bridge. And so I turned and pointed at a crack that ran deep into the chamber's side wall. To Master Juwain, I shouted, "Hide!"

Master Juwain, trapped on the rock shelf on the other side of the chasm, jumped toward the crack and fairly pulled Atara into it. Ymiru followed them a moment later. I was afraid that the dragon, striking sparks with her great claws, might thrust her head into the crack and burn them with her fire. But the dragon's eyes were fixed upon Maram, who was running behind Daj toward the portal. It was he who had wounded the dragon with his fire. And so it would be he, I sensed, whom the dragon would burn first before rending him with her terrible teeth.

"Hurry, Maram!" I shouted.

But there was no way that he, or any of us, could now escape the dragon by running. With great, heaving bounds, she leaped toward us. Her wings beat out just as her huge hind feet struck down upon the center of the bridge. There came a loud cracking of stone and a flurry of driven air. The dragon descended upon the other side of the chasm just as the bridge swayed and shuddered and broke into great pieces in its plummet into the earth's dark and fathomless deeps.

"Val!" Atara called to me from the other side of the chasm. She had stepped out of the crack and had her hands up to her mouth. "Don't attack yet! If you move, you die!"

Behind me, Daj and Maram were still running for the portal. But Kane stood on the huge rock shelf by my right side and Liljana on my left. My sword was drawn, and I had determined that I must charge the dragon to give them time to flee.

The dragon, in her fury of driving feet and beating wings, thundered closer. Liljana waited next to me, staring into her great eyes. Kane had his black stone in hand as his black eyes fixed upon the dragon's snarling face.

"Val!" Atara called again. "Wait until she rises! There will be a moment—you will see the moment!"

Now the dragon, closing quickly upon me from some yards away, opened her jaws. I wondered if I could endure the burning of her fire long enough to put my sword into her before I died. I felt my heart beating out the moments of my life.

The dragon's throat suddenly contracted and tightened even as mine did. And I heard Kane growling at my side, "So . . . so."

The relb spurted at me in a great red jet of jelly. But just then, Kane finally found his way into the depths of his black crystal. The gelstei damped the fires of the relb and kept it from igniting. It splattered upon me like gore hacked out of an enemy's body. It was warm, wet, and sticky, but it burned no worse than blood.

The dragon, catching sight of this miracle, dug her claws into the rock as she reared back and rose up above me. Her long neck drew back like a snake's so that she could strike me dead.

"Val!" Ymiru's voice rang out. He stood on the other side of the chasm, pointing his purple crystal at the dragon. "Can you see the scale?"

I saw the scale, the one just above the dragon's belly that was now darker than all the others. Ymiru had given his arm so that he could work the magic of his gelstei against this stone-hard scale and soften it.

The dragon's eyes stared down at me like searing suns. Her spicy, overpowering stench sickened me as she watched and waited like a giant cobra. I knew that she would never allow me to get close to her exposed belly.

"ANGRABODA!"

With all the power of her stout body, Liljana suddenly shouted out this name that she had wrested from the dragon's mind. It was the dragon's true name, the breath of her soul, and for a moment it chilled her soul and froze her motionless. And in that moment I struck.

I rushed forward, Alkaladur held high. Its bright blade flared with a silver light. It warded off the last, desperate, paralyzing poison of the dragon's mind. And then I thrust it straight through the softened scale, deep into the dragon's insides. It pierced her heart. And a terrible fire, like blood bursting into flames, leaped along the length of my sword, into my blood— straight into my heart. If Atara hadn't cried out for me to move, I would have fallen beneath the dragon even as she fell to the chamber's floor with a tremendous roar of anguish and a crash that shook the mountain's stone.

It took me a long time to return from the dark world that the dragon's death had sent me to. Only my sword's shining silustria, quickened by Flick's twinkling lights, called me back to life. When I opened my eyes again, I found myself lying on the cold stone floor of a cavern deep in the earth. The dragon lay dead ten feet away from me. And Liljana, Kane, Maram, and Daj all knelt above me rubbing my cold limbs.

"Come on," Daj said, pulling at my hand. He pointed at the portal at the far end of the chamber. "We're almost at the stairs."

I sat up slowly, gripping the diamond-studded hilt of my

sword. Strength flowed into me even as the dragon's heart emptied the last of her blood into the great pool of crimson gathering upon the floor. I wanted to weep because I had killed a great, if malignant, being. But instead I stood up and walked over to the lip of the chasm.

"Val—are you all right?" Atara called to me.

She stood with Ymiru and Master Juwain on the other side, thirty feet away. It might as well have been thirty miles. There was nothing left of the stone bridge that had spanned it only a few minutes before.

"Daj," I said, looking at the boy, "how can they get over to us?"

"I don't know," he said. "That was the only way."

He pointed behind us at the portal and added, "That corridor leads right to the stairs to the second level. There's nowhere else we can go."

"Are there any other stairs on this level that lead up to the next?"

As it happened, there was another set of stairs, back through the first level past the dragon's hall. Daj told Master Juwain, Ymiru and Atara how to reach them.

"Then where," I asked Daj, "can we meet on the second level?"

"I don't know," Daj said. "I don't know that level at all."

"But you know the seventh level, don't you?"

"As well as I know this one."

"Is there a place we can meet there?" I asked.

"Yes, there's a fountain near Lord Morjin's palace. It's called the Red Fountain. Everyone knows where it is."

We held quick council then, shouting back and forth across the chasm. We decided to try to find the fountain that Daj had told of and meet there before stealing into Morjin's throne room.

"If something should happen to us and you reach the fountain before us, don't wait too long for us," I called to Atara. "Find your own way into the throne room. Find the cup and take it out of this place, if you can."

"All right," she called back. "And you, too."

With a last look that cut deep into me, she turned to lead Master Juwain and Ymiru out of the chamber the way that they had come. I almost couldn't bear seeing her vanish into cold rock, as it seemed that I was losing not only my eyes and the best of my vision, but my very heart. And then Daj pulled at my hand, pointing toward the portal, and I had to dig deep to find my courage. I had killed one dragon, but I feared with all my soul the Great Red Dragon who dwelt somewhere beyond the dark corridor and stairs leading to Argattha's upper levels.

▪ 14 ▪

THE OPENING TO the stairway proved quite narrow. As in ascending a castle's high tower, we climbed five hundred feet up the winding stairs. In this turning tube of rock, it was cold and dark, with only my sword and Flick's lights providing any illumination. After what seemed forever, the stairs gave out into a deserted corridor leading to a quiet street in the western district of the city. No one was about the street as we debouched onto it. The doors of the apartments along this tunnel of rock were closed. I wondered if it was night; in the twistings of the labyrinth and our fight with the dragon, we had utterly lost the thread of time.

"It is night," Kane said to us as we made our way toward the noise of a larger street ahead of us. "In this accursed city, always night."

Daj was little help to us here. Some days ago, he said, he had made his way up the stairs, even as we just had, only to be captured near this district.

"Lord Morjin's spies," he said, "saw the mark and captured me."

To cover this foul mark inked into his forehead, Master

Juwain had rigged a length of cloth around his head. It looked, Kane told us, something like the flowing kaftafs worn by the tribesmen of the Red Desert.

Soon we reached a street where many people were about. Many of them, I saw, were veterans of Morjin's conquests. They showed signs of service in faraway lands: they had scars upon their faces and arms—that is, if their arms and other limbs hadn't long since been hacked off. Other people— blacksmiths, potters, masons, carpenters, bakers, and especially the tattooed slaves—bore the marks of Morjin's displeasure. The Red Dragon, as Daj told us, had settled upon mutilation as punishment for even minor offenses. As we made our way through the crowds, we saw men and women with branded faces, notched ears, and gouged-out eyes. Thieves who hadn't been given to the dragon lacked hands with which to cut others' purses. In no other city had I seen so many carved-up, burnt, tortured, unfortunate people.

At least, I thought, Ymiru would attract no attention on account of his severed arm. It reassured me as well that we passed several Saryaks hurrying past us. These very tall men were dressed as Ymiru in black robes whose cowls covered their faces. They were girded with maces and curved swords; they served Morjin freely, for pay, as did other mercenaries whose appearance and dress led me to believe that their homelands were Sunguru and Uskudar—and even Surrapam, Delu, and Alonia. Many Sarni warriors, accoutered in leather armor as Atara, rode their steppe ponies boldly through the streets. Kane identified their tribes as Zayak, Marituk, and western Urtuk, all of whom were said to have made alliances with Sakai. As well, we passed a band of Blues with their battle-axes, and companies of marching levies from Hesperu, Karabuk, and Galda, which Morjin's Red Priests had conquered outright in his name. It seemed that Morjin was gathering a great host under his banner and sheltering them here in this dark, impregnable city. If any of Argattha's residents looked our way, I hoped they would think that we were just a few more warriors come to sell our swords.

Daj explained to us that the various levels of the city were mostly devoted to differing activities. Thus on the seventh level were to be found Morjin's palace and throne room, many of Argattha's temples, and other chambers given over to matters of ceremony and state. There lived the Red Priests and nobles, while the higher artisans such as painters and sculptors had shops on the sixth level, with weavers, clothmakers, and dyers on the fifth, and so on down to the second level, the city's largest, where Morjin's armies were quartered in dim, cramped barracks and the blacksmiths and armorers labored over their forges preparing for war.

We saw signs of the coming cataclysm all around us. Carts stacked with yew and horn, bound for the bowmakers' shops, rolled past us. Other carts laden with sheaves of arrows moved the other way. Slaughterhouses laying in pork for long campaigns shook with the squeals of pigs having their throats cut; their blood flowed out into the streets' gutters, there to be drunk by the scurrying rats or the clouds of flies that plagued Argattha. From smithies came the constant hammering of steel as men beat mauls against white-hot metal and made spear points, swords, maces, shields, and suits of mail. From the many forges billowed a thick smoke that choked the streets. Although numerous air shafts opened like chimneys upon the ironworks and dank corridors, they were too few to carry away the fumes and stinks of the city. The foul mixture of smoke, rotting blood and fear was the smell of Argattha, and I worried that it would cling not just to my clothes and hair but to my soul.

After asking directions from a broken, old woman, we found our way onto one of this level's boulevards. This great bore through the mountain's basalt led toward the Zun Gate, named for one of the great Galadin who had joined Angra Mainyu's rebellion against the angelic hosts and had been imprisoned with him on Damoom. All of us, I knew, longed to flee from this gate into the world of fresh air and stars; but our way took us ever deeper into this tomb of stone. We passed bakeries, taverns and mess halls carved out of solid rock. The smell of hot bread mingled with the reek of sewage and the dung that the gong farmers hauled out of the city in wicker baskets.

At last we drew near the central stairs. These great steps, a hundred feet wide, opened onto the boulevard exactly as the old woman had said. Streams of people poured down them on the left, while many others puffed laboriously up them on the right. As we pushed our way toward them, we hoped we might catch sight of Atara, Ymiru, and Master Juwain in the throngs about us.

But just then, Daj caught sight of something else. He pressed himself against my side and pointed toward a doorway giving onto the boulevard across from us. There a cloaked figure stood. "Look! I know that man," Daj said. "He's one of Lord Morjin's spies."

The man he had indicated, tall and blond like the Thalunes and decked in mail like many mercenaries, seemed to be watching the stairs. His cruel blue eyes swept the crowds of people, no doubt looking for a way that he could transmute his betrayal of others into gold.

"Back!" Kane growled. He reversed direction and led us half a block to a side street where we gathered outside of an armorer's shop. In a low voice he said, "Let's hope our friends have found another way to the palace. Or have already gone on ahead of us."

To the sounds of hammering iron, we waited for the spy to leave his post; we waited for most of an hour. Finally, after he had gone, we stole back along the street to the stairs. Then we began our climb up to Argattha's seventh level. With five levels to ascend and five hundred feet per level, we had to work our way up a distance of almost half a mile, straight up through the heart of the mountain. It took us a long time to make this climb. The stairs drove up toward the east until giving way to a great landing, before turning back west on their rise again. And so it went, with many, many turnings as the seemingly endless stairs took us through the black rock past the openings to the third, fourth, fifth, and sixth levels. At last, with Maram fairly wheezing and dripping sweat from his thick brown beard, we came out onto one of the boulevards of the seventh level.

"Here it is," Maram said, puffing as we stepped out onto the huge street. "Well, it doesn't look like much."

Indeed, the street looked like every other tunnel in this unnatural city, save that it was even larger: it was a great, square-cut channel through black rock that was lit with foul-smelling oil lamps and pitted with doorways that opened into dank living spaces and shops. Although we were close to Morjin's throne room, as Daj told us, no vistas of magnificent domed buildings or soaring arches were to be seen, for Morjin's "palace" was just another series of rat holes in a mountain gnawed with thousands of such dark places.

"The palace is that way," Daj said, pointing south at a wall of stone.

To the west of the palace, he said, was the great Garden: a huge hall where flowering plants were bathed in the light of the thousands of glowstones on the walls. To the east of the palace was a passage that only Morjin was permitted to use. This led past a series of private stairs to the lower levels, a mile and a half straight toward an opening cut onto Skartaru's east face. Daj called this opening Morjin's Porch, and there the Red Dragon liked to sit each morning to watch the rising of the sun. There, too, long ago, on the naked rock face, he had nailed the immortal Kalkamesh and tortured him for ten long years.

"I'd like to see this porch of his," Maram said, looking about the dim street. "I'd give anything to feel real light on my face again."

"Don't be a fool!" Kane snapped at him. "You won't be seeing it anytime soon unless Morjin puts you there."

"He may put all of us there," Maram said bravely. "And it may be that someday the poets will sing of us and what we tried to do here. Do you think so, Val?"

"Perhaps," I said to him. "But it would please me more if Alphanderry were here to sing of the stars."

The boulevard led us a quarter-mile toward the east, where it intersected another running from north to south: directly toward the throne room of Morjin's Palace. We walked along this new street until we came to a huge square facing the throne room's north gate. There we found many people milling about the food stalls and fortune-tellers. There, too, at the center of the square, had been built a fountain. Men and women sat around it in the spray of a great plume of water, red as rust, as if it had been forced through ancient iron pipes.

We sat there by this crimson pool, too, waiting for our friends. We watched carts full of silks and wine barrels roll past; one cart, stacked with glowstones that reminded me of the skulls in the dragon's hall, was being taken outside of Argattha so that these gelstei could be refilled with the light of the sun. Hundreds of people from the boulevards promenaded past the fountain. Many of these wore golden robes embroidered with red dragons: the vestments of the Red Priests of the Kallimun. These men—and they were almost all men—strode along with an air of rectitude and dominion, as if all things and peoples about them were their province. More than one of them cast us suspicious looks. And we were, I thought, a suspicious company: three men dressed like mercenaries, a noble-looking woman, and a ragtag child. It was very good, I thought, that only we could see Flick.

After a while, it became clear that there were few mercenaries on this level of the city—but many captains and lords of Morjin's armies. One of these, dressed in a yellow tunic with a broadsword buckled at the waist, swaggered up to us and demanded that we identify ourselves. Only the medallions that we had lifted off the dead knights kept us from being taken and bound in chains.

"That was close," Maram said, after the captain had stalked off. We had hinted that we were spies, and that Morjin would be very displeased if the captain interfered with our mission. "Too, too close."

Liljana sat with her arms thrown around Daj as might his mother. But there was something fierce and unyielding in her gaze, as if she would reluctantly sacrifice him or any of us— or herself—in order to gain the Lightstone.

"We can't wait here much longer," she whispered against the fountain's splatter.

I looked down the boulevard behind us, praying that I might catch sight of Atara and the others.

"With our delay at the stairs, likely they've already come,"

Kane said. "Likely they're trying to find an easier way into the throne room."

He pointed across the square at a wall of basalt into which was set a great gate, with iron doors twenty feet high. Four of Morjin's men stood guard outside it. Daj told us that there were two other gates, on the throne room's east and west sides, and that these were always guarded as well.

It seemed a desperate business to try to fool or force our way into the throne room past the guards. We might simply rush upon them and murder them—and then storm into the throne room to begin our search for the Lightstone. But surely someone would see us and give the alarm.

"Does this street ever grow quiet?" I asked Daj. I looked at the silksellers hawking their wares from their carts and other merchants displaying golden bangles, silver brooches, and jeweled rings.

"At night it does," he said.

Maram pulled at his beard and muttered, "But how can you tell when it's night in this accursed place?"

"Well, the criers come to call out the curfew."

"If our friends have discovered that," Kane said, "then perhaps they're waiting somewhere for night to clear the streets."

"Perhaps," I said. I watched a vendor roasting a baby pig over a fire. The spit and hiss of its dripping fat sent a greasy, black smoke out onto the noisy street. I didn't want to give voice to the fear eating at all of us: that our friends were delayed because they had been discovered and captured.

Maram didn't like the way that one of the silksellers was looking at him, and he pulled his cloak more tightly about him as he muttered, "It's too bad that we can't just turn invisible."

It was then that Daj surprised me, and all of us, saying, "There's another way into the throne room."

Beneath the noise of the square, with what seemed the whole city of Argattha watching us, he told us that inside the throne room a door on its west wall opened upon an unguarded passage leading directly through the palace to Morjin's private quarters.

"Oh, excellent," Maram said to Daj. "And I suppose you

know a way to get inside the Red Dragon's rooms without just knocking at his door?"

"I do," Daj said, and our surprise turned to amazement. "There's a secret passage from Lord Morjin's rooms into the city."

He went on to tell us that Morjin often used this passage to leave his palace unnoticed; he would go about the city in disguise, acting as his own most trusted spy to ferret out any plots or slanders made against him.

"But why didn't you tell us this?" I asked him.

"Because I was afraid," he said, looking at Kane grip his dagger.

"Afraid of what?"

"Afraid that you've come to kill Lord Morjin." He went on to say that an ancient curse had been laid upon anyone who would dare to try to slay the Red Dragon. And so Daj had been afraid to lead us through his private chambers.

"But why are you telling us this now?" I asked him.

"Because I don't care anymore." Daj's dark, youthful face suddenly filled with hate, like Kane's. "About the curse, I mean. I hope you do kill him. I'll never sleep well again until he's dead."

The hurt inside him cut me like a heated knife. And I said to him, "But we haven't come here to kill anyone. We're not assassins, Daj."

As Kane's face seemed to glow like heated iron, I went on to tell him that we meant to enter Morjin's throne room in order to recover something that had once been stolen from the king's palace in Tria.

"What is it then, treasure? There's plenty of that in the throne room."

"Yes, treasure," I said. And then, to myself, I whispered: The greatest treasure in the world.

We decided that Daj should take us to the secret passage that led into Morjin's Palace. Maram, however, counseled waiting a few more hours before embarking on this break-in: "If we're to steal through the Red Dragon's rooms, it would be better to do so at night when he's sleeping."

"But he doesn't sleep," Daj said. "He stays up all night reading his books. Or playing chess with himself. Or . . . other things."

"And during the day?" I asked, looking for some ray of light driving down the airshafts that opened upon the square.

"During the day," Daj said, "he could be anywhere in the city."

I pulled my cloak more tightly about myself as he said this. I felt the eyes of many people about the street watching us.

"Anywhere except the throne room," Liljana said.

"Yes, that's right," Daj said, nodding toward the iron gate. "The doors are almost always open when Lord Morjin is holding court."

"Almost always?" Liljana asked him.

Daj nodded his head. "Yes, sometimes he holds . . . private audiences."

I felt my heart beating like a hammer and sweat running beneath the padding of my armor. I said, "All right, the throne room is likely empty, as we sit here talking. And our friends, if they haven't been taken, are likely waiting somewhere for night to fight their way into it."

"And if they have been taken?" Maram asked.

I tried not to listen to the scream building inside me. I said, "Then all the more reason that we should hasten to find this secret passage that Daj has told of. And if our friends are safe, we'll no doubt find them outside one of the gates tonight, after we've completed our quest."

Everyone agreed that it would be best if we attempted the secret passage now, before we were discovered or our courage failed. And so Daj led the way into the district to the northwest of the palace. Here the streets were narrow and twisted like tunnels that would have confused an ant. Nobles, mostly, lived here between the shops of the bakers, vintners, and others who served their needs. The stares of these people as we quickly passed by disquieted all of us. We pushed through the crowds, and followed Daj onto a dim street that turned toward the north, in the direction of the great stairs. But then it turned again, west and south. We walked on a little way. Then Daj pointed at an open doorway next to a butchery where many flyblown chickens and lambs were hung. It was an unusual doorway, the rock on either side of it being carved with standing dragons that framed it like pillars. It gave into a little chamber that was one of Argattha's many sanctuaries. Inside, as we found, was little more than a single glowstone hanging from the low ceiling. This one light, Daj said, symbolized the light of the One. The meaning of our passage through the pillars was clear: that the way toward the One was through the way of the Dragon.

"People are supposed to come here and meditate," Daj told us. We stood at the center of the deserted chamber, staring at a tapestry of various Elijin and Galadin on the far wall. "But no one ever comes."

"Why not?" Maram asked him.

"Because it's said that Lord Morjin seeks his sacrifices from the most faithful and finds them in the sanctuaries."

Such tales, I thought, were an excellent way of keeping the sanctuaries empty—so that Morjin could reserve them for his private use.

With Maram standing watch in the doorway, we moved over to the tapestry, and Liljana held it away from the wall. Behind it was a door, barely perceptible as such: a crack ran through the black rock just above the level of our heads, while two others cut lengthwise framing a large basalt slab. If pushed against, I thought, it would revolve and open onto the secret passage.

I pushed against it now, but it was like pushing against a solid wall. And Daj said to me, "You have to know the password."

"I presume you know what this is?" Kane said to him.

"Yes, there's a door like this at the other end of the passage—in Lord Morjin's rooms. One time, I hid there and watched him use it. And then followed him here."

"Brave boy," I said, nodding my head at him.

"Yes, you're a brave little spy," Kane said, grinning savagely. "Well, let's see if Morjin has kept the password. What is it?"

"Memoriar-damoom," Daj said softly. "I don't know what it means."

"It means," Kane said, translating the ancient Ardik, " 'Remember Damoom.' "

He stood facing the door and spoke the word clearly, louder this time. And from within the door came a clicking sound as of a lock being slid open.

As Maram hurried across the room to view this marvel, Kane's grin grew larger, and he said, "In the Age of Law, many locks were made thusly. Song stones, keyed to a word or a voice, turn at the touch of the right sound and set the locking mechanism in motion."

Now he set his hand against the edge of the door and leaned his weight into it. The part that he pushed against swung inward while the left edge of the slab revolved out into the room. Beyond the opening lay a dark tunnel.

He started straight into the tunnel, followed by Daj and me. But when it came Maram's turn to step forward, he hesitated and said, "I don't like the look of this at all."

"Come," I said, turning back toward him. "Where's your courage?"

"Ah, where indeed, my friend? I'm afraid that almost all of that coin has been spent."

"There's always more," I said to him.

"For you, perhaps, but not for me. After all, I'm no Valari."

"What do you mean?"

"Well, I mean that for you Valari, courage is a birthright. You breathe it in as easily as others do air."

"No, you are wrong, Maram," I told him, shaking my head. My belly churned as if I had swallowed a nest of writhing snakes. "Courage never gets to be a habit. Each time . . . it gets harder to find. As it is for me now."

"For you?"

"Yes," I said, glancing at Kane and Liljana. Then I looked straight at Maram. "Without you by my side, I don't know how I'd ever be able to do this."

"Do you really mean that?"

I clasped his hand in mine and smiled at him. "Will you come with me this last mile?"

He hesitated another long moment before slowly nodding his head. Then he sighed out, "All right, I'll come. But this has to be the last time."

Then he, too, stepped into the tunnel, followed by Liljana, who had so arrayed the tapestry that it fell back over the door as we pushed it shut. Darkness swallowed us; for a moment we stood nearly blind as beneath a black shroud. Then I drew my sword. Daj stared at the glowing blade in wonder, but seemed too afraid to ask by what miracle it gave light. All that he said was: "The last time I was here, all I had was a candle. But this is better."

He started off down the tunnel, with me, Maram, Liljana, and Kane close behind. The passage seemed empty even of rats. We walked quickly, the scrape of our boots echoing off the bare rocks. After a while we came to a place where another tunnel joined ours. Daj told us that he thought it led to another sanctuary somewhere on the seventh level. Or perhaps, he said, it gave out onto the passage that led to Morjin's Porch on Skartaru's east face. Along that way was to be found Morjin's Stairs, which led down to Argattha's lower levels and the secret escape tunnels that Morjin still kept open.

"Do you know these tunnels?" I asked him.

"Well, I know about them," Daj said. "But I was never able to find out where they were."

We walked on for another two hundred yards and came across two more of these adjoining tunnels. And then, after turning left, toward the east, our tunnel ended abruptly in what seemed a wall of solid rock.

"He's sealed it off!" Maram whispered. "We're trapped!"

I smiled as I brought my sword up close to the wall to reveal the cracks running through it, outlining a door: the door that must open onto Morjin's private chambers. I pressed my ear to the cold rock and listened for any sounds from the room beyond it.

"What do you hear?" Maram whispered, pressing close.

"Only your breath in my ear. Now be quiet."

I continued listening for a murmur of voices, the slap of boots against stone, silverware clacking against a plate—for anything at all. But the rock was as quiet as a skull. The only sound I heard was the drumming of my heart.

"All right," I said, turning back to look at Kane. "Is everyone ready?"

Both Kane and Liljana had their swords drawn, as did Maram. I gripped Alkaladur's hilt more tightly as I faced the door and said softly, "Memoriar-Damoom!"

There came a clicking from within the rock of the door. I placed my hand on the edge of it; it felt wet as from dripping water, but I realized that it was only my sweat. Slowly, I pushed against the door. It opened directly into a cloth that I discovered to be another tapestry. I squeezed out from behind its clinging folds and stepped into a well-lit room.

"This is it," Daj said, joining me there. "Lord's Morjin's room."

I knew that it was. All at once, a sickly sweet odor as of incense mixed with decay made my stomach churn. As the others moved out from behind the tapestry and then pushed the door shut, I looked out at a large, richly furnished room. Intricate tapestries, like the one hiding the door behind us, completely covered the room's four walls so that not a square inch of bare rock remained exposed to remind Morjin that he had chosen to live inside a mountain. We stood with our backs to the room's west wall. To our left, along the north wall, was a heavy bronze door cast with roses and other flowers—the door to the rest of Morjin's palace. Straight ahead stood another door, like in size, but it showed a great tree beneath a bronze sun. Daj said that it opened upon the passage leading to the throne room.

I noticed that three long mirrors, framed in ornate gold, were set into the east, north and west walls, while the floor was covered with a single carpet woven with the shapes of knights on horses, winged lions and ferocious beasts. As before, when Morjin had brought me to this room through the doorway of nightmare and illusion, I looked down to see that I was standing on the head of a fire-breathing dragon.

"Look, Val!" Maram whispered to me as he nudged my side. "That's a touchstone, isn't it!"

I turned to see him pointing at a massive desk on which many books lay open. There, too, set out as if Morjin had been studying them, were warders, wish stones, dragon bones and other lesser gelstei. Maram took a step toward the desk, perhaps intending to touch or take one of these treasures. But I grabbed his elbow and said, "We don't have time for this."

Kane, moving quickly, swept up a few bloodstones glowing with a dreadful red light and pocketed them. Then he pointed his sword at a large stand next to the desk. He snarled out, "We have time for this, then."

I saw that the stand, which looked something like a brazier, held six large eggs thrice the size of an eagle's. Before I could stop him, Kane crossed the room and thrust his sword straight through one of the eggs, breaking open the leathery shell. Five more times he thrust out, and when he was done, the steel of his sword dripped with a thick, blood-orange yolk. Thus did he destroy the eggs of Angraboda, one of the dragons that Morjin had summoned here from Damoom.

"But there were seven eggs!" Daj whispered as he crossed the room to where Kane stood snarling down at the broken, oozing mass of shells.

"Seven, eh? Are you sure?"

Daj nodded his head, looking about the room, as did Kane.

"Kane, there's no time!" I said, making for the door with the great tree. "We've got to go!"

"You go," he said. "This is a rare chance."

"To destroy an egg?"

"Yes, that," he said. He stalked over to the great, canopied bed and stabbed his sword toward its silk coverings. "And to destroy Morjin."

He looked at the door on the north wall that led to the rest of the palace; he gazed fiercely at the tapestry covering the door by which we had entered the room. I found it hard to

bear the wrath welling up inside him then. But I stared straight
at him and said a single word: "Please."

There was a moment when I thought he would turn inward
to that burning ocean of hate that pulled him ever downward
into the hell of his own being. But once, near a little clearing
littered with the bodies of the gray men that we had slain, he
had pledged his sword to my service so long as I sought the
Lightstone. The deep, knowing touch of our eyes told me that
he remembered this promise. And that he would keep it.

"All right," he said, pointing his sword toward the east door
that led to the throne room. "Let's finish this damn quest of
yours then!"

I stepped over and twisted the knob of the door, which was
unlocked and pulled open like any other. Behind it was a hallway, draped with flowing silks, that ran straight east. I led the
way into it, and then Kane shut the door behind us.

We marched forward for a distance of a few hundred yards.
No other doors or passages gave out onto this new tunnel. On
either side of us and above us, Daj said, were the rooms of
Morjin's palace that could only be reached from his room
through its north door. Many people, I sensed, were all about
us through thin walls of rock. As we hurried along, my breath
came more quickly in bursts that seemed to burn my nostrils
and mouth. And yet the air was cold, as was the rock beneath
the thin wall coverings. The door at the opposite end of the
hallway was cold, too. We came upon it in a rush of driving
feet and beating hearts. Like the door to Morjin's room, it was
cast of bronze and unlocked.

With a last look back at Kane and the others, I pushed it
open. And then I stepped out into Morjin's throne room.

"Look!" Maram whispered in my ear. "Oh, my Lord!"

We stood along the west wall of one of the largest enclosed
spaces I had ever beheld. The vast chamber, carved out of
solid rock, must have been three hundred feet high and nearly
as long and wide. Immense pillars rose up from the floor like
giant stone trees and fluted out to support the dark ceiling high
above. Everything about this cold, vaulted hall seemed dark,

with its acres of bare, black basalt. Yet Morjin and the hall's makers had applied all their art toward filling it with light. In the walls and ceiling were set many hundreds of glowstones, throwing out their soft, silky sheen. The pillars were jacketed in gold leaf, which reflected this radiance out into the hall. Various statues, encrusted with rubies, sapphires, and other gems, added to the glitter. And yet it was not quite enough to reach into the farthest corners and drive away the shadows. In the midst of all this ancient and hideous splendor hung an air of dread that seemed to ooze from the exposed rock along the ceiling, floor, and walls; here echoed the memory of torments as old as the ages and the future cries of hopelessness and doom.

For a moment, I pressed back against the bronze door to still my dizziness and orient myself. I noted the three closed gates, along the east, north and west walls. Opposite the door to Morjin's rooms where we gathered, at the center of the hall and toward its southern end, stood a great throne. It had been built, it seemed, in mockery of the king's throne in Tria. Six broad steps led up to it, and each step was framed at either end by the sculptures of Gashur and Zun and other Galadin who had become as monsters. The greatest of these was the red dragon monument to Angra Mainyu into which the throne itself was set. When Morjin took his place on this seat of power, his head would be framed just below the huge dragon's head, which looked out into the room with golden eyes carved out of two huge amber stones.

Leaving the door behind us open should we have to beat a hasty retreat, we moved out into the great hall as we began what I hoped would be the final moments of the quest. But even as Alkaladur's blade shined with a new light, my hope faded. For in truth, the silustria blazed too brightly. In whatever direction I pointed it—north, east, south, and west—I could detect not the slightest change in its luminosity. I knew from this frightful radiance that the Lightstone must be very close: so close that my silver sword could lead us no farther. But how we might otherwise find it in so vast a space, I didn't know.

For there were a thousand places where Sartan Odinan

might have set down a little golden cup. Behind the throne, and in other parts of the room, there were altars and pedestals that might have been the Lightstone's resting place. And cold braziers, lamp stands, cabinets and even the plinths of the great stone pillars holding up the ceiling. Along the huge walls themselves—carved with dragons, demons, and a huge bas-relief of the Baaloch and the dark angels imprisoned with him on Damoom—there were recesses and rocky projections, any one of which might have hidden the Lightstone.

"Well?" Maram said to me as we walked out into the room.

"It is here," I said. "But it's so close, my sword can't tell us where."

"Then how are we to find it?" Maram stopped by the line of pillars running down the hall to the right of the throne. He bent to feel along a pillar's massive, square-cut plinth, tapping his hands along the stone like a blind man. "We can't just hope we'll stumble across it!"

We worked our way across the hall, passing between the throne and an evil-looking, circular area with several great standing stones arising from the floor. We came to the line of pillars running down the hall to the left of the throne. And there, suddenly, Flick appeared. His small, scintillating form, now throwing out sparks of silver and gold, shot up into the air like fireworks. He whirled about ecstatically, then dove down like a firebird and began weaving his way in and out of the mighty pillars in streaks of violet flame.

"Do you think he's trying to tell us where it is?" Maram asked.

Flick looped in and out of the pillars and then spun directly over the circular area with its standing stones, which looked to be used for rituals. Flick, I thought, did know where the Lightstone was. It seemed he was drinking in its presence through every sparkling bit of his being. But I sensed that he couldn't simply tell us where it had been hidden. For whatever Flick really was, it couldn't have occurred to him that for my friends and me, the Lightstone remained invisible.

"Why, why?" I whispered. It was the greatest torment of

Argattha to stand so close to the Lightstone, almost to feel its numinous presence charging the air as before a storm, but not be able to see it.

Daj, watching us look across the room as Flick streaked about, must have thought we had fallen mad. He could not make out the Timpum's fiery shape. And so he was the first of us to behold another sight.

"Val—over there!" he cried as he pulled on my arm. He pointed across the ritual area at the gate on the west side of the hall. "They're coming!"

And even as my eyes fell upon the gate's iron doors, they flew open, swinging inward. Many guards, dressed in mail and yellow livery stained with angry red dragons, charged into the hall. Many of them bore swords and halberds in their hands; some had long, thrusting spears. Their captains arrayed them in four lines, two on either side of the doorway. Almost without thinking, I took a quick count of their numbers: there were about twenty-five of them in each line.

"So," Kane muttered. Just then the door to Morjin's private chamber by which we had entered the hall slammed shut. "Four of us against a hundred—so."

Without any more prompting, Maram ran over to the gate on the east wall behind the pillars where we gathered. He pounded against it, but it was locked.

"Trapped!" he cried out. "Now we're truly trapped!"

So we were. As Maram rejoined us and we stood with our backs to the pillars, there came a flurry of motion from outside the open gate to the throne room. And then a man dressed in a golden tunic, trimmed with black fur and emblazoned with a ferocious red dragon, strode through the doorway. He was almost tall and bore himself with an unshakable air of command. His close-cropped hair shined like gold while the beauty of his form and face seemed almost too perfect. His eyes appeared golden, too. For he was, of course, Morjin the Fair—the Lord of Lies and the Great Beast who had so often come for me with his claws and illusions in the worst of my nightmares.

"Ah, my friend," Maram said to me as we pressed back

against the pillars, preparing for a last stand. "This is the end—finally, the end."

Morjin took another step forward, before pausing to beckon with his hand to his guards. He stared across the room straight at me—and at Kane, Maram, Liljana, and Daj. His hideously beautiful eyes gleamed with utter triumph. And then, without a word, his face fell into a mask of hate as he and his guards began marching toward us.

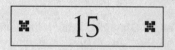

15

MORJIN LEFT HALF of his men to guard the open gate while he deployed the fifty others around the ritual area facing us. I had supposed that he and his guards would simply charge us when they drew close enough. But he stood staring at us across some seventy feet of the bare stone floor.

"Back toward the wall!" Maram hissed at me.

I was reluctant to retreat from the line of the pillars to the wall, for there we would be trapped with no room to maneuver.

"No, hold here," I said to Maram. "Let's see what he's waiting for."

A moment later, six red-robed men walked through the gate, down the line of the guards posted there and crossed the room to join Morjin. They were of various ages, heights, and colorings, but they all had the long, lean, hungry look of wolves.

"The Red Priests!" Kane snarled out. "Damn them all!"

Even as he said this, I felt a sharp stab of despair at the base of my skull, and men that I dreaded even more than these drinkers of blood entered the room. There were thirteen of them, all wearing hooded gray cloaks over their gray garments. Their faces were as gray as rotting flesh, while their eyes—what little we could see of them—were like cold gray marbles empty of life. There was nothing inside them, I thought, except a ravenous desire to drink our lives and our very souls.

"Oh, no!" Maram muttered. "The Stonefaces!"

Liljana held one hand protectively over Daj's heart, while she gripped her gelstei in the other. She watched the thirteen Grays take their places inside the circle with Morjin. She said, "It is they. I'm almost certain it was they who gave us away."

Hearing this, Maram whispered, "Then perhaps our friends are still safe. Perhaps they'll find a way to—"

"Hold your noise!" Kane snapped at him. "And guard your thoughts!"

The leader of the Grays, a tall man with a pitiless contempt stamped into his face, turned his cold gaze upon me. A terrible fear suddenly pinned me back against the pillar as if a dozen lances of ice had pierced my body.

And then Liljana brought her little figurine up to her head, engaging his mind, fighting him and his dreadful company for all our sakes, and the lances suddenly snapped as I felt a new life returning to my chilled limbs.

"Liljana," I said, looking at her. "Can you hold them?"

Liljana stood valiantly facing the Grays. Her wise, willful eyes fought off their soul-sucking stares. Sweat poured down her deeply creased face. And she gasped out, "I think I can . . . for a while."

Mighty was the power of the blue gelstei, I thought, and mighty was the mind of Liljana Ashvaran. A surge of hope shot through me then. But not for us: I could only pray that Atara and the others would discover that we had been taken and that Liljana's valor would give them time to flee Argattha.

And then, as if Morjin could read my mind through the flames of kirax connecting us, he turned toward the still-open gate. His gloat of victory disfigured his fine face. My heart broke to see two guards dragging Atara into the throne room in chains. Another likewise led Master Juwain toward the ritual area. And then five men, each pulling at long chains like leashes on a mad dog, strained to jerk the furiously struggling Ymiru into the room. Five more men followed him with chains pulled tight around the shackles binding his huge wrist, neck, and waist. His black Saryak's robe had been stripped from him. Blood stained his fur where the shackles cut into him. It took all the strength of these ten large men to control him and move him toward the circle where Morjin stood with his priests, his guards, and the terrible Grays.

Seeing the guards manhandle Atara, I lifted up Alkaladur and took a step forward. Its blade radiated my hate. And then Morjin, his eyes fixed fearfully on my bright sword, finally spoke to me. His words rang out like steel through the hall: "If you come any closer, Valashu Elahad, she will be killed."

The Red Priests who were swarming over Atara, I saw, had jeweled knives fastened to their belts. And the Grays, of course, had their knives drawn: gray-steel daggers as sharp as death. The guards deployed around the circle pointed their swords, halberds, and spears at Kane and me.

"Chain her!" Morjin commanded his guards. He turned his golden eyes upon Master Juwain and the raging Ymiru. "Chain them, too!"

Guards came forward with hammers then, and beat at our friends' chains with a dreadful clang of metal against metal. They bound them to the iron rings sunk into the standing stones. With the cruel chains pulling their arms straight out from their sides, they could barely move.

My fear for Atara—and for Master Juwain, Ymiru, and all of us—almost chained me back against the pillar. I could only gaze helplessly into Atara's eyes as I held my sword at my side and waited for Morjin to speak.

The Lord of Lies seemed steeped in thought as he paced around the circle. He had ordered Ymiru's club and Atara's bow and arrows, like the key to Daj's shackles, placed on the floor just beyond their reach. There, too, lay Master Juwain's varistei, Ymiru's purple gelstei, and Atara's crystal sphere. Now Morjin came over and held his hands above the gelstei as if to draw up their power. He bent to slip a feathered arrow from Atara's quiver; he stood staring at the sharp, steel point. Then, as if remembering other times when he had held court here, he looked down at the dark etchings in the floor. I took keen note of what I had so far scarcely perceived: that the stonework of the ritual area was carved with a great, coiled dragon. The dragon's head formed the very center of the circle, and its mouth was open as if to swallow the blood that must run through the grooves in the dark, sticky stone.

"All right then," he called out as the doors closed, "we may begin."

His voice, as I remembered from my nightmares, was clear and strong like the ringing of a silver bell. But now that we had finally met in the flesh, here in the fastness of his hall, he seemed to have abandoned all desire to charm or persuade me. His smiles were chill and full of malice, as little alluring as the stare of a snake. His manner was brusque and cruel as if he had come to mete out justice with an iron hand.

"Stay where you are, Valari!" he suddenly commanded me. "I would speak with you but I don't wish to shout!"

He summoned twenty of his guards and his Red Priests to walk slowly toward us where we stood by the line of pillars. They drew up forty feet away with ten guards on either side of him.

"So," Kane muttered.

I could feel Kane's large body tensing to spring forward like a tiger's; his hands fairly trembled to tear apart Morjin— as did my own.

Morjin turned to nod at the fiercest-looking of his priests, a man with the black skin of Uskudar and the dark, hungry eyes of the damned. He spoke to this priest, and to his other men, saying, "Well, Lord Almalik, it's as I've foretold. The enemy has sent assassins to murder me."

He pointed a long, elegant finger back toward the circle at Ymiru and said, "It's obvious that the Ymanish led them here. No doubt out of vengeance of his people's false claim. Do you see what comes of the bitterness of believing ancient lies?"

"It be you who lies!" Ymiru roared out as he lunged against his chains. "Argattha be our hrome!"

Morjin nodded at a guard, who slammed the butt end of his spear into Ymiru's face, smashing his teeth and bloodying his lips. He shook his dazed head slowly back and forth as Morjin continued to address him:

"Your people were paid good gold for the work they did here," he said. "And they did good work, but there is much we've improved upon."

Ymiru stared down at the dragon carved into the floor, then cast his eyes upon the dragon throne. Finally he turned to look at the Red Dragon himself. "You've taken a hroly place and made it into something horrible!"

Again Morjin nodded at his guard. This time the man thrust the point of his spear into Ymiru's side, tearing open a bloody hole in his fur.

"Thus to assassins," Morjin called out.

His golden eyes now fell upon Master Juwain as he said, "For ages, the Brotherhoods have opposed us. And now the Great White Brotherhood sends one of its Masters—a Master Healer, no less—to slay rather than mend body and soul together."

Master Juwain stared fearlessly at Morjin and opened his mouth as if to gainsay this lie. But, mindful of the guard's bloody spear, he decided that there was little point in disputing Morjin.

"If he touches him," Maram said, looking at Master Juwain, "I'll . . ."

His voice suddenly died as he looked down at the red crystal in his hand. The cracked firestone was now useless and couldn't summon forth even a wooden match's worth of flame.

Now Morjin pointed the arrow that he still held at Atara. He called out, "Princess Atara Ars Narmada, daughter of the usurper of the realm that is still ours! The Manslayer who must have seen me dead beneath her assassin's arrows! Well, scryer, what future do you see now?"

I, too, wondered what Atara saw; she stared at the figures of the fallen Galadin carved into the walls, and her eyes were full of horror.

I recalled the last part of Ayondela Kirriland's prophecy, that the dragon would be slain. Well, the dragon named Angraboda had been slain, but Morjin must have feared that the prophecy really spoke of him. Could it be, I wondered, that he truly thought we were assassins? Was it possible that he didn't know our real reason for entering Argattha?

He mustn't know then, I thought. At all costs, he mustn't know.

Morjin turned toward us where we took shelter beneath the pillars. He pointed at Daj, and spoke with great bitterness: "Well, young Dajarian, I've been merciful, but this time for you, it's the cross."

Daj pulled back behind Liljana, who was still fighting off the Grays. He began trembling as he cast his eyes about the room like a trapped fawn.

"And Prince Maram Marshayk," Morjin said, looking at my best friend. "Why you have joined this conspiracy is a mystery to me."

"Ah, it's a mystery to me as well," Maram muttered. He, too, trembled to flee, but he held his ground bravely even so.

"And Liljana Ashvaran," Morjin said, watching her stare down the leader of the Grays. "At least your motives are more obvious, witch."

He added his dreadful stare to that of the Grays, trying to beat open her mind. And I shouted, "Leave her alone! She's just a poor widow!"

Morjin suddenly smiled at me and said, "Is that what you've thought? She is the Materix of the Maitriche Telu. The ruling witch herself."

Liljana's unyielding gaze fixed on the Grays, but some flicker of pride fired up inside her then, and I knew that Morjin had told true.

"Well, witch, did you keep this a secret from your companions?"

Kane, I thought from the look on his face, might have known Liljana's true rank. And so might have Atara. But this news clearly amazed Maram, Master Juwain, and Ymiru—as it did me.

Morjin nodded at the priest named Almalik and said,

"Maitriche Telu, do you see? Poisoners and assassins, all of them."

At a nod from Morjin, the leader of the Grays looked away from Liljana. And she turned to me and said, "I am the Materix of the Maitriche Telu. Perhaps I should have told you—I'm sorry, Val."

Liljana, I thought, had given me a dozen clues that this was so. Why hadn't I seen this?

"And we have killed," she went on, "but only when we've had to."

My amazement only deepened. The Maitriche Telu, it was said, had secret sanctuaries and chapter houses in almost every land. If Morjin was more powerful than any king, even King Kiritan, then Liljana was the most powerful woman in Ea.

"But Morjin lies," she told me, "when he says that we desire to rule. We seek only to restore Ea to the ancient ways."

"You might want to be careful whom you call a liar, old witch," Morjin snapped at her. He pointed at another iron ring on the side of the standing stone to which Atara was bound. "It's an evil tongue you have, and I might decide to tear it out."

Morjin turned back toward the Grays' leader. Something seemed to pass back and forth unspoken between them. And then, as if explaining this exchange to his Red Priests and guards, Morjin said to the Gray, "Soon enough you shall have the witch's blue gelstei. And the black stone that was stolen from your brother."

Now Morjin whirled about facing Kane. Their eyes locked together like red-hot iron rings hammered into a chain. Emotions as fiery and deep as a volcano's molten rock blasted out into the room. It was impossible for me to tell whose hate was vaster, Morjin's or Kane's.

"You," Morjin said to him. "You dare to come here again."

"So, I do dare."

"What is it you call yourself now—'Kane'?"

"What is it you call yourself now—'King of Kings'? Ha!"

Morjin stood before his priests and snapped at Kane, "I should have torn out your tongue long ago!"

"Do you think it wouldn't have grown back in the mouths of ten thousand others to tell the truth of who you really are?"

"Be careful of what you say!"

"So, I'm free to speak as I will."

"For the moment." Morjin's face flushed with rage, and he pointed at the iron rings sticking out the side of Ymiru's stone. He said, "When you're chained there, who will set you free?"

"Ask that," Kane said, pointing his sword at Morjin, "after you've put me there."

Morjin stared so hard at Kane that his eyes seemed to redden from burst blood vessels. And he demanded, "Give me the stone!"

Kane held up the black gelstei that he had cut from the Gray's forehead on the night of the full moon. Then he snarled out, "Take it from me!"

My old suspicions of Kane came flooding back into me. I wondered for the thousandth time at his grievance against Morjin. It seemed they had known each other long ago in another place.

Morjin saw me looking at Kane, and he turned his spite upon me. He said, "You've taken a madman into your company, Valari."

"Do not speak so," I told him, "of my friends."

"Kane, your friend?" Morjin sneered. He pointed at Alkaladur, which I held gleaming by my side. "He's no more your friend than that is your sword."

I knew from the pounding of his heart that he feared this bright blade as he did death. It seemed that he could hardly bear to look at it.

"Alkaladur," he said softly. "How did you find it?"

"It was given to me," I told him.

I sensed that the sword's shimmering presence made him recall dark moments in dark ages long past, as well as visions yet to come. I knew, as he did, that it had been foretold that the sword would bring his death.

"Surrender the sword to me, Valari!" he shouted. "Surrender it, now!"

This sudden command, breaking from his throat like a clap

of thunder, shocked every nerve in my body. His golden eyes dazzled me; the tremendous power of his will beat at my bones, almost breaking my will to keep my fingers fastened around the hilt of my sword.

"Surrender and save yourself!" he told me. "And save your friends."

The hatred that poured out of him smothered me like burning pitch. The Red Dragon, in the flesh, was far worse than in any of my illusions or dreams. Only my resolve to oppose him—magnified by the shielding powers of my sword—kept me from falling down and groveling at his feet.

"Do you see how strong the Valari are?" Morjin said, turning to the leader of the Grays. Then he looked at Almalik and his other Red Priests. "And so the savages send one of their strongest to murder me."

I stared at him down the length of the shining sword that I pointed at him. I did badly want to murder him. How could I deny this?

"Conspirators, thieves, and murderers," he said. "They defiled my chambers. They would have trapped and tortured me there."

Lord Almalik caught Morjin's eye and said, "Torture, sire?"

Morjin nodded his head and spoke to all gathered in the room: "These seven, save the Ymanish, all journeyed to Tria to the lure of Kiritan's illicit summons. They've made quest for the Lightstone across half of Ea. I'm certain that they've gathered clues as to where it was hidden."

He doesn't know! I thought. He truly doesn't know that the Lightstone lies somewhere in this room!

"And these clues," he continued, "led them here. To me. They must have thought that I possess the key clue to their stealing of what is rightfully mine. And so they came to torture this knowledge from me."

I held myself very still, staring at him. And he said to me, "Do you deny this, Valari?"

No, I thought, I couldn't, lest I give away our true purpose. But neither could I affirm such a lie. And so held myself cloaked in silence.

"Do you see how proud the Valari is?" Morjin said to Salma-lik. "Proud and vain—it is the curse of his kind. Telemesh. Aramesh. Elemesh. Murderers, all. How many have been slaughtered in wars because of them? Because they, who are savages at heart, put their glory above others? Descendants of Elahad they claim to be! Elahad, whom the Valari claim brought the Lightstone to Ea. Elahad, the murderer of his own—"

"Elahad did bring the Lightstone to Ea!" I shouted. "The Valari were it's guardians!"

"Be quiet while I'm speaking!" Morjin roared at me. He turned to look back at the ritual area and nod at his guards, who stood in rapt attention. "Do you see how the Valari twists this false claim of guardianship into an excuse to break into my home and torture me? From such a people, are any out-rages impossible?"

"You lie!" I said to him.

Morjin paused to stare at me as he gathered in his breath. He was working himself up into a frenzy of spite. And now all his hate fell upon me like an infected wound bursting with pus.

"Look at the Valari standing there!" he said to his priests. "So tall, so arrogant! The long sword. The black eyes—who has ever seen such eyes outside nightmares where demons haunt the dark? Many have said that the Valari have made a pact with demons. But I say they are demons themselves—fiends from hell. They are a plague upon the world; they are a corruption of all that is good and true. It is in their blood, like poison. The taint goes back to the beginning of time. But it will have an ending, in time, an antidote of fire and steel. Haven't I foretold that if war comes, this last war we've all been dreading, that the Valari race will disappear from the face of the earth? That race of warlords and savages has on its conscience the dead of every great conflict in Ea's history. Would it be too much to ask that they be given new homes in the Red Desert or on trees that shall grow out of the ground in entire forests to accommodate them?"

How, I wondered, could Morjin speak with such passion and conviction when he must have known the enormity of his deceit? In the agony of his golden eyes, I sensed something about him then: that his hundreds of years of deceiving others had worked an evil alchemy upon him so that he truly believed his lies.

His lies have possessed him. And so he has made of himself a ghul.

For a moment, I was moved to pity him. But this only caused him to further rant and rage at me as he pointed at me and thundered: "The arrogance of the Valari! Who else could steal the Lightstone and keep it behind their mountains for most of an age? Is there a greater crime than this in all of history?"

I felt Morjin's hate beating at me like a hammer, from his heart to mine—as it beat at his guards and Grays and everyone else gathered in the hall.

Morjin stepped over to one of his priests, a young man whose handsome face was marred with patches of scar as if it had been burned in by heated iron. Morjin said to him, "Lord Uilliam, if such criminals came into your care, what would you recommend be done with them?"

Morjin's fervid gaze fell upon Lord Uilliam; his tongue seemed to shoot invisible streams of relb at Lord Uilliam so that the young man's tongue caught up the flames of malice, and he said, "Purify them with fire!"

Morjin breathed out the fire of his approval and set the young man's blood burning with a raging desire to punish his enemies.

And so it went as he paced about the room, here pausing to question one of his guards, there nodding at one of the Grays or his priests. He played to his people: with cunning words that fell easily off his silver tongue, with long, soulful looks, with veiled threats and promises and deceits. One man he flattered; another he frightened; too many his malice opened like a black knife and set loose their animal ferocity. I hated how Morjin perverted the gift we both had been given: he played men like instruments, plucking at their heartstrings as if he were a twisted minstrel making the most evil of music.

Morjin nodded across the hall at one of his guards, who brought a brazier heaped with hot coals into the ritual circle.

He set it down in front of Atara, Ymiru, and Master Juwain. Then he thrust a pincers and three long, pointed irons into the coals to heat them.

"The Lightstone will soon be recovered," Morjin shouted. "Haven't I foretold that this is the time when it will again be seen in this hall? And what should be done with this cup when it returns to its rightful place?"

One of his guards, an old soldier with a grim face and a strange hunger in his eyes, knew the right answer to this question. And he called out, "Pour from it eternal life!"

Now every pair of eyes in the hall fixed on Morjin. His men looked at him with an almost electric anticipation.

"Eternal life!" Morjin cried out. "This is the gift that the Lightstone may bestow upon the chosen."

As Kane glared at Morjin, I understood that the powerful seek power for its own sake because it gives them the illusion they have power over death.

But fear of death, I thought, leads to hate of life.

With these few words, whispered inside my mind, I knew that I had condemned myself should the door that I most feared be flung open before me. For Morjin, with all his vainglory and hate, was like a mirror reflecting back at me a shape that I did not want to see.

"And who are these chosen?" Morjin continued. He nodded sternly at Lord Uilliam and Lord Almalik. "They are the priests who have served the Kallimun so faithfully; they are my guards and soldiers who have given their lives for a greater purpose, and so it is only fitting that they shall have greater life themselves."

Morjin, the sorcerer who had lived thousands of years, stood before his men as the living embodiment that what he promised was possible.

"And who," he quietly asked, "shall be the one to pour the nectar of immortality from the golden cup? Only the Maitreya. But who is this man? That will be determined only when the Lightstone is placed in his hands."

So saying, he reached his hands out to the hundred and twenty men who had followed him into the room. In their many eyes was a terrible lust for the Lightstone and all that Morjin had vowed to give them.

"So," Kane muttered next to me. There came a rumbling sound of hate from deep inside his throat. "So."

Now Morjin turned to me and said, "You've taken a vow to seek the Lightstone. And now you can fulfill it by helping us to recover it. You must help us, Valari."

I gripped my sword more tightly as I fought off the waves of false bliss that Morjin now beamed at me. It was strange to think that he wanted my hate and fear less than he did my love.

"Surrender your sword," he commanded me. "Surrender yourself."

"No," I said, my heart beating fast like a bird's.

"You must surrender, Valari."

All people have a love and longing for the One, for that is our source, at once father and mother and breath of the infinite in which we take our being. Morjin now stood before me with his fingers outstretched as if waiting for me to place my sword in his hands. His eyes called to me. His soul called me to adore him as I would the One's blessed light so that he might feel within himself the ancient heavenly connection that he had long since lost.

"Is it death you want?" he asked me. His eyes now seemed as golden as the Lightstone itself. "Or life?"

I took a few deep breaths to slow the racing of my heart. And then I said, "It is not upon you to give me either."

"Is it not? That we shall see."

I lifted my sword back behind my head in readiness should Morjin send his guards against us. And I told him, "I will never surrender to you!"

My contempt for Morjin burned through my face for all to behold. Even if I hadn't possessed the gift of *valarda,* not a man in the hall would have been spared feeling my defiance.

"Damn you, Valari!" he thundered at me. His face contorted into a mask of ugliness as rage took hold of him. If he couldn't have love, he was ready to embrace hate. "Never surrender, you say? That, too, we shall see."

He shook Atara's arrow at me, and then pointed it directly at Master Juwain. He shouted at him, "What is it you know about the Lightstone?"

"What?" Master Juwain said as if he didn't understand the question.

"Didn't you hear me?" Morjin roared out. Upon beckoning Lord Uilliam to follow him, he turned and strode back into the circle. He plucked one of the irons from the brazier and handed it to Lord Uilliam. "Master Juwain's ear is stopped with wax—clean it out."

As Lord Uilliam gazed at the iron's glowing red point, Morjin commanded the guards still posted near the door to join the others around the circle. They took their places there, and Lord Uilliam looked over at Master Juwain, who was sweating and biting his lip as he pulled at his chains.

"Put it in his ear!" Morjin commanded.

Lord Uilliam still hesitated, and he said, "But he's just an old man!"

"Do it!" Morjin hissed.

Beside me, Maram now had his sword drawn, as did Liljana and Kane. I was ready to charge forward in an effort to cut our way through to Master Juwain. But we were only four against a hundred.

"Be strong," Kane said to me. "You must be strong now, eh?"

Now Morjin breathed the terrible fire of his wrath into Lord Uilliam. The reluctant priest suddenly stiffened as if he could feel the heat of the iron up through his hand and all throughout his body. He turned to step closer to Master Juwain. As one of the guards slammed Master Juwain's head back against the standing stone and held it clamped there, Lord Uilliam pushed the burning point of the iron into the opening of Master Juwain's ear. There came a hissing and the stench of burnt flesh. Lord Uilliam snarled and gnashed his teeth together; he keep pushing the iron deeper, twisting it, reaming it around in circles as his hate poured out of him.

"Master Juwain!" Maram called out, and he burst into tears.

The pain burning through my head was so great that I could

barely keep standing. But the sheer valor with which Master Juwain faced his torture sent a thrill of strength shooting through me. Not once did he cry out for mercy. His whole body quivered with the shock of what the priest was doing to him. Although his face contorted with agony, I saw that it was really beautiful after all—beautiful with a luminous will that overmatched Morjin's and kept him from surrendering his soul to him.

"Master Juwain!" Maram cried out again. "Master Juwain!"

True men, I thought looking at my best friend, didn't need the gift of *valarda* to suffer another's pain.

At last, the iron's point quenched in Master Juwain's blood, Lord Uilliam stood away from him. His face was white; he held the iron in his trembling hand. He could barely stand himself. Morjin stepped closer to him, and wrapped his arm around his back to help hold him up.

"Well done, my priest," Morjin told him. He touched his finger to the iron's bloody point; then he touched his finger to his tongue. "Have I not said many times that the priests of the Kallimun must do the hard things and so sacrifice themselves for the sake of Ea?"

Morjin shook his fist at Master Juwain and shouted, "Is this what you wanted? That you, a healer, should cause such sickness in my priest's soul?"

But I did not think that Master Juwain could hear him, even with his remaining good ear. His head had fallen down against his chest, and the weight of his body pulled against the chains binding him.

"Where is the Lightstone?" Morjin screamed at him. He stepped over and slapped his face. "What have you learned about it?"

Master Juwain finally opened his eyes and lifted up his head. His gray eyes blazed with defiance. And he told Morjin, "Only that you'll never have from it what you wish."

Again Morjin slapped his face, which snapped his head back against the great stone. Then Morjin motioned for his six priests to gather around him. He stood talking to them in hushed tones as the thirteen silent Grays waited nearby and the hundred guards circled the ritual area with the steel of their swords and spears. It was a mortar of torture and blood-crime that bound this evil brotherhood together. It was well for them, I thought, that they hid their secrets inside the windowless vaults of a black mountain.

"Val," Maram whispered to me as he stared at the standing stones. He was sweating even more profusely than Master Juwain. "Stab your sword into my heart—I don't think I have the courage to fall on mine."

"Be strong!" Kane called to him. "Strong as stone now, I say!"

Maram closed his eyes then. It was said that the Brotherhoods taught meditations that could forever still the beating of one's heart. But it seemed that Maram had been too busy with other pursuits to learn them.

"I can't," he finally said, looking at me. "I can't will myself to die."

"Will them to die!" Kane growled out, stabbing his sword at Morjin and his priests.

Now Morjin stepped over to Atara and looked at her, and a new terror struck into me. Atara looked back at him boldly, her eyes as clear as diamonds. There was a terrible fear in their bright blue depths, but something else as well. It seemed that she was seeing the future and trying to surrender herself to what must be. This was her will, as a warrior and a woman, to fulfill her purpose in being born on such a savage world as Ea.

"Don't you ever look at me like that!" Morjin suddenly raged at her. He slapped her face with his left hand, turning her head, and then backhanded her, turning her head again. But she summoned up all her courage and held her head up proudly as she continued to stare at him. I sensed that she was seeing something in him that no one else could see.

"Damn you!" he snarled out, slapping her again and bloodying her mouth. Then he whirled about to face me. "And damn you, Valari!"

I turned to catch Kane's stare and said to him, "Let's charge them now and make an end to this."

Kane eyed the hundred guards waiting around the circle, and he said, "It would be our death."

"There is no help for that now."

"No—there may yet be a chance."

"What, then?"

Kane examined the walls of the room, the great throne, the pillars and the bolted iron doors. Then he said, "I wish I knew."

Morjin, hating to be ignored, waved Atara's arrow at me and shouted: "Lay down your sword and I will spare your woman!"

"No!" Atara cried out to me. "You must never surrender!"

"Do it!" Morjin hissed at me. "Now!"

"No, Val! The sword is his death—can't you see how he fears it?"

Morjin tore his gaze from my flashing sword to stare at Atara. And then he screamed at her, "And what do you fear, scryer? Not death, I think. And scarcely pain. Something worse. What is it you see when you look at my eyes now? Look as long as you can, scryer—look deep."

Atara looked at him in utter loathing and contempt, and then spat the blood from her broken lip straight into his eyes.

"Damn you!" he shouted. He wiped his sleeve across his face and blinked furiously. He shook the arrow at her and cried out, "Is this one of the arrows you shot into my son's eyes?"

I stood almost unable to breathe, watching the rage flow into Morjin's face as I remembered the deadly accuracy of Atara's arrows in the darkness of the Vardaloon.

"Meliadus," Atara said clearly for all to hear, "was a monster."

"HE WAS MY SON!"

Morjin screamed this so loudly that the rock of the archways three hundred feet above the circle rang with his anguish and wrath. He suddenly reached out and grabbed Atara's long hair. He slammed her head back against the standing stone. And then, with blinding speed, he stabbed the arrow's barbed point into her left eye. It took only a moment for him to rip it

free and plunge the bloody steel straight through the center of
her right eye.

A terrible madness seized me then. I surged forward to kill
as many priests and guards as I could in my rage to get at
Morjin. But Kane grabbed me from behind and wrapped his
iron arm around my throat. Maram grasped my right arm; Liljana held fast to my left. From somewhere behind me, I heard
Daj screaming and cursing and gasping out his fear of Morjin,
all at once.

Morjin didn't even pause to glance at me. He cast down the
bloody arrow. And then, like a bird of prey, like a rabid cat, like
the demon he was, he fell upon Atara with all his fury. He spat
and hissed as he drove his clawlike fingers into her face. He
stood fastened to her, shaking and snarling and gouging, pulling
ferociously, tearing at her—driving his fingers beneath her
brows and tearing out her eyes. He suddenly jumped back and
held the bloody orbs up for all to see. Then he crossed over to
the brazier and cast these lumps of flesh into the burning coals.

For a long time, it seemed, my world went dark, and I could
not see for the terrible burning that blinded me. A high,
hideous scream broke upon the hall. At first I thought it was
Atara giving voice to what Morjin had done to her; then I realized that the sound had been torn from deep inside me.
When I could finally see again, it was not by virtue of the
glowstones' dim light but only the hate that filled my heart
and utterly possessed me. I looked over at the circle to see
Atara shaking and sobbing as she wept blood instead of tears
from her reddened eye hollows. Morjin stood holding a cup to
her cheek, catching the blood that flowed out of them. More
blood—a whole ocean of it, it seemed—flowed off Atara's
chin in streams. It fell to the floor and ran through the dark
grooves cut into the stone there; it disappeared into the
dragon's open mouth like water gurgling down a hole.

Kane's arm was an iron collar bound around my throat; his
body behind me was a pillar of stone that I could not break or
pull down. And his breath in my ear was the red-hot flame of
vengeance: "Damn Morjin and all his kind!"

Now Morjin stood back from Atara and gazed at her ruined

face. He took a drink from the cup that he held in his bloody hands. Then he passed it to Lord Almalik, who also drank from it before passing it on to another priest.

With great effort, Atara pulled back her head and oriented it facing Morjin, as if she could smell or sense his presence. Her heart beat with her contempt for him. And then an incredible thing happened. I perceived Morjin as she had, just before her blinding. The mask of illusion was suddenly ripped away from him, and he stood revealed as he truly was: no longer beautiful in face and form, but rather terrible and ghastly to behold. His eyes were not golden at all. They were a sickly red, with pigments of ocher and iron settled into the irises, while the whites were bloodshot as if he was never able to sleep. His pale, mottled skin was likewise disfigured with a webwork of broken blood vessels. There were pouches under his eyes, and much of his limp, grayish hair had fallen out. In the skin that drooped from his neck and in his predatory countenance was a ravenous hunger for vitality and lost love.

I knew that I would never be able to see him otherwise again. As his tongue darted out like a snake's and he licked the blood from his lips, I saw something else: that he had blinded Atara not because of Meliadus but because she had seen through the veil of his most precious illusion and had shown him in the mirror of her eyes what an evil being he truly was.

He knows! I suddenly realized. *All this time, he has known!*

Somewhere, beneath the lies and trickeries that he crafted for himself and others, lived a man who knew very well the wrong of what he did—and chose to do it anyway. And why? Because people were less than animals to him.

What is hate? It is a black abyss full of fire hotter than a dragon's breath. It is a poison that burns a thousand times as painfully as kirax. It is a black and bitter bile that gathers at the center of one's being, seething to a boil. It is a stabbing pain in the heart, a pressure in the head, a gathering in of all the world's anguish and an overwhelming desire to make another suffer as you have. It is lightning. But not the thunderbolt of illumination, but rather its opposite which maims and burns and blinds. And its name is *valarda*.

MORJIN!

As he had once promised I would, I struck out at him with the gift that the angels had bestowed upon me. Something very like a thunderbolt of pure, black hate shot out from my heart along the line of my sword and struck his heart. It staggered him. He gasped as he stared at me in astonishment. He dropped to one knee, gasping and clutching at his chest, even as Kane held me from behind and kept me from collapsing in the sudden agony of what I had done to him.

"Oh, Valari!" Morjin gasped as he struggled to breathe.

I, myself, had stopped breathing. For a few moments, I think, my heart stopped beating, too, and I nearly died. And then, as Morjin regained his strength, I felt hate pouring into my limbs again and firing up my being.

"Oh, Valari!" Morjin said again as he stood up and gazed at me. On his pale, fell face was a look of utter triumph. "That is the last time you'll catch me off-guard. You're stronger than I would have believed, but there's much you have to learn. Shall I show you how it's done?"

So saying, he whirled upon Atara and fixed her with his terrible red eyes. A storm of hate gathered inside him. His heart beat in rhythm with mine.

"No!" I cried.

"Then throw down your sword!"

"No!" I cried again.

"What befalls your woman," he said, pointing at her, "is upon you."

"No, that is not true!"

"You'll see her die, but not until you've died a thousand times." And with that, he stepped over to the brazier and removed the glowing pincers.

"Damn you!" I screamed at him.

"Damn you, Valari, for making me do this!" He looked at the pincers' red-hot iron and shouted, "I'll tear out her vile tongue and roast it on the coals! I'll send lepers to ravish her! I'll give her to the rats and let you watch as they eat what's left of her face!"

The thirteen Grays, with their cold eyes and long knives, stood in the circle of death with Morjin waiting to see what he would do. The six priests of the Kallimun looked pitilessly at Atara as they must have many other victims. The hundred guards ringing the circle waited with their swords and spears and axelike halberds. The whole world, it seemed, waited for me to speak or move.

"You must not surrender!" Atara suddenly called to me. She stood tall and brave and eyeless in eternity.

"In a moment, I'll tear out your tongue," Morjin promised her. "But first you will call for the Elahad to surrender."

He took a step closer to her as I gripped my sword more tightly. I sensed that he wanted to test my compassion for Atara. It was his will to torture her terribly and for a long time. Because he hated her, yes, but more because he wanted to break me utterly. He wanted me to kneel before him in the sight of all the men gathered in the hall almost as much as he wanted the Lightstone itself.

"Atara," I whispered.

What is hate? It is a wall ten thousand feet high surrounding the castle of despair. Since the moment that Morjin had blinded Atara, I had built this wall higher and higher so that I would not have to know what she really suffered. But now, in looking at her as she turned toward me, the blood pooling in her eye hollows and dripping down her cheeks, her face emptied of all hope of that which she most deeply desired, this wall of stone split asunder as if the earth beneath it had cracked open. And I cried out in the greatest anguish I had ever known, for the love that bound Atara and me together was the greatest I had ever known.

"Hold!" I shouted to Morjin. "Take me instead of Atara!"

The world, I knew, was a place of infinite suffering, infinite pain. In the end I was the weakest of our company. I could bear Atara's torture much less than she herself.

"Throw down your sword, then!" Morjin called to me, turning away from Atara.

I shook myself free from Kane, who stared at me, waiting

to see what I would do. And I shouted at Morjin, "First free Atara!"

I looked at Master Juwain bound to his stone and at Ymiru pulling against his chain. "Free my friends, too! Let them leave Argattha!"

"No," Morjin said to me. "First throw down and step forward into our circle, and then I shall do as you ask."

He stared at me, smiling triumphantly.

"Val, don't do it!" Liljana said to me, pulling on my arm. "He lies!"

"So, his promise is worth rat dung," Kane growled out.

I called out to Morjin, "What surety do we have that you will keep your word?"

"I am King of Ea, and what more surety can there be?" he said. "It is we who need surety, Valari. How is it to be believed that a proud Valari knight will go willingly to his death with no sword in his hand?"

Morjin's red eyes now filled with a bloodlust that was terrible to behold.

How is it to be believed? I asked myself. How can I do what I must do?

Kane had said that there still might be a chance for us, and now I saw that there was. But not for me. I might buy my friends' lives with mine. Morjin had given his word before his priests and men, and there was a chance that he might keep it.

"Val!" Atara called to me.

What is love? It is the warm, healing breath of life that melts the bitterest ice. It is the hot pain of joy in one's heart impossible to quench. It is the fire of the stars that burns clean the soul. It is a simple thing—the simplest thing in the world.

"Atara," I whispered as I looked at her. Her bloody, mutilated face, I thought, was the most beautiful thing I had ever seen.

I stood there facing the circle where Atara and my friends were bound, and my hands sweated to feel the diamonds in Alkaladur's hilt for the last time. There was a sickness in my belly; my chest ached with a crushing pain. Death waited there for me. My old enemy was cold and black and terrifying; it was a terrible emptiness that had no end. It didn't matter. In looking at Atara look toward me, so full of love, so full of light, I suddenly wanted to die for her. I burned with a fierce desire to accept any torment and annihilation in order to keep her living in the land of light.

"Well, Valari?" Morjin called out to me.

I glanced at him and nodded my head. Even if there was only one chance in ten thousand that he would spare Atara and my friends, I had to take it.

And then, even as I bent to lay Alkaladur down upon the dark stone of this vast, dark hall, at the darkest moment of my life, the Bright Sword began shining with an intense radiance that I also felt inside myself. At that moment, the world was strangely full of light. For I, and I alone, suddenly saw the Lightstone everywhere: on top of pedestals and gleaming golden in the recesses of the rocky walls; on the altar near the throne and on tables and even shimmering amidst the red-hot coals in the brazier into which Morjin had cast his offering of flesh. The whole of the throne room blazed with a brilliant golden light. It blinded me to the Lightstone's true presence as surely as my flaws of fear and faithlessness had always blinded me to myself.

"Valari!" Morjin called to me.

And then Alkaladur flared silver-white, more brightly than it ever had before. In the mirror of the polished and perfect silustria of my sword, I saw who I really was: Valashu Elahad, son of Shavashar Elahad, who was the direct descendant of Telemesh and Aramesh and all the kings of Mesh going back to the grandsons of Elahad himself. In me still burned the soul of the Valari—we who long ago had brought the Lightstone to earth. The Valari, I remembered, were once guardians of the Lightstone, and would someday be again.

"Damn you, Valari, throw it down now or I'll take your woman's tongue!"

But what or who were we to guard the Lightstone for? Not for glory or the ending of pain. Not for invulnerability or immortality or power. Not for the dreams of the Maitriche Telu or the vengeance of Kane. Nor for great kings such as Kiritan who would give their daughters to triumphant warriors, nor even for wise queens such as the Lady of the Lake. And certainly not for false Maitreyas such as Morjin who would use it to work great evil instead of good.

The Lightstone is for one and one only, I thought. *The true Maitreya told of in the great prophecy, the Lightbringer who will arise from Ea to defeat the Lord of Darkness and lead all the worlds into a new age.*

To gain this cup and guard it so that I could place it in the Maitreya's hands was my purpose; it was my deepest desire and fate.

What is love? It is the radiance of the One; it is the blazing of the Morning Star in the eastern sky that calls men to wake up.

All my life, it seemed, I had worked to polish and sharpen the sword of my soul, rubbing away the rust and honing the steel finer and finer to put on it an exceedingly keen edge. And now, through a love beyond love, with the hand of the One bestowing this final grace, the polishing was at last completed and nothing of myself remained. And yet, paradoxically, everything. And so the true sword was revealed. It cut with an infinitely fine edge and was impossibly bright.

I suddenly stood straight and gripped Alkaladur more tightly. And with the deeper sword that the One had placed in my heart, I finally slayed the great dragon whose names are Vanity and Pride. The evil of my hate left me. And then both swords, the one that I held in my hand and the other inside me, blazed like suns. The light was so intense that it completely outshined the illusions all around me and made the thousands of Lightstones that I saw simply disappear. And in this luminous state, my eyes finally opened and drank in the sight of the Lightstone.

As the songs had told, it was just a plain golden cup that would easily fit into the palm of my hand. And as Sartan Odinan had told, it still remained in the vast, dark hall where he had set it down thousands of years before. Even as Morjin and his priests shielded their eyes against the sheen of my sword, I looked to the south of the ritual circle at the great throne. And there, on top of the eye of the coiled red dragon that framed the throne, the Lightstone waited all golden and glorious as it always had.

"Valari!" Morjin called to me.

I somehow knew that if I could only hold the Lightstone in my hands, everything would come out all right. And so I broke from our shelter by the pillars and sprinted for the throne at the same moment that Morjin's voice filled the hall.

"Guards!" he called out. "He's trying to run away!"

The hundred men of his Dragon Guard, no less his Red Priests and the murderous Grays, waited for him to order an attack. But Morjin, confused at my seeming cowardice, all the while realizing that there was something here that he didn't quite see, hesitated a heartbeat too long.

And in that moment, Flick suddenly appeared. From out of the hall's dark depths he streaked like a bolt of lightning straight toward the ritual circle. As I ran, I looked back over my shoulder to see Flick fall upon Morjin's face in swirls of white and violet sparks. Morjin, his face rigid with astonishment, dropped the iron pincers to the floor and used his hands to try to beat Flick's fiery form away from his head. And he gasped out, "Damn you, Valari! What is this trick of yours?"

It took me only a few seconds to reach the steps to the throne. I bounded up them, taking but little notice of the statues of the fallen Galadin that stared silently at me from their sides. I stood on the hard stone before the seat of the throne itself. I rested my sword there. And then I reached out and grasped the Lightstone in my hands.

Upon its touch, at once cool as grass and warm as Atara's cheek, Morjin's cries and the dark glitter of the hall faded away as in the passing of a dream. A deeper world blazed forth. Everything seemed touched with a single color, and that was glorre. The cup overflowed with shimmering cascades of light that fell over my hands and arms and every part of me. I felt its incredible sweetness through my skin and brightening my blood. Suddenly the cup began ringing with a single, pure note like a great golden bell. Then the gold gelstei of which the Lightstone was wrought turned transparent, and there was an astonishing clarity. Inside it were swirling constellations of stars—all the stars in the universe. Their light was impossibly deep; it was more brilliant and beautiful than anything I had ever beheld. I dissolved like salt into this infinite clear sea of radiance. And at last I knew the indestructible joy and bottomless peace of diving deep into the shimmering waters of the One.

When I returned to the throne room a single moment and ten thousand years later, I knew why the Lightstone's touch had killed Sartan Odinan. For the gold gelstei, far from healing my hurts, quickened my gift of valarda almost infinitely. Inside the cup was all of creation, and so long as I held it, I was open to all of its joy—and all its pain.

Infinite pain, I whispered. And then, as I felt within myself the polishing of the true substance of which I was wrought, there came a greater realization: But infinite capacity to bear it.

And so I finally understand words that I had read once in the *Saganom Elu:* "To drink in the world's suffering, you must become the ocean; to bear the burning of the fire, you must become the flame."

I grasped the Lightstone, and all fear left me. And I smiled to see that I was holding only a small golden cup in my hand.

The others saw it, too. But only for a moment. As the face of everyone in the hall turned toward me, the gold of the Lightstone fell clear as a diamond crystal and began radiating light like the sun. Brighter and brighter grew this light until it poured out like the starfire of ten thousand suns. It dazzled the very soul, and for a few moments, blinded every pair of eyes in the hall save my own.

Morjin was especially stricken by this terrible and beautiful light. He stood at the center of the black circle on top of the dragon's open mouth, gasping in terror because he was suddenly more blind than Atara. And then, finally, with a sickening jolt, he realized why my friends and I had really entered Argattha. He saw that the brilliance of my sword had come not from my hate but from a deeper resonance that he had long been denied. And so he opened his mouth and let loose a terrible cry that filled all the hall:

"VALARIII!"

His raw, outraged voice shook the stones of the pillars to the sides of the throne even as he shook his head about and howled like a mad dog. His hatred was a terrible thing. It blasted out into the hall like the fire of a furnace from hell. He hated me, and all of us, with a black, bitter fury for keeping this secret from him. And even more, he hated his own blindness that had lasted thirty centuries and lasted still.

"Guards!" he screamed. "Kill the Valari! Take the Lightstone!"

I saw that the Lightstone's radiance was now beginning to fade and would soon return to a simple golden sheen. After taking a last look at it, I tucked the little cup down beneath my mail shirt over my heart. And then, lifting up my bright, long sword, I hurried down the steps of the throne and rushed forward to do battle to defend it.

▪ 16 ▪

To BE CAST into darkness is the cruelest of fates. Morjin's sudden blindness struck terror into him. He waved his hand in front of his face and screamed out, "Guards! To me! To me!"

Like writhing, sightless insects, his guards stumbled about and managed to swarm around Morjin and protect him with their frantically waving spears. I sensed that I had only moments before they regained their vision. And so I sprinted from the throne straight across the hall toward the circle where Atara, Ymiru, and Master Juwain were bound.

Three guards, no doubt hearing the pounding of my boots against the floor, stabbed out their spears blindly to stop me. I parried their clumsy thrusts and cut them down. Then I pushed my way through other guards until I came to the standing stone holding up Atara. I swung Alkaladur twice, with great precision; its incredibly sharp silustria cut clean through her chains in a shriek of snapping iron. I wrapped my arm around her back as I led her over to Master Juwain's and Ymiru's stones and likewise freed them.

Four more guards tried to hinder me—or perhaps they were only fleeing into me in their blindness. I reddened my sword in the warm, wet sheaths of their bodies. I led Atara over to the part of the circle where their weapons and gelstei had been heaped. Then the still-blind Master Juwain and Ymiru. It took only a moment for me to grab up Ymiru's great war club and press it into his remaining hand. He suddenly regained his vision even as his huge fingers closed around the haft.

"Now there be blood!" he roared out. He stood glaring at the nearby guards as I tucked his violet crystal into the pouch on his belt. "Now they'll know what real hrorror be!"

As Master Juwain espied his green gelstei lying on the bloodstained floor, Ymiru raised up his club and began laying about Morjin's guards with a terrifying ferocity. Flesh and bones broke like eggshells with a sickening crunch as gouts of flesh sprayed out into the air. Four more men fell like bludgeoned chickens. The gargoyles carved into the walls of the hall—to say nothing of the statues of the fallen Galadin—smiled their hideous smiles to behold a bloody horror that would make even stone itself quail.

And all the while, Morjin kept screaming, "Guards! To me! To me!"

"Master Juwain!" I said as he held his crystal in front of Atara's face to stop the bleeding there. "Stay close!"

Blood still trickled from his ruined ear, and he nodded his head.

"Atara!" I said, putting her sword into her hand. "Stay by me!"

I worried that she would be too weak to stand; I didn't quite see how I could protect both her and the Lightstone in the battle that was building around us. And then she astonished me by moving precisely to gather up her bow and arrows as if she could sense how they lay on the floor. She strapped on her quiver and then turned her eyeless head toward me, saying, "No, Val—stay with the others. I've men to slay."

She smiled grimly and broke away from me; she took off at a run, dodging or stabbing guards who tried to block her way. When she had fought clear of the circle, she began running straight for Morjin's throne.

How is it possible! I wondered. How is it possible that the sightless can see? And what power was she drawing from to do battle after such an injury?

I had no time to ponder this mystery. Even as Atara bounded up the throne's steps, leaped upon the seat of the throne and climbed up the face of the dragon to stand on top of its head, the sight began returning to our enemies, one by one. A few were so bold as to attack Ymiru or me, and these quickly died. But soon the entire host of Morjin's guard would be able to see us and direct their spears in a coordinated assault. And then they would surely cut us down.

"To me!" a strong voice called out like the roar of a lion. "Val, to me!"

Across the circle, at its edge in the direction of the pillars and the hall's eastern gate, Kane had also regained the use of his eyes. He had wasted no time or pity in butchering Morjin's men; at least seven of them lay dead beneath his dripping sword. His efforts, however, weren't directed against these spear carriers and halberd wielders. It seemed that he was trying to slash his way toward Morjin, who stood near the center of the ritual area ringed by several circles of still-dazzled guards.

"Val, kill the Grays first, if you can!" Kane shouted.

Between Morjin and Kane gathered the thirteen Grays. These dreadful men might have paralyzed any and all of us but for the wrath of Liljana, who fought by Kane's side along with Maram. She held her blue gelstei up before her. I could almost feel it resonating with the Lightstone close to my heart and gaining great power. It seemed to pour forth an ethereal radiance like that of a hot blue star. So fierce was Liljana's attack upon the Grays' minds that they grabbed their heads and howled in helplessness. And Kane howled out as well, "To me!" And then, with Maram fighting frantically by his side, he finally broke through the ring of guards around the Grays and began matching their long knives with his much longer sword. It took him only a few moments to slaughter them all.

As the last of them fell, Liljana joined Kane in fixing her eyes on Morjin. And the Beast suddenly bellowed out, "Get out of my mind, witch!"

I could almost feel the blast of pure mental fire that Morjin directed at Liljana. For a moment she stood utterly stricken. It was as if she had been cast into the flames of hell. And then she turned on him a terrible fire of her own.

Now many more of Morjin's guards were able to see, and they closed ranks to protect their lord. Kane, Maram, and Liljana were forced to retreat back a few dozen yards toward the throne. Ymiru and I, with Master Juwain behind us, fought our way around the edge of the circle and joined them a hundred feet from the throne and as far from the line of pillars to the east. It was an exposed position with the bare black stone of the floor all around us. Behind us rose the dragon throne, upon which Atara now stood holding her great curved bow. Ahead of us was the mass of guards shielding Morjin inside the circle. Further retreat, I saw, would be futile. And so I called for us to form up into a five-pointed star: I stood in facing Morjin, with Kane on my right and Ymiru on my left. Maram and Liljana stood farther back, with Master Juwain in the star's center.

At that moment, Atara loosed the first of her arrows. It burned through the air and struck through the face of a tall guard standing in front of Morjin. Atara cried out, "Sixty-one!" Then, in quick succession, three more arrows sang out and found their marks in the guards surrounding Morjin. She would have slain the great Red Dragon himself if he and his priests hadn't ducked down beneath their shields of living flesh.

"Atara!" I cried out. "Kill the captains first!"

I didn't understand how Atara's arrows found these four, steel-clad men. It took her only six more shots to send them on to the stars. As death rained down all about Morjin, he cowered at the center of the circle and his naked fear beat out into the room.

He was perhaps the last person in the hall to regain his sight. As he finally did, and one of his priests pointed out where Atara stood on his throne with her great bow like an angel of death, he shouted, "Kill her!"

"Kane!" I called out. None of Morjin's captains remained standing to lead a charge against Atara. But soon he would choose out guards to send against her. Unless we fell against him first. "Ymiru! Maram! Liljana! Attack!"

I led forth into the clot of men gathered around Morjin and his priests. Four guards stabbed their spears toward me. I swung Alkaladur and cut through the shafts of all the spears in a single stroke; on the backstroke, I took off the head of one of these guards and cut clean through another's arm deep into his chest. Kane, at my right, quickly butchered two more as Ymiru's club fell straight down and crushed a halberd-bearing guard to a bloody pulp.

A few guards, on their own initiative, tried to circle around us. Liljana stabbed one of these through the neck while Maram worked his sword against the sword and spear of two others. I sensed a great strength flowing into him. He cut and parried and thrust, all the while grunting like a bear. Although his gelstei was cracked, the presence of the Lightstone seemed to cause some of its fire to ignite his heart and limbs. He suddenly snarled as he drove his sword clean through the opposing swordman's chest. And then whipping it free, he turned to parry a spear thrust and bury his sword in its owner's eye.

We had slain many but many more stood before us. The stone eyes of Angra Mainyu looking out upon the battle might have recorded that we were still badly outnumbered. But I knew that the numbers favored us. For we were not just six warriors against sixty. Kane fought beside me with the strength and fury of ten men; all that he had taught me came out in the speed and precision of my sword, which flashed and cut as if I wielded ten swords in my hands. My father was there beside me as well, and his weapons master, Lansar Rashaaru, and Asaru, Karshur, Yarashan, and all my brothers. My mother fought with me like a lioness, calling out encouragements and warnings, protecting me, urging me to live at all costs and return home to her. In truth, the entire host of the Valari was in the hall that day, the Ishkans with the Meshians, the Waashians, and the warriors of Kaash, and it was as if we slashed ten thousand bright steel kalamas into the soul of our ancient enemy.

Panic, in battle, is a terrible thing. The victors strike it into the vanquished in the furious clash of steel against steel, in the lionlike roar of their hearts and in the blaze of their eyes. It spreads among the doomed like a disease: here a guard cries out in dismay while another sprays his neighbor in a fountain of blood; there a halberd wavers in the air and a spearman pulls back behind the imagined safety of others around him while many others begin falling back as well and even a few break and run. Panic communicates from commander to commanded like wildfire through dry grass. When a king, on the field of battle, loses heart, he has no hope of victory.

Even as Ymiru's club crumpled steel and my sword cut through the armor as if it were cloth, as Atara's arrows sizzled through the air and struck down guards and priests like lightning falling from the heavens, Morjin was seized with a great fear of death. I felt it come quivering alive within his chest and then spread out in waves through the men bunched around him. In truth, they now fought like maddened beasts rather than men. They bunched and screamed and swarmed about Morjin. And his voice rose above the clamor of the spears and clashing steel: "Retreat! Retreat to the gate!"

The Bright Sword that I held in my hands gave me to see through the cloud of battle boiling around me. In front of me, the mass of men moved a few yards toward the southwest, and I knew that Morjin intended to flee through the door leading to his private chambers rather than through the room's west gate. Already one of his priests had broken from the circle to run and open this door. I heard his boots pounding against the floor even as Atara's bowstring sang out its twanging tune of death. And so I "saw" him clutch his chest against the arrow sticking out of it and fall to the floor. Likewise I became aware of Liljana behind me slipping her sword through a guard's defenses and thrusting its steel point through the mail covering his belly. His scream was all strangled and deep like the knot of his suddenly pierced intestines. Nearby, Maram matched sword against sword with a master warrior. The clanging of steel reverberated with rhythms in my blood as Maram fought with a fury and skill I hadn't known he possessed. In truth, in that moment with his brilliant sword and his heart of fire, he fought like a Valari knight. He suddenly killed his man with a quick thrust and then turned to cross swords with another.

In this most desperate of battles, we even had help from two unexpected sources. At the center of the star whose five points were Kane, Liljana, Maram, Ymiru, and I, Master Juwain stood with his green gelstei blazing and pouring new life into our tired limbs and souls. And as we inched slowing toward the door leading to Morjin's rooms, Daj suddenly darted out from behind a pillar and grabbed up a cast-off spear. He went forth mercilessly finishing off the wounded before they could raise weapons against us again.

"Val!" Kane called out to my right. His sword flashed and a hand flew though the air nearby. "Don't let Morjin escape!"

I was closer to him than was Kane. Now, through the mass of men in front of me, I caught glimpses of Morjin's golden tunic between his frantically battling guards. He still crouched low, taking cover behind them. But as Atara fired off the last of her arrows and her mighty bow fell silent, he stood up straight and drew his sword. His eyes found mine across ten yards of the blood-slick floorstone. His hatred poured out of them and something more: he tried to murder me with a blast of the *valarda*. The shining silustria of my sword, however, shielded me from this deadly assault—as it did my companions. As I raised Alkaladur high above my head, he looked upon it and saw his death.

I fought with a rare fury to kill him then. Although I hated killing even more than I did him, he was a poisonous serpent who must be slain if I was to guard the Lightstone. And more, he was a cracked vessel who could not hold light but only darkness. He had lived ages too long, and it was long past time that the One made a new cup out of this particular clay.

It was the destroying wrath of the One itself that fell upon me and blazed forth through the lightning strokes of my sword. I swung Alkaladur and struck off a guard's head; I lunged and drove its point through the mail covering a guard's chest, clean through his body and into the chest of the guard pressed up close behind him. In wrenching its blade free, I killed two more. A few moments later, another guard tried to parry a quick blow. My sword cut the steel of his—and then cut straight down through his shoulder, spine and opposite side, cleaving his body in two. The terror of my sword caused the guards behind him to panic. But they were bunched around Morjin too close to flee.

At last, I understood the Valari ideal of fearlessness, flawlessness and flowingness, not just with my head, but in the surging of my heart and deep in my soul.

Fearlessness: For a few moments I abided in the One and was at one with the death that I dealt out—and so with wild joy of life that poured into me. I did not flinch from spear thrusts, but rather trusted to the strength of my mail, its steel rings forged by the master armorers of Mesh. Thus I was free to thrust and cut myself, like a whirlwind whipping a silver blade among my foes, lunging and parrying and killing—all the time dancing the wild and delicate dance of death.

Flawlessness: In the grace bestowed upon me, nothing could pierce the perfect diamond clarity of my awareness and will to fulfill my fate. All of my soul was in my sword, and my sword was in me, and so I cut my way through steel and flesh straight toward Morjin.

Flowingness: This desperate fight of guards screaming and hacking and spinning about had a logic and pattern that was not mine to control. But as in a storm at sea, there was a still point around which all the winds of violence whirled, and this quiet place was inside of me. And so I became one with the pattern of the battle, moving among men like water, always flowing down the red channels of death toward the great Red Dragon whose name was Morjin.

As Kane and my other friends battled beside me and guarded my back, I fought my way closer to him. Now only two tall guards, aiming spears at me, stood between us. I looked past them and locked eyes with him; he waited to slash his sword into me. His snarl of rage promised endless torments, but he no longer had the power of illusion to make me feel them, nor would he ever again. His hideousness stunned me. Now that we were so near each other, I knew that he didn't really smell of roses as his illusions suggested. Rather, he gave off the sick reek of fear, fouler than a bloody flux, putrid as death. It drove like the blow of a war hammer deep into my belly. My bones ached with the urge to destroy this twisted being. From the circle of the carved stone beneath us came the gurgle of the blood of many dead men being sucked down the drain of the dragon's mouth; it sounded out like a roaring from deep inside the mountain itself.

"Morjin!" I cried out as I cut my way through these last two guards.

And his cry joined mine in echoing from the cold stone of the hall: "Valari!"

We crossed swords then, and my greater fury bore him back into the guards massed about him. The sharp edge of a halberd slammed into the mail covering my side, but I scarcely felt it. A spear thrust at my face, and I pulled back my head to let it slip harmlessly past a couple of inches from my eyes. I raised back my sword.

"Val!" From on top of the throne, Atara's strong, clear voice rang out like a bell through the hall. "You mustn't kill him!"

I suddenly remembered the prophecy that the death of Morjin would be the death of Ea.

"Val!"

It was said by some that Morjin was the finest swordsman on Ea. And perhaps he was. But now his hatred of me and the rigidness of his lust to take my head betrayed him. I felt his murderous intentions deep in my throat, and ducked beneath the vicious slash of his sword at the last moment. And then, rising quickly, I saw my chance. I thrust my sword over the shoulder of a quickly closing guard into Morjin's neck. It was a terrible wound, a mortal wound—but it failed to kill him.

"His fate is yours!" Atara called to me. "If you kill him, you kill yourself!"

"I don't care!" I cried out.

I knew what she said was true. I stood in the land of death with all the men I had slain. If I now killed Morjin, this great immortal being with whom I was connected by the poison in my blood and the dark weave of fate, I would never leave it. Already, with the muscles and veins of Morjin's neck ripped open into a bloody hole, I could barely stand, barely see. Again, I raised back my sword.

"Val, if your kill yourself, you kill me!"

Atara's warning seemed to crack the stone of the mountain and stop the earth itself from turning. I suddenly knew something else: that Atara's blinding had shocked her to a wholly new level of scrying. Thus, even though eyeless, she had been able to "see" to fire her arrows into Morjin's guards. I sensed that she was seeing things both far and near in space and time. And now she fired a different kind of arrow into me. Even as I hesitated and Morjin's guards closed in and came between us, she called out that she loved me more than life. If I died, she told me, she would die, too.

Her words tore open my heart. How much more must this beautiful, tortured woman be made to lose? I looked through the ring of guards to see Morjin choking on his blood and gasping for breath. His eyes closed even as his guards tried desperately to bear him back away from me.

"Atara," I whispered.

My sword lowered as I cast a terrible look at the nearby guards to warn them away from me. I knew that I couldn't kill Morjin. It was the strangest and bitterest turning of fate that out of compassion for the one I most loved, I must spare Morjin's life.

"Damn it, Val!" Kane thundered from my right. "You're letting him get away!"

He started after the mass of guards, many fewer in number now, who were bearing Morjin's gravely wounded body toward the southwest corner of the room. There, one of his guards had finally managed to open the door to his chambers. I suddenly grabbed Kane's arm and looked into his furious black eyes. I'd had enough of killing for one day.

"Damn you!" Kane said again. "If you can't kill him, I will!"

He wrenched his arm free from my grip to pursue Morjin. He ran across the hall, savagely cutting down the few guards who tried to stop him. I ran after him. By the time I reached his side, however, the guards and remaining priests had succeeded in dragging Morjin through the open doorway. A dozen guards stood in front it, waiting their turn to enter the passageway beyond. Kane fell upon them, all the while stabbing and slashing and howling out his frustration that Morjin was escaping him.

"Let him go!" I shouted. "It would be your death to follow him!"

Not even Kane, I thought, could fight his way through such a narrow passageway held by so many men.

"I don't care!" Kane roared. "Morjin must die!"

Perhaps Morjin would die of his dreadful wound, but it was too late to inflict any other. In order to save Kane's life, I came up behind him and wrapped my arm like an iron band across his chest. He surged against me like an enraged tiger. By the time he again broke free, the last of the guards fled into the passageway, and the door slammed shut in our faces.

"MORJINNN!"

Kane screamed out his great enemy's name as he leaped forward to pound the pommel of his sword against the locked door. Then he whirled about facing me. There was blood in his eyes and dripping from his sword.

"What's wrong with you!" he shouted at me, pointing at the door. "We might have killed them all!"

From across the hall to the east, from on top of the throne, Atara's clear voice called out, "No—if we had pursued them there, they would have killed all of us."

"So you say, scryer," Kane snarled out.

I looked over at the throne to behold Atara. But she, who

had seen clearly enough to shoot her arrows across the dim hall into our enemy's throats or eyes, seemed now to be suddenly and completely blind. She fumbled and groped about with her hands as she tried to climb down from the throne. I ran across the hall to help her. Kane ran after me. And then a few moments later, Maram, Liljana and the others joined us there as well, and we gathered beneath the steps to the throne.

"We're trapped!" Maram cried as he turned about to look at the room's locked gates. "We killed a hundred men, and we're still trapped!"

I stood with my arm around Atara's back, helping her stand. She had spent nearly the last of her strength. Her bloody, beautiful head rested heavily on my shoulder.

"Not quite a hundred," Kane said. He stood looking toward the standing stones and the carnage that we had wrought. Across the blood-soaked ritual circle, the hacked and torn bodies of our enemies lay everywhere. "And not quite enough—never enough death for them."

But it was more than enough death for me. As I gazed at those whom I had slain, only my grip on Alkaladur's diamond-set hilt kept me from falling down and joining them.

"I'm sorry," Atara said to Kane. She managed to lift up her head and orient her face toward him. "But I saw . . . that is, I knew that Val needed to remain alive. You, too, Kane, and myself—all of us. We all must live to guard the Lightstone for the Maitreya."

Upon these words I removed the Lightstone from beneath my armor. It seemed more than a lifetime ago that I had put it there. And it seemed almost a dream that I had finally found it after all. Only the warm hardness of the little golden cup in my hand reassured me that it was real.

"So," Kane said. His black eyes were bright as moons as they drank in the cup's golden sheen. His thirst for its light, I thought, was nearly infinite.

He broke his gaze and turned toward Atara, saying, "Morjin and others have killed every Maitreya born on Ea. Killing him was the best hope we had of putting this cup in the next Maitreya's hands."

"Hrope," Ymiru said bitterly. He leaned over his bloody war club as he turned his attention from the wonder of the Lightstone to the room's great bronze gates. "How long will it be before more guards are summoned? Or before the Red Priests call up the whrole army from the first level?"

Maram, tearing his eyes from the Lightstone, looked at me and asked, "Is there no way out of here, then?"

"There is a way out," Liljana said, staring at the Lightstone. She wiped her sword on a tunic torn from one of the dead and sheathed it. "A secret passage leading from this room—I saw this in Morjin's mind."

"Where is it, then?" Maram shouted at her.

"I saw that it is," she told him, "but not where it is."

I looked at Daj, who was standing behind Liljana. He still held his killing spear in his little hands. "Do you know where this passage is?" I asked him.

"No, Lord Morjin never spoke of it," he said. Then his courage finally failed him, and he began trembling and said, "I want to go home!"

But he had no home that we knew of, and Liljana put her arm around him and pulled him closer to her. Then she said to Atara, "Have you seen the door to this passage, my dear?"

"No, I . . . can see nothing now," Atara murmured, shaking her head.

Maram ran over to the wall near the door to Morjin's chambers and began searching it for the telltale cracks that might demarcate a secret door. But the throne room's acres of walls were everywhere cracked and carved with fissures and swirls that formed the shapes of dragons and other beasts, and so it seemed that Maram had set himself a hopeless task. Master Juwain moved up in front of Atara with his varistei held over the crown of her head. A brilliant green light poured out of it as of a rain shower that has taken on the color of new spring leaves. It gave her new life. But it failed to restore her vision.

Liljana laid her hand on Atara's shoulder as she addressed Master Juwain, saying, "If Atara can't find her way to visions of the otherworld, then perhaps you can restore her sight of this one."

"I?" Master Juwain said. "How?"

"By growing new eyes for her."

Master Juwain looked at his crystal as he sadly shook his head. "As I've said before, I'm afraid my gelstei hasn't that power."

"Not by itself, perhaps. But the Lightstone must have that power."

She turned straight toward Kane and recited the lines from the Song of Kalkamesh and Telemesh:

> *The lightning flashed, struck stone, burned clear;*
> *The prince beheld through rain and tear*
> *The hands that held the golden bowl,*
> *The warrior's hands again were whole.*

"Kalkamesh," she told him, "had touched the Lightstone before his torture—before Telemesh freed him by cutting him away from his crucified hands. But he grew new hands, didn't he?"

"So," Kane said as he stood still as stone. "So the old songs say."

"Kalkamesh," she said again, "gained this power thusly, didn't he?"

"How should I know?" Kane muttered, shaking his head.

"Didn't he?"

"No," Kane snarled, "you're wrong—you know nothing."

"I know what I see."

So saying, Liljana pointed at the side of Kane's head. There, during the ferocity of the battle, the bandage that Master Juwain had fixed after the earlier battle with the knights beneath Skartaru's north face had come loose. I stared through the dim light near the throne, and gasped at what I saw. For beneath Kane's white hair, where the knight's sword had sheared off his ear, a small, pink, new ear the size of a child's was growing from his head.

"Kalkamesh," Liljana said, staring at him. "You are he."

"No," Kane murmured, shaking his head. "No."

"Morjin spoke to you as if you'd known him long ago. As you spoke to him."

"No, no," Kane said.

"And the way you looked at him! Your hate. Who could ever hate him so much?"

Kane looked at Atara and then me but said nothing.

"And the way you fight!" Liljana continued. "Who could ever fight as Kalkamesh did?"

Kane bowed his head to me and said, "Valashu Elahad can."

I returned his bow, then asked him, "Are you really Kalkamesh?"

"No," he said as he stared at the Lightstone. "That is not my name."

"Then what is your name? Your true name? It's not Kane, is it?"

"No, that is not my name either."

I waited for him to say more as my heart pounded like the distant hammering that I could hear from beyond the throne room's doors. A battle a thousand times fiercer than the one we had just fought raged inside him.

"My name," he whispered, "is Kalkin."

He drew himself up as straight as a king and pointed his sword at the door to Morjin's chambers. And a single, terrible cry broke from his throat like thunder and shook the hall:

"KALKIN!

"Do you hear that, Morjin! My name is Kalkin, and I've come to return you to the stars!"

It hurt my ears to hear him shout this name; it hurt my heart. As the hall fell silent again, we all looked at him in amazement. And then Master Juwain, who had a better memory than any of us, turned to him and said, "The *Damitan Elu* speaks of Kalkin. He was one of the heroes of the first Lightstone quest."

I remembered King Kiritan telling of this in his great hall: of how Morjin had led heroes on the first quest, only to fall mad upon beholding the Lightstone and slaying Kalkin and all the others—all except the immortal Kalkamesh.

As Master Juwain began recounting this ancient tale, Kane shook his sword at him and cut him off. He said, "I've warned you that many of these ancient histories do not tell true. Morjin never led that quest. And he did not kill Kalkin, as you can see."

"I don't know what I see," Master Juwain said, looking at him strangely. "If you're not Kalkamesh, then whatever happened to him?"

"I happened to him!" Kane said. "Do you understand? After the first quest, Kalkin became Kalkamesh. And at the end of that age, after the Sarburn, when Kalkamesh cast Alkaladur into the sea, he became Kane, do you understand?"

As I looked down at my sword, my amazement deepened. And then I squeezed the Lightstone more tightly in my hand as I asked him, "But if you are really Kalkin, didn't the touch of this cup bestow upon you immortality?"

Kane, or the man that I had known by that name, began pacing about like a caged tiger as he cast quick, ferocious glances at the doors of the hall. He suddenly stopped and snarled out, "Listen, damn you, and listen well—we haven't much time."

He stared down at the blackish blood pooled on the floor as if looking far into the past. Then he looked up and said, "Once there was a band of brothers, a sacred band."

He nodded at Master Juwain and went on, "We were not of any of your Brotherhoods; ours was much older. So, much older, more glorious, I, you—you can't understand."

From beyond the hall's western gate came a pounding as of many boots against stone. We all pressed closer to Kane to hear what he had to tell us.

"I will say their names, for they should be heard at least once in every age," Kane said. "There were twelve of us: Sarojin, Averin, Manjin, Balakin, and Durrikin. And Iojin, Mayin, Baladin, Nurijin, and Garain."

"That's only ten," Maram pointed out.

"The eleventh was myself," Kane said. He pointed at the door to Morjin's chambers. "And you know the name of the twelfth."

Now many voices shouted from beyond the hall's eastern doors. I knew that we should be searching for the secret passage that Liljana had spoken of. But the gleam of my sword, in whose silver I saw reflected the Lightstone, gave me to know that it was somehow more important to listen to Kane.

"We came to Tria early in the Age of Swords," Kane told us. "So, it was a savage time, even worse than this. Manjin was killed in a Sarni raid. Mayin was murdered on the Gray Prairies looking for clues as to where Aryu had taken the Lightstone. Nurijin, Durrikin, Baladin, and Sarojin, Balakin, too, and then even Iojin, sweet, beloved Iojin—all killed. All except Garain and Averin, who set out with Morjin and Kalkin on a ship captained by Bramu Rologar to seek the Lightstone."

Kane paused to stare at the cup that I held, and then continued, "And find it we did. The Lightstone was made to be found. But on the voyage back to Tria, Morjin enlisted the aid of Captain Rologar to kill Averin and Garain. So, and Kalkin, too. But Kalkin was harder to kill, eh? So, he killed Captain Rologar and four of his men, and damned himself, do you understand? He killed, killed men, before Morjin stabbed him in the back and cast him into the sea."

Now, beyond the hall's northern door, came a clamor as of shields banging together. I knew that I, or all of us, should begin cutting arrows out of the dead in case Atara miraculously regained her second sight.

Instead, I nodded at Kane and asked him, "But how did Kalkin live to tell such a tale?"

"The dolphins saved him. They were friends with men, once a time."

"But that still doesn't explain Kalkin's immortality," I pointed out.

Master Juwain, ever the student of history, caught Kane's eyes and said, "You've recounted that Kalkin and his band of brothers came to Tria early in the Age of Swords. But the first quest took place late in that age, didn't it?"

"So," Kane said, his eyes flashing, "so."

"Hundreds of years later," Master Juwain said. "But if

Kalkin and Morjin, and the others as well, lived all that time, then they didn't gain their immortality by touching—"

"The Lightstone has no such power!" Kane suddenly shouted, cutting him off. "Haven't I made that clear?"

"Then how," Master Juwain asked, "did Kalkin become immortal?"

"The way that men do," Kane said. "By becoming more than men."

It was as if a cold wind had fallen down from the nighttime sky and found the flesh along the back of my neck. A shiver, like a lightning bolt made of ice, ran up and down my spine. I stood staring at Kane, waiting for him to say more.

"It was the Galadin who sent us here to recover the Lightstone," he told us. "For them, who were immortal and could not be killed, Ea was deemed too perilous. For us, who were merely immortal, this world proved to be perilous enough, eh?"

How was it possible, I wondered? How was it possible that this man who stood before us—grim, angry, pained, and still dripping with the blood of those whom he had slain—could be one of the blessed Elijin?

"Five men Kalkin put to the sword, eh? But we were forbidden to kill men. And so in breaking with the Law of the One, Kalkin broke with the One, perhaps forever."

Kane stared at the cup in my hand, and there was an immense and endless blackness inside him waiting to be filled with light. How long he had been waiting, I thought! For he, who had once held the Lightstone and had beheld its perfect radiance even as I had, had been cast into a lightless void and had endured a Dark Night of the Soul that had lasted nearly seven thousand years.

Maram, suddenly understanding this, gazed at Kane in awe. "No wonder you fought so hard to bring us here to recover the Lightstone."

"Ha!" Kane called out. "I never thought we would find the Lightstone here. I never believed the account of Master Aluino's journal. I knew Sartan Odinan, and I never thought that his greed would have permitted him simply to drop the Lightstone down on top of Morjin's damn throne."

Maram looked at him nervously and said, "If that's true, then you must have wanted—"

"Vengeance!" Kane cried out. He raised up his bloody sword and swept it about the hall. "I came here to put this into Morjin's treacherous heart! Does anyone deserve death more? What's one more murder against all those I have slain?"

"Perhaps," I said, remembering Atara's warning, "one too many."

"You say that?" he growled at me, looking at my sword. "How many have you slain with that today?"

"Too many," I said as I looked about the hall. Then I held Alkaladur out toward him and said, "If you are really Kalkamesh, then you forged this sword. And so it is yours."

"No, it's yours now. You're better at killing with it than I ever was."

"But if you were to take it back, the silver gelstei might—"

"It's not your damn bloody sword I want!" he thundered at me. There was a strange, faraway look in his eyes—and the faint fire of madness, too. "It's not the silver gelstei that I want."

Now the red flames in his eyes built hotter as he stared at the Lightstone. His voice filled with anger and a choking desire as he pointed at the cup and called out, "Morjin has escaped me, eh? But it seems that fate has put the Lightstone in my hands."

"In Val's hands," Maram said, stepping forward. "That was the rule we made in Tria, that whoever found the Lightstone would have final say as to what would be done with it."

"So," Kane said, taking a step closer to me. His knuckles were white around the hilt of his sword. "So."

"You pledged your sword to Val's service!" Maram reminded him.

"So I did," Kane said. "I pledged it only so long as he sought the Lightstone. Well, the Lightstone has been found, and so he seeks it no longer."

I didn't know if Kane had fallen so far that he would kill me to claim the Lightstone; I didn't know if I could kill him, even in its defense. I doubted that I could kill him. Despite his words of praise as to my prowess with the Bright Sword that he had forged, he was an angel of death who gripped a killing sword of his own in his hands.

"Kalkin," I said to him.

"Don't call me that!"

"No matter how many you kill, even Morjin, even Angra Mainyu himself, it will never bring back the light."

"Damn you!"

We stared at each other, and the anguish that I saw in him cut open my heart. I knew then that I could never kill this brave, blessed man whom I loved.

Without a further glance at my sword, I quickly sheathed it. I looked deep into Kane's black eyes, so like my own. As the Valari were sons and daughters of the Star People, so were the Elijin—in transcendence and immortality. Kane, I thought, was Valari in his soul, and something more.

I held the Lightstone out to him then. I said, "Take it. If you will promise to guard and keep it for the Maitreya, then I would have the Lightstone go with you."

Kane stepped forward and reached out to grasp the Lightstone with his left hand. My hand, suddenly freed from this slight weight, suddenly felt a thousand times heavier.

"So," he whispered, "so."

He stood looking back and forth between the cup in his left hand and the sword in his right. He blinked his eyes in rhythm with the beating of my heart. His belly tightened into a hard knot, and his hands, first the left and then the right, began to tremble.

"Kalkin," I said.

With a great effort, he broke off gazing at the Lightstone and looked at me. His grim mouth could make no words, but his heart spoke to me all the same. In the quiet deep thunder of the blood that we shared, in the touching of each other's unfathomable suffering and pain, his soul cried out that I had offered him something more precious than a small, golden cup, and that was friendship and trust.

What is it to love a man? This above all: that you want with all the polished silver of your being to show him the glory of his own.

Now Kane's jaws clamped shut as if he were trying to bite back the worst of pains. I felt him swallowing against a hard knot in his throat that would not be dislodged. A great pressure built in his chest and burned up through his eyes. He took a long, deep look at the Lightstone.

"Valashu," he gasped.

He suddenly cast his sword clanging down upon the bare rock floor. I felt tears burning in my eyes a moment before his filled as well. And then, at last, the storm broke. He lifted the Lightstone up high and threw back his head. His mouth opened wide as he let loose a terrible sound: "KALKIN!" No torture of Morjin's could have torn such a cry of agony and despair from a man. He fell down to his knees before me, weeping for himself, weeping for the world. In his racking sobs was all his grief at losing Alphanderry to death and much, much else that he had held inside for years beyond counting. His breath burst out so violently that the stone of the hall seemed to shake and the very heavens open up even through miles of rock and ice. For a moment his tears, and my own, flowed so freely that they seemed almost to wash away the blood spilled here this terrible day.

I rested my hand on top of his thick, white hair as he reached his hand behind my leg and pressed his forehead against the hard rings of steel covering my knee. The tremors ripping through his powerful body took a long time to subside. At last, when he had grown quiet again, as I listened to Atara's pained breaths breaking out into the air behind me and to Maram weeping like a child, he looked up at me. He pulled away from me, slightly, and pressed the Lightstone back into my hand.

"You take it," he said to me. "Guard it for the Maitreya. So, guard it with your life—that is your fate."

I gave the cup to Maram to hold, and his large hand closed around it.

"Some wounds," Kane said, "only he can heal."

I reached out to grasp Kane's hard hand in mine as I helped him to his feet. Then he let go of me and pulled himself up tall and straight. The tears in his eyes were gone. I looked deep into their bright, black depths; as had been the Lightstone, they were full of stars.

"Valashu," he said, smiling at me.

For millennia he had waged the bitterest of wars against himself, but angels cannot so easily be killed. A broken man had knelt before me, but here rose up another. The lines of his face seemed to lose their hardness and rigidity. Years fell from him, untold years, and I saw him as he must have been in his youth when he had walked with the One. His skin gleamed all golden like the sun, and his white hair had taken on the silver tones of silustria; a crown of light surrounded his head and fell about his shoulders like a lion's mane set on fire. He seemed raimented all in glorre, while his whole being was transparent to the hopes and dreams of a deeper world. A man he truly was, like the first man to walk the earth and perhaps the last. And yet he was also something more, for here he stood all noble, wise, beautiful and radiant, blazing like a star, as one of the great Elijin.

But only for a moment. He moved over to Atara and lay his hand on her face to turn her toward him. Then, with infinite gentleness, he touched his thumbs into the hollows of her eyes. And the angel fire passed into her and out of him.

"Val!" Atara cried out. "I know where the passageway is!"

Once, speaking of Morjin, Kane had asked what could be greater than the power to make others see what is not. And here, in this beautiful woman restored for a moment to her vision, the only answer: the power to help them see what really is.

Maram gave the Lightstone to Ymiru, who stood holding it in his single hand a few moments before turning it over to Liljana. Then Maram, looking at Kane in awe, said, "Lord Kalkin, you are—"

"Don't say that name again!" Kane told him. Much of the light had now gone out of him; with its passing, Kane had returned to us—but never quite the same Kane again. "So, you'll call me as you have, do you understand?"

"All right, then," Maram said.

Kane smiled grimly as he bent to pick up his sword.

Liljana, after gazing into the Lightstone as long as she dared, gave the cup to Master Juwain, who held it only a moment before placing it in Atara's hands. While Daj stood close to Liljana, looking on in awe, Flick appeared and looped around the cup as if spinning out strands of a silvery cocoon of light.

"So, the second quest ends," Kane said casting one last look at the Lightstone. As a great noise of pounding boots and shaking steel sounded from outside the hall, his eyes flashed around the throne room's three gates. "And it will be the end of us if we don't find our way out of here soon. It sounds as if they're bringing up the whole damn army!"

"Come," Atara said softly, taking my hand.

She gave the Lightstone back to me, and I returned it to its resting place beneath my armor. Then she led us over to the wall behind the throne. There, set into the fearsome face of a carving of Angra Mainyu, she found the hidden door. It took only a few moments to open it.

"Come," she said again, taking Daj's hand. "Let's go home."

Then she turned into the tunnel beyond the open door and bravely led the way into the bright, black darkness.

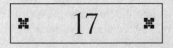

THE PASSAGEWAY TOOK us straight toward the southeast for a distance of a few hundred yards. It gave onto a much larger corridor running east and west. Just at the juncture, however, we found our way blocked by lines of iron bars running from the ceiling down into the floor. An iron door, like one leading from a jail cell, was set into the middle of the bars.

"Locked!" Maram cried out as he rushed forward to try it. "Then we're still trapped in this forsaken place!"

None of us knew how long it would be before Morjin's men burst into the throne room behind us and found their way to this secret passage.

"Hrold your noise!" Ymiru said softly, stepping up to the bars.

Then he brought forth his purple gelstei and worked its magic upon them. Its violet light transformed the crystal within the iron into a softer substance—soft enough so that Ymiru's great strength, with Maram, Kane, and me helping, sufficed to bend them. Daj danced through this opening, and as for the rest of us, only Ymiru had much trouble squeezing through.

"There!" he huffed out after leaving shreds of white fur upon the rough iron bars. "We're not trapped! I'll never allow myself to be taken again."

"But how did Morjin take you?" Maram asked him.

"It was bad chance," he said. "After Val killed the dragon, we made it back to the old throne room and up to the seventh level without much trouble. Then we ran into that company of Grays."

The Grays, as he explained, had scented out the secrets of their minds, and had used their frightful minds to freeze them with fear until Morjin's guards—and Morjin himself—could be summoned to bind them in chains.

"It was hrorrible," Ymiru said, nodding at Atara and Master Juwain. "We fought them as hard as we could, but how long can one hrold against such creatures? And then Morjin suggested taking us into the throne room; he said that the torture of our bodies might help the Grays break into our minds."

"Are you sure they didn't?" Kane asked him.

"I think not," Master Juwain said, stepping up to Ymiru.

"Then it's possible that the enemy doesn't know how we entered Argattha?"

"It's likely," Master Juwain said. "I heard Morjin give orders to double the guard at the city's gates. He berated the captain of his guards for allowing a giant such as Ymiru to pass through unchallenged."

"Then they'll likely look for us at those gates," Maram said.

"If we can find our way back as we came, we may yet have time to make our escape."

"A little time, perhaps," Kane said. "But we must hurry."

And so hurry we did, out into the larger corridor, which was lit with numerous glowstones set at intervals into the black basalt walls. To the west, as Kane told us, the corridor led back toward Morjin's palace. And to the east, this bore through solid rock would take us straight through the mountain to the window carved into its side known as Morjin's Porch.

"But how did you know that?" Daj asked him.

And Kane replied, "Once, a long time ago, one named Kalkamesh was taken this way and crucified on the face of the mountain."

Daj, who apparently hadn't heard this story, stared at Kane in awe.

"If I remember aright," Kane said, "it also leads to Morjin's Stairs."

As Daj had told us, Morjin's Stairs would take us down to Argattha's lower levels, perhaps as far down as the abandoned first level—though not even Daj or Ymiru could say where it might give out.

We had no trouble in finding these stairs about a quarter-mile to our left. They spiraled deep into the dark mountain, turning around and around, and down and down for hundreds of feet. After a while, we came to a landing giving out onto a tunnel, which we supposed led to the secret tunnel system and sanctuaries on the sixth level. It was quiet in that direction. This gave us good hope as we turned the other way and resumed our journey down the endlessly winding stairs. Thus we passed openings to the fifth, fourth, third, and second levels. There, as we had prayed, the stairs didn't end; they led us another five hundred feet down to the first level of Argattha.

"What is this?" Maram said, pointing ahead of us. The stairs let us out onto a short corridor that seemed to end abruptly in a wall. "Another trap?"

"Ha, another secret door, most likely!" Kane said, clapping him on the shoulder. Then he stepped forward and called out, *"Memoriar Damoom!"*

Remember Damoom, I thought as Kane pushed open the carefully concealed door. I looked back at Atara and the one-armed Ymiru, and I knew that all of us, live though we might another thousand years, would always remember Argattha.

By great good fortune, we discovered that the door opened upon Morjin's old throne room. We stepped out into the great hall where we had fought our first battle with the dragon. Here, with its great, cracked columns of basalt and the pyramid of skulls, the floor was still caked with the blood from Ymiru's severed arm. And across from the great portal leading out to the first level, the doorway to the stairs by which we had first entered the hall still stood open.

It was strange and disquieting to cross this vast open space where once had thundered a dragon. We were glad to gain the shelter of the stairwell. And glad, too, to climb down a little way to the corridor leading back toward the labyrinth. Daj, who had explored many of the tunnels of Argattha's first level, had never dared to enter this dark, twisting place. As I held high Alkaladur, now blazing brilliantly in the Lightstone's presence, he and the others followed closely behind me around and through its turnings. At last we came out of it as we had entered it. And so we stepped into the close, foul-smelling, rat-infested tunnel system leading to the cave hidden behind Skartaru's north face.

We found the cave as we had left it: filled with the stone-covered bodies of the knights we had slain, as well as the saddles of their driven-off horses and other accouterments. Here, despite our fear of pursuit, despite the awful fetor of the rotting bodies, we had to pause to search through the knights' gear. We took away as many saddlebags of food as we could carry, and the smallest saddle that we could find. Atara was very happy to lay her hands on a full quiver of arrows; although they were not so well made as those that the Sarni carefully shaped and fletched, she said that they would likely fly straight enough if only she could aim them at our enemies.

When we were finally ready, we rolled aside the great rocks with which we had sealed the cave. We stepped outside into a brilliant night. In all my life, the air that I breathed had never smelled so clean and sweet—even though that air was still of Sakai. A cold wind blew down from the Nagarshath through the valley to the north of the mountain. It set all of us except Ymiru to shivering; even so we were glad for the scent of ice and pines that it carried along in its frigid gusts.

"What time is it?" Maram asked softly as he gazed at the shadowed rockscape of the valley.

I looked up at the sky; to the east of us, above the dark, rolling plains of the Wendrush, the Morning Star stood like a beacon among the bright constellations. "It's nearly dawn," I told him.

"What day is it?"

None of us seemed to know. In the lightless hell of Argattha, we might have journeyed and fought for two days—or two years.

"I would guess the twenty-fourth," Master Juwain said. "Or perhaps the twenty-fifth."

"The twenty-fifth of Ioj?" Maram asked.

Kane came up to him and rumpled his curly hair. "Ioj it still is, my friend. We've still time to make it home before the snows come."

We started walking down through the valley then. First light found us working our way across the ridge that hid the little canyon to the north of Skartaru. With nerves laid bare by what we had endured, we listened and looked for any sign of pursuit. But the brightening foothills rang with the cries of wolves and bluebirds rather than the hoofbeats of Morjin's cavalry. We knew that it would be only a matter of time before he or one of his priests sent out riders to patrol the approaches to Skartaru.

And so we came down into the grassy bowl where we had left the horses; there my heart cried out with what it took to be the greatest stroke of fortune of all our journey. For there, in the center of the bowl, his black coat burning in the light of the rising sun, Altaru stood sniffing the air as for enemies. Atara's roan mare, Fire, was feeding on the lush grass nearby him, while twelve other horses—all of them mares as well—took their breakfast with her. I was sure that these were the mounts of the knights in the cave. Altaru had obviously gathered a harem about him. But he seemed to have driven off the magnificent Iolo, for what stallion will endure another sniffing about his new brides? When Maram discovered this, he wanted to weep bitter tears that he would have to find another horse to carry him homeward. Kane, Liljana, and Master Juwain had better luck: their geldings stood off about a quarter-mile from the herd as if awaiting our return.

We walked down into the bowl, where I whistled for Altaru. His ears pricked up, and he let loose a great whinny in return. I waited to see if he would come to me. It seemed a shame to take him from his newly found freedom, to say nothing of his harem. But he and I had a covenant between us. So long as we had breath in our lungs and blood in our veins, we were fated to face, and fight, our enemies together.

At last he came trotting over to greet me. He nuzzled my face; I breathed into his nostrils and told him that a dragon had been killed—although the Great Red Dragon remained alive. We still had very far to ride together, I said, if he was willing to bear my weight. In answer, he nickered softly and licked my ear. His great heart beat like a war drum. He pawed the ground impatiently as I retrieved his saddle and put it on his back.

The others saddled their horses, too. Maram chose out of the herd a big mare to ride; the smallest we gave to Daj, who had surprised us all by declaring that he could ride.

"My father," he told us, "was a knight."

"In what land, lad?" Kane asked him.

Finally Daj consented to naming his homeland. He looked at Kane and said, "Hesperu. My father, all the knights of the north—there was a rebellion, you see. But we were defeated. Killed and enslaved."

"Hesperu is very far away," Kane told him. "I'm afraid there's no way we can take you home."

"I know," he said. Then a moment later he added, "I have no home."

We spent most of the day in walking along the foothills of the White Mountains. The sun was high in the sky by the time we reached the canyon by which we had come down out of the

Nagarshath. There we said good-bye to Ymiru. He would be traveling west, while we must journey east.

"But it's too dangerous for you to cross the mountains alone!" Maram said to him. He looked at the remains of his arm and shook his head. "And surely you're still too weak from what the dragon did to you."

Ymiru bowed his huge head to Master Juwain, and then said, "I've had the help of Ea's greatest healer—I feel as strong as a bear."

At the mention of Maram's least favorite animal, he cast his eyes about the hills to look for one of the great white bears that were said to haunt the Nagarshath. Then he studied Ymiru. Master Juwain had healed his pierced side, and his green gelstei seemed to have restored him to his great vitality.

"Still," Maram said, "those mountains, two hundred and fifty miles of them, and you alone. And with winter coming on, it's a journey that—"

"Only I can make," Ymiru said, clapping him on the arm. "Don't worry, little man, I shall be all right. But I must go hrome."

He went on to say that he must tell his people the great news that the Lightstone had been found. Such a miracle, he said, surely heralded the return of the Star People, and so Alundil must be prepared for this great event.

"And the Ymanir must prepare for war," he said. "The Great Beast told me that my people would be the next to feel his wrath."

Liljana came forward and laid her hand on his white fur. "I saw this in his mind. His hatred of your land, and the desire to destroy it."

"He has the strength, I think," Ymiru admitted. His sad smile made me recall the hosts of men and the preparations for war that we had seen in Argattha. "But we can still fight a while longer."

"You won't fight alone," I promised him.

Ymiru's face brightened. "Will the Valari take up the sword against him, then?"

"We'll have to," I assured him. "With what we've seen on this journey, what other choice will we have?"

He smiled again as he put down his club; then we clasped hands like brothers.

"I shall miss you, Valashu Elahad."

"And I, you," I told him.

Liljana brought up one of the mares, which she and Master Juwain had heaped with most of the saddlebags of food. Ymiru would need every last biscuit of it on his long journey.

"Farewell," she told him. "May you walk in the light of the One."

The others, too, said their good-byes. And then, one last time, I took out the Lightstone and placed it in Ymiru's hand. Its radiance spilled over him like the gold of the sun.

"Someday," he said, "I'll journey to Mesh to learn this cup's secrets."

"You'll always be welcome," I said to him.

"Or perhaps someday," he added, handing the Lightstone back to me, "you'll bring this to Alundil."

"Perhaps I will," I said.

Gone from his fearsome face was any hint of gloom; I saw there instead only bright, shining hope. He bowed his head to me, and then turned to tie the mare's reins around his mutilated arm. And he called out, "A hrorse! Who would ever have thought that a Ymanir would make company of a hrorse!"

And then, leading his horse, his great war club in his hand, he turned to the west and began his long, lonely walk up into the great white mountains of the Nagarshath.

After he had disappeared around the curve of the canyon, we made our final preparations for our journey. Since we had sixteen horses among the seven of us, we had remounts to tie behind us. And Master Juwain had a bandage to tie around Atara. Because she could not bear us to endure the sight of her missing eyes, she begged Master Juwain to cover them. In his chest, he found a bolt of clean white cloth, which he pulled over her eye hollows and temples. I thought it looked less like a bandage than a blindfold.

At last we were ready to leave Sakai. And so we mounted

our horses and turned them toward the east. Just below the
foothills, the golden plains of the Wendrush gleamed in the
sunlight as far as the eye could see. We rode straight down into
them; there was nothing else to do. Now, as we found ourselves in the middle of a sea of grass or crested a rise, we
would be visible from miles away: clear targets for Morjin's
cavalry or any of the Sarni who might decide to divest us of
our horses, our lives, or more precious treasure.

In truth, on all of Ea there is no other place more perilous to
travelers than the Wendrush. Here, between the Morning
Mountains and the White, prides of lions hunted antelope and
the shaggy sagosk; sometimes a darkness fell upon their
fierce, red hearts, and then they hunted men. Of all the Sarni
tribes, in their plundering for sport or gold, perhaps only the
Kurmak or Niuriu tempered their ferocity with mercy—and
even they had no love of strangers. The worst of the tribes, it
was said, was the Zayak, whose country we now had to cross.
Somehow, Morjin had made allies of them—if it was possible
to enlist the aid of warriors so proudly independent that they
demanded tribute even of Morjin's men should they wish to
ride across their lands.

For all that first day of our flight from Argattha, we saw no
sign of Sarni or of pursuit from Sakai. We rode as fast as we
dared, over the swaying grasses of the soft, black earth. The sky
was an immense blue dome resting upon the fundament of the
far-off horizon; all about us was grass made golden by autumn's last heat. When night came, still we didn't pause in our
rush across the plains. With the rising of the wind, we rode long
past the twilight hour into the falling darkness. The stars came
out like a million candles lighting the black ocean of the heavens. They called us ever onward; their splendor lifted up our
spirits and reminded us how good it was to be free.

The next day, however, as we looked back toward the Black
Mountain still looming over the plain, we found ourselves
pursued by riders. They crested a knoll behind us; there were
twenty of them, bearing neither the shining mail nor lances of
Morjin's knights but rather the leather armor and great curved
bows of the Sarni.

"So," Kane said to Atara, "it's your people."

He turned his horse about and made ready for one last battle. We all knew that it was hopeless to try to outdistance the Zayaks' lithe steppe ponies with our larger mounts—especially with so great and stolid a warhorse as Altaru.

"Please don't call them my people," Atara said to Kane. "Anyone sent by Morjin is as much my enemy as yours."

As we soon discovered, these twenty warriors with their blue-painted faces and wildly streaming yellow hair had been sent by Morjin—or rather by the captains of his cavalry that his priests had sent after us. They charged straight at us, firing arrows as they rode. And we charged them. Two of the warriors underestimated Altaru's speed over short distances; these died quickly beneath my long lance, which had the weight of Altaru's driving body behind it. A third warrior got in the way of Kane's falling sword, and so surrendered his spirit to the sky. A fourth cried out "Give us the treasure that you stole from Lord Morjin!" even as Maram ducked beneath an arrow that he loosed and managed to race forward and duel with him to his death.

Still, the battle would have gone badly for us if Atara hadn't countered the Zayaks' arrows with a murderous stream of her own. She shot off five of them with astonishing accuracy before most of the enemy came close enough to use their bows. And five warriors fell from their ponies with feathered shafts sticking out of their chests. It was the finest archery I had ever seen—and the Zayaks must have thought that, too. The sight of the blinded Atara, whipping her red horse about and firing off death with every crack of her bowstring, utterly unnerved these bold but superstitious warriors. Their leader, a fierce man with a huge, drooping, yellow mustache, cast her an awe-stricken look and cried out: "*Imakla!* The Manslayer is *imakla!*"

And with that, he turned his pony toward the rolling land to the north and led the survivors of his company in a galloping retreat over the plains.

We did not escape this brief but deadly encounter unscathed. An arrow killed Liljana's horse beneath her; she barely managed to avoid being crushed in its fall, and had to choose out another from our remounts. One of the Zayaks' arrows had buried itself in Altaru's flank. It was a bad wound, and Master Juwain drew it only with difficulty. If not for the radiance of the green gelstei, now blazing like emerald fire in its nearness to the Lightstone, it might have been many days before Altaru would have been able to walk without limping. Likewise Master Juwain helped heal Kane of the wound caused by an arrow that had pierced his mail and transfixed his shoulder.

After we had made ready to set out again, I turned to Atara and asked, "What does *imakla* mean?"

She seemed reluctant to answer me. But finally, she turned her blindfolded head toward me and said, "The *imakil* are the immortal dead warriors of ages past, heroes who have done some great deed. Some warriors are said to ride with them and draw upon their strength. They are *imakla,* and may not be touched."

And with that, this brave woman who rode with the dead pointed her horse toward the rising sun and led us through the Zayaks' country. As we trotted along, Maram offered his opinion that we had surely outdistanced Morjin's cavalry, for why else would they have sent the Zayaks after us?

"They spoke of the cup," he said to her. "Do you think they know it's the Lightstone?"

"Hmmph!" Atara said to him. "If they knew that, they'd have called down the entire Zayak host upon us. And then Morjin would have lost all hope of regaining it."

We discovered the next day that the Zayaks almost certainly knew nothing of the treasure that we bore through their land. About seventy miles out onto the plain, we ran into another band of warriors. At the sight of Atara leading us toward them, they turned their horses and fled from us. It seemed that word of a blind *imakla* warrior of the Manslayers had spread ahead of us like fire through dry grass.

Still, we took no assurance from this seeming miracle. We resolved to leave the Zayaks' country as quickly as we could. Our straightest path across the Wendrush would have taken us across most of their land, which was bordered by the White

Mountains in the west, by the Blood River in the north, and by the Jade in the south. It was toward this river that we now turned. We didn't mind adding a few extra miles to our journey. In any case, soon we must cross the Astu River, and it would be much easier first to cross the Jade and then the Astu to the south of where the Jade emptied into it.

And so the following day, with the fording of the cold waters that flowed down from the White Mountains, we passed into the country of the Danladi. Their warriors, too, seemed to have been warned of Atara, for they let us ride through their lands unmolested. They were no friends of Morjin; but neither did they extend amity to a warrior of the Kurmak—and most especially not to Maram or Kane or any of the rest of us. It didn't matter. The weather held fine, with warm days of abundant sunshine and cold, clear nights. Thus we had no need of shelter, for we made our beds on the soft prairie grass and covered ourselves in our cloaks. When our food ran out, Atara shot an antelope, which gave us the sweetest of meats. Maram washed this feast down with the last of the kalvaas that we had brought from Alundil. Then he turned his eyes eastward in anticipation of some good, thick Meshian beer.

It took us three days to cover the hundred and twenty miles between the Jade and the Astu. This great river, here, to the south of where the Jade and the Blood flowed into it, was not nearly so wide as it grew on its course toward the Poru—which eventually wound its way across the plains and forests of Alonia, all the way to Tria. Still, it was wide enough. We had to swim the horses across it. By the time we reached the other side, Maram vowed that he would never swim a river again.

"At least not until we cross the Poru," Atara reminded him.

"Oh, the Poru!" Maram cried out. "I'd forgotten the Poru!"

But this queen of all rivers still lay a hundred and fifty miles to the east. The country to the west of it, here at this latitude, was that of the Niuriu tribe—who were friendly with the Kurmak. When an outrider of one of their clans trotted our way and discovered that Atara was the granddaughter of the great Sajagax, he offered us shelter, meat, and fire.

We spent that night in the great felt tent of his war chief. As

with the other Sarni whom we encountered, Atara remained un-
touchable: any warrior approaching her to offer food or drink
was careful to avert his eyes and very careful not to lay his
hands on her or even brush against her garments. This restraint,
however, did not diminish the Niuriu's hospitality. As we discovered, the Sarni's enmity toward strangers was overmatched
only by the generosity they showed to their friends. The chieftain's warriors and wives brought forth platters heaped with
roasted antelope, sagosk steaks, and coneys grilled over sweet-
grass fire. As well, we had rounds of hot, yellow bread dripping
with butter and honey and bowls of mare's milk. To Maram's
delight, the chieftain himself, who was named Vishakhan,
brought forth a bottle of brandy and poured it into our cups with
his own hand. And before we fell off to a contented sleep, he
presented each of us with a braided leather quirt, with handles
trimmed out in beaten silver.

On the next day—it proved to be the first of Valte—we made
fifty miles over the flat, short-grass steppe. And on the two days
following that, we did as well, riding past the great herds of
sagosk long past sunset. Although the air grew slightly cooler
here in the middle of the Wendrush, the sky deepened to an
even more beautiful blue, and the red-orange paintbush and the
golden leaves of the cottonwood trees along the watercourses
made a great show of color. It would have been the finest leg of
our journey homeward if Atara hadn't thrice lost her way for a
few hours before regaining her sense of the terrain.

On the morning of the fourth of Valte, we came to the
mighty Poru River. Atara assured Maram that the waters were
not nearly so deep as in the spring or summer, when they
raged brown down from the mountains. Even so, Maram
dreaded this immersion. His unease must have communicated
to his horse, because they floated downstream much too far,
and so came out upon the Poru's eastern bank a hundred yards
from the rest of us. This precipitated the only real crisis of this
part of our journey. A great, black-maned lion, lying in wait
by the grasses along the river, decided to chase Maram and his
horse across the steppe. He almost certainly would have sunk
his claws into the flanks of Maram's mare and dragged them

down if Atara hadn't killed him with a single arrow shot into his heart.

"I suppose," Maram said to Atara as we all gathered around the dead lion, "that I should thank you for saving my life."

"I suppose you should," Atara said to him with a broad smile. "But I think we're all long past saying thanks for saving each other's lives."

Atara's feat of shooting down a charging lion was heralded not only by us. As it happened, two warriors of the Manslayer Society, with long hair as yellow as Atara's and wearing leather like hers, were out hunting along the Poru that morning. They immediately thundered our way to greet one of their bloodsisters. It didn't matter that Atara was of the Kurmak while they counted themselves as Urtuk—and eastern Urtuk at that. When they studied the dead lion, killed so cleanly, they insisted that Atara return to their camp and share wine with them. They produced knives and quickly skinned the lion. It was their intention to dress the fur and make for Atara a lion-skin cloak so that all might appreciate her prowess.

They were reluctant, however, for the rest of us to accompany them. Liljana they might have taken into their confidence, but they looked at Kane, Maram, Master Juwain, Daj, and me with the challenge that they reserved for all males. They fired their arrows of suspicion especially at me, for I was a knight of Mesh and therefore the Urtuks' ancient enemy. It cooled their bellicosity not at all that I assured them that I was only returning homeward. Only Atara's claim that we were great warriors who had killed many of Morjin's men softened these two warriors. Atara also insisted that we remain together, and more, that the Manslayers of the Urtuk provide us escort as far as the Morning Mountains. So great had Atara's reputation now grown—to say nothing of her will—that the two Manslayers took a long look at the blindfold wrapped around her face and agreed to her demand.

Later that day, when we returned with them to their camp, their other sisters met in council and decided to honor their decision. They made only a single demand of their own: that Atara remain with them and teach three of the younger sisters her skill with the bow while the older sisters were preparing her lion skin.

And so there, along a stream sheltered by great cottonwoods, we waited for five long days. I felt the passing of time most keenly; an overwhelming sense that I must return home as soon as possible beat like a drum though my blood. Still, I was glad to make friends with these fierce women. At night, we sat around the fire sharing food with them and stories. It amazed them—and us—when one night Flick appeared and entertained them with his dance of silver sparks. We offered them no explanations as to this little miracle. We, ourselves, could only believe that the Lightstone's power had somehow quickened Flick's being and brought forth his colors for all to see.

At last, when the sisters had finished tanning the lion's skin and sewing into it a lining of purest Galdan satin, they brought it to Atara to put on. With the black fur of the lion's mane framing her blond hair and her white blindfold circling her striking face, she did indeed look like one of the *imakil* heroes of past ages come to life.

As I stood by the stream gazing at her, I thought that her count of slain enemies must have exceeded seventy men—I almost didn't want to know the precise number. Then I chanced to give voice to my deepest thoughts, whispering, "She's a great warrior—perhaps the greatest warrior the Sarni have ever seen."

Liljana, who overheard my words and perhaps more, came over to me and told me, "She's a woman. Don't you ever forget that, my dear."

Then she sighed and lowered her voice as if confiding in me a great secret. "A woman," she said, "plays many roles: princess, weaver, mother, warrior, wife. But what she really wants, deep in her heart, is to be someone's beloved."

She looked at me kindly and squeezed my hand. Then she walked over to Atara to admire her new fur.

The next morning, we set out to cross the Urtuks' country. Twelve of the Manslayers, acting as escort, rode out before us. After cutting across a little triangle of the steppe for thirty miles, we came to the Diamond River and followed it east.

This band of clear water, flowing down from the Morning Mountains, reminded me how close I was to my home. I prayed that I would reach it without further incident. I needn't have worried. Although a company of fifty Urtuk warriors rode north from their winter camp farther down along the Poru to witness the strange sight of the Manslayers leading seven outlanders toward Mesh, they did not challenge us or offer battle. Indeed, they offered us cheers in the form of their terrible war cries, for they had heard that we had entered Sakai and had slain many of the Red Dragon's men.

A hundred miles, as the raven flies, it is from the confluence of the Poru and Diamond rivers to Mesh, and we rode nearly as straight. It took us only a day to cover half this distance. By the morning of the eleventh, when we awoke to a few puffy white clouds floating along the sky, the mountains of Mesh were a purplish haze along the horizon. As we urged the horses toward them during that long, long, day, the mountains grew ever greater and more distinct. By noon, I was able to make out the lines of Mount Tarkel's soaring white summit. Although I had never seen it from this vantage, there was only one mountain that stood just south of the Diamond River and overlooking the golden grasses of the Wendrush.

That evening we made camp scarcely three miles from the foothills beneath its western face. The pounding of my heart demanded that we ride up into Mesh even through the falling darkness; but my head told me that it would be foolhardy to brave the wild, rocky approaches to Tarkel at night. And more, such a course would be ungracious and sad beyond thinking because Maram, Master Juwain, and I would have little time to say good-bye to the rest of our friends.

It was only during the five hundred miles of our flight from Argattha that I had gradually come to accept the rightness of the breaking of our company, though I hadn't yet made peace with this difficult decision. After we had thanked the Manslayers for their kindness and they had ridden off back toward their camp, the seven of us gathered around the fire that Maram had made for a last council.

It was a cold, clear night of many stars and a moon just

past full. Flick spun about against the backdrop of the sky, and his swirling form seemed to match the twinkling lights of the constellations. The wind carried down the scents of my homeland and set my heart to beating more quickly. Before us was a little fire of burning sagosk bricks that smelled surprisingly sweet.

We spoke of many things; for a while, we told stories of Alphanderry, whose voice we now listened for in the wind and in the music of the stars. We had decided that Kane should inherit his mandolet, which was all we had left of him—except that we had our memories and a song in our hearts, and that was everything. Kane sat plucking at the mandolet's strings and singing to us. When he wished, he, too, had a fine, clear voice, as strong and beautiful as an eagle soaring across the sky. I thought that he was trying to recapture the words of Alphanderry's last song; I knew that someday he would.

"That's a music that should be heard in Mesh," I said to him. "Are you sure you won't reconsider your plans?"

Kane put down his mandolet and looked at me; I wondered if he would waver in his decision.

"It would be an honor if you could meet my father," I said to him. Then I laid my hand on top of the diamond pommel of the sword that he had forged in Godhra so long ago. "Your name is still remembered in Mesh."

"That name you have promised not to speak, eh?" He bowed his head to me in trust that I would keep this promise. And then he said, "No, I'm sorry but I must return to Tria—I've business there."

Master Juwain, holding his gnarled hands out to the fire, looked up at him and asked, "The business of the Black Brotherhood?"

In all our miles together, Kane had said very little about this secret brotherhood of men whom we supposed he led. And he told us only a little more now, saying, "The Great Beast must be opposed with any weapons we can find."

"Even assassination?" Master Juwain said to him. "Even poison, terror, deceit?"

Kane looked far off into the star-spangled heavens. Somewhere, unseen, golden bands of light streamed out from their center, touching many of the universe's earths.

"No, perhaps not those things," he finally said. He looked over at me and stared at Alkaladur. "Perhaps it's time we found other means of fighting."

"I've said before," Master Juwain told him, "that evil cannot be defeated with the sword."

"No, perhaps not," Kane admitted. "But evil people can."

He cast me a long, sad look, and my hand tightened around Alkaladur's hilt. I feared that fate would once more call me to draw it before the world was rid of such as Morjin. And yet I knew that Master Juwain was right, that even the greatest of swords could never put an end to war.

"There are still battles to be fought," I said. I drew forth the Lightstone and sat gazing at it. "Different kinds of battles."

As I remembered why I had fought so hard for this little cup and why the Galadin had sent it to Ea, it began pouring out an intense, golden radiance. For a moment, I held in my hands a little sun whose light could perhaps have been seen from the mountains to the east of us, if any were looking.

"There will be battles, and soon," Kane assured us. He nodded his head at the Lightstone and added, "Now that we've taken this from the Beast, he'll bend all his will toward getting it back."

"Then you believe he'll recover from his wound?" Maram asked.

"Yes, his kind cannot be killed so easily," Kane said. "A sword through the heart, or the severing of the head—that's almost the only way to kill one of the Elijin."

He went on to say that Morjin would now be forced to accelerate his plans for his conquest: "So, he's always looked to Alonia and to the Nine Kingdoms, Delu as well, for he knows that if they fall, all of Ea falls, too."

The Lightstone's radiance had now faded, and I gave the cup to Maram to hold. I sat staring at the fire. In its flames I saw the conflagration of the great Library and feared that it would soon spread across the whole world.

"No, no, that must never be," Maram told Kane.

I watched the fire's flames gather in the Lightstone's bowl; in Maram there now gathered a different kind of fire.

"We must," he added, "stop Morjin first."

Again, I gripped my sword as a great bitterness ate at my belly. And I said, "Perhaps I should have killed him."

Kane reached over and laid his hand on my shoulder. And then he said a strange thing: "You did what you did out of compassion, and there's nothing to be sorry for in that. Would that we all had such compassion."

Atara, who was now holding the Lightstone, faced me from next to Maram and said, "Not even a scryer can see all ends, you know. If you had died in Argattha, we might never have escaped. And so one of Morjin's Red Priests might have his bloody hands on this even now."

It was one of those moments when the Lightstone's gold seemed to reveal a clear light within its depths—as did Atara. She nodded at me and said, "There's still hope if we stand together."

"Yes," I said, smiling at her, "there's always hrope."

As if she could still see me, she returned my smile and said, "I do hope Ymiru returned safely to his people. Will the Valari come to the Ymanir's aid and fight Morjin?"

"Yes," I told her. "If we don't fight each other."

Maram looked at Kane and then said, "I couldn't bear it if the Beast ever saw Alundil. He would destroy it, I think. Is there no way that the Star People might return and send help?"

We all understood that Kane was forbidden to speak of other worlds around other stars, even as he forbade himself to speak of his past. And so he surprised us, saying, "They did send help, once. But they'll never come again so long as Morjin is free to work his evil. You tell of the glory of Alundil. It's nothing against that of the cities of the Star People and the Elijin. And the Galadin, so, the Galadin. What if Morjin or another were to place the Lightstone in the Dark One's hands? So, they'll not risk the destruction of worlds and a splendor that you cannot imagine."

Liljana, who had been passed the Lightstone, nodded at Kane and said, "And that is why we must first look to this world. And that is why I must return to Tria. The Sisterhood must prepare for what is to come."

She said as little about the Maitriche Telu as Kane did his Black Brotherhood. But it gladdened my heart when she looked at Master Juwain and said, "Perhaps the time has come when our two orders can make our purposes known to each other."

She gave the Lightstone to him, and his ugly face brightened with the most beautiful of smiles. "The time has come, I see. I would like nothing more than for us to call each other Sister and Brother."

As Daj next took the Lightstone, his eyes wide with the wonder of it, Liljana clasped Master Juwain's hand.

Now Master Juwain took out his varistei and sat gazing at it. Seized with inspiration, he held it in front of Daj's forehead. The Lightstone seemed to pour its radiance into the green stone. Then a green light leaped from the crystal, and its rays seared into the tattoo of the red dragon disfiguring Daj. Soon the crystal grew quiet. And we all stared at Daj through the fire's flames to see that the tattoo was gone.

"Is it really?" Daj said, handing the Lightstone to Kane. He scurfed his fingers across his forehead as if feeling for the hated tattoo. "I want to see! Val, will you show me, in your sword?"

I drew Alkaladur so that he could behold himself in its gleaming silver. But the sword, in the Lightstone's presence, suddenly flared so brightly that for a moment none of us could see. After it had returned to only a mirrorlike brilliance, Daj sat looking at himself in wonder.

"It is gone," he said. "Now they won't stare at me in Tria."

We had decided that he would go with Kane and Liljana to Tria, where Liljana would look after him. Atara would accompany them along the mountains facing the Wendrush; she must pay her respects to Sajagax and the Kurmak, she said, before continuing on with Kane and the others to Tria to conclude her business with her father.

"King Kiritan," she said, "must be told that the Lightstone has been found and the quest fulfilled. And I must tell him."

"That I would like to see," Kane said, gazing at the cup that he held. His eyes, like the black stone he kept hidden away, seemed to touch upon the fiery light of creation itself. "Almost as much as I'd like to see his face when Val shows him this."

He passed the Lightstone on to me and asked, "Are you sure you won't reconsider your plans?"

I squeezed the cup between my hands and said, "The Lightstone must first be brought to the Valari. We are its guardians, and we can't guard it if I alone of my people take it into Tria."

"But, Val," Maram reminded me, "King Kiritan is expecting its finder to bring it to him. Our vows—"

"We vowed to seek the Lightstone for all of Ea and not for ourselves," I said. "For Ea, Maram—not for King Kiritan."

"But what about your vow, then?"

Now the gold of the Lightstone suddenly felt as cold as ice in my hands. I remembered too well standing in King Kiritan's hall before thousands of knights and nobles, and promising King Kiritan that I would bring the Lightstone to him and so claim Atara as my bride.

I looked over at Atara sitting rigidly as a statue, and I said, "That vow is not mine to fulfill. Not mine alone."

I longed for her to look at me as she once had and smile brightly with her assurance that we would enjoy a long life together. That she could not cut my heart like a cold knife.

After that, our talk turned toward the remembrance of all that we suffered together, the glories as well as the sorrows. Kane recounted the story of Flick spinning on Alphanderry's nose; this made Daj break open with an easy, boyish laughter that was a delight to hear. We had thought that he would never laugh again. His sudden joy made us weep, especially Liljana, who seemed to have lost her own laughter, even as Atara had warned on the beach of the Bay of Whales. For she had looked too deep into Morjin's mind and seen there an evil so great that her own joy of life seemed forever dimmed. Even the Lightstone's gleaming presence was not enough to restore her peaceable temperament and her lovely smiles.

At last it came time to begin the long and painful rounds of making our good-byes. Master Juwain sat telling Daj of the Great White Brotherhood and gave him his copy of the *Saganom Elu*; Daj promised to read it and someday make the journey to Mesh. I gave Kane the sharpening stone of pressed diamond dust that my brother Mandru had once given me. Alkaladur's edge never needed sharpening, but the kalama that Kane bore would. In return, he gave me one of the bloodstones that he had taken from Morjin's chambers, and instructed me in its use. Much past midnight, with the moon dropping lower in the sky, I spoke with Liljana about a few of the things she had seen in Morjin's mind.

Still later, I walked with Atara through the swishing grass at the edge of our camp. Twice she almost stumbled as the long grasses snared her feet. It was one of those times when she was truly blind. I offered her my arm, but she wouldn't take it.

"I must learn to get on by myself," she told me.

"No one was meant to get on alone," I said to her. "If this quest has taught me anything, it's that."

"Still, you can't walk for me. You can't see for me."

"No," I said, touching the mail over my chest where I had returned the Lightstone. "But now that this has been found, I can marry you."

"I still have my vow," she reminded me.

I stopped to look off across the steppe, west, toward Argattha. I asked her, "How many men have you slain, then? Seventy? Eighty?"

"Would you have me slay more?"

I listened to the beating of my heart, then said, "Your vow isn't what keeps you from wanting to make vows with me."

"No," she said softly, touching the cloth around her face. "I can't marry you like this."

"But your sight will return," I said, speaking of her powers of scrying, which seemed to be growing ever stronger. "In Argattha, when Kane touched you—"

"Kane will go his way, and I will go mine," she told me. "And Kane is still Kane, don't you see?"

I looked back toward the fire where Kane stood like a lonely sentinel surveying the steppe in all directions. Despite our nearness to Mesh, he hadn't ceased his eternal watch for enemies.

"Sometimes now," she said to me, "Kane walks with the One. But too often, he still walks with himself. He hasn't the power to make me see. In Argattha, for a moment, he helped me find my way back to the One. But I . . . can't always remain there. And so then I'm utterly blind."

"I don't care," I told her.

"But I do care," she said to me. "Someday, if I bear your son, as I have wished a thousand times and will, if only I could, my son . . . when I hold him to me and give him my milk, when I look down at him, if I can't see him, if I can't see him seeing me, then it would break my heart."

I stood beneath the blazing stars that she could not perceive. The tears in my eyes nearly blinded me to their light. It was the strangest turn of fate that although I had set out on the quest in order to be relieved of others' suffering, now and forever more I would feel their deepest hurts more keenly.

"I understand," I told her. How could I love this woman if I didn't guard her heart as I would my own heart, as I would the Lightstone itself?

"I know it's vain of me," she said, "I know it's selfish, but I—"

"I understand."

I moved to stroke her hair, gleaming like silver-gold in the starlight. But she shook her head and pulled back from me. And she murmured, "No, no—I'm *imakla* now, haven't you heard? I'm *imakla,* and may not be touched."

"I don't care, Atara."

I knew that she couldn't bear for me to touch her—and even more, that she couldn't bear not being touched. And so one last time, I kissed her. My lips burned with a pain worse than when the dragon had seared me with her fire.

After that, I sat with her on the cold grass holding hands as we waited for the sun to brighten the sky over the mountains to the east. When it came time to say good-bye, she squeezed my hand and said, "I wish you well, Valashu Elahad."

For a moment, my eyes burned and blurred, and I was almost as blind as she. Then I told her, "May you always walk in the light of the One."

She got up to go saddle her horse with the others while I sat staring at the last of the night's stars. After a while Maram came over to me. He somehow knew what had occurred between us, and I loved him for that.

"Take courage, old friend, there may yet be hope," he told me. "If you've taught me anything, it's that."

I slipped the Lightstone out from beneath my armor and held before me. Its hollows suddenly filled with the first rays of the sun rising over Tarkel's slopes, and I knew what he said was true.

"Thank you, Maram," I said as he grabbed my hand and helped pull me to my feet. I pointed east at Tarkel. "Now why don't we go get some of that beer I've promised you for at least the last thousand miles?"

The smile brightening his face reminded me that no matter how fiercely I might miss Atara and the rest of our company, others whom I loved were waiting for me beneath the shining mountains of my home.

18

ABOUT A MILE from our camp, Atara found a ford over the Diamond River and led Liljana, Daj, and Kane across it. Thus they entered the lands of the Adirii tribe, who were presently allied with the Kurmak. As she rode north on her red horse draped in her black-maned lion's skin, my whole being hurt with a great emptiness. I dared not hope that what I most desired would someday come to be. And yet, as I recalled her breath burning over my lips and her blazing passion for life, how could I not hope? Wherever she went, there too would go our star—as it was with me. Someday, I prayed, we would return together to this brightest of heaven's lights.

In the quiet of the morning, I rode with Maram and Master Juwain east along the river. There were no boundary stones to mark the exact place where Altaru first set his hoof upon Meshian soil. But when the steppe gave way to the low foothills fronting the Shoshan range of the Morning Mountains, I knew that we would find no Sarni farming the rocky ground or tending flocks of sheep on the pastures, but only Valari warriors who followed the standard of King Shamesh.

A fortress, built beneath Tarkel's lower slopes, stood looking down upon the Diamond River and the valley through which it cut. It was a great square construction, with thick granite walls—one of the twenty-two kel keeps that ringed my father's kingdom. Politeness demanded that we make our way up to it and pay our respects to its commander. We were met at the north gate by fifty warriors in mail and the keep's commander, a jowly man whose long hair had gone gray. He presented himself as Lord Manthanu of Pushku. He had summoned forth the entire garrison to witness the strange sight of three ragged-looking wanderers, who obviously were not Sarni, coming unscathed out of the Sarni's lands.

"And who," Lord Manthanu called out as we stopped just inside the gate, "are you?"

His men were lined up on either side of the road leading from the gate, their hands gripping their kalamas should they need to draw them. I did not recognize any of them. It seemed that the keep was garrisoned with warriors from the lands along the Sawash River, a part of Mesh I had visited only once ten years before.

"My name," I said, throwing back my cloak to reveal the swan and stars of my much-worn surcoat, "is Valashu Elahad."

Like a lightning flash, Lord Manthanu whipped out his kalama and pointed it at me. And nearly as quickly, his fifty warriors drew their swords, too.

"Impossible!" Lord Manthanu called out. "Sar Valashu was killed last spring in Ishka, in the Black Bog. We had reports of it."

"That is news to me," I said with a smile. "It would seem that the Ishkans reported wrongly. My name is as I have said. And my friends are Prince Maram Marshayk of Delu and Master Juwain of the Brotherhood."

After much discussion we convinced them of who we really were. It turned out that one of the keep's stonemasons making repairs to its walls had once done work for the Brothers at their sanctuary near Silvassu. Upon being summoned, he greeted Master Juwain warmly, for Master Juwain had once healed him of a cataract of the eyes that had nearly blinded him.

"Sar Valashu, my apologies," Lord Manthanu said. He sheathed his sword and clasped my hand. "But the Ishkans did send word that you had perished in the Bog. How did you escape it?"

Maram took this opportunity to say, "That might be a story best told over a glass of beer."

"It might," Lord Manthanu said, "but this is no time for drinkfests."

"How so?" Maram asked.

"Haven't you heard? But of course not—you've been off on that foolish quest. Did you ever make it as far as Tria?"

"Yes," I said, smiling again, "we did. But please tell us these tidings that have all your men drawing swords on their countrymen."

Lord Manthanu paused only a moment before saying, "We received word only yesterday that the Ishkans are marching on Mesh. We're to meet in battle on the fields between the Upper Raaswash and the Lower."

So, I thought, it had finally come to this. Autumn having reached its fullness, and the year's barley safely grown and harvested, the Ishkans had succeeded in calling out the battle that they had long sought.

"Has a date been appointed?" I asked.

"Yes, the sixteenth."

"And today is the twelfth, is that right?"

Lord Manthanu's eyes widened as he asked, "Where have you been that you are in doubt of the date?"

"We have been," I told him, "in a dark place, the darkest of places."

It seemed that while all the Sarni tribes from Galda to the Long Wall knew of our adventure in Argattha, word of this had not penetrated beyond the wall of the Morning Mountains. I decided that this was no time to tell of our journey—and certainly not to show the golden cup that we had brought out of the bowels of Skartaru.

I bowed my head then and said, "Lord Manthanu, as you can see, we haven't much time. Will you supply us with food and drink that we might ride on as soon as possible?"

Maram was quite alarmed by what he heard in my voice. He looked at me and said, "But Val, you can't be thinking of riding to this battle?"

I was thinking exactly that, and he knew it. I told him, "The king has called all free knights and warriors to the Raaswash. And the king himself gave me this ring."

I made a fist to show Maram my knight's ring with its two sparkling diamonds. The fifty warriors lined up by the gate looked on approvingly. And so did Lord Manthanu.

"It's our duty to remain here and miss the greatest battle in years, and more's the pity," he said. "But, Sar Valashu, it seems that fortune has favored you. You've arrived home just in time to seek honor and show brave."

So I had, I thought. But I feared that fate had brought me back to Mesh so that I must witness the death or wounding of my brothers beneath the Ishkans' swords.

Maram, who hadn't reconciled himself to another battle, looked at me and said, "It's a good hundred miles from here to the Raaswash—and mountain miles at that. How can we hope to cover this distance in only four days?"

"By riding fast," I told him. "Very fast."

"Oh, oh," he said, rubbing his hindquarters. Despite Master

Juwain's ministrations, he still complained of hurts taken from the two arrows shot into him in the battle for Khaisham. "My poor body!"

While five of Lord Manthanu's men went to take charge of filling our saddlebags with oats and other supplies, I turned to Maram and said, "This isn't your battle, Maram. No one will think worse of you if you remain here and rest or go straight on to the Brotherhood's sanctuary with Master Juwain."

"No, I suppose they wouldn't," he said. "But I would think worse of myself. Do you think I've ridden by your side across half of Ea to leave you to the Ishkans at the last moment?"

We clasped hands then, and he gripped mine so hard that his fingers squeezed like a vise against my knight's ring.

"I'm afraid I won't be leaving either," Master Juwain said. He rubbed the back of his bald head and sighed. "If a battle must be fought, if it really is, then there will be much healing to be done."

After Lord Manthanu had seen to our provisioning, we thanked him and bade him farewell. Then we rode forth out of the gate and found our way to the Kel Road leading along the border of Ishka. As always, my father's men had kept it in good repair. We urged the horses to a greater effort and so cantered at a fast pace toward the northeast corner of my father's kingdom.

All that day the weather held fair, and we made good time. It was one of the most beautiful seasons of the year with the foliage of the trees just past the most brilliant colors. The maples lining the road waved their bright red leaves in the sun while on the higher slopes, the yellows of the aspens were a blaze against the deep blue sky. We passed by pastures whitened with flocks of sheep and by fields golden with the chaff of freshly cut barley. That night we took shelter in the house of a woman named Fayora. She fed us mutton and black barley bread, and asked us to look for her husband, Sar Laisu, if we should see him on the field of the Raaswash.

The next day—the thirteenth of Valte—found us struggling across and around some of the Shoshan's highest peaks. We pounded across a bridge spanning one of the tributaries of the Diamond, then came to two more kel keeps before crossing over this icy blue river's headwaters where they wound down from the south toward Ishka. We had hoped to make it as far as Mount Raaskel by evening; but for the horses' sake, to say nothing of Maram's poor hindquarters, we felt compelled to spend the night at the kel keep only a few miles from the bridge.

"You'll have some hard travel tomorrow," Master Tadru, the keep's commander, told us. "From here to the North Road, the way is very steep."

And so it was. In the hard frost of the next morning, before the sun had risen, the horses' breath steamed out into the air as they drove forward up the Kel Road. Here, its ice-slicked stones turned away from Mount Raaskel, rising up like a white horn to the north of us. The road led south for a few miles, before turning back north and east again. We passed up a hot meal offered us at the keep where the Kel Road intersected the North Road. On our journey into Ishka, we had stopped here to greet the keep's commander, Lord Avijan. But the keep's new commander, Master Sivar, informed us that we would be hard-pressed to join Lord Avijan in time for the meeting with the Ishkans two days hence.

"The battle is to begin in the morning," he admonished us, "and it won't wait upon one late knight, even if he is King Shamesh's son."

We paused at the keep only long enough to give the horses oats and water—and to gaze up the North Road where it led through the Telemesh Gate into Ishka. There, on the snowfield between Raaskel and Korukel, with its twin peaks and ogre-like humps, the white bear sent by Morjin had attacked us and nearly put an end to our quest at its very beginning. It gave us grim satisfaction to know that the Lord of Illusions would not be making ghuls of animals or men for quite some time to come.

That afternoon we passed through Ki; as on our journey into Ishka, we found that we didn't have time for a hot bath at one of its inns, nor for the beer that I had promised Maram. We left its little chalets and shops quickly behind us. Only one kel keep graced the long stretch of road between Ki and the Raaswash, and I wanted to reach it before nightfall.

We found this cold, spare fortress to be nearly emptied of supplies, which had been sent off in wagons toward the battlefield to the east. Our rest there that night was brief and troubled. For the first time since Argattha, I had bad dreams, none of which had been sent by Morjin. I was only too happy to arise in the darkness before dawn and saddle Altaru for another long day's ride.

It was a good thirty miles from the keep to the Lower Raaswash, and then perhaps another seven to the appointed battlefield. I didn't know how we would be able to cover this distance in a single day. It was a cold morning with wisps of clouds high in the sky and a shifting of the wind that presaged a storm. Although the forest beyond the keep's battlements smelled sweetly of woodsmoke and dry leaves, there hung in the crisp autumn air a certain bitterness: both our remembrance of what we had lost on our long journey and a presentiment of what the following day's battle might still take from us.

I didn't need spurs or the silver-handled quirt that the Niuriu's chieftain, Vishakhan, had given me to hurry Altaru onward. As always, he sensed my urgency to cover ground quickly, and he led the other horses down the road with all the speed their driving hooves could purchase against the worn paving stones. My fierce warhorse smelled battle ahead of us—and not a battle where he must hide behind walls while the Blues and other warriors came howling over battlements, but a great gathering of warriors in long, shining lines and companies of cavalry thundering over grass toward each other. He was a fearless animal, I thought, and I envied him his trust that the future would somehow take care of itself and come out all right.

It grew colder all that day as we rode along; by early afternoon, the sky was growing heavy with clouds. The first snowflakes of the season's first snow began falling a few hours later. Maram, pulling his cloak around himself, offered his opinion that the hand of fate had fallen against us, and now we had no hope of reaching the battlefield by the morrow.

"It's no fun fighting through snow," he said as our horses clopped along the road. "Perhaps they'll call the battle off."

I looked at him past the fluffy white crystals sifting down from the sky. I said to him, "They won't call off the battle, Maram. And so we must ride, even faster, if we can."

"Ride through the snow, then?"

"Yes," I said. "And we'll ride through the night, if we have to."

Although we had suffered much worse cold in the Nagarshath, we had been hoping by this day for the warmth of our home fires and our journey's end. If the storm had proved a heavy one, it might have gone badly for us. As it was, however, it snowed for only a couple of hours. And a couple of hours after that, the clouds began breaking up. By dusk, with the air growing dark and icy, the sky was beginning to fill with stars.

"It seems," I said to Maram, "that fate may yet offer us a chance."

"Yes, to throw ourselves onto the Ishkan's spears," he muttered. He wiped the frost from his moustache, then said to me, "Do you remember that day in Lord Harsha's fields? He said that the next time the Ishkans and Meshians lined up for battle, you'd be there at the front of your army."

Master Juwain, making a rare joke, looked at Maram from on top of his tired horse and said, "I didn't know Mesh produced such scryers. Perhaps we should have taken him with us on our journey as well."

This suggestion produced nothing but groans from Maram. He turned toward me and said, "Lord Harsha is too old to go off to war, isn't he? Now there's a man I don't want to meet decked out for battle."

"Come," I said to him, patting Altaru's neck. "We're likely to meet only the dead on the battlefield if we don't hurry."

That evening we ate our supper in our saddles: a cold meal of cheese, dried cherries, and battle biscuits that nearly broke our teeth. We rode far into the cold night. The many stars and the bright half-moon opened up the black sky and gave enough light so that we could follow the whitened road as it wound like a strand of shimmering silver along the mountains toward the east. It would have been safest for us to cleave to the Kel Road and take it all the way to the keep by the gorge of the Lower Raaswash. There the road from Mir, by which my father's army had marched, came up from the south and followed the river for seven miles as it flowed northeast toward the Upper Raaswash. But for us, coming from the west, this was not the quickest way toward the battlefield. I knew of another road that led straight from the Kel Road down to the Upper Raaswash.

"Are you asking us to cut through the mountains on a snowy night?" Maram asked incredulously when I told him of my plan. "Have you lost your wits?"

"Is this wise?" Master Juwain asked as we stopped the horses for a quick rest. "Your shortcut will save only a few miles."

I looked up at the stars where the Swan constellation was practically flying across the sky. I said, "It may save an hour of our journey—and the difference between life and death."

"Very well," he said, steeling himself for the last leg of a hard ride.

"Ah, I think I've lost my wits," Maram said, "following you this far."

"Come on," I said, smiling at him. "We've dared much worse than this."

The path that gave upon the Kel Road, when we finally found it, proved to be not nearly as bad as Maram had feared. True, it was unpaved and quite steep, leading up and over the side of a small mountain. But there were few rocks to turn the horses' hooves, and the path was quite clear. It took us through a swath of evergreens dusted in white and gleaming in the moonlight. Soon the road began its descent through some elms and oaks mostly bare of leaves; by the time the sky ahead of us began growing lighter, the quiet woods through which we rode were covered with only a couple of inches of snow.

I guessed that the confluence of the two Raaswash rivers lay only four or five miles from here. We rode quickly over ground that gradually fell off toward the northeast, our direction of travel. As we lost elevation, the trees around us showed many more leaves. The rising sun was just beginning to melt the snow from them. The woods around us rang with the patter of falling water, like rain. And from ahead of us came a deeper, more troubling sound: the booming of war drums shaking the air and calling men to battle.

At last we crested a small hill, and through a break in the trees we saw the armies of Ishka and Mesh spread out below us. The clear morning sun cast a great glimmer upon ranks of shields, spears, and polished steel helms. The Upper Raaswash was to our left; the Ishkan lines—perhaps twelve thousand men—were drawn up about five hundred yards to the south of it. They ran along the river, from the base of our hill to the Lower Raaswash, which joined the Upper about a mile father on to the east. There King Hadaru had anchored his left flank, which were all warriors on foot, against these bright waters. He himself had gathered the knights of his cavalry to him on his right flank at the base of our hill. I sensed that Salmelu, Lord Issur, and Lord Nadhru were there, sitting on top of their snorting and stamping mounts as they awaited the command to charge. I counted nearly seven hundred knights around them, all looking toward the standard of the white bear that fluttered near King Hadaru.

Facing them across the snow-covered ground were the lines of the ten thousand warriors and knights of Mesh. A mile away, by the Lower Raaswash, two hundred Meshian knights on horse were massed to the right of the foot warriors. I knew that Asaru would be there leading them, and perhaps Karshur and one or two of my other brothers as well. Although my father always made good use of terrain, he didn't believe in relying upon rivers, hills, or suchlike for protecting his flanks. It gave men, he always said, a false sense of security and weakened their will to fight. And my father's will toward fighting, I knew, was very strong. For a long time he had tried to avoid this battle with all his wiles and good sense, but now that he

had finally taken the field against the Ishkans I pitied any
knight or warrior who dared to cross swords with him.

He sat on top of a great chestnut stallion with five hundred
knights on their horses at the base of our hill, off toward our
right. I couldn't make out his countenance from this distance,
but his flapping standard of the Swan and Stars was clear
enough, as was the white swan crest that graced his helm. I
made out the blazons of the Lords Tomavar, Tanu, and Avijan
nearby him, and of course, the three swords and gold dragon
of his seneschal, Lord Lansar Raasharu. Much to Maram's
chagrin, Lord Harsha had taken a post just to their right. It
seemed that he was not too old for war, after all.

Maram, Master Juwain, and I had only a few moments to
drink in this splendid and terrible sight before a signal was
given and the trumpeters up and down the Meshian lines
sounded the attack. Now the drummers ahead of the lines beat
out a quicker cadence in a great booming thunder as ten thousand men began marching forward. Their long black hair, tied
with brightly colored battle ribbons won in other contests,
flowed out from beneath their helms and streamed out behind
them. Around their ankles they wore silver bells which sounded
the jangling rhythm of their carefully measured steps. This
high-pitched ringing had been known to unnerve whole armies
and put them to flight before a single arrow was fired or spear
clashed against shield. But our enemy that day were Ishkans,
and they sported silver bells of their own, as did all the Valari in
battle. And every man on the field, Ishkan or Meshian, warrior
or king, was dressed in a suit of the marvelous Valari battle
armor: supple black leather encrusted with white diamonds
across the chest and back, covering the neck, and gleaming
along the arms and legs down to the diamond-studded boots.

The brilliance of so many thousands of men, each sparkling
with a covering of thousands of diamonds, dazzled the eye.
Who had ever seen so many diamonds displayed in one place?
The wealth of the Morning Mountains was spread out on the
snowy field below us—and not just her gemstones. For it was
men, I thought, and the women who would grieve for them,
who were the true treasure of this land. Warriors such as

Asaru, pure of heart and noble-souled, born of the fertilest and finest soil—these were the only diamonds that had true worth. And they mustn't, I knew, be squandered.

"Come on!" I said to Maram and Master Juwain. I urged Altaru forward down the hill. "It's nearly too late."

Already, on the battlefield ahead of us through the trees, the archers behind the opposing lines were loosing their arrows. The whine of these hundreds of shafts shivered the air; their points clacked off of armor in a cacophony of steel striking stone. Soon enough, some of these arrows would drive through the chinks between the diamonds and find their way into flesh.

I rode hard for the edge of the woods and the quickly narrowing gap between the two advancing armies. Maram, clinging to his bounding horse, somehow managed to catch up to me. He pointed through the trees off to the right, toward my father's standard and his cavalry. And he gasped out, "Your lines are that way! What are you trying to do?"

"Stop a battle," I said.

And with that I drew forth the Lightstone and charged out onto the field. I held it high above my head. The sun filled the cup with its radiance, and it gave back this splendor a thousandfold. A sudden blaze poured out of it, drenching the warriors of both armies in a brilliant golden sheen. More than twenty thousand pairs of eyes turned my way. With Maram to my right, and Master Juwain to my left, we rode straight past the lines of men to either side of us as down a road. Thus did Lord Harsha's prediction come true as we found ourselves in the middle of the battlefield in front of both advancing armies.

"Hold!" I cried out to the warriors around me as Altaru galloped through the snow. "Hold now!"

An arrow, shot from behind the Ishkans' ranks, whistled past my ear. Then I heard one of the Ishkans shout, "It's the Elahad—back from the dead!"

Many men were now giving voice to their amazement. I recognized Lord Harsha's gruff old voice booming out above others of the knights grouped around my father, "They've returned! The questers have returned! The Lightstone has been found!"

Suddenly the trumpets stopped blowing and the drums fell silent. The captains calling out the cadences up and down the lines gave the order for a halt. The silver bells bound around the warriors' legs ceased their eerie jingling as the twenty thousand men along the Ishkan and Meshian lines drew up waiting to see what their kings would next command.

I stopped Altaru at the middle of the field. Master Juwain and Maram joined me there. The Lightstone was now like the sun itself in my hand. It was a call for a truce, the like of which hadn't been seen among the Valari for three thousand years.

My father, along with Lansar Raasharu, Lord Tomavar, Lord Harsha, and several other lords and master knights, was the first to ride toward us beneath a fluttering white flag. A few moments later, King Hadaru gathered up his most trusted lords and called for one of his squires to hold up a white flag as well. Then he, too, led his men slowly toward us. It was not quite the thundering charge that either the Meshian knights or the Ishkans had anticipated.

"Stop the battle, you said!" Maram muttered at me, holding his hand to his chest. "Stop my heart, I say!"

My father had signaled for Asaru to join the parlay; now he broke from the ranks to the east down by the river and urged his dark brown stallion across the field. It took him only a few minutes to canter across the half mile that separated us. As he drew closer and the Lightstone's radiance showed the long hawk's nose and the noble face that I had nearly given up hope of seeing again, my heart soared and tears filled my eyes.

Then my father, who had drawn up with his lords in a half-circle around Master Juwain, Maram, and me, called out my name, and his voice touched my soul: "Sar Valashu, my son— you have returned to us. And not with empty hands."

He sat straight and grave in his sparkling armor as he regarded the Lightstone with marvel and me even more so. We were like new men to each other. His black eyes, so like Kane's in their brilliance, found mine, and embraced my entire being with gladness and love. In his fierce gaze burned a certainty that he had not lived his life in vain.

As King Hadaru and the Ishkans formed up on the other side of me facing him, my father studied my torn cloak and nearly ragged surcoat. Then he asked me, "Where is the shield that I gave you when you set out on your journey?"

"Gone, sire," I told him. "Consumed in dragon fire."

At this, even the greatest lords of both Ishka and Mesh gasped out their amazement as if they were still unbloodied boys. They all pressed closer. No one seemed to know if what I had said should be taken literally.

"Dragon fire, is it?" King Hadaru said. He sat all bearlike and irritable on top of his huge horse as he looked at me skeptically. His great beak of a nose pointed straight at me as if threatening to pry out the truth. "And where did you fight this dragon?"

"In Argattha," I said.

This name, dreadful and ancient, loosed in the lords another round of gasps and cries. All their eyes now lifted up and fixed on the golden cup still pouring forth its light from above my hand.

"It was in Argattha," Maram said, "that we found the Lightstone."

Prince Salmelu, nudging his horse closer to his father, held his hand covering his eyes as he shook his head. The scar running down the side of his face to his weak chin burned a goldish red. Then he tore his gaze from the Lightstone. He glared at me in challenge. His great hate for me had only grown in poisonousness during the months since I had wounded him in our duel.

"Is it your claim, then," he said to me in a bitter voice, "that this is the Lightstone?"

"There's no claim to be made," I told him. "It is, as you can see, the cup that our ancestors brought to earth."

He pressed his horse a few paces forward as if to get a better look at the cup that I held. His ugly, furtive eyes showed but little of its light. "And you claim to have entered the forbidden city and brought forth this cup?"

"In fulfillment of our quest, yes."

"What proofs can you give us, then?" he called out to me.

"Why should we believe the word of a man who has dishonored himself in fighting duels that he didn't have the courage to finish?"

Despite my resolve to keep a cool head, I found myself gripping Alkaladur's hilt. And Salmelu, moving slightly more slowly due to the wounds I had cut into his arms and chest, curled his fingers around his kalama.

"Val," Master Juwain reminded me with an urgent whisper, "if you truly wish to stop this battle, this is no place for pride."

"Perhaps not pride," I told him, "but certainly honor."

As I fought to turn away from the ever-beckoning and burning black pool of hatred that would consume me if I let it, my father's clear voice rang out: "Sar Valashu, on this day no knight in all of Ea has more honor than you."

His words washed through me like a thrill of cold water. I suddenly let go of my sword.

But my father's praise only inflamed Salmelu and deepened his spite. And so, before two kings and the assembled lords of Ishka and Mesh, with the thousands of warriors of two armies waiting in their lines and looking on, he sneered at me, saying, "And still you lack the courage to test whether the sword stroke that cut me so dishonorably was skill or only evil luck!"

I took a deep breath and said, "We haven't journeyed to the end of Ea and returned here today to make more tests—only to tell of what we've seen."

I informed the assembled lords then of the battle for Surrapam and the conquest of Yarkona by Count Ulanu and his dreadful Blues. I spoke of the armed might that Morjin was assembling behind the rocky shield of Skartaru. And then I called for a peace between Ishka and Mesh. I said that the Valari must now join together and renounce our petty squabbles, duels, and formal combats. For someday Morjin would recover from the wound that I had dealt him. And someday we would have to fight a war without rules or mercy, a terrible war to determine the fate of the world—and perhaps much else.

"A great scryer named Atara Ars Narmada has told that we can die bravely as Ishkans and Meshians," I called out. "Or live as Valari."

Salmelu nudged his horse a step closer as he pointed at the Lightstone. He said, "And still Sar Valashu will say anything to avoid battle. How should we believe anything of what he has told us? How do we know that this is really the cup of our ancestors and not just one of the False Lightstones told of in the ancient chronicles? Or even some glowstone gilded over to fool us?"

Truly, a poisonous serpent was Salmelu. And the time had come to pull his fangs.

"Those who serve the Lord of Lies," I said to him, "will hear lies in the truth that others tell."

As Salmelu froze in a hateful stare, all the Ishkan lords except King Hadaru grabbed at the hilts of their swords. He sat beneath the white flag held by his squire, looking at Salmelu and the others as if to remind them that we had gathered here in sacred truce. Then he turned toward me. In a deathly calm voice, he asked, "Do you accuse my son of treachery?"

"Treachery, yes, and more," I said. I looked straight into Salmelu's black, boiling eyes. I remembered what Liljana had told me on our last night together at the edge of the Wendrush: the truth about Salmelu that she had taken from Morjin's mind. "It was he who shot the poison arrow at me in the woods. He is an assassin, sent by the Red Dragon to—"

I had expected that Salmelu might not be able to bear the shame of his iniquity. And so I was prepared for him to whip free his sword and deliver an underhanded cut at me. But at the last moment, even as he screamed and spurred his horse straight at me, I was seized with a premonition that if I drew forth Alkaladur to defend myself, I would touch off the very battle that I had come here to prevent.

"Damn you, Elahad!" he screamed at me again.

He aimed his kalama in a silvery flash at my hand holding the Lightstone; its razor-sharp edge easily would have cleaved off my arm. But I suddenly gripped the cup tightly and turned it into the plane of his sword stroke. The gold of the gelstei— of the Gelstei—met cold steel in a shiver of shrieking metal. His sword shattered into pieces, and he stared down in disbelief at the hilt-shard sticking out from his spasming fist.

"Hold!" King Hadaru called out, spurring his horse forward. He motioned to Lord Issur, Lord Nadhru, and Lord Mestivan. "Hold him, now! Let it not be said that we Ishkans are trucebreakers!"

As the Ishkan lords and knights swarmed around Salmelu, grabbing at him and the reins of his horse, King Hadaru himself wrested the broken sword from his son's hand. He spat on it and cast it to the ground. Then he raised back his gauntleted hand and struck Salmelu across the face. And he raged at him, "Trucebreaker! You have dishonored yourself in the sight of both friend and foe!"

My father, sitting on his horse between Asaru and Lord Harsha, stared at the livid welt raised up on the side of Salmelu's face. He had little liking for this man, but even less desire to see a king savage his own son.

"And you!" King Hadaru said, whirling about on top of his horse to point at me. "You bring no honor to yourself if you cast careless words at one whom you have already wounded! He who provokes the breaking of a truce may be called a trucebreaker himself!"

"None of my words has been careless, King Hadaru," I said. "Your son has called for war with Mesh at the command of the Red Dragon. He was to weaken your realm and my father's. His reward, after the Red Dragon had sent his armies to conquer us, was to have been the overlordship of both Mesh and Ishka—and eventually all of the Nine Kingdoms."

"No, no," King Hadaru said, his red face falling white with a cold, deadly wrath, "that is not possible!"

Although I pitied him, I looked at him and said, "Your son is one of the Kallimun."

Now a terrible silence descended upon all those assembled beneath the flapping white flags and spread out like death across the battlefield. For a moment, no one dared to move.

"Who has ever heard a Valari knight speak such evil of another?" King Hadaru said, staring at me. "How could you possibly know such a thing?"

"Because," I said, "one of my companions learned this from Morjin himself."

"Proof!" Salmelu suddenly screamed out. "He has no proofs!"

King Hadaru pointed at him and commanded, "Hold him!"

Lord Issur and Lord Nadhru, who had their horses pressed up close to Salmelu's, gripped his arms while Lord Mestivan dismounted and pulled him off his horse. Then three other Ishkan lords dismounted as well, and helped Lord Mestivan subdue the furiously struggling Salmelu.

"There are proofs," I said to King Hadaru. I gave the Lightstone to Maram to hold, then climbed down from Altaru and stepped over to Salmelu. "Watch."

I pulled out the bloodstone that Kane had given me. Its dreadful red light fell upon Salmelu's face. And there, at the center of Salmelu's forehead, was revealed a tattoo of a coiled, red dragon.

"It's the mark of the Kallimun," I said. "The Red Priests affix it to their own with an invisible ink. The bloodstones bring it out into view. Thus do the Red Priests know each other."

"It's a trick!" Salmelu cried out, shaking his head back and forth. "An evil trick of this gelstei!"

"Salmelu's murder of me," I said, ignoring him, "was to have been his final initiation into Morjin's priesthood."

The Ishkan lords murmured among themselves and cast Salmelu looks of loathing. Lansar Raasharu pressed his horse forward as he stared at him. Then he turned toward me and said, "But Sar Valashu, this cannot be! I've already told that I saw Prince Salmelu in the woods by Lake Waskaw on the afternoon you say he shot at you."

Lord Raasharu had told this to Asaru and me, if no other, and it was courageous of him to declaim before two kings what he supposed was the truth—even if it aided Salmelu.

"You did not see Prince Salmelu there as you thought," I told him. "When he failed at my murder, the Lord of Lies sent an illusion to the most trusted man in Mesh so that suspicion wouldn't fall upon his priest."

"What you say disquiets me greatly," Lord Raasharu said. "To think that the Lord of Lies could make me see what is not."

"It has disquieted me, as well," I told him.

"Illusion!" Salmelu cried out again. His squinting at the bloodstone crinkled the red dragon tattooed into his forehead. "What you see is surely an illusion cast by this evil stone!"

I put away the bloodstone then, and watched as the red mark disappeared.

"Do you see?" Salmelu said. "It's gone, isn't it?"

I drew my sword an inch from its sheath. I touched my thumb to its blade, drawing blood. Then I pressed my thumb to the middle of Salmelu's forehead. The ink seared into his flesh grabbed at my blood and held some part of it. When I pulled back, the dragon tattoo now stood out red as blood for all to see.

"A trick!" he called. "Another trick!"

He managed to wrench free his arm, and he clawed his hand furiously at his forehead in a vain attempt to rub away the mark that would remain there to his death.

"Is this a trick?" I asked him.

As the Ishkan lords regained their hold on him, I placed my hand on the dagger at his belt and drew it. I showed it to King Hadaru. Its blade was coated with a dark blue substance that could only be kirax.

"During the battle," I said to him, "if you weren't struck down, he was to have touched you with this."

King Hadaru's gaze fixed on Salmelu in disbelief. "Why?" he asked him softly.

Salmelu, now seeing that his lies would no longer be believed, tried hate and terror instead.

"Because you're a blind old fool who can't see what must be done!" He tried to twist free from the men holding him, but could not. "All the Valari—fools! Can't you see that Morjin will rule Ea? If we oppose him, he'll annihilate us. But if we serve him, he'll make us kings and lords over other men!"

King Hadaru climbed down from his horse. He drew out his sword and stepped in front of me. Then he raised it up above Salmelu's neck. In his wrathful eyes was horror and hate of his son—and a terrible love as well.

"Hold!" my father called out from on top of his horse. "King Hadaru, hold! None of us would see a man slay his own son."

"If not I, then who else?" King Hadaru said. "My son has earned this death—no man more so."

"So he has," my father agreed. "But let there be no blood spilled here today."

His eyes met mine in a twinkle of light, and then he glanced down at my hand. "No more blood, that is."

King Hadaru's sword wavered above Salmelu's neck. I knew that he did not want to kill him. And my father knew this as well.

"May a king ask another king for mercy?"

"Very well," King Hadaru said.

As quickly as he had drawn his sword, he sheathed it. Although it was he who should have thanked my father, his manner suggested that he had granted him a great boon.

"Let me go, then!" Salmelu screamed out.

"Yes, let him go," King Hadaru commanded his men.

As Lord Mestivan and others set Salmelu free, King Hadaru took the tainted dagger from me, then bent and thrust it through the snow into the ground beneath. He walked over to Salmelu's horse. He grabbed up the shield slung there and cast it to the ground as well. His war lance and three throwing lances followed in quick succession. Then, as Salmelu's cold eyes met the even colder stare of his father, King Hadaru commanded that Salmelu's helmet, armor, and ring be stripped from him. This was done. He stood almost naked in his underpadding before the lords of Mesh and Ishka waiting to hear his father pronounce his judgment.

"This is not yet Ishkan soil," King Hadaru said, "and so not even the king of Ishka can banish you from it. But you are so banished from Ishka, forever. No one in my realm is to give you fire, bread, or salt."

"And in my realm as well, Prince Salmelu," my father said, "you are denied fire, bread, and salt."

As twenty thousand men watched the badly shaking

Salmelu, he climbed on top of his horse. Again he rubbed at the red dragon marking his forehead. And then, kicking his heels into his horse, he screamed out, "Damn you, Valari!"

And with that he thundered off across the battlefield cursing and screaming. When he reached the Lower Raaswash, he drove his horse in a savage gallop through its swift waters. From the Raaswash to the Culhadosh was a distance of ten miles. And on the other side of that river was the kingdom of Waas.

After Salmelu had disappeared into the woods beyond the Raaswash, I turned to address his father and my own.

"King Hadaru," I said. Then I looked at my father, "Sire, in all the Morning Mountains, no other kings have so great renown. But a war between Ishka and Mesh will only diminish both realms. It will only please the Lord of Lies—he who has schemed and sent out assassins so that this war might take place. Will you do the bidding of a false king?"

"The King of Ishka," King Hadaru said, touching the white bear of his purple surcoat, "does his own bidding and no other."

With his white hair whipping about in the wind, I could see that he was still wroth over what had occurred with Salmelu. He scowled at my father and said, "The Lord of Lies' schemes notwithstanding, there are still grievances between our kingdoms. There is still the matter of Korukel and its diamonds."

I took back the Lightstone from Maram and stood holding it. Then I looked at my father and said, "Sire, let the Ishkans have the diamonds. They'll need many diamonds to make armor to face the Dragon in the wars that are to come. All the Valari will."

My father, Shavashar Elahad, known throughout the Morning Mountains as King Shamesh, was not a vindictive or grasping man. For a long time, it seemed, he had been looking for a good reason to cede the Ishkans their half of Mount Korukel. Only the stubbornness and ferocity of his lords such as Lord Tanu and Lord Harsha had kept him from this course. But now, in light of all that had occurred here this day, their hearts softened, and the greatest lords of Mesh nodded their heads to my father in assent of what I had suggested.

"Very well," he said to King Hadaru. He dismounted and walked over to him. "You shall have your diamonds."

At this grace, Asaru and others struck their lances against their shields that my father's wisdom had finally prevailed.

King Hadaru inclined his head slightly in acceptance of his offer. And then, most ungraciously, he said, "It is perhaps easy to surrender one treasure when a greater one has so unexpectedly been gained."

And with that, he turned toward me to stare at the Lightstone.

I held the golden cup higher for all to see. Once before in another age, on this same ground, Mesh and Ishka had fought over its possession, and the Ishkan king, Elsu Maruth, had been killed. As I looked upon the thousands of warriors who had taken the field here this day, I prayed that we would not fight over it again.

"King Hadaru," I said, "the Lightstone is to be kept by all the Valari. We are its guardians."

And with that, much to his astonishment, I stepped forward and placed it in his hands.

While Ishkan lords and Meshians came down from their horses and pressed closer, he gazed at the cup in wonder. His grim, old eyes were wide like a child's. Something coiled tightly inside him seemed suddenly to let go. Then he raised his head up and stood straight and tall, looking like one of the Valari kings of old. In a clear voice he called out, "Ishka will not make war with Mesh."

He surprised even himself, I thought, in surrendering the Lightstone to my father. As his hands closed upon it, a golden radiance fell upon him. And in his noble countenance were revealed the lineaments of Telemesh, Aramesh, and even Elahad himself.

"And Mesh," my father told the assembled lords and knights, "will not make war with Ishka."

Holding the cup in one hand, he stepped forward and clasped King Hadaru's hand with his other.

As squires were sent off to report this news to the captains of the two armies, my father looked at the Lightstone and asked me, "How were you led to find it?"

"This led me," I said. And with that I drew Alkaladur and held it shining brilliantly before the Lightstone.

"There are stories to be told here," my father said. His awe at the ancient silver sword was no less than that of the other lords staring at it. "Great stories, it seems."

As he passed the cup to Lord Issur, I began giving an account of our quest. I told of our nightmare journey through the Black Bog and the even greater nightmare of being pursued by the fearsome Grays. I told of meeting Kane and Atara, Liljana and Alphanderry. His death in the Kul Moroth was still a raw wound inside me; it opened in my father and in King Hadaru the anguish of sacrifice, for in their long lives they had witnessed many feats of heroism, and none had touched them quite like this. Both of them were surprised—as were Asaru and Lord Harsha—when they heard of how Maram had almost single-handedly saved the day at the siege of Khaisham. They nodded their heads when I declared that a great Maitreya had been born somewhere on Ea, and that the Lightstone must be guarded for him. They smiled to hear of Master Juwain's brilliant solving of the final clue that had led us into Argattha. And of the gaining of the seven gelstei and Atara's blinding that sometimes helped her truly to see, they listened with amazement.

Now it was Asaru's turn to hold the Lightstone; he gazed at the cup as if he couldn't quite believe it was real. Then he turned to me with a great smile and said, "You've done well, little brother."

"They've all done well," my father said. "It is too bad their other companions aren't here to see this."

He suddenly turned his head and called out, "Ringbearer! Send squires to summon the ringbearer! And Sar Valashu's brothers, too."

At that moment Flick appeared and settled his sparkling form down into the bowl of the Lightstone like a bird into his nest. Asaru blinked his eyes, not quite daring to credit what they beheld. A dozen lords and knights shook their heads in awe.

"It seems," Asaru said, "that you've yet many more stories to tell."

While he gave the Lightstone to Lord Nadhru, a thunder of hooves announced the arrival of my father's ringbearer and my other brothers. As they reined in and dismounted, I ran forward to greet them.

"Karshur!" I cried out, throwing my arms around his solid body. "Ravar! Yarashan!"

Quick-witted Ravar cast a glance at the Lightstone as if he thought that I had proved quite clever in finding it, after all. Yarashan, of course, was envious of my feat; but his pride in being my brother was greater still. He embraced me warmly and kissed my forehead, as did the fierce and valorous Mandru. Jonathay, when he saw Lord Tomavar holding the Lightstone, let loose a great laugh of triumph as sweet and clear as a mountain stream.

With King Hadaru holding up his hand for silence, my father approached Master Juwain and said, "Without your guidance, Sar Valashu might never have found the road that led him to seek the Lightstone. And without your courage and insight, none of you would have found your way to Argattha. Therefore it is my wish that the treasure that would have been wasted upon this battle be spent in raising up a new building for your sanctuary. There you shall gather gelstei to you that their secrets might be revealed. There, from time to time, the Lightstone shall be brought. And it shall be as it was in another and better age."

Master Juwain bowed his head and said, "Thank you, King Shamesh."

My father next turned to Maram and said, "Prince Maram Marshayk! Your courage at Khaisham and in Argattha was extraordinary; your prowess with the sword was the equal of great warriors; your faithfulness on this quest was as adamantine as diamond and worthy of a Valari."

Then he smiled and said, "Ringbearer!"

A young knight named Jushur stepped up to my father

holding a broad, flat wooden case. He opened it to reveal four rows of silver rings pressed into a lining of black velvet. The rings in the first row were set with a single diamond, while those in the second row showed two, and so on. It was my father's pride and pleasure, as king, to reward heroism by promoting knights and master warriors on the field of battle.

After studying Maram's fat fingers, he chose out the largest ring from the second row. Its two diamonds sparkled in the strengthening sun. My father grasped Maram's hand and slipped the ring onto his finger. It was the ring of a Valari knight, even as the one that I wore.

"For your service to my son," he said, clasping Maram's hand. "For your service to Mesh and all of Ea."

As the lords of Mesh and Ishka crowded around Maram to stare at his knight's ring, Maram flushed with pride and thanked my father. For a hundred years, none but Valari warriors had been bestowed with such an honor.

Now my father turned to me and pulled off my knight's ring. He selected another from the case's fourth row. Then he placed this silver band with its four bright diamonds on my finger; he kissed my forehead and said, "Lord Valashu, Knight of the Swan, Guardian of the Lightstone."

The golden cup, I saw, was now being held by one of the Ishkans whom I did not know. Others were whispering that they had never heard of a Valari knight being made directly into a lord.

Master Juwain came over to Maram to get a better look at his new ring. He said to him, "I'm afraid that now you're a Valari in spirit."

"Ah, I'm afraid I am, sir." The diamonds of his ring dazzled his eyes. "I'm afraid that I must formally renounce my vows to the Brotherhood."

At this, Master Juwain smiled and bowed his head in acceptance. He said, "I think you renounced them many miles ago."

As the two kings sent squires to call for their armies to come closer and view the Lightstone, Lord Harsha limped over to us. On his bluff, old face was the brightest of smiles.

His single eye fell upon me, and he said, "Lord Valashu—you can't know how glad it makes me to say that."

Maram, I saw, had pulled back behind the cover of Karshur's thick body. He looked away from Lord Harsha like a child at school who is afraid that his master might call upon him.

"And Sar Maram!" Lord Harsha said, finding him easily enough. "We're all glad to see you."

"You are?" Maram said. "I had thought you might be distressed, ah, about things that had distressed you."

Lord Harsha looked at the two diamonds of Maram's ring and said, "It might have been so. But my poor daughter has talked of little else but you since you went away. And that distresses me."

"Behira," Maram said as if struggling to remember her name, "is a lovely woman."

"Yes, the loveliest. And she will be delighted to see that you've been knighted. What honor could we bestow upon you to equal that which you've brought to us?"

"Perhaps some of your excellent beer, sir."

"That you shall have, Sar Maram. And much else as well. The month of Ashte is a lovely time for a wedding, don't you think?"

"Sir?"

"Yes, a lovely time." Lord Harsha stepped forward favoring his crippled leg. He embraced Maram and said, "My son!"

"Ah, Lord Harsha, I—"

"There is only one thing in the world that could distress me on such a fine day as this," Lord Harsha added. He smiled at Maram as he rested his hand on his kalama. "And that would be to see my daughter further distressed. Do you understand?"

Maram did understand, and he looked at me as if pleading that I might come to his rescue. But this one time, I was powerless to help him.

"Ashte," I said to him, as Lord Harsha walked off, "is half a year away. Much might happen between now and then."

"Yes," Maram said optimistically, "I might come to love Behira, mightn't I?"

"You might," I told him. "Isn't it love that you really sought?"

Now, as the Lightstone was passed back and forth between knights arriving at our encampment in the middle of the field, as my father stood conferring with King Hadaru, and Maram showed Yarashan the rock with the hole that he had burned with his red gelstei in the Vardaloon, Asaru took my hand. Our lord's rings clicked together, and he said, "My apologies for doubting that the Lightstone might be found. Our grandfather would have been proud of you."

"Thank you, Asaru," I told him.

"But you had me worried. When the news came from Ishka, about the Bog, we all gave up hope."

I looked deep into the essential innocence gathering in his dark eyes, and I said, "All except you."

We clasped hands so tightly that my fingers hurt. And he said, "You've changed, Valashu."

All at once, as if ice were breaking beneath me, I felt myself plunging into unbearably cold waters. There pooled all the pain of Atara's blinding, of Kane's darkened soul, of Alphanderry's death.

"Valashu," my brother said.

I blinked my eyes to see him suddenly weeping as all the anguish inside me flowed into him. I knew then that the gift of *valarda* that my grandfather had bestowed upon me had not left Asaru untouched. It lay waiting to be awakened in all Valari, perhaps in all men.

Now the twelve thousand warriors of Ishka and the ten thousand of Mesh had finally closed and met all about us in the middle of the field. At the commands of the warlords and captains, they laid their spears and shields down upon the snow. Its white crystals, like millions of diamonds, shimmered with blues and golds and reds. Soon the morning sun would melt the ground's cold covering, even as the Lightstone melted six thousand years of hatred, envy, and suspicion. I turned to watch the warriors of King Hadaru and King Shamesh passing it from hand to hand, along the ranks, up one file and then down another. The Valari drank in its radiance through their bright eyes and through their hands. It blazed like the sun through their beings. In each of them, as in Asaru, I saw a golden cup pouring out its light from inside their hearts. It melted them open, melted the very diamond armor encasing them. And in this miracle that seemed almost an illusion but was as real as the water in my eyes, as real as my love for Asaru and for my brothers, for my father and King Hadaru and all the Ishkans, it melted even me.

"Look," Asaru said, pointing up at the sky, "there's a good sign."

I followed the line of his finger to see a great flock of swans winging their way south as they flew over the Upper Raaswash into Mesh. As my heart opened to this glorious sight, and to the hearts of the twenty thousand jubilant Valari all around me, I knew that the *valarda* was truly the greatest of gifts. For the joy of my brothers-in-arms and fellow guardians came flooding into me, and I felt myself soaring through the sky as well.

"Tonight," Asaru said, still looking at the swans, "they'll sleep at home. As we will soon enough, since there will be no war. What will you do, Valashu, now that you've found the Lightstone?"

What would I do, I wondered?

I turned to watch the swans disappear over the mountains to the south. In that direction lay the Valley of the Swans and the three great peaks above my father's castle. My mother and grandmother would be waiting for me there—even as my grandfather waited in another place. Atara was waiting in darkness for our son to be born and behold the beauty of the world. Where the stars burned cold and clean and bright, there the Elijin and Galadin waited for the Shining One to come forth. All people everywhere, and all things, always waiting.

And I must wait a little longer, too. The quest had been fulfilled, but one task remained: I must show my grandfather the golden cup that he knew would one day be found. And so soon, on a clear winter night, I would climb Mount Telshar or Arakel and stand upon the summit with the Lightstone in my hand. I would breathe the cold breath of all those who had come before me; I would dream my fiery dreams and speak my promise to the stars: that darkness would be defeated, that men and women would soar the heavens with wings of light, that someday the Lightstone would be returned to that bright, blazing place from which it came.

Turn the page and read a preview of

✖ LORD OF LIES ✖

David Zindell

Available now from
Tom Doherty Associates

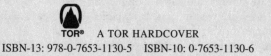

TOR® A TOR HARDCOVER

ISBN-13: 978-0-7653-1130-5   ISBN-10: 0-7653-1130-6

MASTER JUWAIN NOW brought forth the book from beneath his arm. As he opened it and began turning its yellow pages with great care, I noticed the title, written in ancient Ardik: *The Coming of the Shining One*. At last, he reached the page he had been seeking. He smiled as he set down the book next to the second parchment.

"I found this in the library of the Brotherhood's sanctuary at Nar. It was always a rare book, and with the burning of Khaisham's Library, it might be the last copy remaining in the world." He tapped his finger against the symbol-written circle inscribed on the book's open page. "This is the horoscope of Godavanni the Glorious. Look, Val, look!"

Godavanni had been the greatest of Ea's Maitreyas, born at the end of the great Age of Law three thousand years before. He had also been, as I remembered, a great King of Kings. I gasped in wonder because the two horoscopes, Godavanni's and mine, were exactly the same.

"No," I murmured, "it cannot be."

For my grandmother's sake, Master Juwain explained again the features of my horoscope—and Godavanni's. Then he turned to Maram and said, "You see, our quest to find the new Maitreya might already be completed."

"Ah, Val," Maram said as he pulled at his beard and gazed at me. "Ah, Val, Val."

My grandmother reached out her hand and squeezed mine. Then she set it on top of the parchments, fumbling to feel the lines of the symbols written on them.

"Here," I said, gently pressing her fingertip against the rays denoting the Morning Star. "Is this what you wanted?"

There was both joy and sadness in her smile as she turned to face me. Her ivory skin was so worn and old that it seemed almost transparent. The smell of lilacs emanated from her wispy white hair. The cataracts over her eyes clouded their deep sable color, but could not conceal the bright thing inside her, almost too bright to bear. Her breath poured like a warm wind from her lips, and I could feel the way that she had breathed it into me at my birth, pressing her lips over mine. I could feel the beating of her heart. There was a sharp pain there. It hurt me to feel her hurting so, with sorrow because she was blind and could not look upon me in what seemed my hour of glory. My eyes filled with water and burning salt a moment before hers did, too. And then, as if she knew well enough what had passed between us, she reached out her hand to touch away the tears on my cheek that she could not see.

"It was this way with your grandfather, too," she said. "You have his gift."

She gave voice to a thing that we had never spoken of before. For many years it had remained our secret. During the quest, however, Master Juwain and Maram—and my other companions—had discovered what my grandmother called my gift: that what others feel, I feel as well. If I let myself, their joy became my joy, their love flowed into me like the warm, onstreaming rays of the sun. But I was open to darker passions as well: hatred, pain, fury, fear. For my gift was also a curse. How many times on the journey to Argattha, I wondered, had Master Juwain and Maram watched me nearly die with every enemy I had sent on to the otherworld in the screaming agony of death?

My grandmother, as if explaining to Master Juwain and Maram something that she thought it was time for them to know, smiled sadly and said, "It was this way with Valashu from his first breath: it was as if he were breathing in all the pain in the world. It was why, at first, he failed to quicken and almost died."

For what seemed an hour, I sat next to her in silence holding her hand in mine. And then, to Master Juwain and Maram, to me—to the whole world—she cried out: "He's my grandson and has the heart of an angel—shouldn't this be enough?"

My gift, this mysterious soul force within me, had a name,

an ancient name, and that was *valarda*. I remembered that this meant "the heart of the stars."

As Master Juwain looked down at the two parchments, and Maram's soft, brown eyes searched in mine, I kissed my grandmother's forehead, then excused myself. I stood up and moved over to the open window. The warm wind brought the smell of pine trees and earth into the room. It called me to remember who I really was. And that could *not* be, I thought, the Maitreya. Was I a great healer? No, I was a knight of the sword, a great slayer of men. Who knew as well as I did the realm of death where I had sent so many? In the last moment of life, each of my enemies had grasped at me and pulled me down toward that lightless land. I remembered lines of the poem that had tormented me since the day I had killed Morjin's assassin in the woods below the castle:

> *The stealing of the gold,*
> *The evil knife, the cold—*
> *The cold that freezes breath,*
> *The nothingness of death.*
>
> *And down into the dark,*
> *No eyes, no lips, no spark.*
> *The dying of the light,*
> *The neverness of night.*

Even now, in the warmth of a fine spring day, I felt this everlasting cold chilling my limbs and filling me with dread: The night that knows no end called to me, even as the voices of the dead carried along the wind. They spoke to me in grave tones, telling me that I waited to be one of them—and that I could not be the Shining One, for he was of the sun and earth and all the things of life. A deeper voice, like the fire of the far-off stars, whispered this inside me, too. I did not listen. For just then, with my quick breath burning my lips and Telshar's diamond peak so beautiful against the sky, I recalled the words to another poem, about the Maitreya:

To mortal men on planets bound
Who dream and die on darkened ground,
To bold and bright Valari knights
Who cross the starry heavens' heights,
To all: immortal Elijin
As well the quenchless Galadin,
He brings the light that slays the Lie:
The light of love makes death to die.

" 'It is said that the Maitreya shall have eternal life,' " I whispered, quoting from the *Book of Ages* of the *Saganom Elu*.

It was also said that he would show this way to others. How else, I wondered, did men gain the long lives of the Star People and learn to sail the glittering heavens? And how did the Star People advance to the order of the immortal Elijin, and the Elijin become the great Galadin, they who could not be killed or harmed in any way? Men called these beings angels, but they were of flesh and blood—and perhaps something more. Once, in the depths of the black mountain called Skartaru, I had seen a great Elijin lord unveiled in all his glory. Had the hand of a Maitreya once touched him and passed on the inextinguishable flame?

Master Juwain stood up and came over to me, laying his hand on my arm. I turned to him and asked, "If I were the Maitreya, wouldn't I know this?"

He smiled as he hefted his copy of the *Saganom Elu* and began thumbing through its pages. Whether by chance or intuition, he came upon words that were close to the questioning of my heart:

The Shining One
In innocence sleeps
Inside his heart
Angel fire sleeps
And when he wakes
The fire leaps

About the Maitreya
One thing is known:
That to himself
He always is known
When the moment comes
To claim the Lightstone.

"But that's just it, sir," I said to him. "I *don't* know this."

He closed his book and looked deep into my eyes. He said, "In you, Val, there is such a fire. And such an innocence that you've never seen it."

"But, sir, I—"

"I think we *do* know," he told me. "The evidence is overwhelming. First, there is your horoscope, the Swan rising, which purifies—wasn't it only by purifying yourself that you were able to find the Lightstone? And you are the seventh son of a king of the most noble and ancient line. And there is the mark." He paused to touch the lightning bolt scar above my eye. "The mark of Valoreth—the mark of the Galadin."

Just then a swirl of little, twinkling lights fell out of the air as of a storm of shooting stars. In its spiraling patterns were colors of silver, cerulean and scarlet. It hovered near my forehead as if studying the scar there. Joy and faith and other fiery emotions seemed to pour from its center in bursts of radiance. This strange being was one of the Timpum, and Maram had named him Flick. He had attached himself to me in a magical wood deep in the wild forest of Alonia. It was said that once, many ages ago, the bright Galadin had walked there, perhaps looking for the greatest and last of Ea's Maitreyas: the Cosmic Maitreya who might lead all the worlds across the stars into the Age of Light. It was also said that the Galadin had left part of their essence shimmering among the wood's flowers and great trees. Whatever the origins of the Timpum truly were, they did indeed seem to possess the fire of the angels.

"And of course," Master Juwain said, pointing at the space above my forehead, "there is Flick. Of all the Timpum, only he has ever made such friends with a man. And only he left the Lokilani's wood—to follow you."

I looked over toward the tea table, where Maram sat squeezing my grandmother's hand. Then I turned back to Master Juwain and said, "There is evidence, yes, but it's not *known* . . . how the Maitreya will be known."

"I believe," Master Juwain said, "that the Maitreya, alone of all those on earth, will have a true resonance with the Lightstone."

"But how is this resonance to be accomplished?"

"That is one mystery I am trying to solve. As you must, too."

"But *when* will I solve it?"

In answer, he pointed out the window at the clouds glowing with colors in the slanting rays of the sun. "Soon, you will. This is the time, Valashu. The Golden Band grows stronger."

As men such as he and I lived out our lives on far-flung worlds like Ea, the Star People built their great, glittering cities on other worlds closer to the center of the universe. And the Elijin walked on worlds closer still, while the Galadin—Ashtoreth and Valoreth and others—dwelled nearest the stellar heart, on Agathad, which they called Star Home. It was said that they made their abode by an ancient lake, the source of the great river, Ar. The lake was a perfect silver, like liquid silustria, and it reflected the image of the ageless astor tree, Irdrasil, that grew above it. Irdrasil's golden leaves never fell, and they shone even through the night.

For beyond Agathad, at the center of all things, lay Ninsun, a black and utter emptiness out of which eternally poured a brilliant and beautiful light. It was the light of the Ieldra, beings of pure light who dwelled there. This numinous radiance streamed out like the rays of the sun toward all of creation. The Golden Band, it was called, and it fell most strongly on Agathad, there to touch all living things with a glory that never failed.

But other worlds around other stars, on their slow turn through the universe, moved into its splendor more rarely: with Ea, only once every three thousand years, at the end of old ages or the beginning of new ones. The Brotherhood's astrologers had divined that, some twenty years before, Ea had entered the Golden Band. And it was waxing ever stronger, like the wind before a storm, like a river in late spring gathering waters to nourish the land. Now men and women, if they listened, might hear the voices of the Ieldra calling them closer to their source, even as they called to the Star People on their worlds and to the Elijin on theirs—and called eternally to the angels on Agathad to free the light of their beings and return home as newly created Ieldra themselves.

"The Golden Band," Master Juwain explained, "is like a river of light that men do not usually see. It shimmers, the scryers say. There are eddies and currents, and a place where it swells and flows most deeply."

He gazed out the window for a moment, then shook his head as if all that *he* could see was the blazing sun and the drifting clouds—and two golden eagles that soared among them.

"The constellations," he said to me, "somehow affect the Band's strength—and direct it, too. It's known that the Band flared with great intensity on the ninth of Triolet, at the time of your birth."

I, too, looked out the window for this angel fire that remained invisible to me.

"I believe," Master Juwain said, "that a Maitreya is chosen. By the One's grace, through the light of the Ieldra where it falls most brightly."

I looked back to the tea table to see that Maram and my grandmother were attending his every word.

"The Maitreya is made, Val. Made to come forth and take his place in the world. And he must come *soon*, don't you see?"

Soon, he said, the Golden Band would begin to weaken, and a great chance might be lost. For men's hearts, now open to the light that the Maitreya would bring, would soon close and harden their wills yet again toward evil and war.

"You see," he said, "all the other Maitreyas failed. Of those of the Lost Ages, of course, we know almost nothing. But at the end of the Age of the Mother, it's said that Alesar Tal entered the Brotherhood and grew old and died without ever setting eyes upon the Lightstone. And at the end of the Age of

Swords, Issayu was enslaved by Morjin and the Lightstone kept from him. Godavanni was murdered at the moment that the Lightstone was placed into his hands. Now we are in the last years of the Age of the Dragon. This terrible time, the darkest of ages. How will it end, Val? In even greater darkness or in light?"

Out of the window I saw cloud shadows dappling the court-yard below and darkening the white stone walls of the castle. The foothills rising above them were marked with indenta-tions and undulations, their northern slopes invisible to the eye, lost in shadow and perhaps concealing eagles' aeries and bears' caves and the secret powers of the earth. I marveled at the way the sunlight caught the rocky faces of these hills: half standing out clearly in the strong Soldru light, half darkened into the deeper shades of green and gray and black. I saw that there was always a vivid line between the dark and the light, but strangely this line shifted and moved across the naked rock even as the sun moved slowly on its arc across the sky from east to west.

"Val? Are you all right?"

Master Juwain's voice brought me back to his comfortable room high in the Adami tower. I bowed my head to him, then asked if I could borrow his copy of the *Saganom Elu*. It took me only a moment to flip through its pages and find the pas-sage I was seeking. I read it aloud word by word, even though I knew it by heart:

" 'If men look upon the stars and see only cinders, if the sun should be seen to set in the east—if a man comes forth in falseness as the Shining One concealing darkness in his heart, if he claims the Lightstone for his own, then he shall become a new Red Dragon, only mightier and more terrible. Then red will burn black and all colors die; the heavens' lights will be veiled as if by smoke, and the sun will rise no more.' "

I closed the book and gave it back to him. I said, "I must know, sir. If I am truly this one who shines, I must know."

We returned to the table to rejoin Maram and my grand-mother. Master Juwain made us more tea, which we sat drink-ing as the sun fell behind the mountains and twilight stole across the world. Master Juwain reasserted his wish that I might come forth as Maitreya in sight of the emissaries who had assembled in my father's castle; it was why, he said, he had hurried home to Mesh. As much as I might need to know if I were really the Lord of Light foreseen in the prophecies, the world needed to be told of this miracle even more.

At last, as it grew dark and the hour deepened into full night, I went over to the window one last time. The sky was now almost clear. The dying of the sun had revealed the stars that always blazed there, against the immense black vault of the heavens. The constellations that my grandfather had first named for me many years before shimmered like ancient signposts: the Great Bear, the Archer, the Dragon, with its sinuous form and two great, red stars for eyes. I searched a long time in these glittering arrays for any certainty that I was the one whom Master Juwain hoped me to be. I did not find it. There was only light and stars, infinite in number and nearly as old as time.

Then Maram came up to me and clapped me on the shoulder. "It's time for the feast, my friend. You *might* very well be this Maitreya, but you're a man first, and you have to eat."

We walked back across the room, where I helped my grandmother out of her chair and took her arm in mine. Then we all went down to the great hall to take food and wine with many others and view the wonder of the Lightstone.